101 Damnations

D1418980

101
DAMNATIONS

Andrew Harman

LEGEND

Published in the United Kingdom in 1995 by
Legend Books

1 3 5 7 9 10 8 6 4 2

First published in the United Kingdom in 1995 by
Legend Books

Random House UK
20 Vauxhall Bridge Road, London SW1V 2SA

Random House Australia (Pty) Limited
20 Alfred Street, Milsons Point, Sydney,
New South Wales 2061, Australia

Random House New Zealand Limited
18 Poland Road, Glenfield
Auckland 10, New Zealand

Random House South Africa (Pty) Limited
PO Box 337, Bergvlei, South Africa

Random House UK Limited Reg. No. 954009

Typeset by Deltatype Ltd, Ellesmere Port, Cheshire
Printed and bound in Great Britain by
Cox & Wyman Ltd, Reading, Berkshire

ISBN: 0 09 949881 0

Ooooh a familial one!
A great big, all-embracing 'helloooooo' to Nicola and
Andy, Stephen, Trish and Charlotte, Beryl and Roy and
Mandy, Paul, Peter and Samuel.
And not forgetting Charles Bernard Harman who's gone
for a chat.

Contents

'Can you do armadillos?'

Viewed in the correct light, the iguana was perfect.

It squatted on the workbench, gleaming in its scaly skin-tight body stocking of head-turning waterproof finery. Smugly it admired its flawless claws, buffing each in turn against its chest, polishing them to the peak of glinting reptilian perfection. Oozing with conceit, it cast a self-appreciatory glance over its perfect physique, its gaze lingering on the muscles honed to the heights of lean, cold-blooded evolution. In short it was a glorious, shining example of unalloyed technical lizardry. But only for the terminally colourblind.

Snookums the currently custard-yellow Iguana flicked its whip-like tail casually and rolled over onto its side, admiring itself narcissistically in a polished brass plate. It was only then it realised that its favourite crimson, brushed-velvet lounging cushion was nowhere to be seen. Suddenly vexed, and feeling in need of a slice of gently poached Ammorettan Death Lizard on a bed of diced Cranachan lettuce to calm its mounting nerves, it peered around, frowning with a growing sense of anxious pique. Where had all the servants gone? And *what* had happened to the embossed pale blue stucco wall decorations?

From beneath a densely furrowed brow and an unkempt mop of wiry grey hair, a pair of eyes the colour of angry mud on a moonlit night glared at the supercilious reptile with a sense of mounting disgust.

'Definitely overfed,' growled the scowling Alchemist scornfully. 'And I bet it had gout. *Some* people just shouldn't be allowed to keep pets!' And that included Baronesses, he added to himself.

A low rumbling sound seeped into earshot through the thin walls of the hut.

'It's going to take a lot of work to get this creature looking mean and hungry! Cost her five groats at least . . . if I can get it the right colour.' With a flashed grin of lucrative delight he snatched a long bamboo screwdriver from an untidy heap of equipment and advanced, wiping his hand on the front of his cloak. 'She deserves an extra charge for such extensive body reworking!' he grumbled as the floor of the hut began to shake and rattle seismically, tipping several large boxes and half a dozen black bags off the rickety shelves with a sickening splat. Screwdriver at the ready, the Alchemist cursed volubly, coughing as a blast of dust exploded through the window in the wake of a thundering forty-ton wagon train.

Helplessly, the iguana squinted up at the silhouette lurching through the plumes of red dust, gulped a deep breath to hail the servants, choked and winced as no sound came out.

In a second the screwdriver arced down through the eddies of swirling motes, plunging towards the carved wooden plinth, slicing unstoppably through the side of the virtual lizard.

Just outside the hut a small, wiry youth squatted on his haunches, adjusted the bandana over his face and waited for the dust to settle. As usual Knapp was eagerly scanning the roughly rutted surface of Knavesbridge* for the latest TransTalpino Trade Route casualties.

With an evil chuckle he spotted a black and white armadillo snuffling its way slowly along the far side of the track, his grin widening as he instantly recognised it as another of Baroness Eglantine's ill-disciplined menagerie. That would be worth a few groats on its return! he thought smugly, rummaging in his small sack for a tasty tit-bit. Now, what would attract an armadillo's attention? Smoked salmon? Caviar? Probably both if Baroness Eglantine had anything to do with it! Shrugging, Knapp began flicking

---

* or 'Death Valley', as the steep-sided dip was commonly known in the village of Venasht.

through the squirming compartments of his comprehensively stocked pack for something suitable. With a grin he made his choice and deftly flicked three maggots and a bloodworm in a perfect, tempting line across the rutted track. And settled down to wait.

Apparently up to his wrist in iguana, Cheiro Mancini, the Alchemist, wiggled his screwdriver, cursing and tutting miserably as the chrominence filter changed the lizard from custard yellow to sky-blue, then a tasteful cerise and finally a far more normal greeny-grey with a subtle hint of brown. He consulted the small, battered watercolour, contented himself that it was 'near enough for the old bag', tugged his hands clear and sat back to admire the end product of the last three days' work.

Baffled, the lizard licked experimentally at its perfectly reformed side, scowled at the Alchemist with a practised expression of utter distaste and winked out of existence. Again.

It was too much for Mancini. How dare it vanish? What right had it got to deprive him of his five groats' reassembly fee? Five whole groats! Venting his frustration in an inhuman squeal of rage, he hurled himself to the floor, pounding the dust-bedevilled boards with frantic fists and frenzied feet.

'My Snookums!' bellowed a vast fur-clad woman, her expression of tense waiting-room worry clouding into black limb-removing anger. 'What *is* he doing to my poor Snookums?' she demanded, stamping over to the receptionist.

'Oooh! S'Technical,' answered the receptionist boredly from behind a growing mound of nail filings as she honed her crimson talons to ever increasing degrees of sharpness.

'Is the screaming *absolutely* necessary?'

'Vital,' murmured the receptionist, dripping disinterest.

In the 'surgery', tugging at his beard in acute annoyance, Cheiro Mancini glared through red-rimmed eyes at a tiny translucent pink crystal glowing dimly beneath a pile of tangled wire and chalk pentagrams. How dare the infernal

3

creature vanish like that? Damned iguana. Damned woman!

He could never work properly when the owners were outside, waiting. It was so off-putting. Like someone breathing over your shoulder or blowing down your ear.

Miserably he picked up the tastefully carved wooden plinth that held the empathic transmission projector and poked a screwdriver inside. Got to be a dodgy chrominence amplifier, he thought as he carefully replaced the translucent psychoterrin crystal and reconnected the potato. With a surge of microvolts, the crystal glowed brighter and the lizard flickered, shimmered and reappeared with a slight 'phoof'.

Where's my lounging cushion? What's happened to my nice comfy vivarium? it thought with practised conceit. Who's that grinning at me? Why isn't my lower intestine lying next to me any more?

With a small crackle, Snookums the Iguana winked out of existence again. This non-event was followed almost immediately by a frantic bout of waggling the wires poking out of the potato and another hail of oaths cursing the inexactitude of the Science of Projected Empathic Taxidermy.

A second and a half later a vast expanse of fur-clad female exploded into the room and avalanched towards the Alchemist as the iguana on the plinth phoofed reluctantly back into 'life'.

'Snookums! I've brought your favourite lounging cushion,' gushed Baroness Eglantine, trembling with a highly volatile mixture of delight and intense suspicion. With her arms wide and her lips actively pursing she reached for the lizard with the overenthusiasm of a long-lost great auntie. 'Snookums?' she squealed in sudden alarm as her fleshy arms passed straight through the deceased reptile and it vanished again. 'My Snookums?' she squealed, turning on Mancini. 'What have you done to my Snookums?' she demanded, fists clenching angrily as they took up battle positions on her hips. Her face began an alarming transition into crimson fury. Miffed, feisty and rising . . .

4

The hut rumbled – Mancini was uncertain whether this was the effect of another forty-ton wagon train breasting the top of the hill, or Baroness Eglantine's fulminating anger.

Outside the hut, Knapp grinned secretly behind his bandana as the armadillo sniffed the maggot, changed direction and trundled onto the track, blissfully unaware of the vast wagon train crawling over the horizon. With a fanfare of whip-cracks, shrieks and bellows the driver spurred his team of beasts into a gallop, thundering down the half-mile one-in-four in a frantic, uncontrollable, momentum-building dash.

'I did all I could . . .' whimpered Mancini.

Baroness Eglantine's face suddenly contorted in a screaming picture of horror as she caught sight of a glistening heap of familiar-coloured iguana skin. Mancini turned and stared at the black bag where it had fallen off the shelf. 'No, no! Don't look!' he cried. 'It's better if you remember Snookums the way he . . .'

He was too late.

'My Snookums!' screamed the Baroness, staring at the very real and very ex-lizard on the floor. 'You've killed him!' she squealed in a voice that could etch glass at three miles. The rumbling increased in intensity.

Unseen, the iguanoid doppelgänger flashed back into existence and opened its mouth in disbelief. What was all the fuss about? He felt fine! A bit light-headed, but fine nonetheless. Couple of juicy salmon steaks and he'd be right as rain.

'Baroness Egla . . .' began Mancini, convinced his ears were bleeding.

'Murderer! I brought him here with a slight bruising and you've . . .'

'Slight bruising? He was run over by a wagon train on Dea . . . er, Knavesbridge.'

Now I remember, thought Snookums, recalling the joyous feeling of freedom, the strange rumbling sound, the huge wheels bearing down in horizon-filling terror . . . crushing his midriff, and expected to wince. He didn't. In fact, he didn't feel a thing. Healed up nicely.

Outside the hut, a second maggot was about to be devoured by a peckish armadillo. Knapp's gaze flicked nervously between it and the thundering wagon train screaming down into the valley. The armadillo had better hurry up . . .

'If you'd have been a better VET . . .' screamed the Baroness.

'If you'd have brought *all* of his lower intestine instead of . . .' countered Mancini.

'What? *All* that filthy stuff? How *dare* you suggest I sully my ermine gloves with all that . . .'

'Contrary to popular belief,' shouted Mancini, his face reddening, 'iguanas *need* their lower intestines. Nature didn't just throw it in there for padding!'

The lizard nodded sagely. Necessary for the complete digestion of Tepid Sea Beluga caviar.

'I *know* what my Snookums needs and it is patently obvious the dear creature shan't find it here!' Baroness Eglantine's face registered squally tantrums imminent.

The armadillo trundled into the middle of the Trans-Talpino Trade Route. And stopped to chew at the maggot. Forty tons of wagon train and the pounding hooves of the haulage rhinos thundered unstoppably closer.

'All your darling Snookums was fit for,' continued Mancini while he could still get a word in, 'was a handbag.'

The iguana cringed. He really shouldn't have said that.

'A handbag?' squealed the Baroness as rage crowned her face with crimson. 'A handbag!' The table shook. 'How dare you suggest that my beloved Snookums was only fit to become a fashion item? He was a living, breathing . . . !'

'Until it met a forty-ton wagon train,' added the receptionist, peering round the doorframe as she honed her nails still further.

Crackling anger from every pore, the fur-clad woman turned suddenly on her heels. 'I have never been *so* insulted!' she yelled, storming out at the head of a vapour trail of vitriolic abuse.

'What about my fee? I'm not a charity, you know!' shouted

Mancini plaintively and received several suggestions, not all of which were entirely helpful or, indeed, expected from the mouth of a Baroness.

As if it understood, the iguana vanished again. And so did Mancini's last hopes of ever getting the five groats he could have charged for such extensive iguana repair.

'Five groats!' he whimpered, images of debt collectors lurking in the shadows flashing across his mind. If he didn't scrape some cash together soon, there'd be trouble. He hadn't paid his receptionist for months. It was probably best not to consider what personal damage she could inflict with those nails of hers.

Suddenly the door was kicked open and a small, wiry youth staggered in, clutching a black bag. With a lurch he dropped it on the floor and grinned.

'Can you do armadillos?' asked Knapp, stifling a chuckle.

Push back the mists of time, if you will, and peer through the clouds of chronology. Squint between the cotton-wool obscurity of the cumulus tempus and peek at the unseen world of History beyond record . . .

The sandy bed of a warm shallow sea teems with prehistoric life. A trilobite crawls by. Ancient bivalves sip at the primordial cordial surrounding them, nurturing, readying them for the next struggling shin up the infinite length of Evolution's pole. The trilobite's antennae leap erect, suddenly somehow aware that ahead lies food. It bulldozers forward, reeled in by the telepathic hunting skills of the creature buried inches below these ancient sands.

Born countless centuries before the invention of taxonomy, this ancient antecedent of the manta ray lies in nameless cover, patiently waiting, telepathically baiting, just anticipating. Ramrod piston legs drive our trilobite on, unresisting, unsuspecting. In a swirling fountain of sand the rectangular hunter strikes. Rearing out of its sea bed like an angry bath mat, it grabs our trilobite and drags it down.

But today the hunter is the hunted.

The waiting primordial mage sees the flick of the sand, his

desperate eyes lock onto the ambush. Correcting for parallax, he plunges his hands into the ancient salty sea. He snatches at the flat, rectangular sea-scrole, catching and pulling, forcing it to drop our startled trilobite, wrenching it into the alien world of air. He holds the writhing bath mat and begins to talk, to chant secrets at the scrole with his fading twilight breaths. Implanting detailed facts into the sponge-like mind, he writes in the fossil records, filling the molluscan mind in a moment. He flips the ancient hunter onto a waiting barbecue and the secret facts are sealed within the dead sea-scrole for ever.

With a final desperation, this, the last of the primordial mages, raked with battle-scars, riddled with thaumic lance strikes, seals the lid of a waiting terracotta pot, flicks a label around the neck saying 'Please look after these jars, thank you' and draws the knife from his belt. The blade glints faintly in the pale sun as he slices into the pad of his thumb, wincing for the last time.

'Go,' we watch him whisper as the blood cells disperse in the tepid sea, each disc carrying the vital code of life. With a final gasp the mage collapses, sure in the knowledge that every living organism within a one-mile radius will receive its copy of the code. Evolution will attempt to weed it out, but when the time is right a Guardian will emerge. It must. For the sake of the future.

Our trilobite trundles off on another day in the ancient seas.

The sun rose late over the once frequented coach halt of Venasht. It always did. Every day it struggled wearily over the horizon just in time for lunch, beamed into the valley for a couple of hours, then vanished behind the western wall of the half-mile deep trough.

Venasht had prospered once, thriving on the passing trade of wagon drivers feeding and watering their horses before the haul out of the valley. But, since the introduction of sextets of powerful haulage rhinos and the invention of the Snack-on-the-Track slow-release nosebag, wagon trains

8

could cross the Talpa Mountains without stopping. And did – thundering recklessly down the valley wall in a wild momentum-gathering dash, screaming unstoppably through Venasht and just clawing their way over the far lip.

But there were times they didn't make it. Sometimes a wagon train failed to reach escape velocity and half a dozen runaway carts would come to a thundering halt, embedded in the side of a building. There had been a time a few years ago when this happened more than once a month, tons of builder's rubble regularly flattening Baroness Eglantine's partially rebuilt mansion. Precisely why anyone would *want* to transport builder's rubble over the Talpa Mountains and why it was only the Baroness' Mansion that was ritually demolished were two great unanswered questions. Fortunately for the Baroness they were questions the fifty-five different companies with which she was insured failed to ask. The resulting cash settlement set her up for life and bought the continued silence of a certain close friend who just happened to specialise in moving builder's rubble.

At the moment silence was the last thing on a certain Alchemist's mind. Cheiro Mancini pounded his forehead on the floor of his hut and cursed a string of his bluest oaths. What customer care! There was so much he could, and should, have said yesterday about Projected Empathic Taxidermy.

'Your pet iguana is dead, long live your PET iguana. Yes, Baroness Eglantine, an exact, thaumically enhanced copy of all your favourite companion's endearing qualities. Thrill as it catches flies like the real thing. Applaud as it performs the tricks you know and love. Just as affectionate as the real thing; twice as easy to keep. A quick dusting and a new potato every month or so will keep your PET for ever in its prime.'

Did that idiot woman *have* to try and hug the stupid thing? One day they'd have mass.

Outside, a cart careered into the valley, its handbrake smoking as the driver attempted to control its velocity.

'Who'd be a VET?' moaned Mancini. Thankless job being

9

a Virtual Ecology Technician, he thought miserably. Why won't people realise that when an iguana's guts are spread all over the King's Highway then short of opening up a pact with the devil there's nothing else to do but mount it? People should thank him! Alright, so a projected image of the beloved animal isn't as good as having the thankless creature back in full glowing health, but they do look good on the mantelpiece. Some of Cheiro Mancini's finest work had been reptilian, once. What a way to earn a living.

Living? That was a laugh, scowled Mancini. Borderline starvation, more like. His financial stomach rumbled as he mentally wrote off the five groats he would have charged for extensive iguana repair.

With a screech of steel-rimmed wheels and the smell of burning brake pads, the cart slid to a halt and a stocky figure leapt off.

Miserably Mancini looked at the name tag on a recently flattened armadillo. 'Come on then, tiddles,' he said to the heap of armoured limbs. 'Time for a new lease of life as a mantelpiece decoration.'

He rolled up the capacious sleeves of his cloak, flicked back his wiry hair, snatched his scalpel from the doorframe and stopped. Raised voices echoed through the door in heated argument.

'Look, *I* don't make the rules! He doesn't do house calls, alright?' shouted the receptionist, sounding angry and bored at the same time.

Mancini shuddered. The Baroness was back. It had to be her. After all, she was his only customer, the only person in the whole of Venasht who was rich enough to keep pets. And the only one stupid enough to have a catflap as big as a barn door.

'I've travelled a long way to see Mr Mancini,' said a deep, rich-sounding voice. A man's voice. It was accompanied by a strange tinkling sound. Mancini's interest rose a notch, his ear twitching at the door.

'I have heard a lot about Mr Mancini's skills,' continued the voice. 'I really would like to have a word with him.'

10

That didn't sound good. That was the type of thing tax inspectors said. He looked at the armadillo on the bench and saw it as a small stack of gleaming groats.

'I'm sorry, he's in surgery' said the receptionist with a swift accompanying rasp of a nail-file.

'I wish to talk about the future,' said the man.

That's it! thought Mancini. Talk doesn't pay. Especially about the future and all that nonsensical alchemical rubbish. If he's heard so much about me he must *know* I don't do that any more. Not since 'gloomy Tuesday', anyway.

Mancini yelled from within the 'Surgery', 'Tell him to go away! I'm too busy for a palm-reading. Come back next century!'

'Mr Mancini? Is that you?' called the voice with a gentle tinkling.

'Yes, and I'm busy. My crystal ball's at the pawnbroker's! Leave your patient's details and I'll get around to it when I have a chance.'

'I don't have a patient. I don't want a palm-reading or a seance or anything,' answered the stranger and made the chinking sound again. Sort of metallic. A soft yellow metallic . . . Mancini suddenly found that his interest in the dead armadillo had inexplicably vanished . . . Lots of small, round, soft yellow metallic discs . . . 'I merely wish to talk with the finest Virtual Ecology Technician in the shadow of the Talpa Mountains!' he continued in the tone of voice of a man whose dictionary of acceptable responses to demands issued by him contained nothing in the negative. A man who meant business. And a man who knew what he was talking about.

Almost before he realised what was happening, Cheiro Mancini was on his feet and heading for the door, the sound of dangling carats tugging him greedily forward. His vision clouded yellow as if the sun had suddenly risen behind his eyes.

In a second, the 'surgery' door was tugged open, hands clamoured out, snatched frantically and almost as rapidly slammed the portal shut. A flake of ancient paint fluttered down into the waiting room now suddenly empty of the gold, the ferruled cane and the large man.

11

'Cheiro Mancini, Alchemist and VET?' asked the stranger and shook the bag for effect.

Mancini's eyes winked up and down as the sack moved, his attention held tighter than a starving pointer slavering after a well-hung brace of pheasant. 'That's me. But less of the alchemist if you wouldn't mind,' he said absently as he furiously estimated the volume of the sack, divided it by the density of gold, multiplied that figure by the conversion into carats, exchanged that into groats and came to a figure that had a reassuringly large number of noughts behind it.

Nervously he coughed and sprinted through the door.

'That will be all, dear,' he said, staring through greedy eyes at the receptionist.

'But he ain't got an appointment . . .'

'That *will* be all.'

'. . . or a patient . . .'

'Go home.'

'But it's not time . . .'

'Home!' barked Mancini, waving the scalpel and pointing to the door.

Once the short-skirted receptionist had vanished, after clearing the nail-files and sundry cosmetics which inhabited her desk into a bag made from one of the Baroness' smaller lurchers, Mancini barred and bolted the door and returned to the mysteriously chinking stranger.

'Such a way with minions,' said the man, clutching an expensively ferruled staff in one hand and a small velvet pouch in the other. 'I like that in a man,' he added and handed over a business card.

Mancini rubbed his hands together, bowed and thought about tugging his forelock as he surveyed the visitor. He decided against it. Instead, he fell on the floor and grovelled. 'The words that I spoke, sir, were aimed at another.' His eyes totalled the estimated cost of the clothes and began to cloud over with added monetary admiration. 'Forgive my haste, my Lord. What task may I be humbly allowed to carry out for you?'

The stranger ignored the grovelling Alchemist and stared

at a wire and string apparatus wobbling precariously on the table. 'Is this what you use?'

'Is sir interested in a PET? Stick insects are very popular at present. Only twelve . . .' began Mancini, rubbing his hands eagerly.

'I was hoping for something a little larger,' came the reply. 'Preferably with teeth.' The stranger strode towards the shelves.

'A rat, sir?' offered Mancini, crawling after him.

'Ooh, no. Meaner!'

'Weasel? I can offer very good terms on weasels, sir.'

'A little more avant-garde, perhaps?'

'Ah! I should have spotted that. A discerning gentleman like yourself would certainly require something a little more . . . A griffin, perhaps?' Mancini fawned, rubbed his hands and leapt to his feet.

The stranger shook his head.

'Phoenix? With optional flame programme?'

'Can you do dragons?'

Mancini's face dropped. Not even Baroness Eglantine could afford to keep a dragon as a pet. 'd . . . d . . . Basilisks, no problem,' he hedged.

'Dragon.'

He swallowed and watched the stranger place the chinking velvet bag on the table, just out of reach. 'D . . . dragons, now, let me see . . . Hah! Don't get much call for them round here. Wagon trains tend to come off worse. See?'

'Can you do dragons?' snapped the stranger.

Mancini swallowed guiltily, nudged the stubbornly non-functional PET iguana, stared at the sack and launched into a bare-faced lie. 'Oh. Dragons! Of course. Silly me, what *was* I thinking of . . .'

'I want it installed in a week. As well as this little lot,' said the stranger and handed over a parchment list with a flourish of expensive sleeve.

'A week?' shrieked Mancini. 'I'll need a Malpin Emp-Power Driver for a dragon . . . series six at least. And a matched pair of psychoterrins if you want it in 3-D.'

'Well, if you don't want *this* . . .' said the stranger, poking the sack.

'Ah! No! I mean, yes. Yes, I do!' pleaded the impoverished VET.

'One week?'

'Ten days! I'll need to go to Fort Knumm.'

The stranger reached for the bag and turned to leave.

'Okay. Okay. One week!' screamed Mancini as the gold was in danger of slipping away.

"Well done!' said the Thaumaturgical Physicist and flicked the large bag of chinking yellow coins into the air with a flourish of his staff.

As Cheiro Mancini snatched it from its arcing parabola, unfastened the neck and stared transfixed at the gold, the stranger unbarred and unbolted the door and vanished.

'See you in Losa Llamas in a week,' shouted the stranger over his shoulder as he skipped down the stairs. 'There's a wagon outside – use it. Oh, and a map on the back of the card, memorise it. It will self-destruct in fifteen seconds!'

Mancini looked up in a guilty gold-ridden daze, picked up the card and turned it over. As he looked, the lines on the surface glistened then ignited in a sudden magnesium flash, burning the map onto his retina, setting it into his short-term memory and turning the card to a small heap of ash.

A dragon? he cringed, blinking. Nobody in the short history of Virtual Ecology had ever mounted a PET dragon before! The iguana flashed on and off. A whole dragon!

He swallowed nervously. It would be just like a lizard . . . only much, much bigger.

Wouldn't it?

Ah! Who cares? he thought as he emptied the sack on the floor and began feverishly to count.

On one of the toes of the foothills of the Kholan Heights, fifteen hundred feet below the summit of Mount Hofollives, a curse floated in the warm afternoon sun of a spring day. It hummed, resonated and spat briefly above the bleating of a small herd of grey and white goats before disappearing into

14

the higher valleys to join the others.

'The bells,' yelled a solitary figure, twitching. 'The bells! They make me m . . . mmad!' A small boy, dressed in what looked like several sacks huddling together around him, glared accusingly at the herd of goats and hurled a rock at the one with the cracked bell that scraped endlessly at his nerves. A beetle diving repetitively into an ancient tin can would hold more melodic appeal.

'Stand still!' he yelled. 'How am I supposed to count you if you insist on bouncing around the rocks? Move again and it'll end in kebabs!' For the five hundredth time that morning Whaiyn the D'vanouin Goatherd clenched his fists, his teeth, swore through them and started counting again. And for the five hundredth time that day he fervently wished he had never become a goatherd. Especially at times like this.

He leapt forward across the scree field, snatched a goat by the neck, stared into its dumb eyes and screamed. 'Where's Old Git? C'mon, talk! Where's Old Git now?'

The goat returned a bored stare of utter incomprehension as its yellow teeth continued their chewing. Angrily throwing the animal aside, he headed off around the rocky outcrop beneath an aura of abuse.

Whaiyn did not, it is fair to say, find a great degree of job satisfaction in his work. He longed for the day when he could cheerfully wave two fingers at all the bleating tribes of goatdom and do something far more rewarding with his time. Like lying in the sun all day, drinking and eating goat pasties.

He rounded the rock, stared up at the precipice before him and almost wept.

'No. Not up there. *Surely* not!' he yelled, but inside he *knew* that the tiny black opening almost a hundred feet above him just *had* to be the place. One of the things he had learned in his time as a goatherd was never to discount any situation as too inaccessible or unexpected in which to find a missing goat. Anywhere offering the slimmest hope of offering something edible and they were off like a shot. Quite what inexplicable aspect of caprine mentality drove them, over and over again, to scale vertical cliff faces, or sprint along inch-wide ledges for half a handful of heather, Whaiyn hadn't the foggiest. Experience had shown him the intense stupidity possessed by all of goatkind.

Old Git would be in *that* cave. Up there!

Vowing to hurl the bleating animal down the hundred-foot precipice, Whaiyn the goatherd spat on his hands, swore a string of blasphemies that would melt a priest's ears and began to climb.

In spite of the fact that the land-locked Murrhovian Empire stretched across eight thousand ells of the Ghuppi Desert at its narrowest, there was one point that was never far away. The tip of the gleaming blade of Empress Tau's favourite katana. One slip; the tiniest faux pas; just fall out of favour for one second and you'd be carrying your head home in a bag.

One would have to be acutely stupid, hopelessly optimistic or patently depraved even to consider contradicting Empress Tau. Unfortunately, Dewlap, the five-hundred-and-thirty-third Court Livestock Image Consultant, was all three – the results of a lifetime spent at Fashion College.

'No, no, no!' screamed Empress Tau, slamming her fist onto the arm of the obsidian throne and causing two sharp inhalations of breath from the squatting figures of General Lehrt and Admiral Ti.

'But, your Veritable Excellency, it is *ever* so lovable!' defended Dewlap as he adjusted the huge pink ribbon on the tiny dog. '*And* fully Palace trained.' He fiddled with the dog's lace collar. Then tweaked his own.

'I don't want "lovable",' growled the Empress, her teeth squeaking as she ground enamel from her back molars.

'Oh, but your Exquisite Tyrannicality, "lovable" is in. Observe!' The Court Livestock Image Consultant clapped his pale hands effeminately. He beamed as the terrier sprang onto its hind feet, pirouetting gracefully on tip-paws. The only sound in the vast hall was the clicking of claws on polished marble, the shimmering tinkling of the terrier's ankle bells and the grinding of Tau's teeth.

General Lehrt shuffled uneasily in his ceremonial bamboo armour as the tendons in the back of the Empress' hand creaked with irritation in her attempt to tear the armrest off the throne. 'I want mean and nasty! I want fangs and claws! I want three hundred pounds of angry musculature held back with an alligator shoulder harness and brute force!' shrieked Empress Tau, her eyes flashing red with acute fashion-conscious fury.

Dewlap adjusted his rose-tinted pince-nez and dabbed at his mouth with a small square of silk. 'Your Draconimity, alligator is *so* gauche. "Mean and nasty" is passé. Terriers are *so* popular with the lower members of Court . . .'

Admiral Ti winced.

'That is *precisely* why I will not have one resident in my Palace unless it is about to be made into Imperial slippers. That performing rodent enhances one's Imperial status less than halitosis. Take it away!' snarled Tau, fingering the ridged handle of her favourite katana.

'As you wish, but terriers *are* in this season!' said Dewlap, fussing with the rim of his yellow beret and then gesturing limply to the hound. With a jingle, the dog leapt onto its forepaws and proceeded to trot, head down, towards the fuming Empress.

'I said *away!*' shrieked Tau, the eight-inch veranda of her starched eyebrows arching into a V of intense rage.

Dewlap's eyes lit with horror as she exploded from her obsidian throne, bounded to her feet and spun round with a deadly footsweep and a flash of glistening metal and bamboo. With a shriek she somersaulted over a short-legged table bedecked with tea utensils, bringing her curved katana blade down with a flourish towards the performing canine. There was a yelp of surprise and a few strands of stray white fur floated gently towards the polished marble floor. Then deathly silence.

The Court Livestock Image Consultant's hands were in his mouth up to the wrists, fighting to hold back the shrieks of hysteria racing up his throat, surging for freedom.

Growling menacingly behind her ceremonial moustache,

the Empress stood slowly and advanced on Dewlap, bamboo armour creaking malevolently, her Imperial katana aimed unwaveringly at the throat of the Consultant. On the tip of the blade dangled a small white bundle of fur sporting a large pink ribbon. 'When I say "away",' growled Tau in a whisper that could freeze nitrogen at five miles, 'I do *not* mean perform another set of tricks.'

'Aaaahh . . .' whimpered Dewlap, staring at the twitching form dangling grotesquely from the approaching weapon.

The Empress flicked her ostensibly delicate wrist in a series of complex curves, severing the collar and sending the terrier flying. Dewlap watched in quivering shock as the animal hit the floor yelping and went spinning spreadeagled out of the Imperial Presence, sporting a single completely shaven ear.

'Do you *like* life?' growled Tau, snatching at the silk collar of Dewlap's batik-printed kimono and lifting him off the floor. With her other hand she casually resheathed the katana across her back.

'Urgghhhhh . . .' answered Dewlap, the toes of his brushed ermine slippers dangling six inches above the tiles. Fear resonated through the Consultant's mind. Those nails! he screamed inside the pattern-book of his mind. My collar! How will I possibly get all the creases out?

'Eighteen different scrapings from the bottom of nature's evolutionary barrel you have been parading before me,' snarled Tau, her breath vibrating the length of her thin, black ceremonial moustache with every explosive consonant. 'Eighteen! It was forty-five yesterday!'

Dewlap foolishly attempted to nod in agreement and nearly throttled himself.

'I would have expected even you to have been capable of understanding my instructions. But no! The Rotating Emperors of Froul will turn up, as usual, with their growing herds of albino elephants. The Chief of the Raft-People of the Eastern Tepid Seas will parade that infernal piebald octopus, delighting in squirting pouches of sticky ink at everyone. And what do you offer me, Grand Empress Tau,

18

Draconian Ruler of the Murrhovian Empire, She-whose-sword-arm-moves-faster-than-a-gecko-on-coals? Hmmmm? What image-enhancing creatures do you offer me?' She shook Dewlap just in case he had forgotten that he was being addressed.

'Stick insects and white mice!' screamed the Empress, not waiting for an answer. 'Did you seriously expect me to host the Tyrants' Institute Annual Charity Fancy Pets Party with white mice and stick insects in tow? I'd be the laughing stock. It would *ruin* my reputation!'

'I just thought . . .'

'Just thought! Mental activity had *nothing* to do with this shabby selection. Can you *imagine* the Ceremonial Banners – white mouse rampant atop crossed stick insects salient, within a chevron of erminois? It would clash horribly with the napkins!' she wined as her red nails closed tighter around Dewlap's collar. 'It seems I shall have to find a new Court Livestock Image Consultant. Kneel!' commanded Tau, dropping Dewlap in a fit of choking and unsheathing her katana once more.

'If thy head offends me,' scowled the Empress, quoting one of the Entrenched Rules of Murrha, 'cut it off!'

'Excellency, wait!' cried the kneeling figure, his arms flapping desperately, beads of sweat glistening on his flushed brow. 'Please, not my head . . . !'

'Have you ever used a katana?' Tau asked Dewlap, ignoring his protestations. 'Perfectly balanced. Honed to screaming sharpness. Give yourself a nasty nick if you're not careful. I could have your head in a bag before you even noticed.' She grinned mercilessly, staring at the Image Consultant's neck and mentally drawing a dotted line across it.

'Please! Not my head! Excellency, have I not pleased you before? W . . . what about the shimmering Ammorettan Death Lizard with matching belt and sequins? It was just you!' choked Dewlap, pleading profusely from every pore.

'That was *last* year. I want something new. Something never seen before. Unique! I want everyone's jaws on the floor! Is that too much for the Empress Tau to request?' she demanded, twirling the katana inches away from the Consultant's nose.

'Er . . . well. No,' confessed Dewlap.

'Well? What plans have you hatching in that head of yours? Should I remove it and find out?' squealed Tau, shaking the Consultant furiously. General Lehrt fingered the collar of his bamboo armour nervously.

'Please. *Not* my head. Not yet!' whimpered Dewlap.

'Give me *one* reason why not?'

'Excellency . . . I . . . In three days I'm taking delivery of *the* Star of the Gu-Chi Autumn Beret Collection.'

For a split millisecond Empress Tau's nerve twitched as a pang of jealousy nibbled at her insides. *That* beret had stolen the show. Nothing on the catwalk could touch it for pertly rakish panache. Even Xiao-Nel's mirror-silk fedora looked limp beside it. It was *the* finest piece of millinery ever to appear this side of the Gleaming Imperial Tiaras of the Thing Dynasty. Some people would covet such an item more desperately than . . . ooh, life itself . . .

'Well, why didn't you say before?' whispered the Empress, her starched eyebrows fractions of an inch away from Dewlap's trembling brow. She was suddenly calm, suddenly friendly, suddenly even more unnervingly terrifying.

Admiral Ti flashed a querulous glance across at Lehrt.

Empress Tau's upper lip curled back slowly as she grasped Dewlap's right earlobe. 'Very well. You can keep your head.'

'Excellency! May the Gods bless you and all who sail in you!' gushed Dewlap as he covered Tau's steel toecap sandals with kisses.

'However . . .' she snapped, trapping the gushing Consultant's tongue with a deft twist of her ankle. 'Fail to bring me a companion for the Tyrants' Party and you lose your ears . . .'

A yelp of anguish floated up from the vicinity of Tau's heel. What use was the Gu-Chi Beret without earlobes? It would ruin its line!

'. . . *Then* you lose your head. Do I make myself clear?'
Dewlap attempted to nod agreement.

'Well. Go and fetch. You have three days.' And with an almost casual footsweep Empress Tau kicked the Consultant after the still yelping dog, resheathed her trusty blade and stomped back to her throne between the motionless figures of General Lehrt and Admiral Ti.

Having hauled his sweat-ridden body over the lip of the tiny cave entrance with a final grunted oath, Whaiyn the Goatherd was now crawling through the gloom. Right now the most important thing in his life was to find Old Git. Oooh, that goat would suffer when he got his hands around its neck! One hundred feet up a vertical sandstone precipice was no picnic. He had lost count of the number of times the idea of just kicking the damned thing into mid-air, laughing hysterically as it plunged rapidly screewards, had crossed his mind. It was definitely into double figures . . . or possibly even ten.

His knees scraped on the rock floor as he squeezed claustrophobically through the passage, and was almost deafened by the scream he let out as his hand struck deep black nothing ahead. The bottom of the passage had disappeared. He lay on his belly and stared into the black velvet gloom, waiting impatiently as the rhodopsin amplifiers at the back of his retina struggled to grasp at images submerged in the darkness.

A murky picture of a set of very non-goat-like stone jars arranged neatly on a stone shelf swam reluctantly into view. Whaiyn stared in utter confusion.

Who could have accidentally lost a set of stone jars in the back of a cave, one hundred feet up a precipice, miles from anywhere? And whoever it was, were they offering a reward?

It was this last part that made Whaiyn reach out into the darkness towards the nearest jar. With a few minor oaths, for once not directed at goats, he hauled it into the passage and wriggled out into the light. There was no way, no matter how

21

curious he felt, that he was going to put his hand inside that terracotta receptacle without seeing inside it first. Who knows what people put in jars!

After a few minutes he was at the entrance. Maybe the jars had been hidden, perhaps they contained treasure? Gold and jewels, to make him rich forever! Taking a nervous breath, he removed the lid and peered expectantly inside. Sparkles of light glistening off the facets of a diamond the size of his fist; coronas of dazzling wealth coruscating hypnotically above oceans of coins; the sapphire glow of fortunes unimaginable . . . all this and more were nowhere to be seen. Just a crumpled, aging roll of parchment.

The other four jars contained the same: sheets of thick, yellowing parchments decorated with random scribblings and deformed pictures with no sense of scale. Men with big horns and wispy tails towered over hundreds of running stick figures. Whaiyn stared in bewilderment at the scrolls, tutted and folded them into his shirt, utterly oblivious of the fact that these parchments contained information that no mortal should ever possess. In the wrong hands the results could be terrible.

Fortunately for the world at large, one of the many life-enhancing skills that Whaiyn the D'vanouin Goatherd had failed to acquire was the ability to read.

It was probably for this reason more than anything that Whaiyn totally ignored the faded label plaintively requesting that somebody, anybody, 'Please look after these jars, thank you.'

The only thing missing was the smell.

Cheiro Mancini was overwhelmed by it every time he visited the Scale and Claw salesfloor of Hashe's Fur and Feather Fayre. And today was no exception. So many animals, so little aroma. His jaw dropped open in total amazement as he stared at the shelves and racks of designer wildlife baying for attention, mewling desperately for anyone to shell out and take them home. Under this one roof was jammed everything that any self-respecting Virtual

Ecology Technician could ever want. From ready-assembled aardvarks to lounge lizards; Hare-fix kits to newts-on-cradles for the stressed executive. There was seemingly no end to the list of shapes, colours and skin types a projected empathic field could not be twisted into. And Hashe was taking full advantage of it all.

Ever since the day he sold his sister Lotte's pet Talpine Rock Mouse for a slice and a half of Ammorettan Fudge at the tender age of two and three-quarters, Annz Hashe had been fascinated by animals of all kinds. Or more specifically he had been fascinated by other people's fascination with animals of all kinds. Generally the monetary kind. With an incisive insight rare in one so young Hashe realised he could cash in on nature's rich bounty; he could turn mountain goats into mountains of groats, one might say.

Just over a decade later and things had changed gear. He'd moved on from Talpine Rock Mice and could now be found anywhere from struggling through the most hostile environs of the Angstarktik in search of such rare quarries as the legendary katana-clawed wolverine of Upper Thhk; to scouring the Eastern Tepid Seas for double-horned narwhals or decanter-nosed dolphins, netting them and flogging them off to the highest bidder. And netting himself a healthy fortune in the process.

It was only after serving prison sentences in numerous kingdoms for breach of import-export licences, flouting shipping regulations, and contravening countless quarantine by-laws that he saw the error of his ways. Livestock was hard work. There was only one answer. Virtual Ecology – the ability to preserve thaumically any organism's spirit and appearance at any time up to three days after its demise.

For Annz Hashe this was an answer to all his dreams. Dead things don't need half as much parchment work. And they're far easier to stack. It may be ecologically unfriendly . . . but, boy, the profit margins!

Hashe was now the Undisputed King of Virtual Ecology, with fifteen thousand creature patents under his belt and always on the lookout for more. A slight tweak to a lizard's colouring here, nip an elephant's trunk there and call it a tapir. It would only be a matter of months before Hashe reinvented the eel.

'I see you're admiring our latest line,' said an expensively dressed man in khaki strolling up to the awestruck figures of Cheiro Mancini and Knapp staring at the range of death lizards. 'Any colour you like, as long as it's black,' he said and smiled. 'Very friendly, ideal for children's parties, All Hallows' Eve and the like. Roar- or growl-o-matic voice-box options and realistic flight simulation. They're on special offer . . .'

'They're PET's?' spluttered Mancini as one roared. Knapp whimpered and hid behind the VET's cloak.

'Oh yes! Proving very popular, too,' answered Annz Hashe, examining the end of his riding crop. 'A snip at only three thousand groats.'

'But they're so . . .'

'Realistic? Yes, aren't they?' Hashe slid a companionable arm around Mancini's shoulder. 'Hate to admit it, but they even give me the willies! Not like the early days, eh? How I ever got away with selling some of those first versions, I'll never know.'

Mancini grinned. 'Like the king penguins?'

'Too right! The rockhoppers were the worst. Whole range kept falling through their ice floes. And the colour matching was dreadful! Those cheap verdance valves are *such* a nuisance.'

Knapp squeaked nervously once more as a death lizard leaned forward, stared straight at him and roared through a tiny grille in its plinth.

'It's alright, son, they won't bite. Look!' Hashe reached out and waved his hand through the middle of the scaly creature. The death lizard flickered, shook its head, then pulled itself together. 'One day they'll have mass. Bigger psychoterrin crystals and two slightly detuned empathy fields and it'll work. It's got to! What the market wants. Harness mass and they can really roar. Something to do with air and solid vocal chords. Technical . . .'

'Will it breathe fire?' said Mancini, his eyes transfixed by the creatures, his jaw barely closing as he spoke.

'Oh no, sir. Not real fire. I'm afraid that the use of volatile substances within transmitted empathy fields is strictly prohibited,' answered Hashe, sounding not a little disappointed. 'However, for an extra two hundred and eighty-six groats we do have an optical subsidiary empathic flame generator. Free fitting while current stocks last!'

'I'll take six! Discount for cash?' asked Mancini, smiling at Hashe. With a flourish the VET pulled a long shopping list out of a pocket and jingled a small velvet sack.

'Come into my office, sir,' oozed Hashe, his eyes popping as the list unravelled before him. 'I'm sure we can accommodate your wishes!'

As Knapp followed them through the noisy virtual menagerie, snatching a glossy catalogue from a shelf and shoving it in his sack, Mancini's heart leapt for joy. A visit to Hashe's Fur and Feather Fayre and for once he would come away with more than just a bag of rivets for his growing frog collection.

'I'm sorry, sir. Rules is rules,' said the Murrhovian Police Officer, glaring boredly over the pile of parchment on the desk at Dewlap.

'But, it's a murder plot!' screamed the Court Livestock Image Consultant, hopping up and down ineffectually.

'So you've said, sir, but without a body . . .'

'We've been through that already! Haven't you been listening?' shouted Dewlap, pummelling the desk with his tightly clenched fists.

'I'm all ears, sir,' replied the uniformed man, barely stifling a yawn of weary indifference.

'Well? What are you going to do about it?' shrieked a red-faced Dewlap, the Empress' threat ringing loud in his short-term memory.

'Do, sir?'

'Yes. Action. Protection. Arrests! That sort of thing! You do *make* arrests?' fumed the Consultant, the tassel on his yellow beret trembling.

'I've written it all down,' explained Constable Poh, pointing proudly at the large book.

'And?' urged Dewlap.

'*And*, sir?' asked the constable, baffled.

'What are you going to do next? This is urgent!'

Constable Poh thought hard, closing his eyes to show how hard he was thinking. 'Oh yes, sir. You're right, sir.' A look of urgency passed suddenly across the officer's face as realisation blossomed. 'Dead right. Something *should* be done. Urgent, like you say!'

'At last!'

'Should've thought of it sooner,' continued Poh. 'It's no good me just writin' it all down. Action, that's what we need.' He reached out, grabbed a large pinkish sheet of absorbent parchment and dabbed the book thoroughly. 'There. Thanks for reminding me.' A wash of relief flooded his face. 'Might've gone all smudgy an' unreadable.'

Dewlap pounded his forehead on the desktop. He was past caring about the fact that he might end up with a nasty bruise and that purple and yellow was out this season.

'This stuff's terrible if you don't blot it quick,' Poh continued, ignoring the screaming Dewlap as nothing unusual. In his experience people often resorted to screaming and bashing things when they came to see him at the station. Funny, that. Constable Poh turned the leaf and looked at the next page. 'See? Already startin' to come through. Would've caused a right mess, that. Don't know why they get this cheap ink. Really don't.'

'I didn't come here to waste my time discussing ink blots!' shouted Dewlap, fear boiling within him as an imaginary katana blade curved out of the sky and headed for his neck. 'What about this murder? *I'm* the victim!'

'Well, not to put too fine a point on it, sir. That's the problem, see?' Constable Poh scowled at Dewlap, examining his body carefully.

'No, I don't see!'

'Evidence, sir! Witnesses . . . it's your body!'

'How *dare* you! There's nothing wrong with my body!'

shouted Dewlap, ruffling his batik-printed kimono petulantly.

'Exactly. I've seen a few murder victims in my time and, well, you're just a teensy bit too lively, see?'

'That's 'cause it hasn't happened yet. In three days' time the Empress will murder me!'

A small youth pulled his ear quickly away from the door and stepped into the shadows.

'Ah, well, that's that, then,' grunted Poh, putting down the quill and folding his arms. 'Wish you'd said before. Would've saved all that parchment. Doesn't grow on trees, you know,' he added and picked up a pencil. 'Look, best thing you can do is come back in three days' time with all the information an' we'll look into it then. If you could bring the murder weapon and a chief suspect it'll speed things up. Is twelve-thirty alright for you and the Empress, sir? You do mean Empress Tau, sir? Sir?'

Constable Poh looked up as the door slammed shut behind the screaming heels of Dewlap dashing into the crowded streets.

'Timewasters,' he tutted, picked up the quill once more and drew a line through the most recent entry in the book. 'The stupidity of some people. Shocking! Doesn't he know it's a tyranny?'

Dewlap ran blindly, curving mental katanas slicing out of the sky from his left and right.

Three days! he panicked, ducking around a cart. Three days to come up with *the* star of the Tyrants' Institute Ball. Or else . . .

Another razor-edged blade lashed at him from the wildest corners of his fearful imagination as he swung into a dark alley – a timorous rodent running to ground. Options flicked through his mind and were rejected: hide, and sentence anyone found harbouring him to their very own Imperial katana in the throat: emigrate, and he'd be tracked down in hours by any one of the countless unknown Imperial spies; curl up, and die! They all led one way.

Suddenly, as he sprinted past, a hand flashed out from a

side alley, tapped him on the shoulder and drew back. He spun reflexively, left leg caught under right ankle, and then crashed into the far wall. The hand, followed closely by the rest of a small body, exploded out of the side alley, sprang onto the prone figure, drew a knife and held it threateningly at Dewlap's throat.

'Got somethin' you want,' whispered the lithe figure gruffly, well aware of the needs of Dewlap from eaves-dropping.

'You're too soon!' whimpered Dewlap, shaking with terror and confusion, trying to rid himself of the imaginary katanas. 'I've still got three days!'

'An' I got somethin' you want.' The knife pressed harder.

'No! I'm not being picky but . . .'

'You come get it.'

'No thanks. I'm sure you're very good at assassinating but . . .'

The figure with the knife stared at Dewlap, momentarily confused, then shook its head and barked, 'Gimme good price. You live long!'

'I . . . I . . .'

The weight on Dewlap's chest lessened as the youth leapt off and tugged him upright, somehow managing to keep the knife firmly at his throat all the time.

'Have no choice. Go with Itto,' insisted the knife-wielding silhouette.

He had no choice.

He went, frowning as he noticed a dirty stain on his kimono. What a day!

It took a while, but Whaiyn the D'vanouin Goatherd eventually found Old Git – in a narrow cleft in the rocks engaged in illicit carnal activities with a wild ibex less than half his age. Extracting the wayward goat with a large stick and a lot of leverage, Whaiyn rounded up the rest of the herd, tied them to a small clump of trees and dashed into the town of Khomun. For today was market day and unless he was *very* much mistaken he should be able to wheedle a few shekels out of 'Genuine' Sham Cantrip, Purveyor of Ancient Artifacts, Treasures and Exquisite Perfidy.

In a network of dark backstreets, hundreds of feet below the sand-blasted tips of countless ancient minarets, cowered the rug-strewn chaos of the Khomun Market. For centuries, deep in the choking incense fog, traders had squabbled and haggled noisily, their camels idly chewing tobacco behind them. And seemingly for almost as long, Sham Cantrip had carefully added the finishing touches to an inexhaustible stream of 'genuine' three-thousand-year-old magic lanterns. Today was no exception. Around him lay piles of recently completed ancient manuscripts, boxes of carved marble friezes (cast from finest limestone, sharp sand and water) and sacks of freshly baked ancient manna from heaven. Cantrip's tongue darted out across his lips as he flung yet another magic lantern across the tiny, cluttered workshop, picked it up, grunted critically and repeated the process. Obtaining the correct degree of 'aging' was a difficult and highly skilled operation.

Skipping around the swaying head of a hooded serpent captivated by the reedy squeaking of a small pipe, Whaiyn squeezed through a tiny gap in a gabbling knot of sword-toting traders arguing over the ashes of a suspiciously torched rug. Barely avoiding a mountain of precariously balanced baskets he finally ducked between the legs of a stall, brushed a gaudy curtain aside and entered the world of 'Genuine' Sham Cantrip. And almost instantly wished he hadn't.

Before his reflexes knew there was something to react to, a spinning magic lantern whistled out of the gloom and bounced off his head with a dull clang. In a flash of 'authentic' D'vanouin desert garb, a hunched wild-eyed figure erupted from the hazy gloom and pounced on it. Sham Cantrip turned the lantern slowly, inches from the tip of his hooked nose, his eyes bulging through a huge lens in hypercritical examination.

'Perfect!' he concluded, rubbing his hands together enthusiastically. 'A beautiful dent. So enigmatic, so

29

authentic. *So* sellable! Add at least eight shekels!' He spun around and snatched a second lantern from the stack behind him, eager for another value-enhancing dent. 'Just stand still,' he said, lining his sights up on the vital tool of Whaiyn's forehead and drawing back his throwing arm for another whistling pitch.

Without warning he hurled the lantern, grinning as it curved towards its target. Whaiyn squealed, leapt sideways for cover and landed in a heap of blank parchments. The lantern screamed past, inches away from his ear, and struck a small statue of a squatting sphinx, shattering its nose.

'What are you *doing*? Don't you recognise me? Stop trying to kill me!' shrieked Whaiyn. Sham dashed across the tiny workshop, stared at the lantern, then at the sphinx and cursed.

'Look at this!' shouted the stall owner, waving the statue angrily and glaring over the hooked horizon of his nose. 'Just look. Ruined! Four days' work, wasted.' He hurled it over his shoulder and snatched at the lantern.

'Should be more careful,' snapped Whaiyn as Cantrip tried, and failed, to return the mangled spout to something at least theoretically capable of decanting genies.

'What do you want?' he snarled irritably, scowling at Whaiyn with his piercing eyes, then returning his attention to the mangled lantern. In that moment Whaiyn was convinced the stall owner had weighed him, searched him for the slightest sign of anything valuable, totalled it up and dismissed him as worthless.

Generally that would have been true. But not today.

'I've got something for you,' began the goatherd, eagerly unbuttoning his shirt and staring intently at Cantrip wrestling with the spout, grumbling as it slipped in his grip.

'Ruined,' he moaned. 'Why couldn't you have stood still?'

'Forget about the lantern, this is far better!' Whaiyn waved a scroll impatiently.

'I'll never sell this, now,' Sham mourned. 'Never! A valuable antique destroyed. Lost forever!'

'In that case, you'll be interested in a valuable antique

found,' said Whaiyn, waving a pair of scrolls under the acquiline hook of the stall owner's nose.

'Am I hearing right? Are *you* trying to sell me something?' asked Cantrip suspiciously. 'It's a miracle!'

Whaiyn waved the complete bunch of five parchment scrolls and held them out. A look of intense curiosity flashed across Sham's calculating face. His hand snatched out reflexively. Whaiyn jerked the scrolls out of reach and stood grinning. 'Not so fast,' he said. 'I want five shekels.'

The stall owner made a show of trying to look sceptically at the parchment, certain inside that these were not just your average bits of scrotty parchment. These were *old* bits of scrotty parchment. And that meant money. 'For the lot?' he asked.

'Each,' demanded Whaiyn.

Cantrip took a sharp intake of breath, grunted and unravelled one bath mat-sized scroll, staring critically at the illuminated text, examining the texture of the yellowed surface, thrilling at the ancient feel of it, his hooked nose twitching with the aroma of the musty temporal conditioner from a genuinely time-washed manuscript. His fingertips quivered as the trapped centuries ached for release.

'Fake,' he grunted and handed it back to the goatherd.

'What?' protested Whaiyn, genuinely shocked. 'But look at the colour of them. They're ancient!'

'Lemon juice,' answered the stall owner, returning his attention to the lantern. 'Soak for twenty-four hours then bake in a low oven for two days. Works every time. Fakes, all of them.'

'But why were they all in pots in a cave?'

Pots in a cave? thought Cantrip, bursting with questions. What cave?

'To give them the right smell? Don't ask me,' he grunted, a study of burning indifference. Shrugging his shoulders, he peered at his lantern once more, desperate to know why parchment should smell so fishy.

'But, I thought . . .'

'Sorry, Whaiyn. They're fakes. You've been had.' Deep

inside, the stall owner was quivering. Five real antiques! So close. 'I can tell you're disappointed. Tell you what, as I've known you for so long I'll give you three shekels.'

'Each?' asked Whaiyn, hope sparking briefly to life amongst the rocks of disappointment.

'The lot,' grunted Sham, ostensibly staring at the spout, but gauging Whaiyn's reaction perfectly.

'Three?' squeaked the goatherd with incredulity.

'. . . as it's you, yes.'

'But, I struggled a hundred feet up a rock face to find them!'

'Yes. But you *found* them,' answered Cantrip. *Found* them? he screamed inside, fighting with the desperate urge for information and the skinflint monetary desire for a bargain. 'Er . . . No investment to recoup, see? This is a commercial world. Three shekels for something you just picked up is a *very* good deal! Now, if you were to allow me to hire your head,' he said, deftly changing the subject, weighing the lantern in his hand and staring at Whaiyn's reddening forehead, 'I'm sure we could reach a better price!'

'Ahh, no way!' answered Whaiyn, throwing the scrolls onto the floor and holding out his hand. 'Three shekels,' he demanded.

In a flash, before the goatherd could even consider changing his mind, Sham had plucked three battered coins from within the folds of his coloured gown, dropped them in the waiting palm and snatched the scrolls up hungrily.

Just as swiftly, the goatherd ceased to exist in his calculating consciousness. The stall owner's mind was already teaming with greedy joy. Five real antiques, and they were all his. His first *real* antiques! Miserably, Whaiyn turned and left.

They could be shopping lists as far as Sham was concerned. All that mattered was that they were old, *genuinely* old. That meant they'd fetch a better price.

Cheerfully he hurled another lantern at the wall, swooped through the curtain, arranged the scrolls carefully on his stall and waited for his first customer of the day.

With a deadly mixture of barked instructions and sharp prods to his left and right kidneys from the gleaming knife blade, Dewlap was expertly steered through the throbbing warren of Murrhovian backstreets.

Fed by the nutritional compost of pure fear, his thoughts were racing. Where was he being led? Why hadn't the assassin killed him there and then? And why had he introduced himself?

Dewlap was certain that assassins didn't as a rule go spreading their name around with such gay abandon.

Eventually a sharp stab to his right turned him left into a narrow street, made even narrower by the crates, boxes and sacks which spilled out from the front of what passed for shops around this less than wealthy region of Murrha. Dewlap let out a squeak of alarm – take one pace in there and his brushed ermine Gu-Chi slippers would be ruined. Unrecognisable vegetables vied for Dewlap's attention against the dried remains of ducks, deep-fried eels and a host of stringy, begristled flesh which he shuddered to imagine anyone even considering eating. Nervously, he swallowed. Was this it – death by dried squid?

There was a sharp flick of knife blade to his left kidney, then Itto the knife-wielder leapt to one side, snatched a handle from between a crate of long green vegetables and several sacks of rice and tugged hard. With a gasp Dewlap stared at the endless flight of stairs that was revealed. He couldn't go down there. His batik-print kimono would clash unbearably with the pink and yellow paisley wallpaper! Itto's knife blade made it alarmingly clear that Dewlap must lose either his perfectly manicured sense of taste, or several fingers . . .

How many flights they descended he couldn't tell (he lost count after a few minutes and didn't dare risk opening his eyes) but, ably encouraged by a volley of sharp whispers and short stabs, he stepped out into what should have been a far larger space. It was in fact a very large room, but crammed with precarious piles of unidentifiable objects, stacked high from floor to crumbling ceiling – a claustrophobic nightmare incarnate. Almost no room to move. And even less to breathe. The air was thick with the unmistakable aroma of mice.

Panic chewed nervously at his fingernails as feet dashed unseen behind him, scampering away, twisting and turning expertly around the columns of wicker baskets and cages. There was the sound of fevered rummaging, boxes crashing to the floor as they were searched through, shaken and rejected by Itto.

Given several million more lumens by which to see and a passing hint as to where he was and how to get away from there, Dewlap would have been out of that door and up the stairs faster than a rat up a downspout. Instead, the Imperial Court Livestock Image Consultant stared about him uselessly, in total confusion, unable to see beyond a few inches, which, judging by the decor on the stairs, was probably for the best.

Abruptly there was a snarling sound followed by a grunt of satisfaction then dashing feet approaching. Panic's cold teeth chewed at his quivering hands.

'Here. Very precious!' whispered Itto harshly in Dewlap's ear, igniting a match and lighting a candle with it. Dewlap winced as the light exploded, burning at his eyes, making green circles as he blinked afterimages of mounting terror. 'Good money. Live long!' grated the knife-welder harshly, picked up a box and held it out. 'You need. You like. Tau like. Very precious,' spluttered Itto in pidgin Murrhovian.

Dewlap's beret trembled, telegraphing his fear-laden confusion as panic sucked at his elbows.

'Not like?' whispered Itto waving the knife meaningfully.

'Haha! No, er . . . yes. I not understand,' suggested Dewlap.

'Damnation,' snarled the youth, trying to keep his voice low and glancing behind him nervously.

'That's precisely what I want to avoid,' he confessed, staring at the knife's tip, glinting in the candlelight.

'Damnation? Not like? Tau like!'

The snarling sound appeared again, closer this time. Right

under his nose, in fact. He looked around in terror, the dark giving his imagination claws and teeth. It didn't need to.

'Damnation!' repeated Itto urgently, shaking the box and snatching it open under Dewlap's already quivering nose. He screamed as he stared at a jungle of thrashing black and white fur and searing red eyes. Nine-inch teeth and countless claws fought for release from beneath a steel mesh that suddenly looked far too flimsy for its purpose. The Consultant whimpered pathetically, backing away, flapping his hands and knocking over a stack of incense sticks.

His imagination, defeated by the reality in the box, packed up in a huff and left him to his own devices. How could it compete with *that*?

'Damnation! Good price, eh?' Itto grinned, his teeth shining in the gloom as he held out the box. 'You like? You buy?'

Suddenly, a wave of curiosity surged upon the seas of Dewlap's self-preservation, the heady froth of comprehension bubbling across its leading edge. He held his breath, cringed and peered once more into the box.

One of the faculties that Dewlap prided himself on was the ability to look at one of the thousands of Nature's Creations and not only instantly recognise and name it, but classify it, list its relatives, assess its image enhancement quotient, recall all its previous private and public appearances and work out a quote for its hire fee. He was therefore utterly horrified when he stared at the creature in the box and came up with a string of absolute blanks. With a jolt he realised that he was nose to muzzle with something he had never seen before . . . and if *he* hadn't seen it before . . . Suddenly a blank was filled in – image enhancement quotient for appearance with never-before-seen creature . . . immense! An imaginary katana was miserably resheathed.

Whatever that thing was, Dewlap simply had to have it. It was a matter of life or death.

'You like?' whispered Itto, staring intently at Dewlap's wide-eyed expression of awe. 'Good price!'

'How much?' pleaded Dewlap.

Before Itto could open his mouth a rapid-fire barrage of angry local dialect launched itself wildly into earshot. Syllables and consonants tumbled so swiftly and heavily accented that Dewlap caught perhaps one word in three. But the message was perfectly clear. Itto answered in fluent protesting gibberish, was chastised in acute rebuke, began to wheedle, was cut off and sulkily vanished into the gloom with the box.

'I'm afraid your journey has been a waste of time,' said the age-cracked voice switching easily to a perfect Imperial accent, and a frail-looking man stepped out from behind a column of wicker baskets. 'We are closed for redecoration.' The old man's eyes stared at Dewlap from behind centuries of cataracts.

'You need it! Whe . . . when will you be open?' stuttered Dewlap, searching for the youth.

'Some time yet,' answered the paper-thin man. 'Trouble choosing the colour scheme.'

'I could help!'

'That would not be a good idea.'

'But the animal . . .'

'. . . are not for sale. Now, leave.'

'I'll give you a good price,' said Dewlap, his thoughts racing. *Are* not for sale? There's more than one!

'Leave.'

'Hire?' wheedled Dewlap.

'They are not for hire. Too mean and nasty! You cannot begin to understand,' growled the man, his hands tucked inside the sleeves of his robe.

Empress Tau's face flashed into Dewlap's mind. 'Mean and nasty! I want mean and nasty! . . . nasty! . . . nasty!'

'If you don't let me have them I'll be dead in three days!' blurted Dewlap frantically.

'Small price to pay. Leave!' The old man's eyes flared with anger.

'Name your price . . .' grovelled Dewlap.

The frail man snapped a series of percussive commands in guttural dialect and a shadow, which Dewlap had taken to be a rather large and garish wardrobe, moved. The light level seemed to drop. A vast hand snatched at Dewlap's arm, spinning him around easily and jamming it up his back, lifting his ermine slippers off the floor.

'Ha! I was just leaving,' he whimpered, wincing as his shoulder joint made a noise he was certain it wasn't supposed to. Ponderously, and with the inevitable unstoppability of a calving glacier, the 'wardrobe' opened the door to the stairs and ejected Dewlap with sufficient momentum to send him crashing through the trap door and arcing across the street to land unceremoniously amongst several crates of mysterious and evil-smelling spiked fruits.

The imaginary katana of the Empress slowly unsheathed itself and waggled its point at him with relish.

Through the tangled undergrowth of a dense forest far to the south of the Talpa Mountains, two cold green somethings roared. They hurled themselves together in a tumultuous clash, one leaping one hundred and fifty feet off a cliff to land in a torrent of spitting, frothing frenzy, as it had done for countless centuries.

Had the spectacular confluence of the Rivers Gharial and Caman been anywhere less inaccessible than the middle of a vast tract of uncharted sub-tropical forest it would certainly have been way up in the top ten natural wonders for eager tourists to visit. As it was, apart from the local peculiar wildlife and the odd madman, the only eyes ever to have stared admiringly at the vast cataract were those of the contractors who had built the village three miles away. And that had been a *long* time ago.

They had never found out why they had trekked countless miles through unknown jungle, blindfolded, to build the small collection of ill-matched dwellings which huddled around a neat checkerboard lawn. They had never blinked their collective eye as the plaster veneers were painted garish pink, sky blue and mustard yellow. And they had never even thought about scratching their collective head and daring to ask why such a small community should need so immense an

37

underground system of cavernous drains and connecting passages. Well, why should they – each of them received a two-hundred groat bonus for not finding out, scratching heads or daring to ask.

The real reasons behind the construction of the tiny village of Losa Llamas were lost somewhere in a musty heap of mouldering red tape and gossamer whispers of hurriedly hushed conspiracy. It was something to do with the Ultimate Deterrent – but who the King of Rhyngill had wanted to ultimately deter, and why, had also been lost in an ancient web of impenetrable subterfuge.

The people who undoubtedly knew most about the workings of Losa Llamas and high-energy thaumaturgy were currently four and a half miles away from the Roaring Falls, buried the best part of two hundred feet down in a vast cavern. And some of them were swearing. Profusely.

'This isn't right, you know!' yelled Thurgia, sweating liberally as he strained on the end of a complicated block and tackle arrangement. A lifetime's study to become the Head of Demonic Possession and an overfondness for steak pies had done nothing to prepare him for swinging nigh on twenty tons of highly sensitive thaumic apparatus into position. And he wanted to let everyone else in the thaumatron bay know about it. 'Haven't you got one of those fancy spells to do this?' he complained, hauling on the rope with as much enthusiasm as an amateur bell-ringer with a slipped disc.

'Yes,' answered chief technician Wat, gesturing furiously with what looked like two yellow table tennis bats and slotting his answer between a hail of barked orders. 'C'mon. Up a bit more! A fifteen-kilothaum Daedelian Lift Harness would do the trick in a couple of minutes.'

'Well, why am I struggling with this . . . this *thing* like some galley slave? And *don't* tell me it's to lose weight!' flustered Thurgia, another wave of sweat cascading down his brow.

'Left. Left! Thurgia, I've told you!' insisted Wat. 'That "thing" is a wandbrake. Left, I said. Once we get it bolted in place we can fire up the thaumatron again.'

'I *know* that. I'm not a three-year-old!' grizzled Thurgia, yanking grumpily on a large hessian rope.

'Too far. Swing it right! So what's the problem?'

'Ahhh! Spare me! *Why* can't you use a Daedelian Lift Harness to shift this?'

'*Slowly*!' snapped Wat, waving the table tennis bats with a flourish. 'Don't swing it! 'Cause it's too heavy, that's why. Didn't you hear me, I said "a fifteen *kilo*thaum Harness"? Can you produce that much power yourself? I know I can't!'

Thurgia blushed. He was as guiltily aware as any of the Thaumaturgical Physicists just how little magic he himself could produce now. Oh, give him a couple of dozen kilothaums at his fingertip's disposal and he could pull any number of rabbits out of anyone's favourite topper; he could rustle up a piping hot meal in seconds by just jamming his thumb in the socket and clicking his finger. But ask him to do it without being within reach of a Thaumatron Access Point and you'd wait a long time for your rabbit stew. Throughout Losa Llamas' vast length of subterranean labyrinth, convenience atrophy had taken its pernicious hold. Well, why bother eating a diet of spinach, liver and sprouts three days a week to keep up one's own personal levels of thaumaglobin when just down the corridor a naffing great magi-kinetic field and a humming flux of accelerating particles could produce all the thaums one would ever need? The Thaumaturgical Physicists were magically unfit couch potatoes.

It was inevitable. Just like giving an undergraduate computer programmer unlimited access to *the* highest technology numbercruncher available, updating it every year, building in automatic sub-routines, parallel processing, networking capabilities . . . then snatching it away and asking him to calculate pi from first principles. In his head.

Suddenly Thurgia had an idea. 'What about this backpack thaumatron you've been wittering on about, eh Wat? I thought that was supposed to be perfectly self-contained in a go-anywhere, rear-mounted harness? Won't that produce fifteen kilothaums?'

'More to the right! Oh, yes,' Wat added smugly, thinking

about the advances that he and Phlim had made. 'I've had almost twenty out of it.'

'Well, why isn't it here instead of me?'

'Hold it there. No, *hold* it! Pull the other one! The backpack's a prototype. Still unstable at times,' explained Wat wearily. 'Daren't risk anything as delicate as a wand-brake on it! You know as well as I how fragile these things are. I've spent weeks calibrating it. One knock and the damping field'll be ruined. Then we'll never be able to control the thaumatron feedback generator properly. *Careful*! . . .'

'Oops!' whimpered Thurgia as the doughnut of technical wizardry lurched a foot and a half straight down towards the gaping hole in the squatting toroid of the thaumatron. Hyperensorcelled steam tubes crisscrossed its bulky outline, making it look almost like a drift net of scrap metal hauled off a river bed. Interestingly, there were bits that looked surprisingly not unlike old tyres and shopping trolleys.

'Lower it gently,' insisted Wat, waving his bats wildly. 'Gently!' The wandbrake lurched once more then slid into the slot with only the slightest clang and squeal of grinding metal and nerves.

'Rutger!' yelled Wat as the ropes went slack and Thurgia exhaled with acute relief. 'Unhook it, will you!' A short, almost dwarvish figure in a lab-cloak squirmed across the Thaumatron and began wrestling with the complexities of a very tight half-hitch. Thurgia sat down with a thump. Nerves, and far more physical exercise than he'd had in the last six years put together, were taking their toll gleefully.

Wat dashed up to the thaumatron, tugged a pair of wire looms out of a small inspection hatch and thrust them into their corresponding sockets. With a flickering crackle the damping field of the wandbrake flashed into life – the magical asbestos padding capable of halting a runaway thaumatron.

Two months ago, following Phlim's nightmare realisation that common graphite damping rods could never mop up enough charged particles to prevent meltdown in a runaway thaumatron, he had invented the wandbrake. By adapting the simple magi-kinetic fields that were used as particle accelerators, tweaking the phase angle and mucking about with a whole host of other jiggery-pokery, he had produced a self-contained magical tourniquet capable of controlling terrathaums of screaming magical energy. At least, that was what it did in theory.

Wat thrust a few more wires into holes and pulled a ratchet lever. With a sharp increase in humming the wandbrake sprung into the full glowing aura of reassuring safety. It looked as if it was working.

'Super!' squeaked Wat, rubbing his hands together gleefully. 'Alright, Thurgia, time for the other one.'

The rotund Head of Demonic Possession made a pathetic, whimpering objection and ached desperately for a small individual steak pudding. Wat couldn't be serious. Another one!

'Rutger, attach number two to the pulley, there's a good chap!' yelled Wat. Thurgia cringed. He *was* serious.

The dwarvish figure of Rutger waved a chirpy salute, skipped off across the curving arc of the thaumatron, snatched the rope and swung onto the wandbrake. For a moment he imagined himself to be Clint Machismo the moustachioed hero of the magic lantern shows, swooping gallantly across the chasm to save the heroine in full 80mm Superthaumination, his sword arm ready to swash any buckles that dared get in his way.

Down below Thurgia struggled miserably to his feet as an inch-thick oak-ply door creaked open and a stocky figure stomped imperiously in, his cloak billowing around his ankles. 'Who's nicked my favourite table tennis bats?' shouted Practz, the self-elected head of Losa Llamas.

Wat shrugged and found a vital adjustment to make inside the inspection cover, hoping Practz would go away before he needed to guide the second wandbrake into place.

'Ho there, Cap'n, mainsail's trussed'n'ready for haulin' ' shouted Rutger from on top of the second wandbrake, vividly reliving yesterday's showing of 'Pirates on Parade'.

'Rutger! Why are you still here?' yelled Practz, his bushy

41

eyebrows frowning fluffily as he scowled at the gyroscopically mounted figure-of-eight shaped tube strapped to his wrist. With a grunt he glared at the sand flowing into the bottom half, tutting as it reached above the third graduation. 'It's past three. You should have gone ages ago. It's not good to keep guests waiting!'

'Aye, cap'n . . . er, yes,' spluttered Rutger, the pale, windswept horizon of the Eastern Tepid Sea turning back into the cavern wall. 'I'd best be off then,' he grunted, all traces of Clint Machismo dissolving as he slid off the thaumatron and sprinted out of the door.

'Spending too long in the magic lantern palace, that boy. He'll get square eyes,' growled Practz. 'About time he grew up. Sitting in the dark all day, it's not natural!'

Wat looked around at the cavern and shook his head.

'Well, come on then!' shouted Practz. 'Can't sit around all day talking. Is that wandbrake ready for fitting, or not?'

'Ready,' said Wat.

'Well, come on, me hearties! Jump to it. Man those ropes!' bellowed Practz, hands on hips, feet apart.

Wat shook his head and wondered, not for the first time, whether it was Practz or Rutger who had the squarer eyes.

'My table tennis bats!' shrieked Practz as Wat issued a series of barked orders and began to guide another twenty tons of cutting-edge thaumic engineering into place. 'Give me them back.'

'And on your right you can see one of the traditional market stalls which have been plying their trade throughout centuries of the Khomun Market,' shouted the guide to the knot of people milling behind her in the smoky clutter of the backstreets. 'The bright blue patterns on the crockery are traditional to this area and legend has it that during the reign of . . .'

At the back of the clump of tourists straining to squint over each other's shoulders at the gaudy collection of pots and vases inhabiting the stall, a bored-looking figure tutted and brushed a strand of brown hair out of his eyes.

'Traditional pots. Typical local pans. Load of rubbish!' grumbled Phlim miserably. How many more markets can we possibly visit in the next three days? he thought desperately. The dark corridors and familiar faces of Losa Llamas began to look more and more attractive. Idly he wondered how the Thaumatron refit was going.

But the familiar sound of haggling dragged his attention kicking and screaming to the scene before him. A throng of greying fellow tourists were clamouring for a bargain buy to add to their already bulging cases. In a flash Phlim realised why it was called a package tour. They had hundreds of them. Each. One couple had even hired their very own sherpa to struggle beneath an ever growing mountain of gaudy gifts and stupid souvenirs each individually packaged for the journey home.

If Phlim had really wanted a fortnight's shopping trip, traipsing through one sweltering market after yet another endlessly heaving fayre, feigning incomprehension to escape droves of beggars and sitting through interminable displays of hastily invented 'traditional' rhythmic rituals performed by dancers whose dedicated studies had lasted minutes – if he'd wanted all that then he would have booked a bed and breakfast in Fort Knumm during the St Swindling's Day celebrations. But, he didn't, he hadn't and he was becoming increasingly annoyed about it.

He'd spent good money on this much needed chance of rest and recuperation. Inventing the wandbrake had taken it out of him. Rest! That was a joke. He'd already shuffled the best part of three miles today through these heaving, acrid markets, and *paid* for the privilege, shelling out loads of money he'd worked dashed hard to get. Finding new sources of sufficient supplies of lead piping at short notice, and finding a time when the Thaumatron was free to turn it into gold could be very tricky. It wasn't as if being a Thaumaturgical Physicist was a licence to make gold, but it helped, he admitted secretly.

He really had needed a holiday. Any holiday. After all the trouble that had gone on at Losa Llamas over the last few months he was surprised the whole place wasn't deserted with people snatching well-deserved breaks here and there. One did need to unwind after such a major refit. And it wasn't just the thaumatron that had been stripped and rebuilt. After discovering that half a dozen of the local tree-climbing fish had set up home in the library and were having teething troubles with their sixth litter, Practz had taken stock of the security systems and set about having them tweaked. It seemed that onomatopedes and gerunds just weren't good enough these days.* The fish were now happily into their seventh generation on the twelfth shelf up in Practz's study.

'Come along,' shrieked the guide, waving her tour flag, 'we haven't got all day!'

Obediently, Phlim shuffled after the struggling sherpa frantically attempting to cope with the added weight of a large blue and white pot and three brass doorstops in the shape of hissing vipers. As usual, the guide was pointing out myriad items of fascinating local interest, gabbling incessantly in full verbal flow about the archway overhead which had to be raised in the year . . . blahdyblah . . . following a decree from King . . . blah . . . whose camel was ever so slightly taller than average, or the engrossing inscription on

* Two branches of high-energy linguistic research had produced the onomatopede and the gerund.

Ten foot long, three feet high, coated in a hard exoskeleton and possessed of the most complex array of glisteningly lethal mandibles ever seen, the onomatopede could terrorise even the most hard-hearted of invaders with its deadly accurate barrage of sound effects. It could bark, scream, squeal, roar and utter a million other blood-curdling sounds at the drop of a hat. Unfortunately it was totally useless against an invading force armed with earplugs.

However, the gerund was a completely different beastie. Born out of extensive verbal-noun interbreeding programmes, it had the ability to snap onto the nounal root of an object and will it to behave as an adjective. Thus, the more enarmoured an invading force was, the more effective the gerund proved to be. Hammers would begin hammering; pikes would metamorphose into wildly snapping fifteen-pound fish; and lichen on rocks could be changed into million-kilowat bolts of lichening.

Unfortunately, for some inexplicable reason, the gerund had an insatiable desire for the one soft fruit that didn't grow in Losa Llamas forest. A gerund would do anything for a banana.

Practz felt certain that it was only a matter of time before this became common knowledge amongst the criminal fraternity.

the corner of . . . blah . . . which marked it as a meeting place for the illicit monks of the pre-Emptic era of the post-sympathetic epoch . . . blah . . . blah.

Phlim let the constant gush of words flow through his ears, listening for the tiniest of breaks as the guide took a breath, and idly attempted to calculated her lung capacity. He concluded that she would almost certainly suffer no lasting ill effects if she were to be submerged in a tank of water to a depth of six feet and held there for twelve and a half minutes. He wondered absently if there were a tank nearby in which to try it. Twelve and a half minutes of silence would be bliss.

He was about to ask a squatting fakir the way to the local swimming baths when disaster struck. The knees of the heavily overladen sherpa, which had been trembling on the very brink of collapse for the last five hours, finally gave way, in spectacular fashion. Brass snakes leapt for freedom as the tower of baggage trembled, wobbled and subsided in a shower of straw hats, shell animals and local 'delicacies' prepared from all the parts of certain herbivores which the locals were far too choosy to eat. Packages sprang in all directions, spinning and looping into spatial freedom with exquisite abandon. Screams of horror erupted from the couple whose belongings they were and roars of delight blossomed hysterically amongst the heaving local throng. Including Phlim. Well, he just couldn't help himself.

In a flash seemingly hundreds of bodies appeared, leapt gleefully into the heap and almost as rapidly vanished, each carrying an item which particularly caught their eye or perhaps which they had sold in the first place. Within seconds the entire, once mobile mountain range of souvenirs had ceased to exist, instantly spread amongst the poor of Khomun.

The middle-aged couple stared at the spot in red-faced disbelief, jaws hanging limply in acute shock. Phlim had to turn away, splutters of barely contained mirth escaping from his lips. He didn't think that bending double in peals of helpless belly-laughter would change their mood for the better.

45

It was then that the Thaumaturgical Physicist felt a tug on his sleeve. 'Sir, come closer, come closer!' beckoned a stall owner clad in what looked like a white hessian sack and open-toed sandals. 'Real antiques, ancient treasures, bargain prices! All major currencies accepted. Gold, frankincense, Myrrhican Express.'

Unable to face the tourists, Phlim looked.

'I see Sir is admiring the ancient lantern. An unassuming piece, found washed up on the Northern shore of the Eastern Tepid Seas,' began 'Genuine' Sham Cantrip. 'Quite, quite unique,' he said, kicking a box of identical lanterns under the stall. 'Has been on show in the National Museum of Arts in Khiro. Fifteen shekels?'

Phlim smirked and allowed his eyes to wander idly over the stall.

'Thirteen? And I shall personally gift-wrap it, sir,' babbled Cantrip. 'It is *very* popular!'

Phlim grinned. 'Thought it was unique.'

'Ah. Ahhahha . . . Lots of people come to, er . . . look. Yes, look! It is famous. Can cure baldness.'

'What can it do for lying?' quipped Phlim, looking down momentarily at the turbaned head and the corner of the box of 'unique' lanterns.

'Sir, I am an honest trader in a wide variety of new and used antiques. You insult me!' protested the stall owner, drawing a knife with a sharply curling blade and a handle encrusted with jewels. 'You make amends!'

'Hey! That was a joke!' squeaked Phlim, stepping back.

Cantrip brandished the knife with overexaggerated flourishes. 'You upset me. Only two things cheer me when I'm upset. Blood!' he snarled, making slicing motions in the air inches away from Phlim's spleen, then grinned widely. 'Or money! You buy knife, eighteen shekels with matching slippers, see? Real imitation diamonds and rubies. I wrap it for you?'

'No, no!'

'You buy. You insulted me!'

Phlim looked around on the stall for anything harmless.

His eyes landed on five rolls of parchment. 'Alright. I'll take them.' He pointed.

'A wise decision, sir. Beautiful quality. Twenty shekels.'

Behind him, the tour guide stared at the unbroken circle of squabbling marketeers and cut-throats surrounding them and swiftly reached the decision that the Khomun Market had definitely lost its quaint ethnic charms. Nothing like this had *ever* happened before. She waved her flag and bellowed loudly, turning on her heel and trotting away at double speed.

Phlim grunted, rummaged in his purse, threw twenty shekels at Cantrip, grabbed the parchment scrolls and ran off.

'Hey! Sir, no!' shrieked the turbaned stall holder, leaping up and down. 'Twenty shekels. *Each*!'

As he helplessly watched the back of Phlim disappear into the crowd Sham Cantrip cursed the offspring of every camel which the Thaumaturgical Physicist would ever own. Twice. Not only had he virtually stolen those parchments at twenty shekels for five but he hadn't even haggled for them.

Tourists. No sense of shopping etiquette!

Cheiro Mancini's eyelids flickered as his rapidly moving pupils dashed about inside. His mind whirled, dreaming of 'Gloomy Tuesday' as the horses frothed and hauled the cart wildly onwards.

'Sorry, dear,' he grunted, staring into the alchemical burner at the lump of brownish sludge in the bottom. 'It did look like it might be Philosopher's Mercury. Would have fooled me.' He glanced at the twelve-year-old girl staring expectantly at him. 'Pay on the way out and send the next one in,' he added and patted her gently on the head.

The sleeping Mancini twitched as he recalled that day four years ago with the crisp clarity of yesterday's breakfast.

She was a good customer, always turning up with some strange ore found in her father's mine and handing over her money, expectantly, excitedly hoping that *this* time it was the real thing. Philosopher's Mercury. The vital ingredient for

47

commercially turning lead into gold, and the rarest element ever known. It wasn't that it was impossible to turn lead into gold without it, mind. Every alchemist knew that if you heat a couple of tons of lead for long enough, it fuses, then boils. Catch the vapour in a jar, keep it at something approaching the temperature of a small star and zap it with a sixteen thousand-kilovolt stab of lightning on a moonless night and bingo! Gold. Alright, so 'hot fusion' was fiddly, dirty and the piddling scrap of gold you got at the end of it all was so impure that it wouldn't even pay for the heating bills, but it was gold. It could be done. And with a few sackfuls of Philosopher's Mercury it might just be possible to do it at room temperature. The snag was actually finding a seam of the stuff. It would be worth ten times its weight in gold. Ten thousand if it actually *did* turn lead into gold.

The door in Mancini's swirling dreamworld creaked open and the next customer strolled in, bags of ore held eagerly ahead of him.

Suddenly there was a sound of uproar from outside and a vast prospector stormed through the door sending the customer and his bags of unknown ores flying.

'Charlatan. Liar!' screamed the prospector, waving a scrunched copy of *Trends in Alchemical Sciences* under Mancini's nose. 'What d'you think of this?' he yelled, flinging the parchment journal onto the desk.

The Mancini on the hurtling cart twitched and writhed as he relived the memory of that Tuesday. That headline. That disastrous headline!

'Philosopher's Mercury a hoax!'

Professor Flyshmanan Pohns, the highly regarded – and remarkably vocal – Murrhovian Court Alchemist had just published yet another article. In a massive change to his normal direction he produced tables of figures that killed off the centuries-old Alchemist's dream of Philosopher's Mercury; he formed theories that nailed the coffin lid down and drew conclusions that gleefully flung several tons of soil on top. The room temperature conversion of lead into gold

48

was now 'officially impossible': 'Cold fusion' was dead.

With that headline everything that Mancini had been striving for since he had been big enough to stir the Junior Cauldron of his first alchemistry set had vanished in a puff of truth. He had dreamed the impossible dream, stirred the improbable vat, lost the unwinnable fight with reality. Lead is lead, iron is iron and mercury is a freezing lump of rock on the far edge of space. And nobody, nobody can change that. Well, not at room temperature, anyway.

In a flash on that 'Gloomy Tuesday', all the hundreds of groats' worth of Mancini's alchemical equipment had turned into shelves of misshapen reject pottery. His Patented Philosopher's Funnel had metamorphosed into a grubby glass cone before his very eyes; his Ashmolean Kleenburn Athanor had suddenly become a battered, nondescript ether burner available from any backstreet camping shop and, worst of all, his treasured Nay-Stick Nay-Burn Aludel had almost gleefully transmutated into a terracotta soup-bowl readily available from any of the hundreds of market traders in Fort Knumm for – not the sixteen groats that he had paid, not eight groats, not five . . . they wouldn't even ask three for it . . . three for it . . . three . . .

The thundering progress of the large cart and the induced dozing of its two passengers was suddenly, and rudely, interrupted as the rear wheel slipped sideways off a loose stone. Cheiro Mancini sat immediately bolt upright, swore and failed totally to recognise where he was. Knapp stared about him in bewilderment as the scenery slid rapidly by.

The last thing Mancini remembered was grinning smugly at Annz Hashe outside his Fur and Feather Fayre, cracking his whip across the back of the horses and setting off for . . . well, come to think of it, he wasn't sure.

'Are we there yet?' asked Knapp, staring at the dense blur of countless tracts of foliage huddled at the edge of the track. Millions of leaves coloured the light green, filling the air with the musty aroma of decades of unchallenged arboreal dominance.

'Course not!' barked Mancini, pinching himself as the

horses reached a junction and swerved unerringly around the unmarked left turn.

'Is it much further?'

'Ask the horses! I haven't a clue!' protested Mancini, feeling distinctly uncomfortable around his cloak collar. The delicate peal of alarm bells began to scream inside his head. Panic rising, he tugged hard on the reins, snapping the bits tight into the horses' mouths, calling for an immediate screeching halt. He was completely ignored. Knapp watched in dumb confusion as Mancini squealed and leapt off the cart, barely overtaking it as he dashed alongside.

'Stop!' he cried, sprinting backwards, waving frantically at the relentlessly advancing beasts. 'Halt. Cease. Whoa!' If it hadn't been for a nifty leap into a convenient rhododendron bush Mancini would now be wearing a series of tasteful mud-coloured horseshoe designs across his jerkin.

Knapp grabbed his sack, leapt off the cart and helped him up, tugging branches out of Mancini's cloak as they sprinted head-down after their vanishing transport. Unseen, a short figure swooped out of a tree on the end of a vine and landed in the cart.

With a grunt of sweating frustration Mancini snatched at the side of the rattling cart and vaulted in. And nearly fell out again with shock.

'Oh, sorry. Did I startle you?' asked the squat figure in the cart. 'You were heading my way so I thought I'd hop in and hitch a ride. Don't mind, do you? Name's Rutger, by the way.'

'Who the . . . ? Where the . . . ?'

'We all thought you weren't coming,' continued the solidly built, but undersized hitcher. 'You're about half a day late, you know. But you're here now, that's the important bit. And I'm so glad you are. Here, that is. It's miles back to Losa Llamas, hard work on my legs.' He waved a pair of short, stocky limbs, a child's in everything but bristling musculature and forests of red hair.

'Come back!' shouted the fading voice of Knapp behind.

'Oh. Hang on,' said Rutger, grabbing the reins and giving them a quick flick. The horses stopped instantly.

'How did you do that?' squawked Mancini. 'I tried . . . Did you say Losa Llamas? But . . . I was heading back to Venasht to get my toothbrush. What do you mean by hijacking me?'

'Oh no. It's nothing that sinister. You drove here,' said Rutger as Knapp struggled onto the cart, panting. 'Hi ho, slither on away!' bellowed Rutger in his favourite Clint Machismo cry and cracked the reins across a pair of fetlocks.

'How could I drive here?' protested Mancini, ignoring the grinning technician. 'I was asleep!'

'Hmmm, yes. Practz got a bit carried away, I'm afraid. He shouldn't really have used a SMART Card on you but we're so short of time.'

'A what?'

'SMART Card. They're new. Subliminal Memory-Aided Remote Tracking. It's a way of getting people to come here without knowing where "here" is! Sticks an image of the directions in the subconscious which pops up when we want it to. It'd be deadly if advertisers got hold of it. People would buy anything you wanted them to. Speaking of which, did you get everything?' Rutger hooked a finger over his shoulder at the bulging tarpaulin. Knapp nodded as he gasped for breath.

'Yes, I think so,' said Mancini, sounding very unsure of everything.

'Pricey?' queried Rutger.

'Fifty-three thousand, eight hundred and ninety-six groats,' answered Mancini, still utterly baffled, wondering how he had managed to buy everything. Truth to tell he wasn't even sure what he had bought. If the card was SMART, Mancini certainly wasn't.

Rutger whistled appreciatively. 'I told 'em it'd be well over thirty thou. There goes another eighteen bidets,' he added thoughtfully, his stubby fingers wriggling against each other as he calculated the exchange rate.

Cheiro Mancini shook his head. 'Bidets?' he repeated, staring at the stranger in the cart as if he had eight nostrils. 'What've bidets got to do with it?'

'Plumbing.'

'Eh?'

'Lead plumbing,' answered Rutger cheerfully. 'Fifty-three thousand, eight hundred and ninety-six groats is about equal to twelve ells of half-inch lead piping which in turn is just about enough to supply eighteen bidets.' Knapp scratched his head.

'That's a very good price for scrap,' whimpered Mancini suspiciously, his eyebrows furrowing into bewildered question marks. How long had he been asleep? Was inflation *that* bad?

'No, no! Wouldn't get a fraction of that as scrap. I'm talking gold!' grinned Rutger.

Both Mancini's and Knapp's eyes lit up. Had they heard right? Did he say gold? Despite the fact that he was sweating and he still had several feet of rhododendron sticking out of his cloak pocket, Mancini was sure he was still dreaming. Surely this almost dwarvish figure sitting next to him couldn't know the secret of every alchemist's wildest greed-driven dreams? Could it possibly be true?

'You can turn lea . . . lea . . .' struggled Mancini, his tongue sticking to the roof of his greedy mouth.

'. . . lead into gold?' offered Rutger. 'Oh yeah. Easy peasy!'

Mancini turned a very strange shade of green as envy wrestled with his complexion.

'You can't?' asked Rutger, swallowing nervously.

Mancini shook his head numbly, his jaw limply wagging. Knapp stifled a snigger and snatched every word that came oug of Rutger's mouth.

'You're having me on? It's one of the first things you learn on the Basic Transmogrification Course in the first term. If you can't do that you don't deserve to call yourself a Thaumaturgical Physicist.'

Mancini stared blankly at Rutger, the trees and undergrowth slipping by unseen. 'A what?' he croaked.

'Whoops! You're not a Thaumaturg . . . ?' Rutger grinned the grin of a man sitting on a freshly painted park bench. 'Er, look. Just forget I said anything, alright? Don't say anything to Practz . . . Hah! I thought everybody knew . . . ahem. Nice weather we're having, er, just right for dahlias . . .'

Mancini's mind was a kaleidoscope of gyrating, glistening greed. Lead into gold! Pipes into piles! 'Easy peasy!' he'd said. Cold mutation *was* possible. And he was about to enter the place that held the secret!

An image of himself spread on a silk-sheeted bed, surrounded by droves of nubile maidens, gallons of wine, bunches of exotic fruit and gently strumming minstrels flashed eagerly into his mind. Dreamily he licked his lips. Oh yes, he thought, filthy rich for me.

Welcome to the Treasure Dome!

Drop the Dead Dragon

With a jolt of panic and a profusely sweating brow, Dewlap sat bolt upright in his room and stared about him in the pale morning light. His eyes widened into pools of nightmare panic as a gleaming katana surged out of the ceiling. The screaming blade whistled towards the vicinity of his chin, slashed once, twice, then receded into his terrified subconscious. Nervously he felt his neck, fearing the worst, the fatal gush of warm stickiness. Deflating with relief he exhaled a huge sigh and collapsed back onto the futon. Still intact. Oh joy, Praise be to Omo, the Bright White God of Coloureds Forty. Blood was *so* hard to remove from the collars of batik kimonos – all the scrubbing faded the colours dreadfully.

Suddenly he caught sight of the train of filthy footprints staggering across his favourite alpaca rug. Somebody had entered his room *without* taking their shoes off! Well, actually, they had removed one. One! The ultimate insult. Dewlap's temper rose exponentially, anger flooding through every vein. His alpaca rug! . . . destroyed by an act of wanton vandalism. Dip any piece of alpaca ware in the slightest amount of water and the natural oils congeal into something that looks like a week-old omelette. Who could *do* such a thing? Snarling, he followed the zig-zagging trail and squealed as he stared at his feet, still dripping durian juice, mango peel and mud from five toes, and a destroyed ermine court slipper. What had happened . . . ?

In a torrent of horror, last night's escapades came flooding back. The mouse-smelling storeroom, the mobile wardrobe, the exit, the frantic pursuit by a club-wielding shop owner. How had he escaped? How had he found his way back to the Palace? Where was his other shoe? Had anyone seen him in *such* a state?

Abruptly there was an officious pounding at his door and a voice yelled, 'Her Exaltedness, The Empress Tau demands your presence immediately. If not sooner!'

A tidal wave of apprehension surged up Dewlap's emotional tributaries, bursting their banks and flooding his plains of alarm knee-deep in torrents of bubbling worry. His mouth gaped as he fought for a reply. Too soon!

The door was struck again.

'Yes, yes! Just coming!' lied Dewlap, trying to hold his voice steady as he began to divest himself of the tattered garments, mourning every torn thread, weeping over every stain.

'You are wanted immediately,' reminded the caller. 'I did say immediately, didn't I? That means now!'

'A few moments . . .' came the squeaked reply as a shirt button steadfastly refused to be undone.

'Now!'

'I can't . . . I'm not ready!' The button pinged across the room as Dewlap tugged hard. 'I . . . I . . .' His mind whirred for an excuse. 'I'm in . . . conference!' he blurted and cringed, reaching for a rack of clean clothes, his leggings dangling around one ankle. Would he believe the lie?

There was a pause.

'Shall I inform Her Exaltedness of this fact?' pressed the voice in the corridor.

'No! I . . .' Suddenly, out of the ashes of despair rose an idea, a shadow of a plan which, given a mountain of gullibility down which to propel it, followed by a tropical storm of misplaced belief and an earthquake of pure luck to drive it home, might *just* work. Dewlap cleared his throat and tugged on a sock. 'Yes! Tell her I will be along shortly. With news!'

Now you've done it, he thought grimly to himself. Staring interrogatively at the wall, he said aloud, 'So you can supply two of these creatures? And they have never been seen at any public or private function previous to this? Oh, they're outside even as we speak, yes, I'd love to take a look!' Dewlap shook hands across the table with the imaginary animal trader.

The messenger on the other side of the door, listening to

the conference, shook his head doubtfully, turned and strode off to inform the Empress.

Pulling the rest of his clothes on in a rush, offering a minute's silence for the alpaca rug and each of his court slippers, Dewlap waited a period of time which he deemed was about right to go into the courtyard and haggle with the imaginary animal trader for a better deal. During this time he took two leads and carefully wound them around a pair of convenient microfilament bamboo hat-pins and held them out admiringly before him. Then he stalked towards his door, took one last look around and stepped into the corridor, the smell of burning bridges stabbing at the inside of his fear-stricken nose.

He couldn't believe he was even going to attempt such a ridiculous act of unsubstantiated bluffery.

But what choice did he have?

'Done yet?' demanded Practz, shutting the three-ply oak door behind him as he strode into the thaumatron bay.

'Just about completed the second wandbrake interface networking,' answered Wat, stifling a yawn.

'Eh?' grunted Practz.

'Nearly finished plugging it in,' explained the chief technician with a groan, rubbing the back of his neck. It had been a hard day, alright; he should be sleeping like a log.

'Well, why isn't it finished?' said Practz eagerly.

'There's an open circuit on the secondary hypertaurus subcomplex loom,' murmured Wat.

Practz stared gazedly at him. 'Is that serious?'

'If you reckon that shinning up there and plugging that bunch of wires into that socket is serious, then yes,' groaned Wat, pointing to a swinging string of multicoloured multicore. 'There's a ladder over there . . .'

'Ooh no. That's a tech's job,' whimpered Practz. 'I wouldn't dare.' A streak of icicles screamed up his spine as he thought of climbing the twenty feet up to that inspection panel. His head spun vertiginously at the prospect of just one tiny ladder rung being the only thing stopping him from plunging twenty feet straight down . . .

A hand appeared over the horizon of the thaumatron and a technician clambered into view. Practz heaved and looked away. How could anyone stand being so far above the floor? It was unnatural.

'This one?' shouted the technician, waving the clump of wires.

'Shove that in and we're done!' shouted Wat, a flutter of relief tinging the edge of his voice. The technician grinned, snatched the wires and jammed them enthusiastically into the waiting socket, closed the inspection panel and disappeared over the horizon.

'Has he finished?' asked Practz, investigating his feet. 'Can we start it up now?'

'What's the hurry?' whined Wat.

'We've got guests coming and I want everything ready . . .' began Practz.

'So you've got something to pay them with,' grunted Wat, looking meaningfully from the pile of lead plumbing in the corner to the thaumatron to Practz.

The Head grinned sheepishly. 'Well, is it ready, or not?'

'It needs a diagnostic first, just to check it out, make sure we haven't plugged something up the wrong way,' answered Wat. He spun on his heel and marched off across the bay to a row of small hooks on the wall. Removing a key he unlocked a small door, withdrew a larger, far more elaborate key, walked back across the chamber, unlocked another door, moved several sheets of lead and took out a small black box of nano-sprites.

The diagnostic tools of Thaumaturgical physics, nano-sprites were the microscopic relatives of naiads and nixes, but with an almost infinite technical superiority. While nixes were content to frolick tweely in babbling forest brooks, nano-sprites romped in the surging torrents of multi-gigathaum flux fields. While Naiads cavorted in the gentle flow of rivers, nano-sprites surfed on the heady currents of power. They could control and reorder matter at the micro-quantum level, recharging tired electrons, charming strange quarks and unsticking incorrectly attached gluons. No self-respecting Thaumaturgical Physicist should leave home without at least half a dozen sewn into his turn-ups.

Sucking one of the glowing creatures into a syringe-like device, Wat strolled over to a small port and pushed the plunger home, injecting the nano-sprite into the vast bulk of the thaumatron.

'Half an hour or so and we can fire it up,' announced Wat, much to the relief of Practz, who was hopping impatiently from foot to foot and glancing at his wrist timer.

'Cutting it fine,' he said with a sharp intake of breath. 'Have to leave the honours to you. Must dash!' And with that Practz spun on his heel, sprinted out of the thaumatron bay and away towards the upper levels.

It was not surprising that Cheiro Mancino and Knapp had never in their lives seen anywhere quite like Losa Llamas. Because there *was* nowhere quite like Losa Llamas.

The first thing that struck Mancini as the wagon trundled out of the dense greenery and into the clearing in which the village stood was, 'Who could possibly keep a pet dragon in one of *those* huts?' They were so small!

He stared, momentarily flummoxed, at the random collection of gaudily decorated dwellings. Blue and white buildings sporting vases and gourds nestled around a central pond which had once been stocked with a comprehensive range of local fish. Unfortunately, several species had been highly carnivorous and, following a period of intense digestive activity, the total number remaining alive within the pond totalled marginally less than one. However, since no-one ever stared into its murky green depths it didn't matter.

Losa Llamas had the air of an Angstarktik coastal resort in winter, bypassed, ignored, erased from the map of essential visits; a long forgotten tourist trap. Its springs rusted beyond use, its bait mouldy, its turnstiles – if it had possessed any – corroded into immobility.

Cheiro Mancini stared around in disbelief, half-expecting to see a waterlogged crazy-golf course or a set of rusting swings creaking in the breeze.

His mind flew back to the visit by the richly dressed man

with the sack of gold and tried to fit him into this scene. But, no matter how much his mental fists hammered at the image, attempting to force it into the swirling jigsaw of images and feelings around him, it didn't compute.

Rutger could sense the cloud of buzzing queries swirling wildly in the Virtual Ecology Technician's brain and spoke swiftly to head it off at the proverbial pass.

'Who d'you think's going to win the Cranachan All-comers Cow-toppling Championship this year? My money's on "Black" Achonite,' he blurted. Mancini and Knapp, like anyone not involved in the work of Losa Llamas, were a gaping security hazard; a disaster waiting to spill the cat out of the beans, as one of the lower grade technicians had insisted, ineloquently mixing his metaphors. So the more distractions Rutger could throw at the two guests, the better.

'Ever seen Flossie the Wonder Hound at the magic lantern palaces?' Rutger asked Knapp. 'I love the way she wags her tail and whimpers and always saves the day. Have you seen her?'

Why Practz had insisted that bringing in outside help was a necessary risk Rutger hadn't a clue. It was never this complicated in 80mm Superthaumination.

Mancini stared about him. Already surprised by the lack of people and the theatrical feel to the place, he was utterly spellbound when the wagon turned and headed straight for a steep outcrop of rocks crowned with a mohican of trees. Before his very eyes two seemingly natural columns of elder twitched, swayed momentarily, then suddenly bent away from each other. It was as if some offensive arboreal argument had broken out and each row, with sap rising, found it absolutely intolerable to be rooted so close to such petty-minded examples of overgrown shrubbery. The trees hinged at ground level, lying flat and allowing a clear path to the immense moss-coated outcrop squatting ahead. Moments later the ancient stone itself began to move as forces way beyond Mancini's limited ken began to reshape the very metamorphic rock itself. A vast section of it rumbled seismically as it descended into the ground, revealing a huge cavern. Rutger grinned as he steered the horses through the entrance into a space big enough not only for the wagon but several more cathedrals and a dozen elephants besides.

The horses slid smoothly inside and the grinning gap in the cliff face sealed behind them.

'Welcome to Losa Llamas,' said Rutger, gesturing as expansively as his short arms would allow and leaping off the wagon.

'Ah! There you are,' shouted a familiar figure crossing the cavern floor with a determined stride, the vast bulk of a Losa Llaman porter and part-time guard behind him. 'So glad you could make it! Traffic bad on the Trans-Talpino Trade Route, eh?' said Practz, glancing at the complex arrangement of glass jars and sand strapped to his wrist. 'You're late. We expected you almost five turns ago.' He rotated one of the smaller jars as he spoke and flicked a bead across on the abacus.

Mancini recognised the speaker instantly. One of the things he prided himself on was his ability never to forget a face which belonged to someone who recently handed over sacks of money. Especially one so generous! It was a skill born out of years of absolute poverty.

Unfortunately he hadn't much of a clue why he was late. For that matter, he hadn't much of a clue where he had been or what he had been up to for the past . . . he calculated quickly . . . three days. He couldn't remember a thing.

'Be careful with that stuff, Uhrnest,' yelled Practz over his shoulder at the struggling porter-guard. 'Cost a packet, that did.'

'Sack,' corrected Mancini, grinning nervously. Knapp looked up and hugged his sack.

'Eh? Oh yes, very good.' Practz shrugged at Rutger behind Mancini's back, leading the VET through a large opening in the cave wall.

As he descended an enormous flight of stairs hewn out of the solid rock, sandwiched between an amiably chatting Practz and his dwarvish colleague, Cheiro Mancini began to wonder if he had made the right decision.

He also began to wonder if he'd really had any choice.

And a tiny voice inside his head pondered the chances of ever seeing daylight again.

With his nerves clenched tight and his heart pounding faster than the buttocks of a mating stoat, Dewlap heaved open a pair of doors, strode into the huge courtyard and barely missed crashing into the backside of a vast horse. Shaking his head he looked up and, despite lacking any formal qualifications in gynaecology, realised that the beast was definitely a stallion. He quickly averted his gaze and searched for the Empress, taking several shocked steps backwards as he realised that two huge armies were massed in the Murrhovian Imperial Palace Central Courtyard.

Two enormous bamboo siege towers were drawn up facing one other across the arena, each raising a single figure high above the melee below, each displaying a huge banner fluttering gently in the morning air. Above the gleaming green- and red-tiled roofs, the toothed symbol of the Imperial Murrhovian Dragon curled lazily in its customary snarling fashion. Dewlap looked up at the nearest siege tower and with a baffled gasp recognised Empress Tau's steel toecapped sandals danging over the edge. As he watched she raised a large cone to her mouth, pointed down and yelled, 'Knight to King's Pawn Three!'

Immediately, eight Imperial Guards swarmed out of nowhere, grabbed the horse, two to a leg, and hopped the terracotta beast two squares forward and one to the side. The crowd went wild. Mate in two moves.

At the far end of the courtyard General Lehrt bellowed a series of commands and a swarm of squaddies began to shift a vast castle tower towards Tau's terracotta army. An inhuman scream issued from fifty feet above Dewlap's head as the Empress watched one of her ten-foot pawns being dragged out of the courtyard.

'Bring that back now!' she squealed angrily, her voice echoing shrilly off the curving roofs.

'You can't. I took it!' yelled General Lehrt through his megaphone.

'And I want it back!'

'But the rules state . . .'

'That *I* can remove your head between moves if I wish,' screamed Tau, cutting the General's words off in mid-flow. 'Would you *like* me to remove your head between moves, hmmm? Would you?'

Even across the half-mile span of the courtyard, General Lehrt could sense the Empress fiddling with the handle of her katana.

'Bring back the pawn,' commanded Lehrt miserably.

Suddenly Empress Tau's eagle eye spotted Dewlap fidgeting nervously behind her twelve foot-tall terracotta bishop. 'Well?' she demanded, her starched eyebrows knitting into V's of anger. 'What news? Shall kitty taste your neck today?' she growled through her megaphone as she fondled her katana's handle.

Dewlap swallowed, cringing deep inside as the charred remains of a burning bridge crumbled and collapsed. Here goes! 'Your Exquisite Draconimity, good news! I have two . . .'

'What? Shout up. Louder, man!'

Dewlap shuddered. It was bad enough having to lie to the Empress, but having to shout it out . . . 'Your Exquisite Draco . . .'

'Can't hear you!' bellowed Tau.

Dewlap wheeled around, snatched a megaphone from an Imperial Guard's belt and yelled, 'Empress, I have two of the finest, most splendid creatures ever to exist. I can guarantee that as hostess of this year's Tyrants' Institute Fancy Pets Party *you*, O Dreadful One, shall be looked upon with gazes of envy to be rivalled only by the sneers of tyrannical power which you can return. Indeed, you shall . . .'

'Get to the point! What are they?' snapped Empress Tau.

'A pair of . . .' Could he really go through with this? Would it work? A ripple of expectant murmurings vibrated around the courtyard. Could he possibly impress the Empress? Dewlap tried to swallow in a dry mouth. '. . . A pair of sloths.'

'Sloths! You presented me with sloths two years ago!' shrieked Tau. 'Kept hiding under the tables as I recall. Slowed the party down no end. Have you forgotten how I detested them then? I refuse to accept such pathetically hairy lumps of derisable . . . derisable . . . sloth-hood!'

Dewlap winced as the crowd sniggered. 'These are . . . different . . .'

'A sloth is a sloth!'

'These are new sloths. Believe me, O Merciless One, you'll love them! These are just you!'

Empress Tau made a deep noise in her throat, her bamboo armour squeaking as she moved forward to scowl from on high. 'Very well, bring them in. If you dare!' she growled, her finger toying with her katana's handle. A gesture which Dewlap and the entire gathered crowd couldn't possibly fail to see.

He gulped, held up a quivering palm and said, 'Your Imperial Greatness, I must beg a few fleeting moments prior to their entrance in order to acquaint you with *all* of their capabilities. Factors which I feel sure will turn an evening of pleasure into one of immense strategic use.'

The Empress grunted and leant back in her siege tower, tutting, 'Very well, get your wheedling excuses out of the way first. Just make them good!'

'Your Splendidity, I am painfully aware that it is not my place to question but, have you ever wondered at the suitability of other Tyrants to hold their position?'

The crowd took a sharp breath and settled forward in their seats. He was on dangerous ground here – all the more interesting.

Dewlap continued; he had no choice. The flames from the bridges behind him were scorching the back of his neck. 'Have you ever seen the effeminate flick of a supposed warrior's wrist that has raised an eyebrow of inquiry? Or witnessed a kingdom-crushing Impaler, whose list of victories stretches for centuries before him, wince if the herbed wine is too hot? Ever wondered how you may find out if your rivals in the world of tyranny are really cut out for it?'

General Lehrt pricked up an ear. The silence in the courtyard dripped with pent expectation. They were either going to witness something very, very special or it would end in execution.

'What has this to do with sloths?' snarled Tau.

'These sloths, which I am about to present, have been raised on a diet of pure courage, weaned onto hatred at an early age, bathed in ruthlessness daily. None but the most tyrannical, the most dictatorial, the most *wicked*, and I say that in the nicest way, will be able to see the creatures I shall introduce.'

The Empress' eyes burned with curiosity and cunning as she rolled this concept around in her mind. It sounded good.

'With one glance, Your Dictatoriality, you shall see the heart of your rivals . . .'

'Bring them in!' she cried suddenly, her breath blasting the black strands of the moustache of honour glued firmly to her upper lip.

Dewlap needed no second bidding. He fled for the doors in a cloud of dust.

Almost immediately, Tau clapped her hands and four vast guards snapped into action. They hitched up their sumo belts, dashed for the Imperial Open-Top Sedan Chair and sprinted with it towards the base of the siege tower. Fifty feet above their heads the end of a silk rope was launched over the bamboo banister, followed seconds later by the Empress abseiling rapidly into position on her red sedan.

Half a mile away General Lehrt swallowed and headed for the ladder, quickly recalling that Rule Twelve of the Six Thousand and Three Entrenched Murrhovian laws said something about everyone having to look up to the Empress or else . . .

With a gasp of anticipation from the crowd, the doors were kicked open and Dewlap lurched in, leaning back from two empty leads as if angry rottweilers in them could sense flesh ahead. 'May I present,' he screamed, 'the Empress' New Sloths!'

A scream of applause erupted as the crowd, desperate to

be seen as tyrannical, dictatorial and above all wicked, yelled their appreciation.

Dewlap marched slowly forward, the creatures supposedly straining at their collars, he acting restraint against the leads horizontal before him.

The Empress stared. At nothing. She couldn't believe it. Why could everyone see the creatures and yet she – the most tyrannical of the lot of them, more raw despotism surging through her little toe than in all of them put together – she saw nothing?

A sudden flash of extreme active oppression crossed her furious mind, demanding instant relief. She stood, leapt off her sedan chair, dashed forward, knifed a cheering attendant and stared at the approaching figure again. Still nothing!

It couldn't be true. An act of such evil should have given rise to at least a little glimpse of them.

Dewlap halted before the Empress as she wiped her six-inch knife absently against her thigh.

'Such a beautiful colour, aren't they?' he said matter of factly. 'I think they like you – look, he's wagging his tail!'

Tau's shoulders tensed as she stared at the two collars restraining the invisible sloths. In a flash she turned, snatched Admiral Ti by the throat and glared into his eyes. 'What colour are they?' she demanded, the tendons on the back of her hand standing like cables.

'B . . . b . . . brown,' choked Ti, turning red as General Lehrt muscled his way around the vast terracotta horse.

Tau whirled on her heel, discarding Ti with a flick of her wrist and snatching General Lehrt's Adam's apple in her vice-like grip. 'What colour?' she growled, pointing at the empty collars in Dewlap's hands.

Lehrt panicked. What had Ti answered? What if he contradicted? What would happen?

'What colour?' squealed Tau, shaking the General, lifting him off his haunches.

'Ghhh . . .' began Lehrt, choking. Admiral Ti shook his head wildly.

'Answer!' squealed Empress Tau.

'B . . . b . . .' croaked Lehrt, glancing over her shoulder at the Admiral of the Fleet mouthing colours at him. 'B . . . blue!' he croaked, praying he was right. Admiral Ti covered his ears, but, instead of the tirade he was expecting the Empress gently put Lehrt down, turned in ostensible serenity and moved slowly towards Dewlap, growling.

General Lerht rubbed his throat, thanking the Lucky Pin-Holes in the Canopy of Night that he had guessed correctly.

Her Imperial Empress Tau glared at Dewlap, smiled a smile that would put a crocodile to shame and whispered in a voice that somehow everyone in the courtyard could hear, 'Admiral Ti says that they are brown and General Lehrt says that they are blue. Which one is right, Dewlap?'

A drip of cold sweat trickled from his temple as a menu of possible replies flicked into his head:

'You mean you don't know, Empress?' . . . instant death!

'Blue. I never did trust Admiral Ti' . . . death of Ti, certain death for him from one of the Admiral's henchmen.

'Brown. Lehrt always struck me as a wimp!' . . . death of Lehrt, a life of terror for him.

'Pink!' . . . death of Ti *and* Lehrt. Rioting, civil war . . .

He opted for, 'Both! They're brown and blue! Tasteful, hmmm?'

Tau made a strange noise in her throat and bent down as if to pat the head of one of the sloths. In a flash she drew her katana and plunged it through where she expected the throat to be. Unsurprisingly, it passed straight through.

'If it were not for the fact that I still have nothing with which to go to the ball, you would have been strung up by your tongue and peeled for lying to me!' growled Tau, the point of her katana pressing against the throat of the trembling Dewlap. 'Against my better judgement, you still have two days! Find something or kitty's teeth will find your ears, remember!' she snarled, drumming her fingers along the handle.

Dewlap squeaked and sprinted out of the courtyard, his head filled with lobeless images of himself attempting to look good in the Gu-Chi beret.

The Empress turned and swooped on Lehrt and Ti. 'And

what have I told you about lying?' she shrieked as the Central Courtyard mysteriously emptied. If Tau was about to have a tantrum it would not do to be within three miles of her.

Within a matter of seconds the familiar din of Imperial female fists could just be distinguished above the sound of high-ranking military sobbing.

More as an antidote to the unnervingly unfamiliar surroundings of Losa Llamas than from any desire to try and impress, Cheiro Mancini spread out a growing comfort zone of the familiar tools of his trade. Knapp clutched at his sack, fetched things and looked for anything portable and not nailed down that might be useful in the future. They had walked what felt like miles through a labyrinth of twisting corridors, spiral staircases and half-glimpsed passages scurrying away into the gloom punctuated by vast, echoing caverns or clumps of rooms bristling with throbbing equipment. It was all as disconcerting as it was incomprehensible. And nobody appeared willing to make it less so.

Under the steady gaze of Practz and a few other vaguely interested Thaumaturgical Physicists who floated into view, scrutinised, then drifted aware barely hiding stifled giggles of derision, Mancini arranged the equipment which Uhrnest had manhandled down from the wagon.

Incredibly it was all there. And intact. More virtual ecology hardware than he had ever had the chance to play with.

Attempting to calm himself with the thought of all the promised money arising from this job and revelling in the idle contemplation of how he was going to spend it, he picked out a Malpin Emp-Power Driver Series 6 and told himself 'the quicker you start, the quicker you get paid.' He took a deep breath and from beneath a constant stream of low-level blessings and incantations, which somehow managed to squeeze their way around his constantly waving tongue, his hands began the work of constructing an empathic projector array. Practz looked on with a twitch of admiration as the Virtual Ecology Technologist tied the wave guides from the taxidermal pre-amp to the focusing ring and the hypertaurus accelerator, thus linking the psychoterrin crystals to the micropentagram buffers. Knapp played with a string of maggots and looked for anything to bait with them.

After three hours' work Mancini sat back and stared at the untidy shrub of wires and chalk markings, then looked up at Practz and asked, 'May I see the patient now?'

Practz was taken aback. 'Patient?'

'Er . . . dearly beloved?' suggested Mancini euphemistically. 'Faithful companion? Trusted friend?'

Practz stared in utter bafflement as he was watched eagerly by Knapp, suddenly feeling naked without a large black bag for the dragon.

'Recently deceased?' added Mancini, racking his brain for any other way of saying it. 'I can't do any more without your . . . your dead dragon!'

Practz's face creased up and burst into laughter.

Mancini had seen a great many different reactions from a whole host of various people when he had requested to 'see the patient'. Anything from the slight twitch of a stiff upper lip as dignity overrode sadness, right the way up to grown men dissolving into complete dribbling wrecks within milliseconds. But never, in his entire career, had he been *laughed* at.

Anger flared within him. He'd had a hard day, in strange surroundings. He hadn't trekked untold miles through jungle, been hijacked and dragged into what was no better than a fetishistic potholer's speleological heaven, merely to be laughed at!

'Look,' he shouted, 'just drop the dead dragon over there and I'll have it up and running in a few hours, alright? Alright? What are you laughing at? Something on my nose?' he ranted as Practz attempted to calm his humour. Knapp scratched his head.

'I . . . I'm sorry,' answered the Thaumaturgical Physicist. 'Ahem . . . I don't have a dead dragon,' he confessed.

'Whoa now! Look, mate. I'm not into cryogenics, it's too dangerous! Have you tried shoving a cat into a freezing bath of ice? Teeth, claws and spitting everywhere! If that's what you brought me here for . . .'

'Let me explain. We've been having a little trouble with . . .'

Mancini waved his hands dismissively and backed away. 'Forget it, forget it! Bit of trouble? Yeah, poor old dragon's lost her marbles! Torched too many of next door's prize dahlias? Dribbling evil-smelling lighter fuel all over the carpet? "Let's get a man in, dear, it's for the best, darling!" ' he mocked. 'Saurian euthanasia? Right out! Call me back when it's snuffed it, an' I'll be glad to oblige. Dragons are for life, not just barbecues! People like you shouldn't be allowed to have drag . . .'

'I've never had a dragon!' snapped Practz. 'That's why *you're* here!'

'. . . eh? . . .'

'I want one,' said Practz.

'You don't want me, then. You want a breeder. I know a great guy, ex-wizard, won Kruffs five times with his dragons, should see his little fire-lizards . . .'

'No, no!' interrupted Practz, feeling another tirade coming on, 'I don't want a *real* one.'

'Oh, make your mind up. What *do* you want?'

'A PET dragon!'

Now it was the turn of Cheiro Mancini's lip to twitch into a smirk; his stomach's opportunity to convulse with rising mirth; his head's chance to hurl itself backwards, open its mouth and shriek with incredulous laughter. And right on cue they all did exactly that. Practz glared at the twitching VET.

'Oh, that's a good one!' Mancini cried a few minutes later, clutching at his ribs. 'A PET dragon.' He dissolved once more into a fit of quivering giggles under the increasingly stern glare of Practz, struggled to contain himself, wiped his mouth and got up off the floor.

'Ahem . . . I'm sorry,' said Mancini, his cheek muscles aching. 'I don't think you understand. Projected Empathic Taxidermy, the preservation of a faithful companion by thaumic means, relies on the bond between a pet and its owner. Empathy, see? The owner's got to want it to exist,

69

otherwise . . . phoof! Gone. So, if it hasn't ever existed . . .'

'. . . it can't be preserved!' finished Practz. Quietly Knapp pulled the catalogue he had pinched from Annz Hashe's Fur and Feather Fayre out of his sack and stared at the definitions on the inside cover.

Mancini looked suspiciously at the Thaumaturgical Physicist. 'If you try to preserve nothing . . .' he began, testing as Knapp followed the sparring quote with his finger.

'. . . you have an empty pot of vinegar,' completed Practz. 'Ancient VET's proverb!'

'How the . . .'

'I don't want you to preserve anything,' interrupted Practz with a grin. 'The Rhoil VET College's standard introductory lecture, as written by Prof. Rhoil himself, and remarkably well remembered by yourself, states, "The owner has got to want it to exist, whether through the love of a faithful companion or the desire to show off." '

Mancini nodded, grinning slightly with the flush of the compliment. Exactly as Practz had intended.

'As a Virtual Ecology Technician yourself,' continued Practz, 'what, in your esteemed opinion, is the difference between desiring the return of, say, a long-loved Talpine Rock Mouse for purely sentimental reasons or the need to create a PET dragon for the sake of lasting interkingdomnal peace and high security?'

'Well, I . . .'

'Is it better to have loved a mouse than never own a dragon at all?' urged Practz dramatically.

In the centre of the greyish collection of cells that called itself Cheiro Mancini's brain, currently positioned in the middle of that vast cave in Losa Llamas, untold miles from the familiar surroundings of his 'surgery' in Death Valley, Venasht, a shy, almost embarrassed concept stepped onto a small box, stared fixedly at its pigeoning toes, and began to whisper what it thought *might* be something to try if anyone was willing to give it a go cos it wasn't too much trouble and it wasn't going to cost much so if anyone *wanted* to . . .

Two passing neurons glanced up from the leaves and

stared, axon in axon, at the concept. In a moment three more joined them to listen. A flock of fifteen thoughts swooped in, settled down and joined the growing crowd. Within a few minutes, as the shy concept finished talking and looked up, thousands of neurons put their synapses together in a huge round of appreciative applause, cheered and carried the struggling concept to the Action Centre, hailing it a hero. Practz and Knapp watched silently as Mancini's brain struggled to adjust to the uproar within, kicking itself as it wondered whether it *could* be done, and had it been tried, and why had he never thought of it before!

Abruptly, his eyes cleared, his head came up and he stared fixedly at Practz. 'Just one question,' he said, 'how big d'you want it?'

To provoke one sentence of death from the Empress Tau of Murrha could be considered unfortunate, but to receive two, in as many days, could only be considered as carelessness in the extreme. That's it! thought Dewlap as he fled from the Central Courtyard in a flurry of designer kimono, his arms windmilling frantically as he tore down the corridors, the sound of Tau's punitive pummelling fading. No more pay rises, no chance of promotion. The end of a promising life!

A tiny figure zapped into existence, looped around his head and settled on his rapidly hurtling right shoulder. It folded its wings and tapped its foot angrily.

'Now look what you've done!' shouted the white figure in his ear. 'Are you satisfied, hmm? You and your big mouth! I *told* you it'd get us all into trouble one day, didn't I? Sloths! I ask you. Did you *really* expect to get away with lying to the Empress in public? Nobody gets away with lying to the Empress in public, especially through a megaphone! Well, except for politicians. But they don't really count . . .'

Just above Dewlap's left shoulder a flash of red sprang into existence. An inch-high crimson figure carrying a flaming three-pronged spear kicked the sprinting consultant's mother-of-pearl earring out of the way and swung on his lobe.

71

'Damned shame, old boy,' shouted the crimson one, smouldering provocatively. 'So close, so close. What you going to do now, eh laddie? Only a few hours left, got to make every moment count. Pleasures of the flesh, nudge, nudge! What'll it be? All that booze you've been savin' for a rainy day? Or that maid over in . . .'

'Stop that. It's disgusting!' shouted the white one, fluttering her wings irritatedly, clinging to the collar of Dewlap's kimono. 'This isn't the time to be leading him astray with your crude brand of lechery. He should be begging for mercy, offering sacrifices, praying. It's not too late!'

'Pah! Takes way too long, ducky. You know what I always say, it's better to burn out than kneel and pray!' screamed the red one, spinning around manically and laughing evilly as it bounced off Dewlap's shoulder, swooped round and soared in front of the other figure on a blazing trail of infernal exhaust gases. The angel fluffed her wings and tutted.

The soon-to-be-ex-Court Livestock Image Consultant's mind whirred almost as frantically as his arms, ripping and tearing at the blankets of forgetfulness, searching for a memory he knew he needed. Something dark and *very* embarrassing.

'And I suppose that a few hours of drunken orgiastic behaviour will set him up nicely for an eternity of damnation!' countered the angel through teeth clenched in piety, a barrage of words strafing the air behind the red target.

Dewlap's mind lifted the hazy corner of a blanket and spotted the edge of his required recollection. Quivering, he reached out for it . . .

'Damnation? Hell, no. But what a way to go!' taunted the crimson guardian devil, flopping out his tongue and parading his red buttocks as he climbed vertically before the angel.

'Disgusting! So juvenile,' tutted the angel, folding her arms and tapping her foot again.

'That's right!' shouted Dewlap, screeching to a panting halt, the memory there in all its glory before him. He winced as he recalled the state of his kimono and the stains on his alpaca rug . . .

'See?' snapped the angel, glaring at her rising opponent. 'He doesn't *need* you!'

'No! It's you!' snapped the soaring red devil, stall-turning and diving joyously ahead of a blue spiralling smoke trail.

'It's *both* of you!' shouted Dewlap.

'I hear a drinks cabinet calling!' cackled the devil, poking Dewlap's nose with his spear as he tumbled past in free-fall.

'Confessional!' shouted the angel, horrified, waving the smoke away with her wings.

'Drinks! Wimmin!' letched the devil, inches from Dewlap's chin.

'Prayers! Forgiveness!' pleaded the angel, fluttering in desperate piety, secretly wishing that she had one of those spears to poke that devil, just once! Just there in those offensive crimson buttocks!

'Oh no! Time for all that later. Right now, I'm heading straight for damnation!' cried Dewlap, turning unexpectedly on his heel and accelerating away.

'Now look what you've done!' shouted the angel, fluttering after the rapidly diminishing figure in camel hair slippers.

'Me?' cried the devil, pulling out of the sharp dive. 'How can it be me? I didn't even mention fornication, and the women are *that* way.' He waved his spear behind him.

Dewlap's guardian angel swooped around the corner, out of sight, close on the kimono-tails of her sprinting charge.

'Hey! Hang on, wait for me! He's not getting out of temptation *that* easily!' shrieked the devil. 'Come back. If he's on to something better than fornication, *I* want to know about it!'

It had taken the best part of two hours for Cheiro Mancini to finish off the empathic projector. He'd delved into the deepest nooks and murkiest crannies of his memory. He'd flashed inquisitorial torches round dark corners, mentally winkling out every last scrap of accumulated virtual ecology experience, like some seafood-starved gastronome scraping frantically at the last white flesh in a half-dressed crab. He'd adjusted everything as best he could, setting the chrominence filter to where he hoped greenish was, tweaking the alignment of the psychoterrin crystal to compensate for the lack of a real subject, and finally whacking the Emp-Power Amp up to full. And he still hadn't the foggiest pea-soup of an idea if the damned thing would actually work.

Privately Mancini wished he'd shelled out a few extra groats and gone for a Malpin series 7 with its optional emotion filter. He really could do with something to screen out his nerves. A triple glass of Jag'd Anyuls on the rocks wouldn't go amiss, either.

He had turned the whole concept over in his mind and couldn't see a flaw in Practz's logic – to create rather than simply preserve; invent rather than resurrect! It seemed so simple. But he still had a million doubts nagging at the back of his mind, like a trawlerful of fishwives, standing behind him, arms tightly folded, peering over his shoulder, wagging fingers, criticising in cracked falsetto (. . .oooh, Gladys, you wouldn't catch me using pure imagination instead of readily available empathy! Pass that haddock . . .)

A million questions spun around his head, each with enough potential PhD projects to give a thousand grant-funding bodies the screaming abdabs. But to Mancini, there was only one question that needed answering, one soaring monolith of uncertainty marring a perfect horizon of happiness, one fly in the ointment of delight.

If it didn't work . . . would he get paid?

Well, he'd find out pretty soon.

'Ready?' called Practz as he strode purposefully across the cavern floor.

Mancini shrugged his shoulders doubtfully.

'Such confidence,' grunted Practz. 'I'm underwhelmed!'

Mancini tutted, clicked his fingers and Knapp hurled him the largest potato he could find in his sack. Resignedly the VET thrust two electrodes into the biological power supply and took a step backwards. Knapp squinted expectantly over the top of the table, took a particular fancy to two large purple rocks and vanished them into a secret pocket in his sack.

A pale red glow spluttered in one of the hyperreality valves as a trickle of microvolts dribbled in, attempting to warm it up. Mancini scowled at it, struggling to muster every last dreg of optimism. He reached out, grabbed a strange device and handed it to Practz, grunting, 'Put that on.'

'Where?' the boss of Losa Llamos asked, turning what looked like a chicken wire bob-cap over in his hands.

'On your head. Where else?' grumbled Mancini.

'Do I have to? It looks silly. What if someone comes in?'

'If you don't put it on it won't work.'

Reluctantly, after checking the corridor outside for any sign of anyone lurking in the shadows, Practz donned the psychic funnel cap, arranging the clump of wires sprouting from the crown in a way he hoped didn't look too ridiculous. Knapp stifled a giggle.

'Now, concentrate on the dragon you want,' said Mancini to Practz and started tweaking the empathic pre-amp. 'Form it in your mind and hold it there. The more details you can think of the better.'

'Like colour and stuff?' asked the stocky Thaumaturgical Physicist.

'Everything. Colour of eyes, number of teeth. Inside leg measurement if you can.'

Practz closed his eyes, screwed his face up and tried to conjure a nightmare dragon inside his mind. Briefly he wondered whether to call Rutger. That head was so stuffed with fantastic images in 80mm Superthaumination there was bound to be a dragon in amongst Flossie the Wonder Hound and Clint Machismo. There'd probably even be a choice.

Practz shook off the idea with a shrug, slipped the reins off his imagination, whacked it firmly across the buttocks and watched as it gambolled freely in the field of dreams, kicking barefoot at the nightmarish lupins of madness . . .

His mind's eyes widened in surprised fear as a dark shape unfurled its wings and dropped ponderously off its perch, accelerating as it extended its snake-like neck in a huge curl. Ridges of serrated scales ran like a bandsaw down its spine, glinting almost as menacingly as the vast claws which curled from the end of its toes. Enormous black holes of nostrils belched smoke into his head as the worm swooped and snorted, zooming towards him, yellow slitted eyes fixing him with deadly saurian precision, claws ready to rake a furrow red, licensed to mutilate.

And as he concentrated, Mancini tweaked and tuned the psychic funnel, homing in on the ephemeral mental waves of Practz's subconscious, dredging the mental mud with a drifting ethernet. Incredibly, something appeared in the projected field, each detail appearing as Practz conjured it in his raving imagination. It stood on top of the carved elm plinth, drew itself up to its full height, glared angrily behind double-barrelled nostrils, shimmered, then vanished with a curse from Mancini.

Practz opened his eyes and snatched the psychic funnel off his head. 'Did it work?'

'If you imagined a three-inch monster exuding as much malevolence as a toothless newt with gout, then, yes, it was a complete success!' grumbled Mancini, his face dropping as the hyperreality valves dimmed and went out. 'It's no good, I need more power!'

'I've got another potato,' offered Knapp helpfully.

'No. I mean loads more power,' snarled Mancini in frustration, as an image of a bag of gold hitched up its skirts and hightailed it over the horizon.

'Swede?' suggested Knapp, up to his elbows in his sack.

Practz scratched his chin thoughtfully. 'How much more?' he asked, ignoring Knapp.

'Hundreds of thousands times more than I'll ever get from *this*,' sobbed Mancini, waving the electrically dead King Edward. 'It's impossible! I need about twelve volts.'

'What's that in gigathaums?' asked Practz.

'Eh?' suggested Mancini intelligently.

Practz stared at his fingers, mumbling to himself, trying to calculate through a haze of muddled conversion factors. 'Fifteen coulombs to a gigathaum. No, no, no. *Twelve* amps to a . . . a . . . ?'

'What?' grunted Mancini.

'No. It's five ohms to a watt, or is it? Twelve long hundreds to a bushel and three french hens in a pear tree. No, no! That's shillings . . . isn't it? Oh, dammit! I can never remember all this nonsense. Wat'll know for sure, but I reckon a quarter of a gigathaum ought to be plenty . . . give or take a couple of . . .'

'What are you on about?' pleaded Mancini desperately.

'You said you needed more power?' Practz's face creased into a grin.

'Well . . . I . . . yes,' answered the bewildered VET.

'Come on, then,' said Practz cheerfully, turning on his heel. 'I'll introduce you to the thaumatron!'

'I've got three swedes and a turnip, if you want them,' offered Knapp forlornly.

If the tiny red devil on Dewlap's shoulder knew what trouble was going to be caused by the box the sprinting figure was carrying, he would have been cartwheeling for joy and soaring blue smoke trails of wicked delight around Dewlap's panting head. Instead he just thrilled at the crime that had just been commited.

'Now you've done it!' shrieked Dewlap's guardian angel. 'That's *stealing*, you know! Put it back, now!'

'Ah, shut up!' cackled the devil. 'Face it, darlin', I won! He's on my side now! He handled that like a pro. In and out in a few seconds. Lovely job!'

Dewlap dashed panting through the darkened streets of downtown Murrha clutching the box and trying to ignore the teeth and claws within which were lashing at the metal mesh of the grille, struggling for release or revenge. Or both. It was hard to tell from the look in those eyes. Red fury shrieked from the pupils of the damnation.

Suddenly the adrenaline buzz of the theft faded and reaction to the sprinting getaway caught up. Dewlap stopped and leant against a wall, his chest heaving desperately. The chest of a thief!

He strained an ear to listen for any pursuit as he caught his breath. No angry footsteps sounded, no irate horde was surging towards him flashing cleavers and shrieking wildly. He had done it. He was in the clear. A guilty surge of pride swept through him making him grin smugly.

Abruptly a single blood-curdling yell sounded, howling in heart-stopping ululation. A sound to threaten the very bowel control of all that heard it.

And it was answered by a chorus of distant replies.

With a sickening jolt, Dewlap realised that the first call had come from inside the box in his arms. The damnation was calling.

Calling for what?

Dewlap whimpered nervously and dashed away towards the palace, and as he did so a wave of black and white spotted creatures burst forth from the underground storeroom and surged after their kidnapped companion.

In a smallish cavern strewn with the myriad bits and bobs of high-level thaumic research – you know, the usual hypertaurus densitometers, psychic screwdrivers and a plethora of wires and crystal sets and countless unfinished projects – a heated discussion was under way.

'But is it safe?' whimpered Thurgia, trying to be heard above the squealing hum of what sounded like half a million extremely angry mosquitos in a tin can.

'Probably,' answered Wat the technician, staring doubt-fully at the fizzing backpack thaumatron mounted squarely on the shoulders of the Head of Demonic Possession. Wires and thaumic wave guides glowed aquamarine.

'Are you *sure*?' insisted Thurgia as the humming increased rapidly.

'Mostly,' replied Wat, hands placed firmly in his lab-cloak pockets. 'At least, it *should* be.'

'Look, I didn't volunteer to become a martyr for the advancement of Thaumatronics, you know,' whimpered Thurgia nervously as the aquamarine turned fifty fathoms deeper.

'Stop fussing and whack the power up a bit. If there were

any snags the nano-sprites will have sorted them.'

'You trust those things?' screeched Thurgia, as countless torrents of thaumic power throbbed within the device presently residing, none too comfortably, upon his back.

'Sure, they checked out the big thaumatron alright. Running fine now,' reassured Wat.

Oh well, if Wat said it was alright, then there was a good chance that it was . . . possibly . . . maybe. One of the things Thurgia admired about Wat was his ability to take such endless care over each of the tiny details of safety involved in high-energy thaumic research. Admired it, that is, approximately as much as he admired your average slime mould. Deep down Thurgia was certain that nobody could throw together a piece of high-powered technology which sat ten microns ahead of the cutting edge of thaumaturgical physics without hacking off a few safety corners along the way. He wished fervently, and not for the first time, that all the technical wizardry had been left up to Phlim. He *was* the Technical Wizard, after all. Why did he have to be on holiday?

Still, he thought in as spirit-bolstering a voice as possible, faint heart never caught the early worm. Or something.

Thurgia cringed, reached down to the knob on the right of the pack and cautiously turned it clockwise. The fountain of sapphire sparks above his head increased in intensity. So did the noise – the mosquitos turned to bees.

'What's that din?' protested Thurgia.

'Sounds fine from here!' cried Wat, popping meerkat-like from behind an upturned table.

'But the big one isn't this loud!' he protested, yelling over the humming fizz as the bees metamorphosed into wasps. And turned angry.

'It's 'cause you're so close!' bellowed Wat. 'Inverse square law and all that stuff.' He vanished once more behind the relative safety of the table as he spotted a destiny valve glowing white-hot behind Thurgia's ear.

Forty yards beyond the reinforced doors of the lab a pair of boots trundled wearily along the corridor, their owner suffering from the early effects of a long and extremely tedious journey on horseback. Miserably he looked about the dimly lit corridors.

'Welcome back, Phlim,' he grumbled to himself. 'Good holiday? Nice weather? Pah! Should've stayed away.'

The backpack thaumatron's glow increased by several thousand angst-filled lumens as Thurgia turned the knob a little more. Above him, sparks of thaumic energy whizzed and spluttered as they leaked from the accelerating magi-kinetic field on his back. Wat, and even Phlim, had attempted to explain the theory of the gizmo behind his head on numerous occasions and he had failed utterly to understand. But then he failed to understand pretty much anything that didn't involve the spirits of long dead souls repossessing living bodies in sudden acts of psychic squatting.

He did recall that the whole project sounded more than a trifle dodgy. Something to do with a thaumatron being like a magical ring, only bigger, better and almost infinitely more powerful.

It did work, though. Most, if not all, of the research in Losa Llamas was supplied with energy from the thaumatron – the big new twenty-eight terrathaum jobby in the basement – with stacks left over for lighting, heating and all the hot water you could shake a divining rod at.

Thurgia glared at the five-ton block of marble before him, looked at the picture of the sculpture in his left hand and nervously loosed the pent up energy from the device. A million sapphire hornets exploded in a hovering swarm above him, buzzed, flitted and then dived as one at the top of his head.

Ten yards from the door Phlim trudged onward. 'Like I've never been away,' he mumbled. 'All that time, vanished. And what have I got to show for it?' Grimly, he surveyed the five rolls under his arm and the stack of filthy washing in the cases.

Beneath a shower of ricocheting thaumic particles Thurgia trembled and shook nervously. His eyes shone with reflected blue as the energy fizzed off his eyebrows. Unconsciously he shrieked as the power surge hit – a million-gallon shock of ice-watered underwear.

Three yards to the door. 'I hope they like these,' Phlim mumbled grimly at the scrolls.

Wat risked a peek over the table as lightning surges bolted around the trembling, stocky figure of Thurgia. It was working!

The Head of Demonic Possession fixed his flashing eyes on the five-ton slab, preparing to turn it into a statue of an athletic young man, just like in the picture. His hands flexed before him, moulding the sizzling magic, caressing the power, fondling the thaums. With a jolt he flicked the force towards the stone, yelling as the fireball of phosphorescent power shot towards its target.

Wat ducked behind the table again, bracing himself for the hailstones of marble chips that had to come, catching his fleeing breath before the avalanche struck.

Thurgia cried out, his voice filling the room.

The torrent of flying white shrapnel exploded from the marble stone . . . and vanished.

Thurgia leapt up and down with intense relief and joy as he stared at the beautiful figure in gleaming white, marble muscles rippling beneath a sheen of stone.

'Look at that!' he cried. 'Look at it. Perfect! Oh, what an artist. Applause please!'

'No!' shrieked Wat, leaping from the cover of the table, 'Don't clap your hands. You'll short yourself!'

Suddenly, the door opened. 'Hi folks, I'm back!' shouted Phlim, attempting to sound cheery. 'Did you miss me? Here's a pressie.' Casually, not taking in the scene before him, he tossed one of the scrolls to Wat and one to Thurgia.

'No!' yelled Wat.

'Well, thank you *very* much!' snapped Phlim haughtily as the scroll tumbled end over end towards the enthauma-tronned wizard. 'There's gratitude!'

Thurgia reached out with both hands eagerly, clawing at the air as Wat struggled to scramble over the table.

Thurgia's hands closed in on the scroll and each other. As

81

his fingers wrapped around the cylinder fifteen kilothaums of pure thaumic energy shorted itself in a blinding corona of light, straight through the centre of the parchment-coloured gift. Wat swung the thaumatron knob a fraction of a second too late, shutting off the power as Thurgia screamed in shock and flung the scroll into a far corner, releasing a final blast of power and shearing the arms off the statue just above the elbows.

'My statue!' he squealed.

'My ear!' protested Wat, rubbing a singed and smarting lobe.

'My word!' whimpered Phlim. 'It works.'

As the smoke cleared and the shock subsided, in the far corner of the test lab a twitch of life sparked through the scroll. A corner of parchment-coloured, age-dried flesh jerked. The dead sea-scrole breathed again for the first time in eighty-five thousand centuries. In a flash it sensed minds, consciousness clamouring in clattering emotion. It remembered its task, counted the minds. Bum! it thought. Too many of them.

Shrugging its non-existent shoulders in confusion and wonder at the new tattoos it appeared to have gained in the last eighty-five thousand centuries, it headed off to find some water, smacking its primordial lips.

Sprinting as casually as he dared in the feeble light of a late dawn, with the box tucked beneath his cloak, Dewlap nodded to the guard on the gates as he flashed past. The yelp of the caged damnation dropped a good semitone as he hurtled around the corner and dashed frantically for the Empress' Quarters. Fear pounded in his chest as he wondered precisely when his own personal deadline was. Had he crossed it? And would this little snarling darling put him back in Tau's good books?'

Just out of sight of the guard four hundred legs back-pedalled to a screeching halt, two hundred clawed paws grasped at the edge of the ramshackle building which they hid behind and two hundred fiery red eyes glared around the corner, assessing, calculating. One hundred low growls sounded quietly as they communed and discussed, a hundred heads nodded. And they charged.

Dewlap hurtled through the palace, stuffing his cloak into the grilles of the box, attempting to hush the screaming creature. Corridors flashed by, intersections were glimpsed momentarily in his mad dash until, with his mind reeling in terror and excitement, he ploughed into the Empress' Quarters unnanounced.

Instantly, as the warm smell of goats hit him full force, he realised his folly.

'Get out, you idiot!' screamed Empress Tau, her head just visible above the surface of her sunken bath of goat's milk, her eyebrows knotting in anger at the sudden entrance. 'Nobody enters whilst I am bathing!' she cried angrily, exploding from the milk to stand suddenly and glare up at him. Dewlap stood watching the drips run in rivulets down the length of her full dress armour and swallowed.

'I . . . I . . . For you!' he stammered and held out the box.

'At last! Open it!' she demanded, temporarily postponing any further punitive action against Dewlap until she had seen what was in the box. She sprang up the steps, leaving a trail of white translucent drips from her armour, bringing the smell of goats even nearer.

Dewlap felt the damnation moving wildly inside. Something was exciting it. Something in the air.

'I haven't got all day!' shrieked Tau in a growing puddle.

With his heart in his mouth Dewlap's fingers fumbled at the catch on the side. Now that he had come this far: lying to the Empress in public, breaking and entering, stealing an unknown (and probably very dangerous) creature, and making a gift of said creature to the Empress in the full knowledge that he hadn't a clue how it, or the Empress, would react upon its receipt . . . well, he wasn't really sure that it was such a good idea, now.

If the guard at the gate had blinked he could have missed the black and white tide of damnations as they surged through the gate and swarmed, tooth and claw bare, into the

Palace. He hadn't, and was found several hours later curled in a terrified ball in his hut staring accusingly at a half-empty bottle of spirits, gibbering.

The hundred damnations leapt and cavorted along the corridors, their paws skittering on the marble floors, howling as they clawed for traction on the sharp corners, homing in on their companion.

'Are you going to open it?' yelled Tau at the quivering figure with the thrashing box.

He loosened the catch and the damnation exploded out of the box, arcing through the air, straight at the Empress, slavering and baying wildly. The recoil knocked Dewlap flying, snatching at a tapestry for balance and yanking it from the wall. The last terrifying sight he saw was the damnation, mouth open, hurtling rapidly Tau-wards.

A second later, the chaotic sound of a hundred more of the livid beasts surging into the Empress' Quarters blasted through the heap of tapestry. There was a scream, a splat. Then . . .

Somehow the thick and heavy almost-silence that fell was worse than the wild howling yelps of destruction a second before. The wet, slimy sounds of creatures feeding filled his terrified ears.

Apprehension dripping from every pore, Dewlap struggled to extricate himself from the heavy folds of dusty embroidery and with unutterable shock stared at the scene before him.

The Empress had managed to fight off one or two of the raging beasts, but even she had been simply overwhelmed by their number. The Head of the Murrhovian Empire was now completely lost beneath a wave of thrashing black and white bodies, swamped under a tide of terrifying claws and teeth and fiery eyes and she was . . . giggling.

'No! Stop it. That tickles!' she squealed as fifty tongues licked feverishly at the goat's milk on her armour, their rasping tongues flicking between the bamboo sections. Fifty others had discovered the bath and were either gaily lapping at the surface or leaping down the three marble steps into the white pool.

Dewlap collapsed beneath the tapestry.

Of the wildly excited threesome that sprinted down the corridor towards the thaumatron bay, brimming with news that a backpack thaumatron actually worked, Wat was the first to see it. And the first to wish instantly he hadn't.

He'd never experienced such a complete reversal of emotion in his life. His body turned from bubbling, yelling enthusiasm to blubbering, shrieking terror in the space of a nanosecond. He screamed, attempted to spring backwards, skidded and ended up flat on his back staring straight up into the smouldering double-barrelled nostrils of one hundred and eight thousand pounds of verdant dragon.

His mouth opened and closed like a beached goldfish in a vacuum as he tried to form some words, any words. He got as far as 'Wh . . . Wh . . . WAAAAH!' and then fainted.

Thurgia and Phlim stood trembling at the door about to flee in alarm-raising terror when Practz's calm voice floated over the hum of the Thaumatron. 'It's alright,' he said, stepping through the belly of the vast fire lizard and causing a slight shadow in its projection. 'My new toy!' he continued, waving an expansive arm proudly. 'Do you approve?'

'I like that!' shouted Phlim in disgust. 'My back's turned for a few days and I come back to . . . to . . . dragons running about the place causing mayhem. If you want to get rid of me I'd prefer not to be frightened to death, alright? I'll leave, retire, emigrate . . .'

'No, no,' soothed Practz. 'I didn't intend to scare *you*. But you should have seen your faces!'

There was movement from Wat on the floor. He twitched, opened his eyes, looked up and collapsed again.

'Oh dear. Erm . . . switch him off, will you, Cheiro?' shouted Practz at a point somewhere near the dragon's left leg. In a second the vast monster shrank into a tiny glowing spot which floated for a moment at the height of its navel, then winked out.

Thurgia's jaw dropped as Mancini was revealed, the VET's face almost splitting with a huge self-congratulatory grin of smugness.

Phlim pointed. 'Who the . . . ?'

'Ah, yes. That is Cheiro Mancini. He's going to give us a few dragons and things.'

'Dragons!' shrieked Phlim, the colour draining from his face. 'You want dragons . . . after all the trouble we've had with frogs? I can't believe . . .'

Practz waved his hands at Phlim to be quiet, put a finger to his lips, gestured at Mancini and flicked his ears.

Phlim stared blankly at the VET. 'What's wrong with his ears?' he asked. 'They look alright to me!'

Practz slapped a frustrated palm against his forehead. 'They hear things,' he whispered. 'Secret things!'

'Yeah . . . Oh . . .' said Phlim as it dawned on him that Mancini didn't know their guilty secret. 'But what've dragons got to do with . . . well, anything, really?'

'You've been on the beach too long,' grunted Practz. 'Do I have to spell it out?'

Phlim and Thurgia nodded.

'It is precisely to prevent another breach of security that I am proposing to install a whole set of guard dragons. They seemed to work on Wat, eh?' said Practz, jerking a thumb at the unconscious figure. 'If the wrong hands happened to get hold of *anything* we have here . . . well, I don't need to spell it out,' he ended grimly.

Phlim shivered as he thought of the eight-foot amphibians lurking in the lower levels. The eyes, the tongues, the teeth!

And besides possessing a colony of ruthlessly vicious, all-terrain attack amphibians in the basement, Losa Llamas was home to some of the most dangerously potent military magic secrets ever written. The library was humming with them.

Suddenly Wat sat bolt upright and looked around in sheer bewildered confusion. 'It's gone!' he whimpered. 'It was there in front of my . . . did anyone see a . . . a . . . ?' As everyone stared at him he blushed, suddenly unsure if he had actually witnessed the mythical beast. 'Nah! Don't exist anyway,' he added, attempting to reassure himself. 'Must've been working too hard.'

'Ah, yes,' shouted Practz a little too enthusiastically,

sensing Mancini approaching and desperately changing the subject, 'How is your backpack thaumatron coming on?' He turned to Phlim, adding slyly, 'He's been making some good progress while you've been away. He'll have your job if you're not careful.'

Phlim grinned uncomfortably as Wat leaped up and began to enthuse about the trial he had just performed and the repeat performance tomorrow, all thoughts of dragons swept from his mind.

As the technician raved and led the small group away to show them the results of his work, passing unnoticed along the wall behind them, what looked like an animated bath mat slithered and waved its corner, trying to attract someone's attention.

Oi! it yelled telepathically. Hey! You lot. Come back. I've got a message!

Mumbling a favourite ancient trilobite oath, it slunk towards the pool of cooling water in the far corner of the Thaumatron Bay. With a centuries-old grunt the sea-scrole slid into the water and bubbled a primeval sigh of relief. Eighty-five centuries was a long time between baths. Ahhh . . . bliss!

Bliss was one of the last words that could be used to describe the scene in the basement of Itto's grandfather.

Blitzed would be a smidgin nearer.

But even that couldn't possibly begin to convey the slightest fraction of the destruction that had been wreaked on the storeroom. It was as if a hundred or so frenzied prize bulls had whirlwinded their angry way through the most fragile of tableware stores. Only much worse.

The wall opposite the gently swinging remnant of the ruptured door to the staircase had been blown in. Bricks and plaster dust covered the wreckage of crushed baskets and smashed packing cases trampled beneath the four hundred rabid paws as they had hurled their damned owners out into the night on their uncontrolled mission of destruction.

'I thought you said they'd just popped out!' shrieked a voice aghast with shock.

Itto looked at his feet, trying to avoid the solar glare of his grandfather's furious gaze, and held up a single uncracked bowl with a wavering hand. 'I help tidy up?'

'Don't bother! If we don't find them soon this'll be about the tidiest place in the whole of Murrha. If anybody realises what they are . . .' His voice quaking, he turned and struggled up the debris-strewn staircase.

'As mean as you can make it, alright?' reminded Practz as Mancini unpacked the last of his aging tools outside the library of Losa Llamas. 'I don't want *anything* getting in there!' he added.

So it *is* true. It is in there, screamed Mancini's greedy mind, desperately victorious.

'But of course,' blurted Mancini.

He could feel Practz staring at him in those frantic few seconds as he struggled to think, working hard to calm himself and, more importantly, damp down the fires of suspicion smouldering behind the Wizard's eyes.

'If you think . . . If you . . . think . . .' *Think*! screamed Mancini's whirling mind. 'Er . . . that the nasty in the Thaumatron Bay was good, well, ha, just you wait! I've been thinking hard overnight about some interesting updates.' Mancini grinned as reassuring a grin as he could muster. Behind him Knapp nodded his enthusiastic agreement.

'Look forward to it!' smiled Practz with a slightly quizzical look. 'Must dash, though. Wat's got his backpack thaumatron demo to show me.' He turned to leave.

'Erm . . .' said Mancini, struggling to keep his voice calm. 'Just one thing?'

Practz wheeled around quickly, his cloak brushing the edges of the dimly lit corridor, and raised a questioning eyebrow.

'Where do I get power?' asked Mancini, making a show of staring along the wall, his insides churning with pent up excitement and nerves.

Practz slapped his forehead. 'Hah! Of course. Silly me!' he headed towards the vast, reinforced wood door that led into the library, withdrew a key from his pocket and opened it. 'Just down there on the left. Can't miss it! Must dash!' And he was gone.

Suddenly, Mancini and Knapp were alone with only the diminishing sound of Practz's feet for temporary company. That and the open door into the library of Losa Llamas. Virtual Ecology wasn't the only thing Mancini's mental jaws had been chewing over last night. He'd heard the whispered secrets dropped by the Thaumaturgical Physicists, caught the tiny pearls of silently falling clues, hoarded them carefully in the apron of his mind and cautiously, gradually assembled them. It had taken only the final addition of the two facts he knew and . . . Robert was indeed his father's brother.

'Remember this moment well, Knapp,' whispered Mancini, rubbing his hands eagerly. 'Our future starts here!' he growled and leapt into the library.

'Hang on. What are you on about?' squeaked Knapp, sprinting to catch up.

Mancini stood amongst the endless rows of shelves and stared at the countless spines stretching away into the gloom.

'What future?' pressed Knapp, tugging eagerly on Mancini's lab-cloak sleeve.

'Think, lad,' he snarled greedily. 'What's the most valuable thing you can have?'

Knapp thought hard. 'Er. Maggots! They're really good for attracting armadillos an' you give me half a groat for every armadillo I . . .'

'No, no! Better than that . . .' Mancini's voice trailed away as he swivelled slowly around in the centre of the library.

'Meal worms?'

'No! Have you learnt nothing from me? Gold!' croaked Mancini in an avaricious whisper.

'Does that attract armadillos, too?'

'Look! Forget about rotten armadillos, will you! The key to our future is in here, just waiting to be freed.' An evil glint stole across Mancini's face as he thought of the millions of groats that would soon be at his fingertips. No more VET work. Freedom!

'You sure?' asked Knapp, scowling doubtfully at the cobwebby shelves.

'Course I am! Why would a library be guarded unless it contained something valuable, eh? Why would a whole new type of security system be invented for that guarding unless that something being guarded was very, *very* valuable, eh? Eh?'

The conversation with Rutger on the cart soared greedily back to Mancini's mind, over the currents of his memory, and settled there, flapping and urging him on, spurring Avarice into action. In this library was the secret . . . *The* Secret he had craved for longer than he could remember. The Alchemist's Dream. Mancini's Desire.

'All I've got to do is walk down one of those lines of shelves and the secret is mine. The Secret of turning Lead into shining, yellow, spendable, twenty-eight carat lovelies! Gold. Gold! Where's "G"?'

Shaking with greedy excitement he began to search the shelves of ancient tomes, running his finger along the spines, mouthing the names of subjects as they flashed before him, bewildering in their unfamiliarity . . . The Gramaraye . . . Gazing, Crystals . . . Gastrognomes.

With a stifled shriek, he stopped dead in his tracks as his gaze fell on the letter 'H'. Knapp ran into the small of his back.

Mancini whirled around, snatching his trusty assistant by the collar and shaking him. 'It's not here! No mention of gold. Nothing!' Panicky frustration surged inside him. 'That dwarf on the cart *said* they knew how to do it. It's here somewhere, it *has* to be. Where is it? Lead to Gold, where?'

'How about "L" for lead?' suggested Knapp, turning very blue.

Suddenly Mancini dropped him and dashed off across the library, his cloak tails stirring up eddies of dust. He began to search frantically under under 'L', clamouring through the titles on the spines.

All he got was another dusty finger and the start of a headache.

Misery flooded over him. Not under 'G' or 'L'! He slunk down against a wall, chin in hands, and stared at the shelves stretching away into the gloom. Where in this mass of idiotic filing would he find the secret of . . . The secret of . . .

A vague memory of his early alchemy sparked in the misery of his brain. Of course! The Secret of Transmogrification!

Within seconds his gaze stopped dead, quivering unbelievingly on the dull brown spine of a tome under 'T'. There it was. *Transmogrification: Everything You Ever Wanted To Turn Into Something Else But Were Afraid To Try.*

A praying mantis couldn't have snatched it from the shelf faster. He flicked through the parchment euphorically . . . Lead into pencils . . . Lead into Pipes . . . Lead into Gold! He almost fainted.

As Mancini pored over his dream tome something shaped not entirely unlike a rubber bath mat squelched its way into the library. The vat of cooling water, as wonderfully refreshing as it had been, wasn't right for the sea-scrole. Fresh water just would not do. The ancient creature yearned for the tidal undulations of a clear tepid sea, lined with swaying palms and miles of untrodden golden sand. It had to escape this dull subterranean world.

'Found it?' croaked Knapp, rubbing his neck as he followed Mancini. He didn't really need an answer. There was something about the way the VET was clutching the tome and staring into the middle distance that spoke volumes.

'Gold,' whispered Mancini, his mind whirring and plotting. What to do with all this gold? His thoughts swam through an idyllic tropical sea edged with gleaming white sand, ice-cold cocktails and a plethora of scantily clad waitresses . . .

The sea-scrole's telepathic centres flashed into excited life as its long neglected hunting instincts were reactivated. *Somewhere* close by *someone* was thinking about *something* very close to paradise.

Hello! it shouted neuronally. Look, I've got a message for you! It squelched eagerly towards Mancini.

Suddenly Mancini slammed the tome shut and thrust it back on the shelf.

'You haven't found it?' groaned Knapp, backing away, wondering which part of his anatomy Mancini would take his frustration out on next.

'Oh, yes. It's perfect!'

'Here. Stick it in my sack, then,' urged Knapp, opening it eagerly.

'Don't be stupid! Take this now and we're bound to be caught!' schemed Mancini, his mind burning with only one thought. 'They'll search us.' Affectionately he stroked the tome's spine. 'I'll be back for you!' he crooned. 'Not today, not tomorrow, but soon! Oh, the things we'll do together!'

The sea-scole thrilled. Contact!

With the lightest of final caresses, Mancini left, his brain whirring with scheming demons, plotting . . . plotting. Knapp scurried after him, bewildered.

The mentally eavesdropping sea-scrole didn't understand the words, only the emotions. But instinctively it knew that here was a way out, an end, a chance to retire and grow really old gracefully.

Struggling for clammy traction on the wood, the animated bath mat squelched up the shelf marked 'T' and slipped inside a tome's dust jacket.

'His Royal Rotating Highness, the King Vyrnwing of Froul* and Beanoh,' yelled the Master of Rolls as a vast albino elephant trundled into the Imperial Murrhovian Ballroom. A remarkably insignificant-looking ruler waved cheerfully from its back in response to the wave of apathy that rumbled and broke in his direction. King Vyrnwing *always* came to the Tyrants' Insititute Annual Fancy Pets Ball with Beanoh. If his rulership was as imaginative as his animal companions then he had no right to call himself a tyrant.

* Depending on which calendar system you chose to believe, it was either sixty-three or five hundred and eighty-six years since the Rulers of Froul began rotating.

With a swift kick to the kidneys of his mahout, the Froulian Ruler spurred the aging elephant towards the Imperial Pedestal of Honour, his jaw sagging as the crowd parted to reveal the Empress Tau.

It was an unbelievable sight.

She sat straight-backed atop the diamond-studded throne, glistening in the splendid purple paisley of her Xiao-Nel Party Armour and spiked knee-pads. Her jet black hair was starched and dyed into a corona of hissing Murrhovian puff-vipers, rounding on her eyebrows which had been crafted into a pair of rabid mongoose. Kitty, her favourite Going-Out Katana, lay nonchalantly across her muscled thighs below a gleaming waterfall of weaponry trailing from her yellow leather arms-belt. A matching pair of spear-fans crowned her shoulders, barely inches clear of the long, thin strands of her Imperial State Moustache, which was glued perfectly to her stiff upper lip. Each ceremonial titanium toe-nail extension had been honed to screaming sharpness and gleamed malevolently between the straps of her stainless steel sandals.

Both she and the throne were surrounded by a livid living carpet of one hundred and one of the meanest, red-eyed, black-spotted creatures ever to stalk the surface of . . . well, anywhere, really. Their razor teeth were bared, their claws unsheathed, their eyes terrifying.

To all the Guest Tyrants at the Annual Charity Ball the appearance of Empress Tau and her one hundred and one

After the accidental death of the Last Froulian Emperor whilst he was sharpening his favourite gutting knife, the ensuing series of bloody elections to choose the next Emperor from the thirteen state Kings, and the spate of civil uprisings and attempted coups which resulted, it was decided that the kings should each occupy the throne for one month. The inconvenience of a calendar system that slipped dramatically out of phase with the rest of 'civilisation' was more than compensated for by the saving on first aid supplies and the all-day investiture parties that happened every month.

And so a type of peace reigned nervously in Froul. Oh, there were minor interstate wars, the occasional regicide, the odd half dozen invasions and petty decapitations of complete royal families, but that was to be expected.

Gradually, over the years, the number of Rotating Kings of Froul dropped to three.

As a result the Froulian Calendar is now one thousand five hundred and five years ahead of the rest of the world. And rising.

damnations was overbearing in the extreme. She would definitely receive the rosette of first prize.

But to the terrified gaze of General Lehrt and Admiral Ti there was more. Much more. It wasn't the fact that Wrag Narrok the Extremely Un-Lax from the Mountain Kingdoms of Khutsk dropped his drinking horn of lizard's blood and with a shriek of delight threw himself at the feet of the Empress begging for any part of her body in unholy wedlock. It wasn't the fact that they had never seen anything move quite as fast as the one hundred and one creatures seething around her feet. It wasn't even the surprisingly small amount of Narrok which remained after the damnations had wiped their claws and cleaned their teeth. None of these made too much impression on the battle-hardened Murrhovian War Veterans.

What made the Hostess of this year's Tyrants' Institute Annual Charity Ball look so truly unbelievable, so totally unique in the history of Murrhovian Imperialism, so terrifying to behold, was the fact that she, Empress Tau, was smiling!

Whilst heavily armoured Oppressor waltzed warily with alarmingly enweaponed Dictator and intensely bodyguarded Despot goose-stepped cagily with power-mad Martinet, Empress Tau smiled and stroked the largest damnation affectionately behind its sharply pointed ears. The musicians found it difficult to be heard over the deep bass rumbling of the creature's malevolent contentment, growling as it rolled over and was tickled on the belly. And the host of paparazzi reporters found it hard to paint good enough pictures for their rival newsparchments from the distance at which they considered themselves safe.

But Empress Tau didn't care. And at that exact moment, in the deepest dungeons of the Murrhovian Imperial Marble Extraction Company (Slave Division), only hours since the shackles had been welded shut around his ankles, neither did Dewlap. He stared at his face in a tiny shard of mirror and grinned.

Tau had been so, literally, bowled over by the damnations

that she had ignored the breaking of the delivery deadline and didn't seem to mind that the red of the damnations' eyes clashed dreadfully with the purple of her Party Armour. She had even been lenient on Dewlap's sentence arising from the sloth incident. He breathed a deep sigh of relief and grinned again. Fifteen years' hard labour . . . ahhh, bliss! It could have been twenty, he just didn't care. Twisting the shard of mirror slightly, he picked out his best side, tilted the yellow cap to its jauntiest angle and swelled with pride. He had his Gu-Chi beret *and* his ears. Life was good. Alright, fashionally challenged by the black and white arrows of prison-wear it might be, but with *the* Gu-Chi beret on his head it just didn't matter.

The Misfortune of Being Uhrnest

With his brown-gloved fingers spread on the tunnel wall like an eager gecko on a nocturnal mate-hunting expedition, Cheiro Mancini peered around the dark corner. He squinted into the gloom of the complex system of familiar passages, lit only by the faint blue glow from his staff, and smirked confidently.

'I said I'd be back, and here I am,' he whispered smugly to himself. 'Have they got a surprise on the way!' It was a rhetorical statement of intent but Knapp found himself nodding enthusiastically in the dark.

Just around the corner, as Mancini had so accurately predicted, slouched the bulk of a single enormous guard. Brushing mental fingernails on his cerebral chest, Mancini thrilled as he recognised it as Uhrnest.

Perfect, he thought. Perfect!

The VET peered at his auto-illumined wrist sundial – bought especially for this job out of the gold so generously supplied by Practz – and counted off the arc-seconds. Three . . . two . . .

Uhrnest shrugged resignedly, heaved himself upright and trudged off on the remainder of his rounds. Life, he thought dully, such a heady whirl of unrivalled excitement.

Mancini smirked once again, gestured urgently to Knapp and received a weighty sockful of damp sand. Silently he slung around the corner and sprinted after the Losa Llaman guard. With a sickening crunch he coshed Uhrnest across the back of the neck and leapt out of the way. The vast guard stopped in his tracks, swayed for a moment then plunged forward like an ancient monolithic carving. Knapp somehow resisted the temptation to yell 'timber!'. Instead, within a matter of seconds he had pulled two lengths of rope from his sack, slung one to Mancini and was busily trussing the unfortunate Uhrnest as swiftly and effectively as possible.

Moments later, the intruders dashed across the corridor to the sound of unheard footsteps and plunged excitedly down a stone spiral staircase. Mancini counted off the exits as they sank deeper into the enormous complex of tunnels that was Losa Llamas; a pair of magic bullets, armed, ready and willing.

'Twenty-seven . . . twenty-eight . . . here. This way,' whispered Mancini, pointing to a corridor in the gloom of his staff light.

He dashed around the corner, Knapp hard on his heels, their soft-soled feet raising tiny clouds of dust, nerves peeled for the slightest unexpected sound.

Suddenly, Mancini screeched to a halt, both feet back-pedalling frantically as if a bottomless chasm had opened in the corridor before them. Knapp slammed into his back at full tilt, pushing the VET several inches forwards and bruising his nose.

'Whad d'you do dat for?' growled Knapp, rubbing his proboscis irritably.

Mancini raised his staff and shone the low blue light into the gloom beyond. Cautiously, Knapp edged forward and stared in wonder at the bottomless chasm yawning hungrily at his feet. Engineered edges plunged away from him, vanishing into fathomless black, with no ledge around, too far to leap, impossible.

'I don't remember that being there,' grunted Mancini, peering at the chasm.

'Don't suppose you've got a ladder in your pocket, have you?' snarled Knapp as he rummaged in his sack. 'I seem to have forgotten to pack one.'

'It's very, very good,' whispered Mancini admiringly.

'Have you gone mad? It's a disaster!' whispered Knapp, squinting down into the lower intestines of the earth, like a keyhole geophysicist. 'We can't get over that! I thought you'd mapped all these things?'

'I did. I don't remember it being there,' mused Mancini, staring at a very slight chrominence shift on the far edge. 'Hah! They've moved it!'

'What? This is one you put in? A PET chasm?'

Mancini grinned, made a mental note to check on the reality lock and stepped out into nothingness with the sure confidence to disbelieve everything his eyes were telling him. Well, why should he believe them? Only two weeks ago he'd created and fitted this PET chasm himself. Not here, mind, but that didn't matter.

Having learnt the scientific art of creating rather than preserving, his imagination had leapt into overdrive to devise the most comprehensive security system ever known. As well as PET chasms, he had installed huge PET rocks to rattle and roll down corridors threatening to crush the unwary burglar; PET demons shrieking and lashing barbed poisonous tongues from hidden corners; PET unicorns ready to burst from the wall at any moment and hurl themselves in hot pursuit of any invader, their horns flashing menace, their hooves willing to crush . . .

And the beautiful, fantastic thing was that he knew they weren't real! What an Achilles heel! Smugly he congratulated himself on the fact that he could just walk through all these psychological barriers and head straight for the library, his prize and the security of a fortune! He smirked at the chasm, placed his foot squarely in mid-air where he expected the real floor to be, screamed and fell.

A small cloud of dust billowed around him as he landed in the all-too-real two-foot deep trough, twisting his ankle. His adrenaline levels shot through the roof as he spat dust and launched a series of curses in ancient Venashtian. Damned meddling wizards! Weren't they happy with the way it looked?

Behind him Knapp choked as he held back the series of shrieking guffaws jostling for freedom in his windpipe.

Mancini flashed the youth a scowl laden with daggers and whirling cutlasses, made a mental note to deal with him later and scrambled out of the far side of the chasm.

Pulling a large stick out of his sack and tapping the ground like a blind man on a tightrope, Knapp nervously waded through the jaws of the pit, fighting bouts of vertigo at every step.

Mancini snarled as he glanced quickly at his sundial. 'Get a move on,' he growled, clipping Knapp across the ear, 'time's slipping away!' How much further? he thought, as he dashed off down the corridor. Third left . . . second right . . .

Half running, half hopping, Mancini struggled round a corner and almost slammed into the largest dragon he or Knapp had ever seen. It stood, glistening green, filling the entire tunnel. Wafts of smoke drifted lazily from its pilot gland as it sized up the intruders, mentally calculating the required heat output to effect total and instant incineration. A deep rumbling issued from its stomach as the acid-base heat exchangers fired up.

Mancini began to sweat, Knapp whimpered. The dragon lurched forward. Its head lashed out, jaws slashing inches above the VET's pointy leather hat. He hadn't programmed it to do that! And that heat . . . was it real? Or was it mimickry? Had Practz been lying when he'd said he hadn't owned a dragon? Mancini squealed as he ducked sideways and rolled away. In a flash of hydrocarbons the dragon whirled after Knapp, its neck arching violently in the cramped tunnel.

It was only then that Mancini's eagle eye spotted the lack of footprints in the dust. It was almost perfect, had almost fooled him.

Grinning broadly to himself and giggling at the expression on Knapp's face as six-foot jaws chomped inches away from his neck, Mancini stood, fixed the dragon with a hard stare and walked forward into the hail of slashing talons and teeth. In a second he vanished, much to the irritation of Knapp.

A PET Dragon. Projected Empathic Transmission – the Ultimate in Virtual Security. He should know!

Having reappeared on the post dragon side of the tunnel, Mancini waved at Knapp and sprinted off down the corridor. Knapp swore swiftly and very effectively, held his breath, wrapped his arms around his head, shut his eyes and sprinted at the flailing dragon. Bouncing off the rock wall only twice, Knapp quickened his pace, flashed past several doors in quick succession and finally skidded to an excited halt outside a huge oak door. This was turning out to be much more fun than he had expected.

'Well, come on. Get them out,' growled Mancini, scowling at the door. 'It's locked. Quick, quick!'

Knapp snatched a small metal box out of his sack, rattled the contents briefly and smirked as he handed it to Mancini. With a grin the VET poured the thirty or so hyperborers onto the door handle and stepped back. Their razor-sharp mandibles glistened momentarily in the gloomy blue light from his staff, twitched as they sensed wood and vanished in a screaming fountain of jawdust. With insectile excitement the hyperborers attacked the surface of the door, illustrating perfectly the effect that several generations of thaumically enhanced interbreeding can have on the humble woodworm. Look at them go! he thought smugly as they dived below the lignified surface in a hail of wood chips.

As they worked Knapp rummaged in his sack, withdrew a scrappy-looking collection of wires, chalk marks and two pink psychoterrin crystals, fitted the crystals into their holders and waited for Mancini to turn the device on.

Those crystals were Knapp's finest acquisition in recent weeks. A thrill of pride surged through him as he recalled Mancini's face on seeing them back in Venasht. Two of the biggest psychoterrin crystals the VET had ever seen, flawless and perfectly matched. It hadn't taken Mancini long to link them up to two slightly detuned outputs from a stereo Emp-Power Amplifier, ramp up the energy and thrill as each image began to support the other, positively interfering, creating the first PET with mass. Within a week he'd tweaked it so that it was solid enough to appear in three dimensions and, crucially, carry small objects. It hadn't taken long for the rest of his plan to drop conveniently into place . . . and in a few moments the prize would be his!

With a swift flurry of fingers, and a slight hum, a glow appeared in the Emp-power Amp. Winking at the large figure that appeared in the corridor, Mancini turned back to the library door, impatiently waggling the handle.

Suddenly he was aware of a low rumbling off to his left and

a frantic tugging on the sleeve of his cloak. He turned almost instinctively, squinting beyond the light from his staff as a white-faced Knapp pointed horrified into the dark. Then Mancini saw it. An enormous spherical boulder careering down the corridor towards them, picking up speed, blocking the passage and leaving no room to escape. He shuddered, icicles of terror racing up the glacier of his horrified spine as tons of rock thundered forward, hellbent on crushing them where they stood. Mancini rattled at the handle of the library door, suddenly horribly aware of the changes that the Thaumaturgical Physicists had made. He had definitely not fitted a PET boulder here. Had they simply moved one of his? Or was this actually fifty tons of rapidly accelerating genuine granite boulder?

With a terrified jerk he suddenly realised that he had been thinking far too long. The boulder was too close to escape from, bearing down on them ready and eager to claim its first victims. Surging adrenaline levels peaked throughout Mancini's body, firing the muscles in his legs. He spun round, raised his knees to flee and tripped over Knapp. In the instant that the rocky rumbling reached maximum and the rough spinning surface of the rock smashed against his body, Mancini opened his mouth, filled his lungs and collapsed as the rock passed straight through him.

'Bat-turds!' he cursed as Knapp whimpered underneath him. 'Those utter, utter bat-turds! They'll pay for that!' With an immense effort of will he pulled himself together and hoped the hyperborers hadn't been as terrified by the PET boulder. With fear turning rapidly to anger, Mancini stared at the heap of jawdust that had formed at the base of the door. In a second he had the entire handle, mortice and lock assembly in his hand. The door swung quietly open and he crawled into the room he had come all this way to reach.

His goal! The library of Losa Llamas. Home of the greatest stores of magical knowledge, practical and theoretical, known in the whole of . . . well, anywhere, really. Vast tracts of information so potentially dangerous that they had to be guarded by the Thaumaturgical Physicists.

Pressed inside the dust jacket of a book called *Transmogrification: All You've Ever Wanted To Turn Into Something Else But Were Afraid To Try*, an ancient creature, shaped not entirely unlike a bath mat, sensed the end of its waiting.

Mancini's heart pounded as he scanned the shelves for the second time. They almost hummed with collected intellect; he buzzed with avarice. His finger brushed along a shelf, stroking the spines, caressing the covers. He'd waited so long for this, ached for a fraction of the information held here. One spell and he'd be set for life. And there it was on the shelf marked 'T'. With a flurry the book was vanishing inside a dark fold in his cloak.

Suddenly a click, a contact, and a damburst of white light flooded the library, chasing shadows in an instant. Applause rattled out from behind the spots, cheers of congratulation mingled with wolf whistles of genuine admiration.

'Well done!' shouted a grinning man, turning a figure of eight-shaped device on his arm and totalling something on his wrist abacus. 'Three hours! I must admit, I didn't think you'd do it, you know! After all the changes we've made . . .'

'It was touch and go,' admitted Mancini, externally calm, internally whirling. 'You've been tweaking things. That chasm's moved, for one thing. And that boulder!'

'Of course,' grinned Practz. 'No disrespect, but we couldn't resist a little, er . . . enhancement. What do you think of Flambe?'

'What?' grunted the VET.

'The Dragon!' said Practz smugly.

Knapp whimpered.

'That thing? How did you get it so big?' squeaked Mancini, his voice quivering with admiration. 'You must've boosted the pre-empathic power amp? Got to be a Malpin series Ten, at least.'

'Yup!' grinned Phlim, butting in smugly as he brushed a strand of brown hair from his eyes. 'And I replaced the psychoterrin crystals. We've found a way of growing them far bigger now! And we're using close tolerance pairs for enhanced 3-D imaging.'

102

'What? Oh, come on! You'll put me out of business,' complained Mancini, the palms of his hands sweating as he thought, 'So what. I've got it made now! I've got the book!' 'Nobody'll want my PETs if they see the ones you've got here!' he added quickly.

'Hey! Nobody makes PETs like Cheiro Mancini,' grinned Practz, slapping him on the back. 'When you make them, they're almost alive. And besides, anybody who sets foot in here won't get out to advertise. This place is going to be totally thiefproof soon.'

Too late! thought Mancini, and stifled a grin.

Suddenly, Rutger appeared at his elbow, 'Excuse me, but the celebratory buffet is ready. If you would like to go through.'

'So soon?' grumbled Practz. 'Thanks, Rutger.' He turned to Cheiro Mancini, 'Well, I think I can say that our new security system is fully operational. Would you agree?'

'There's a slight fault with the reality lock on the level twenty-eight chasm . . . and that dragon's too damned scary!' said Mancini, his face creasing into a nervous grin.

Practz and Phlim laughed and clapped him across the shoulder.

'To lunch!' shouted Rutger.

'To lunch,' agreed Mancini, stepping towards the dust heap that had once been a door. 'Hmmm, sorry about that,' he apologised. 'I never was very good with locks. Maybe a stone door there, next time?'

'Stone? Pah! We have other things in mind,' smiled Practz, and tapped the side of his nose. 'Makes granite look like cream cheese!'

Just as Mancini and Knapp stepped into the corridor a vast muscular hand swung out of the air onto the shoulder of the Virtual Security Designer. 'Ahem!' said the voice, rattling Mancini's socks. 'I think you've still got something of ours, sir!' growled Uhrnest, staring meaningfully at the inside pocket of Mancini's cloak.

'What *do* you mean?' he protested in a voice that sounded far less than convincing to him.

'Book!' snarled Uhrnest.

'Oh, surely not!' whimpered Mancini as near to innocently as he could manage. 'In here? I . . .' he rummaged in his pocket and, with a theatrical expression of heavily rehearsed shock, withdrew the book. 'How did *that* get there?'

'Give!' growled Uhrnest as a rumbling sounded in the corridor behind him.

Cheiro Mancini flushed then handed it over.

'Tut, tut! Sticky fingers!' grunted Practz as Uhrnest disappeared into the library and the PET boulder surged onwards.

'I, er . . .' whimpered a, supposedly, defeated Mancini as he was led away to the buffet. 'Look,' he pleaded, attempting to excuse himself from the act of theft, 'after your contract I've got to go back to straight alchemy. It doesn't pay so good, you know? You can't deprive me of a little pocket money.'

'A little pocket money's one thing. Some of the books down here could cause utter chaos if they were to fall into the wrong hands!' growled Practz, wincing slightly as fifty tons of virtual boulder surged through the assembled crowd and crashed away down the corridor. 'But, as you can see, now we've got our fully uprated system we can breathe a lot easier.' He grinned, slapped Mancini around the shoulder and headed off towards the buffet. 'One day I'll get used to that thing trying to crush me every time I use the library!'

Having spent eighty-five thousand centuries inside a terracotta pot, suddenly found itself being discovered, then sold, then bought, then given away and finally been so rudely awakened, the sea-scrole was now totally confused and frustrated. Up until very recently its life had been simple and it had done what it was supposed to do as best it could. In fact, if the truth were known, the sea-scrole was quite proud of the fact that it had managed to retain the information entrusted to it so well, holding the secrets, waiting for the coming of the One.

It only had one worry, though, just one black mark on an

otherwise pristine career record. It had forgotten what the One looked like. Well, eighty-five thousand centuries was quite a long time to remember a description of someone you'd never met, especially when you'd no idea what things like five foot eight, brown curly hair and long fuzzy beard actually meant. The sad truth was that after only fifteen thousand centuries or so the memory net containing the description of the One had given up, totally. Seventy thousand centuries ago the sea-scrole had twitched in alarm, then sighed an ancient sigh and decided that it would all turn out right in the end. It would tell its secret to the first person that it happened to meet.

The only snag was that everyone kept running away.

Forlornly the sea-scrole reached out with its mind and tried to probe the creature now lugging it to who knew where. It searched and prodded and poked its primordial mental fingers into the consciousness of the being referred to as Uhrnest. And found nothing.

Ah well, shrugged the sea-scrole, after eighty-five thousand centuries a few more hours shouldn't make any difference.

It was difficult to control the tilapia vol-au-vents whilst he was shaking so much. Crumbs of flaky pastry exploded in tiny savoury detonations, decorating Cheiro Mancini's wiry beard as he lost momentary control of his overwrought jaw muscles and bit far too hard. Practz was certain to notice, he thought nervously, as the strain of making polite conversation grew heavier on his emotional shoulders.

'Are you alright?' asked Practz, sounding genuinely concerned.

'Just a bit over-excited, I suppose,' he answered, brushing at his cloak in tiny nervous flicks. 'Ha! I'm not used to breaking and entering.'

Knapp helped himself to several dozen vol-au-vents, secreting them into his sack.

'I prefer to think of it as "bug-hunting",' said Practz. 'Who better to try out our updates than the man who installed the system in the first place?'

'Speaking of which,' Mancini began, desperate for any chance to steer the conversation away from the all-too-recent criminal activities of himself and Knapp, 'I noticed a slight chrominence shift on the chasm. It could be a glitch in the reality prison . . . prism. D'you want me to check it out?' He cringed, his butterfly-infested stomach writhing in embarrassment at his slip.

'No, no. You're our guest, now. Phlim can take care of that. Would you care for a slice of frog's leg?' asked Practz, holding out a large tranche of meat. 'We've been force-feeding them.'

Phlim scowled, thinking of the trouble he'd had catching that beast: those eyes . . . that tongue! Swiftly he changed the subject. 'How's the PET business, Mr Mancini?'

'Can't complain,' the Alchemist grunted round a large beaker of ale. 'Picking up a bit, especially in the mythical department. Had an order for twenty-five self-contained basilisks the other day and I've got another for three amphisbanes and a mantichora. It's funny, I used to think that griffins were a bit special, but now . . .' He raised his eyes. 'They'll be asking me for purple panthers next.'

'I think pink would be nicer, Mr Mancini,' said Phlim. 'Purple is just not panthery enough.'

'Hmmm, don't really like pink. That was last season's colour. Pink elephants were big last year, ha ha!'

Practz cringed at the VET's attempt at humour. 'Argh! You ought to be locked up . . . !'

Cheiro stared at the Losa Llamas head of security and swallowed nervously. 'Wha . . . what d'you mean?' he stuttered, turning pale. Had he given himself away? Knapp looked up in fear.

'Jokes like that are a health hazard,' complained Practz.

'Ha! Yes, sorry,' cringed the VET. 'Well, I've er, taken up far too much of your time already. I really must be going. Amphisbanes don't grow on trees, you know. C'mon, Knapp.'

'The night is still young,' said Phlim, staring at the barrel of beer and getting ready for a good drinking session.

'No, I really ought to go. It's a long way back to Venasht,' Mancini excused himself, desperate to leave.

'Very well. Keep in touch!' said Practz, shaking his hand.

'If you need any more PETs, give me a call.' Mancini grinned, turned and scarpered through the door with Knapp hard on his heels. He led the dash down the tunnel and then stopped, panting against the wall. Bare-faced lying was such hard work.

Suddenly a hand flashed around the corner and grabbed him on the shoulder in a vice-like grip. 'Not yet, Uhrnest. You know the plan.'

'No! I'm Rholf. Uhrnest didn't show up, Mr Mancini,' growled the deep voice of a guard. Mancini squealed and stared at the figure clutching at his shoulder. Terror snatched at him. He knows! he panicked, I'll confess . . . I'll tell him everything . . . there's just not enough money in alchemy . . . it's not my fault . . . I had to steal it . . . In a flash he turned on the huge hand, bit the finger hard, wriggled frantically loose and sprinted away.

'Oi! Come back!' shouted Rholf accelerating after him, pounding hard against the forces of inertia and sucking his finger.

Mancini and Knapp vanished down a side passage, turned left and sprinted up a spiral staircase, Knapp clutching feverishly at his vol-au-vent filled sack. The guard was hard on their heels, leaping two steps at a time, gaining rapidly.

'Come back, I won't hurt you!'

'You'll never catch me!' squealed Mancini, panting hard, lifelong stretches behind bars flashing through his mind.

'Oh no!' grunted Rholf, leaping forward, his hand catching the VET's fleeing ankle, pulling him down in a crumpled heap. 'Give me your pockets! C'mon, turn 'em out.'

'Never!' puffed Mancini.

'Come on, open up!'

'You'll have to make me! I'm innocent. There's nothing in there!'

'I know. That's why I was told to bring these.' The guard held out a large bag of cakes and beer.

'What?' croaked Mancini. 'For us?'

'Yeah, boss thought you deserved it seeing as you didn't eat much before. Take it or leave it.'

'I thought . . . I . . . thank you!' He almost screamed with relief as the guard saluted and strolled off down the staircase.

Cheiro Mancini struggled to his feet, swung the bag over his shoulder and crept out of Losa Llamas, his heart pounding. He had done it. Right under their noses!

Riches beyond my wildest dreams here we come! he screamed quietly to himself as they passed through a small cave entrance and into the forest air. They leapt aboard the cart and spurred it into action, Mancini mentally rubbing his hands and tossing gold coins into the air. The forest of Losa Llamas slipped by unseen. In the distance an onomatopede howled, shrieked and snarled, its best efforts ignored by Mancini and Knapp. They had far better things to think about. Mancini dreamt of gold and Knapp scoffed several dozen vol-au-vents as he kicked the horses into a galloping frenzy.

'Soon I'll be able to do it,' thrilled Mancini. 'Turn lead into gold!' His eyes flashed with greedy glee, his tongue tasted the victory of turning dull, soft, malleable metal into carats of shining yellow beauty. Scrap into covetable, spendable coinage! His hands glistened moistly with anticipation. No more palmistry; an end to crystal gazing; PETs would be a thing of the past! Gold, gold, and more gold from now on! He mentally flung a few more glistering handfuls skywards.

Suddenly, Knapp tugged hard on the reins and the cart slewed to a rapid halt.

'What is it?' snapped Mancini, clipping Knapp across the back of his head. 'Why've we stopped?'

Before Knapp could answer a branch snapped over to their right.

Ice skates of terror screeched down Mancini's spine, casting white flakes of fear in all directions. They had been followed, already. Another branch cracked, and guilt seized the sound, translating it into a thousand pursuing Losa Llaman Guards. They had found the book missing, discovered the bound body of Uhrnest . . . They were coming.

'Move!' shouted Mancini, snatching the reins off Knapp and slapping the horses' backs with terror. 'Get galloping or it's the knacker's yard for you!' he screamed.

Suddenly a hail of sticks and leaves exploded in the forest as a wood pigeon struggled skywards through a holly bush. Mancini's eyes locked onto its wing-whacking struggle, staring feverishly as his body fought an emotional civil war, dithering between screaming and laughing with blind relief.

A wood pigeon! Calm down, he told himself. The cracking branches were suddenly innocent, no longer indicative of the careless footfall of countless guards. 'Stay calm. Just ride away!' he told himself.

Knapp tugged on his sleeve as a tree ahead rustled menacingly. 'Stop it, Knapp,' growled Mancini. 'Get a grip on yourself, it's only a pigeon.' He slapped the reins across the horses' backs and leapt out of his skin as a figure swung from a tree and landed next to him in the cart, blocking out the entire light as effectively as a solar eclipse – the figure of a Losa Llaman guard. Weapons hung from every available inch of his massive torso and a vast second generation backpack thaumatron was slung across his glistening muscular shoulders, throbbing and humming with massed flux density. Mancini dived for the tarpaulin, pleading.

'Boo!' said the guard, rummaged in his pocket and held out an aging tome. 'Did I frighten you?'

'Idiot!' shouted Mancini. 'You're supposed to meet us *outside* the forest!'

'Well, I saw you stop and I thought . . .'

'You weren't designed to think!' he snapped, snatching the proffered tome and thrusting it into his pack. 'You nearly scared me to death!' he added, tugging a Malpin Empathy Generator out of his cloak pocket.

'Sorry, I won't do it ag . . .'

The figure of Uhrnest shimmered, turned suddenly translucent and vanished with a small 'fhoof' as Mancini broke the thaumic contact. He stared at the scrappy-looking collection of wires, chalk marks and two pink psychoterrin crystals, and despite his terror-hidden state, grinned happily. What a stroke of sheer genius, he thought, linking two detuned psychoterrins to create enough mass to mount a PET core inside its very own Projected Empathy Transmission. The first PET to take itself for a walk. And it looked so good – it almost fooled me!

Chuckling greedily and still shaking with fear, he shoved the core in his pack, spurring the cart towards the edge of the forest.

What a genius! I deserve it all! I'm too good for mere alchemy! he shrieked inside his head. Filthy rich, here I come!!! Sanity and Cheiro Mancini were swiftly becoming little more than nodding acquaintances.

One of the last things that Rholf expected to fall over in the gloomy corridors of level twenty-eight was the gagged and bound bulk of the real Uhrnest.

Rholf brushed the dirt off his uniform and scowled. 'There you are!' he shouted. 'Lyin' around as usual. Well, I hope you're satisfied with yourself, I've had to do your blinkin' shift.'

'Mmmmf mmf mmmffmmm!' replied Uhrnest, squirming to illustrate the point.

'Excuses, excuses!'

'Mmmf mmf mmffmmm!' protested Uhrnest.

'What kind of a state would we be in if we all lay around complainin' of headaches,' snarled Rholf.

'MMMMMMMMMMFF!'

'And the same to you!' snapped Rholf, swivelling on his heel and heading back to the buffet. 'With bells on!' he added over his huge shoulder.

Uhrnest squirmed pathetically and wondered what he had said to upset Rholf quite so much.

Mancini spurred the horses on relentlessly, reached the edge of Losa Llamas forest, swung on the cart's handbrake and leapt off. With a swift glint of steel he hacked the panting horses free, whacking a stick across their flanks, and dashed across the track. Tugging frantically at an innocent-looking mound of leaves and branches, casually piled just out of sight, he and Knapp revealed a small red sporty getaway cart stacked high with carefully wrapped equipment, and a pair of leaf-littered horses scowling miserably at them. Eagerly the criminals leapt into the cart, cracked the whips and thrilled as they felt the tug of the two horse-power acceleration and the screech of low-profile Peerhelly Tyres on the gravel. Freedom! They'd never catch them now that they had changed carts.

Next stop the secret hideout high in the mountains . . . and pots and pots of gold!

Whether it was the relaxed atmosphere, the vast quantities of mulled ale which he had eagerly quaffed or the sight of one of the porters struggling out of the cavern beneath a mountainous heap of precariously quivering cups and plates that reminded him of a certain afternoon in the Khomun Market, Phlim couldn't be certain. It could have been all three. But suddenly he realised he was rabbiting uncontrollably about his recent holiday and the events leading up to the purchase of the dead sea-scrolls.

'You haven't got a spare one, have you?' asked Thurgia when he had finished.

'Eh?' answered Phlim. 'Why? You've got yours!'

'Well, it's a funny thing, you know,' confessed Thurgia, 'but, I never did find mine after you threw it at me.'

'It rolled under the table, I saw it.'

'I looked. No sign of it. Not even any bits of ash. Almost as if it grew legs and ran off.'

Phlim and Wat burst into peals of laughter at such a ridiculous idea. No rolled up bit of parchment could just grow legs and squirm away. Ridiculous idea!

Just within earshot Practz's face clouded over as a host of sudden nagging doubts whinnied into life inside his head and crashed the fences of trust. When Practz had received his scroll from Phlim something hadn't felt quite right about it; it

111

hadn't felt *really* parchmenty. But that was just because they were cheap foreign fakes . . . wasn't it?

With a shudder he mulled over all the possible explanations as to why an innocent piece of fake parchment scroll should not only fail to explode into a million blackened fragments upon having countless gigathaums of pure magical energy shorted through it, but also appear to have generated its very own perambulatory properties. The answers he came up with he didn't like. At all.

Either three of his staff were victims of a small and very potent localised attack of mass hysteria. Or they weren't *parchment* scrolls that Phlim had brought back.

Draining his ale with a gulp, he left the party chamber and sprinted to his quarters, panic growing as he accelerated through the deserted corridors. His thoughts whirled. If they're not parchment, then what are they? Could the legends be true? Could a once dead sea-scrole be loose within Losa Llamas? It seemed too scary to consider.

Almost before he realised it he was screeching to a frantic halt outside his door and bursting in. In a second he had cast a practised spell at the hex-ray panel on the wall, snatched his scroll from the shelf and was unrolling it. Now he came to think about it, the surface didn't feel entirely like parchment . . . and what about that tiny thin line and two dots on the back? A mouth and two nostrils? Surely not.

He thrust the corners of the scroll into the clips on the hex-ray box and stared. Blue light glowed around the rectangular edges of the scroll. Practz moved closer, his jaws dropping as his eyes picked out the details, his heart pounding faster as the truth was revealed for the first time in eighty-five thousand centuries.

There before him, finer than the purest of watermarks, exposed by the hex-rays, was a fine tracery of cartilaginous bones standing proud in all their primeval glory. Practz's finger traced the dead sea-scrole's ribcage, its flat skull and even some preserved organs. So it was true!

Shuddering nervously, he flicked his wrist, the hex-ray panel dimmed and he collapsed into his chair, truth draining his energy, snippets of ancient legend spinning and screaming in his head.

The equivocal evidence for the existence of Mesozoic Mages held true. The legends were fact! Practz gasped. And if it was true that those pre-Cambrian conjurors lived and breathed and wove spells, then it was probably also true that the souvenir fossil record he was staring at held an awful truth, an ancient and deadly string of facts that, if unleashed could cause untold . . . what?

Rumours and speculations abounded as to what was contained within the dead sea-scroles, and they all had a sickeningly unhelpful common theme. Destruction, death, chaos, mayhem, pestilence. And that was just chapter one.

Practz dropped his head into his hands and moaned. He had just discovered the answer to every Thaumic Historian's greatest conundrum. He should be happy. He was the only person to know, with undeniable certainty, not only that a race of magic-users existed way back in the dim and distant echoes of the past, but that they stored valuable and dangerous spells on Read Only Marine-life and Random Access Molluscs.

And one of them was alive and well and slirming its ancient way around Losa Llamas.

If the information it contained should fall into the wrong hands . . . Practz shuddered, stood and sprinted back to the party. They had to find it. Now!

It had taken three days to get there, trekking across leagues of windswept tundra, getting lost, struggling up mountain tracks into the depths of the Eastern Talpa Mountains, getting lost again, pushing the sporty red getaway cart up ever steepening paths away from the Foh Pass, thinking they were going to die as the wind ripped through their clothes, getting lost yet again . . . but finally Cheiro Mancini and Knapp arrived at the collection of sticks and rusty nails that was their secret hideout.

The advertisement n *Criminal Weekly* under 'Out of Town Secret Residences' was correct. It did have running water and washing facilities. It did have plenty of sporting opportunities to offer the outdoor type. And it did have a fully operational self-catering facility offering grilling and toasting potential. These were respectively five hundred feet from the back door, straight down; the entire Eastern Arm of the Talpa Mountains; and a pile of sticks and a toasting fork.

But Mancini didn't care about a short period of creature discomforts. He knew that the Thaumaturgical Physicists of Losa Llamas would be searching for him, thus he had to lay low. He also knew that by the time he had spent a week up here he would have transmogrified more lead piping into gold than he had ever dreamed of.

He was only half right.

Eagerly he and Knapp unloaded a stack of half-inch piping, a small athanor burner and a brand-new alchemist's flask – one of the finest that the Murrhovian Empire could produce, especially imported for him. He grinned as he ripped the layers of packing newsparchment from it and threw them in the corner.

As he set the apparatus up on the cold floor of the hired hideout, secure in the knowledge that no-one had followed him, he relaxed, thrilling on the very edge of a brand-new way of life. Knapp chewed on a three-day-old vol-au-vent that had somehow not been devoured by the other residents of his sack.

Mancini pulled the tome out of his cloak pocket and a wave of nervous excitement flashed up his spine as he clutched it to his chest. Here was the key. *Transmogrification: All You Ever Wanted To Turn Into Anything Else But Were Afraid To Try* and it was his. Such geniu . . .

'Oi! Stop squeezing!'

'Eh?' grunted Mancini, scowling at Knapp.

'What?' the youth mumbled around another mouthful of vol-au-vent.

'What d'you say?' snapped the VET.

'Stop squeezing. It hurts!' came the voice, as Knapp shrugged and swallowed.

Mancini shrieked and dropped the tome, staring frantically around for the source of the voice. They'd been followed, they'd been found, this was it! The end. Life could be such a b . . .

A tiny part of Mancini's mind waved its axons and tried to ask why a Losa Llaman guard, if he'd tracked you down to this godforsaken hideout quite so soon, would be demanding that you stop squeezing? It was ignored.

'You'll never take me alive!' shrieked Mancini to the unseen threat as he peered through cracks in the fabric of the hut. Knapp stared in utter confusion.

Behind him the surface of the tome writhed and contorted as the sea-scrole slimed its way out from under the dust cover.

'I say! It's awfully dry up here,' came the voice in Mancini's head. 'You couldn't be an angel and pour me a bath? Could you?'

Mancini swivelled on his heel. He'd heard the voice but it sounded too close, too dry, not decorated by any echoes off rocks, no ambience.

'Three days in your cloak pocket is a bit much!' came the voice. Mancini screamed, trying to see who was talking to him. None of this made any sense. A Losa Llaman guard in his pocket? he thought as panic stirred the sediment of his mind once more.

'No, no! Not guard. Guardian. Of the Message for the One. For You!' answered the sea-scrole, its telepathic tendrils reaching out to the terrified Mancini.

'Knapp! If this is supposed to be some kind of joke, stop it now. It's not funny.'

The wiry youth fished in his sack for anything else that hadn't crossed the borders of inedibility.

'I'm down here!' telepathed the sea-scrole. 'And I'd kill for a bath. You've no idea what this atmosphere's doing to my skin. I feel so itchy.'

Suddenly Mancini realised that there was an object on the floor that looked not entirely dissimilar to a rubber bath mat. And it was waving at him.

'Cooee! Scrole to Mancini, come in please!'

He turned and sprinted out of the hut, crashed into one of the horses and laid himself out cold.

It had never happened before.

In the entire history of High Energy Thaumic Research in Losa Llamas this was the first time that all research had totally stopped. Even on the day that a band of Cranachan Imperial Stealth Troopers had smashed their way into the complex of tunnels on their mission to steal the Frogs of War, a small clump of desperate Thaumaturgical Physicists had still been furiously studying the potential defensive properties of atomised psychoterrin suspensions and fifteen-pound lump hammers.

Practz had split the entire Losa Llamas workforce into five groups, each led by one Thaumaturgical Physicist, and upon his command they had had strip-searched every inch of the complex. Three times.

Within minutes they had found something very odd. It was called Uhrnest and it was lying in an extremely angry heap on level twenty-eight 'Mmmmf'-ing and blinding profusely. It took eight technicians sitting on his chest and the promise of several gallons of beer to calm him sufficiently to untie him. Sadly, he hadn't a clue who had hit him and trussed him so neatly and he didn't recall seeing any animated bath mats in this particular stretch of corridor.

After three days of crossing and recrossing the same ground, upturning tables, emptying cupboards and removing all the U-bends in every single washroom, they came across two other very strange things. The first was that a tome was long overdue in the library and no-one knew who had borrowed it.

And the second was Practz's reaction to the news that they had found that a tome was long overdue in the library and no-one knew who had borrowed it.

He turned very pale, quivered, slapped an angst-ridden palm against a rapidly furrowing brow and dragged Phlim away down a corridor yelling at him to ready the Sneeke for action.

All this fuss for an overdue library tome.

Out of a swirling miasma of distorted thoughts and warped ideas a comforting trilling purr wheedled into his consciousness. At almost the same time Mancini became aware of a cold flannel being laid upon his head and encouraging words swimming towards him.

'There, there,' it oozed. 'Did ickle Cheiro bash his teeny-weeny headsy-wedsy, den? Who's a poor ickle chippy-chappy?'

He groaned and opened his eyes. White clouds scudded casually unconcerned beneath a dark curtain of rubber bath mat. *Rubber bath mat?*

In a flash he was on his feet, his back against the cart, glaring at the crumpled rectangular creature struggling to smooth itself out on the rocky ground.

'Get away from me!' screamed Mancini. 'Leave me alone!'

'Awww. That's not nice. I've been waiting eighty-five thousand centuries to talk to you!' answered the sea-scrole as it sploomed slowly forward.

Knapp popped his head out of the hut. 'You alright?'

'Go away! Shoo!' shouted Mancini, backing away.

'Only asked,' tutted Knapp and vanished inside to count his maggots.

'Don't you want to hear my message?' telepathed the sea-scrole, squelching forward a little more.

'No! Leave me alone, you mangy bathmat!'

'Leave you for what? Just so you can turn one worthless metal into another?'

'Yes! I mean no! Gold's valuable!' Suddenly he stopped and shook his head. What was happening to him? He was actually defending his actions to a scrappy piece of bathroom furniture!

'Oh, well. If you're happy with mere gold then I'll just have to find someone else who wants to behold the most awesome power ever seen in eight-five thousand centuries. I mean, if you're totally happy to deal in bullion when entire kingdoms are at stake, that's up to you. But I know what I'd rather have.'

Mancini was sure the thing winked at him.

'See you around, bub!' telepathed the sea-scrole as it began to floop away.

'No, no! Hang on a bit,' pleaded Mancini, suddenly feeling that just listening to what this creature had to say might be useful. 'What was that you were saying about a bath?' he added.

The sea-scrole grinned to itself. 'Ideally just warm enough so you can dip your elbow in. Oh, and don't forget to put three tablespoons of salt per gallon in. Osmosis can be a real pain.'

Despite the best efforts of the elemental gusts of icy winds through the narrow Foh Pass bottleneck, tempers were rising in the two opposing, and very stationary, wagon trains. Horns blared in the thin air of the Talpa Mountains as strings of threats and peals of choice insults were exchanged.

'Get that overladen pile of junk out of my way!' screamed the fuming figure of Magnus the Carter, standing hands on angry hips in the front of his wagon.

'No chance! You're supposed to give way to up-traffic!' yelled Hassock the haulage contractor, snarling and looking uglier by the minute.

'I was here first, left Cranachan hours ago! There's a passing place just round that corner!' bawled Magnus, his hands wringing at his whip. The six harnessed beasts shuffled and snorted restlessly.

'Hah! Sure. And there's a five-hundred-foot drop down there. Or hadn't you noticed?' argued Hassock, clenching his fists and pointing over the edge of the cliff track.

'So what? Can't control your wagon train, eh?' growled Magnus. 'That why you've had so many damaged goods lately?'

'I got my licence when it was a *tough* test. I can put all seven wagons of this beauty anywhere I want to, turn it on a groat,' grinned Hassock, slapping the thick flank of his rear haulage rhinoceros. 'But only if I *want* to!'

Magnus snarled a string of choice Cranachan oaths,

vaulted off his wagon and advanced on Hassock whirling his rhino-whip threateningly. 'Time for a bit of persuasion, then!'

'You and whose army?' shouted Hassock, rolling up the sleeves of his leather jacket, snatching the handbrake on and leaping down. With a practised move he grabbed a vast club out from behind the driver's seat and whirled it round his head. 'Now, why don't you back up before I rearrange your nose?'

Unnoticed by the two imminently warring hauliers, eight mounted figures rounded a corner on the Cranachan side, tugged on their reins and stopped. The seven members of the Small Bore Drainage Company leapt off their llamas and began unloading a whole plethora of mystical surveying and divining equipment. The eighth figure squatted on his horse and stared at the warily circling hauliers. It suddenly became blindingly clear to Rosch Mh'tonnay, Chief Civil Engineer and Project Leader of the Trans-Talpino Trade Route Improvement Scheme, why a small trundle-thru instalment offering hot beverages, refreshments and rhino watering facilities was so urgently required. A sickening thump of seasoned elm on nasal cartilage served as a graphic punctuation mark.

Mh'tonnay turned at Proph, the leader of the survey team, pointed open-mouthed at the hauliers and pleaded, 'Aren't you going to stop them?'

'Those two?' answered the red-bearded dwarf, his moustache sticking out beyond his shoulders and ending scant inches above the ground. 'Hell, no way! Shoot! 'F I had to stop those two each time they pick fights up 'ere I wouldn't get no work done.' He rolled his tongue around the inside of his mouth and spat a vast glob of sticky saliva twenty feet across the track. ' 'Sides, you wouldn't catch me standin' in the way 'f hauliers expressin' theys rights.'

'What rights?' squeaked Mh'tonnay as Hassock's head collided with a large rock in Magnus' hand.

'Rights 'f Way.'

'But they're fighting!'

119

'Yup!' answered Proph. 'Why d'you think it's called a duel carriageway? Heee heee.'

Suddenly Magnus leapt out of Hassock's reach, slashed his whip at his rival's wagon train, caught the handbrake and pulled. The six rhinos staggered backwards a pace as the grip released, issuing startled pachyderm snorts of panic as they tried to take the strain against the momentum of the wagon train on the incline.

Proph, so called because of his PHD (Prophecyship in High-altitude Drainage), ignored the dispute and gathered his team together. Three years ago he had set up the Small Bore Drainage Company and peopled it with dwarves. With centuries of mining experience in his blood, not to mention his diminutive stature, love of burrowing in confined spaces and nose for rooting out underground streams and aquifers, one dwarf could lay eight times the amount of piping in one day that a team of the less vertically challenged could in a week.

Squealing, Hassock sprinted towards his wagon train as it slowly lurched backwards, potential energy outmatching rhino power. Magnus grinned and leapt into his driving seat. He cracked his whip, eased off his handbrake and advanced with a hail of abuse.

'Awlreet, Digger,' shouted Proph, launching a salvo of sticky saliva at a shovel and grinning as he heard the metallic ring of a direct hit. He handed the muscular dwarf what looked like a pair of bent coat hangers and pointed towards Cranachan. 'Start over yonder. Rhett, you over there!' In a matter of moments, the seven dwarves were spread out around the Foh Pass, waving small metal wires at the ground and chanting low investigative incantations and surveying spells.

Rosch Mh'tonnay watched helplessly as Hassock's wagon train slowly retreated backwards around the corner, the air above it rapidly turning blue. Magnus whipped his rhinos onwards.

Proph relaxed into his divining, scouring the rocks of the Foh Pass, his elbows tingling as he quartered and searched for running underground water with which to supply the proposed Happy Chef franchise. His shoulders twitched as he passed over a rough section, vibrating itchy harmonics down his spine.

Hassock's runaway cart vanished around a column of rock.

Proph turned back and concentrated on the rough spot, fascination and curiosity raising their heads. In a flash his divining rods twitched, spun wildly, then stopped dead, pointing straight down. The dwarf let out a squeal as a purple spark arced from the ground, struck the rods and welded them firmly together.

'What is it?' panted Rosch Mh'tonnay, sprinting up and choking on the smell of burning metal. The other six dwarves followed.

'Jumpin' jiminy . . . !' croaked Proph, shaking as a corona of purple sparks earthed themselves from the ends of his moustache. 'Either *the* biggest underground stream ever found in th'history 'f divinin'. Or . . .'

Around the corner of the bottleneck a raging blasphemy of curses exploded as Hassock somehow steered his runaway wagon train into the gravel catchway, scrunching to a noisy halt. Magnus waved two fingers cheerfully as he rumbled by, chalking up a victory and heading off towards Rhyngill and a waiting market.

'Or what?' pressed Mh'tonnay, staring eagerly at Proph and his arc-welded divining rods.

Or something else . . . something a whole lot more interesting, Proph almost answered, a distant memory from his PHD course pricking for attention. He glanced at the eager faces of his Drainage Company.

'Or . . . or a faulty divinin' rod,' he actually said, covering up until he knew for sure. You don't just go blabbing about things like *this* in front of mere employees. Not until you're certain. 'Happens sometimes, nothin' t' worry 'bout,' he lied, dismissing the other six.

He gestured at Rosch Mh'tonnay to come closer. 'Tell me,' he whispered, barely audible over the ranting of

Hassock around the corner. 'As Chief Engineer you 'ave full say where the porta-hovels go, don't you?'

Mh'tonnay nodded.

'Put yours there,' insisted Proph, winking meaningfully and pointing to the rough spot.

It was probably the happiest the sea-scrole had been for at least . . . oooh, eighty-five thousand centuries. It flipped and cavorted in the shallow tepid bath of salty water and almost managed to convince itself that it was home in the primordial tom-yum soup of the pre-cambrian. It rolled onto its back and began to telepath a jaunty little sea-scrole shanty, splashing and thrilling as some of the thought waves bounced off the walls of the bath, echoing in its mind.

There were only two things that could possibly mar its newfound animational joy. One was the deadly secret locked into the fibres of its cerebellum and the other was glaring at it over the side of the bath.

'But what is it?' snarled Knapp, resentfully topping up the bath. 'And where did it come from? And where's all this gold, eh? I didn't lug all that lead piping in here just for fun, you know.'

'Questions, questions,' grumbled Mancini almost to himself.

'How about some answers?'

'Impatient, isn't he?' telepathed the scrole.

'Always has been,' sighed Mancini.

'What?' snapped Knapp. 'Stop talking to yourself.'

'I'm not. I'm talking to the . . .' Mancini's gaze hardened as he turned from Knapp and scowled at the scrole. 'You mean you can't hear . . . ?'

'Can't hear what?' pressed Knapp, hurling several gallons of water into the bath.

'Course he can't,' telepathed the scrole smugly. 'I don't want him to. Besides, I've been waiting with a message for the One.'

'What is this message?' snarled Mancini.

'You're doing it again,' moaned Knapp. 'When can we do the gold?'

'Look, go and count your maggots again. I'm *thinking*!' shouted Mancini. 'You can't just jump in and start transmogrifying willy-nilly. There's more to it than that!'

Miserably, Knapp picked up his sack and shuffled out of the hut.

And then the sea-scrole made the mistake of actually handing over the message to Mancini.

'What's that supposed to mean?' snapped Mancini as he glared at the sea-scrole in the bath.

'You mean you don't know?'

'Would I be asking if I knew?' shouted the VET, frustration scratching at his nerves.

'Maybe,' hedged the sea-scrole, splashing a corner thoughtfully in the warm, salty water.

'Is there no more of it? An extra verse or something? A bit of a clue?'

'Er . . . Nope.'

'Well, what's the point of keeping that slice of doggerel in your head for eighty-five thousand centuries?' shrieked Mancini. 'I mean, it doesn't even rhyme properly!'

'Okay, so it's doggerel. Don't blame me. I didn't write it!'

'It's nonsense!' shouted Mancini. 'How's that supposed to release untold power and be the key to the rise and fall of kingdoms? How's that supposed to be better than gold, eh? You said it'd be better than gold!'

'If I knew that do you think I'd be flapping about here in this poxy bath on the top of a mountain? I'd be ruling my very own kingdom!'

'You couldn't rule a . . . a . . . thumb!'

'Says who . . .'

'Me!'

'And why . . .'

'Well, look at you. You're nothing but a . . . a . . . bath mat!'

'Speciesist!'

'How dare you call me a . . .'

'Listen to your arguments. Based purely on the premise that appearance is all . . .'

'Oh no! I'm saying you couldn't rule a kingdom because, er . . . the crown wouldn't fit! See!'

'Oh, very clever!'

'Of course,' said Mancini smugly.

'If you're so clever what does the rhyme mean?'

'I was close to working it out . . . but you put me off. Remind me how it goes.'

The sea-scrole grinned to itself, knowing that it had won, and telepathed the message once more.

> 'Bah, ba, blacknyss,
> Havyn't any sowel,
> To Hel, sire, Hel, sire, ye hundryd and won.
> Powyr from ye rocks and,
> Fohcuss threw ye stone,
> onto ye boddey of ye damned-naytion.'

Mancini shook his head. 'And you reckon that's worth more than gold! You're out of your fishy mind!'

'How dare you call me a fish!'

'Because you're wet and stupid, that's why!' mumbled Mancini, folding his arms petulantly.

'That's eels!' snapped the scrole in his mind.

'Shut up!'

'You don't know what it means, do you?'

'I'm not telling you. I've got work to do!' Mancini waved the stolen tome, turned his back and stared blankly at the page.

A stray thought waved an irritating finger in his head. Something in that message was familiar. But what did it mean?

And why was he thinking of black sheep?

'Left, left, left!' shrieked the man in the yellow jacket and hard hat, bellowing directions and waving what looked like small table tennis bats at the man backing up the last of the porta-hovel delivery carts.

'You deaf? I said "left" ' he screamed as it turned to the right, dropped a wheel into the trough, emptied its contents onto the half-set section of the Trans-Talpino Trade Route and ended up swaying precariously above a five-hundred-foot drop.

'What you playin' at directin' me over the edge?' shouted the cart driver angrily. 'Some kinda joke, eh? Tryin' to kill me?'

'I said left!' yelled Grike, the site foreman, drawing himself up to his full height and bellowing down the rolled up tube he used for directing.

'I went left,' barked the cart driver, rolling up his sleeves and bristling.

'My left!' shrieked Grike and pointed. 'That way!'

'It was my left,' snarled the cart driver.

'You take directions from me so it's my left, right?'

There was a terrified snort from the creature trapped in the shafts of the cart as it slid closer to the edge.

'Look. Now you've upset Dubbin!' shouted the cart driver, shoving his sleeves further up and exposing a pair of very hairy arms. 'I don't have no truck wi' people who upset my Dubbin!'

'If you'd paid attention to my instructions then nobody would be upset. Least of all that rhino of yours!' shouted Grike, pointing at the terrified haulage pachyderm.

'You sayin' my Dubbin don't matter, eh?' growled the cart driver, stamping forward menacingly.

'No, no, I like rhinos,' whimpered Grike, backing away. 'Some of my best frinds are rh . . .'

Rosch Mh'tonnay cringed at the sound of a breaking nose drifting up into earshot as he surveyed the progress from above. He shook his head and wandered back into his Project Leader's Hut, tutting. It was like this every day. Arguments breaking out, petty squabbles about overtime, yellow-jacketed workers filling in holes that another team had only just completed moments before . . . He was sure it was getting worse. Whoever named this sort of work Civil Engineering had never set foot on a working site. Five days into a nine-month contract, cooped up in a hut in the Talpa Mountains, adding an extra lane and a trundle-thru Happy

125

Chef to the Trade Routes, and all because some groat-pinching accountant in Cranachan had got the traffic figures wrong. What a life!

Slamming the door on the rapidly expanding fight below his balcony, Rosch Mh'tonnay locked the door of his porta-hovel and headed for the stove. Picking the carefully shaped planks out from behind his desk he wedged them under the edges of the stove, then lifted and eased the burner off the trap door. In a second the square section had flipped back revealing the eagerly beaming red-bearded face of a dwarf.

'Well?' snapped Mh'tonnay.

The dwarf squirmed out of the hole and held up an ornately carved wooden box, pointed at the dial with a quivering stubby finger and spat a glob of brown saliva across the room. A shovel rang with a direct hit. 'Heee doggy! 'S a big one! Thought they were myths, but not 'ny more, no siree!' he babbled excitedly.

'What?'

' 'S huge! Thaumometer shows eighty . . . 'f it's fifty feet down, then . . . whoooeee, that's . . . ! Damn . . . what's thaumoclude shieldin' coefficient 'f granite? Twenty-six or sixty-two, I can never remember. Say it's sixty . . .'

'What are you talking about?' growled Mh'tonnay, rapidly losing patience.

' 'Bout two and a half gigs, that's what! Hot Jiminy! If it's a fully fledged thaumafer an' not just a thaumolith . . .'

Mh'tonnay threw his hands up, waving them frantically to stop the gushing drainage engineer. 'Stop! Explain! A fully fledged what?'

'You ain't never heard 'f a thaumafer?'

'No!'

'Shoot! What 'bout geothaumal energy, earth-magic . . .'

'They're just fairy tales . . .' began Mh'tonnay.

' 'S what I thought. Look what happened t' my divinin' rods.'

'You said that was a fault . . .' stuttered Mh'tonnay, rapidly losing track of the conversation.

'Said that t' get rid 'f others. How c'n two bits 'f coat

126

hanger arc-weld theyselves t'gether while looking f' water? No way. Thought I must've tapped into more than jus' an underground stream. This proves it!' the dwarf cried, waving the thaumometer. ' 'F my calculations right there's two an' half gigathaums down there, at least.' The Proph's eyes lit up as he thought of it all.

'So what?' grumbled Mh'tonnay. 'What use is it?'

'You no imagination, boy?' tutted the dwarf. 'Harness the arts 'f geomancy an' any civil engineering project'll be a piece of cake.'

Mh'tonnay's eyes lit up.

'Explosives'll be obsolete,' continued the dwarf. 'Quarrying? Shoot! Forget it. Pickaxes? Cement mixers? No need!'

Mh'tonnay stared, his jaw dropping as he listened to the fight outside. 'You mean I won't need to employ anyone?'

'Sure y' won't! Why stop there?' ranted Proph. 'Kill th' Trade Route Improvement Scheme. Hail th' Trans-Talpino Canal Initiative! Locks. Dry-docks, Straight through th' middle of Tor Teehya. Easy-peasy.'

Mh'tonnay stared through the window of the porta-hovel as another epidemic of squabbling erupted between the cement mixers and the delivery men.

'Geomancy can do all that?' he asked dreamily, gazing into a nirvanic future.

'Yes siree, an' no messin',' insisted Proph. 'How d'you think all those stone circles got built, huh? I mean, can you imagine your lot co-operating long enough t' hoick those big stones on top 'f the others? An' what 'bout the Blikni Yogis in the Meanlayla Mountains? Think that lot could excavate their cave temples on their own? Fat chance! Couldn't even build a sand castle if they were given the instructions.'

Mh'tonnay wheeled around, grabbing the dwarf by the beard, staring imploringly into his eyes. 'Give!' he croaked. 'I need it.'

'Whoa! Hold on, man. It'll take a while. We've got t' dig it out first.'

'How long?' pleaded the Chief Engineer.

Proph considered for a moment. 'Fifty feet 'f solid granite. Just li'l ol' me. Ahhh. Couple of days.'

'Do it!' snapped Mh'tonnay, shoving the dwarf down the hole, slamming shut the trap door, replacing the stove and staring out at the heaving melee of 'civil' engineers.

'Told you!' telepathed the sea-scrole smugly, several curse-laden hours later. 'Said it wouldn't work. Didn't I?'

'Shut up!' growled Mancini, glaring at the small but perfectly formed toad staring up at him.

'Thought it was supposed to be gold!' grumbled Knapp, sulkily scowling at the glistening amphibian. 'You can't spend that!'

'How am I supposed to concentrate with you rabbiting away inside my head?' snapped Mancini, glaring at the scrole. 'It would have been gold if I'd had peace and quiet,' he whined and scowled at Knapp for good measure.

The toad hopped a few steps forward, snatched a maggot from Knapp's sack and received a swift clip across the head for its trouble. Mancini glared miserably from the tome to the toad, scratching his head as he tried to figure where he had gone wrong. It had all seemed so easy. Just take it in four little stages, altering one piece at a time – LEAD to LOAD to GOAD to GOLD. No problem! It was just that last stage . . . LEAD to LOAD to GOAD to TOAD! Damn!

The whole hideout was littered with his previous mistakes. LEAD to LOAD to LOAF . . . LEAD to LEAF to LEECH . . . that one had really confused him!

'Told you it was a waste of time. Really going to make your fortune turning lead into toads, aren't you?' smarmed the scrole. 'Wealth beyond your wildest dreams. I don't think!'

'Shut up! I've nearly got it.'

The toad croaked and hopped off the table.

'You've been saying that for the last five days,' sniffed Knapp.

'I really don't understand you,' telepathed the scrole. 'I offer you the chance to . . .'

'Rubbish!' shouted Mancini, leaping up from the table and

staring into the bath. 'You spout a few lines of nonsense and expect me to know what it means. I understand this stuff. I can't do it, but I know what I'm doing wrong. The garbage you've had in your head for the last million years or so . . .'

Knapp stared open-mouthed as Mancini ranted at the creature. It almost sounded as if he was having an argument.

'Eighty-five thousand centuries . . .' interrupted the scrole pedantically.

'. . . whatever. It's incomprehensible. I don't know where to begin!' finished Mancini, grabbing the toad and putting in a bucket with thirty-five others. Knapp shook his head. Been working too hard, he thought.

'Aha!' thought the scrole triumphantly.

'What's that supposed to mean?'

'I might know where to begin!' came the offhand reply.

'You said you didn't have a clue before,' protested Mancini, rapidly losing patience with the rectangular creature in the bath. 'You trying to tell me that after eighty-five thousand centuries without a clue you've suddenly worked it out in the last five days? How convenient!'

'Things weren't delivered in layers of newsparchment in my day,' thought the scrole, waving a nonchalant corner towards a heap of discarded wrappings.

'What?'

'Just look over there, will you, and tell me what you see!'

'A heap of parchment!'

'Cha! Look closer!'

'Give me a clue!'

'Do I have to do everything?' protested the scrole, flopping out of the bath and slooping towards the heap. Knapp's eyes bulged. Something weird was going on here. It was as if the creature understood.

'Here!' thought the scrole a few seconds later, grabbing a sheet in its teeth and waving it petulantly.

Knapp began to consider giggling hysterically as Mancini took the parchment, shook off the drips offered by the scrole and read it. 'So what? Some Mad Murrhovian Empress hosts a Tyrants' Charity Ball?'

'Look at the illustration. What's lurking around her feet, eh?'

'Vicious-looking black and white things. So what?'

'How did you ever get to become an alchemist? They're damnations!' The scrole stared at Mancini's blank expression. 'Lordy!' If it had a palm and a forehead it would have been slapping it furiously. 'The rhyme . . . onto ye boddey of ye damned-naytion . . . remember? Do I have to spell it out?'

Mancini stared at the parchment then at the scrole then at the heap of lead piping outside. Miserably he shook his head, shrugged his shoulders and said, 'Yes, please.'

'Ye damned-naytion. Damnation. Same thing! See? Eighty-five thousand centuries does things to language.'

'Are you trying to tell me that I need one of those to release untold power and be the key to the rise and fall of kingdoms, like it says in the rhyme . . .'

'Yup!'

'Don't even think about it!' growled Mancini, screwing the parchment up, hurling it across the hut and grabbing a length of tubing. Knapp was on the tumbling parchment in a second, staring dumbfounded at the illustration. Questions and dreads flooded wildly into his mind, whirling and screaming as he began to draw conclusions that he really didn't like the look of. Frantically he tried to rub them out. He failed.

'I may be thick but I'm not totally stupid!' ranted Mancini at the scrole. 'An Empress' pets cannot be that important. She'd be in charge of everything if that was the case!'

'If she knew . . .' thought the scrole.

'Pah! You're making it up!' snarled Mancini, opening the tome again and laying the tubing in the pentagram.

Knapp whimpered and hoped fervently that his future wasn't going to involve one of those things in the picture.

'Have you found anything yet?' snapped the fuming stocky figure of Practz as he burst into a small cubic cavern in the lower intestines of Losa Llamas.

Phlim looked up from the racing images of trees and foliage in the viewing crystal. 'If I knew what exactly I'm supposed to be looking for, I might be able to answer.' He frowned as he brushed the stray strand of brown hair out of his eyes. 'I can't see how a library tome can end up out here.'

'Have you searched where I said?'

'Just about quartered the whole blinkin' forest and there's nothing out of the ordinary.' Phlim waved his hands over the crystal controlling the flight path of the Sneeke – the tiny insect-like creature with fish-eye lenses, specially created for covert missions of this very nature. Waving his hands pentagrammatically above the runic dials, he instructed it to swoop low over the last few trees of the forest's northern aspect, angling swiftly and stall-turning around the last tree in a flash. There was a brief image of acres of featureless tundra stretching away to the Talpa Mountains and then sky as the Sneeke performed a neat wing-over turn. Practz turned slightly green as he watched the vertigo-inducing image flashing in the sphere.

The Technical Wizard turned and glared at Practz. 'Nothing! Now will you tell me what I've wasted my time . . .'

'There! There! Go back. Under that tree!' Practz was hopping up and down, pointing. Phlim cast a series of course-correcting spells and stared at the swirling crystal ball images.

'Take it lower, lower. *Please*! There! See it?' snapped Practz fanatically.

'What? Those branches scattered under the tree?' asked Phlim doubtfully.

'Yes. That's it!' nodded Practz, relieved to be below the tops of the trees.

'You mean I've wasted all this time and effort to find the results of someone's illegal pruning?'

Suddenly Practz slammed his fist into his palm. 'We're too late! Missed him!'

'Don't worry, he's bound to strike again,' said Phlim, his voice dripping with sarcasm. 'With a whole forest of helpless trees to choose from, the Phantom Pruner's certain to slash a few shrubs, hack a copse about a bit, engage in a bit of grievous boughly harm. Worse than a cereal killer, that is.'

'What are you on about?' flustered Practz as the Sneeke's eye-view hovered above the site of the herbicide.

'The Phantom Pruner. Isn't that who I've been looking for?'

'Cheiro Mancini!' snapped Practz.

'He's the Phantom Pruner?'

'What Phantom Pruner?' Practz shook a suddenly bewildered head. 'No! He's got the tome. And we've missed him.'

'What does it matter? As far as I can remember there's only a couple of minor matter rearrangement spells in that tome anyhow. If you're worried I'm sure I can recall how to change lead into gold . . .'

'It's not that!' Practz said. 'He's got Thurgia's scroll!'

'Oh, come on! He was searched when he left!'

'I don't know how he's got it but he has and . . . Look! That proves it!' Practz pointed wildly at the crystal sphere as a hastily hidden cart swam nauseously into view.

'Damn him! He had it planned! He's changed carts. Widen the sweep! We've got to find him before it's too late!'

'Too late for what?'

'I don't know,' confessed Practz. 'That's what's worrying me.'

Mancini's brow dripped with the sweat of intense concentration. Eyes closed, his thoughts focused like lasers on the heap of gradually metamorphosing lead piping before him. Mental fingers tweaked and massaged, warping and bending the plasticine of reality. His head quivered with the strain of the final surge of willpower and his chanting ended. He opened his eyes.

Five loaves and two toads blinked back at him.

He swore profusely and flung the stolen book across the room. It was hopeless. At this rate, his fortune would have to rely on an upswing in the toad sandwich market. Knapp looked up from the heap of bread and amphibians and swallowed nervously.

'Alright, you win!' moaned Mancini at the sea-scrole. 'We'll try it your way. But if they're not what you say they are, you'll be a handbag before you know what's hit you. Understand?'

'Perfectly,' thought the scrole.

'Good. So which way's the Murrhovian Empire?' said Mancini, putting on a brave voice. Knapp whimpered and jammed the tome into his sack.

The scrole flopped in the bath, dredged the back of its mind and began to telepath at Mancini. Brown lines swirled concentrically in the Alchemist's head, tracks crossed them, green patches superimposed across blue snakes and letters sprung themselves randomly across the whole mess.

Mancini stared at the perfect mental map, tutted and set off to pack the horse and fill his saddle bath for the scrole.

Knapp fished about in his sack, unravelled a piece of parchment and stared at the image of piebald malevolence around the Empress Tau's toes. In a spot-on expression of confidence-building speechifying, he grunted 'Uh-oh.'

'It's alive!'

At the far western end of the Murrhovian Empire, a fast moving Fraree Sports cart screeched to a dusty halt behind a small copse of spiky trees and two figures leapt out. In a flash they'd snatched a collection of sheets from a trunk and had wrapped them around their heads, securing them firmly with leather belts. The taller of the two picked up a hip flask, unscrewed the lid and appeared to have a brief conversation with the contents before hiding it in the folds of his flowing sheet and striding off towards the gleaming gates of the city ahead of them.

'Slow down!' shouted the smaller one after half an hour's sprinting across the sandhills. 'Where are we going?' pleaded Knapp.

'There!' declared Cheiro Mancini significantly, pointing at the square tower set into the seemingly endless wall stretching to the far horizons. 'The Murrhovian Empire.'

'Why couldn't we have ridden there?'

'Because if anyone asks, we are D'vanouin Tribesmen, and D'vanouin Tribesmen are not famed for owning brand-new Fraree Sports carts, alright?'

'S'pose so,' grumbled Knapp. 'But you could've parked a bit closer!'

'Shut up,' snapped Mancini, and strode on towards the gleaming gates.

It wasn't long before he realised they weren't the only ones heading that way. From miles around, all sorts of other people hiked excitedly into the capitol, crowding into the streets around the Imperial Palace, hauling rickety handcarts laden with offerings of all kinds – gifts and sacrifices to the fish-headed chicken god of the inflamed tongues, Sahmbal Uhlek.

It was a fundamental belief of the Murrhovian people that

the poisons of lies and falsehoods told throughout one's life remained within the mouth of the fabricator, causing ulcers, plaque and halitosis. Only by drinking of the cleansing unction of Sahmbal Uklek could these stains be removed.

And so every Sahmbal Uhlek's Day, once every nine years, the gates to the Murrhovian Empire were flung altruistically wide, allowing all comers access to the holy cleansing unction. Had Mancini and Knapp attempted to gain entry on any other day they would have been strip-searched at katana-point by any number of the twenty-stone guards lining the entrance gate, had anything of even remote worth removed and been slung into the Murrhovian Jails until the next Sahmbal Uhlek's Day when they would have been allowed to declare why they had wished access in the first place.

It was only when the last of the guards had remained unmoved and uninterested in Mancini and Knapp's entry that the sea-scrole bubbled an acute sigh of relief in the halfpint of brine in the hip flask. Relief that it had managed to calculate the date correctly and relief that Mancini hadn't the foggiest how dangerous just strolling up to the gate would normally be.

Within the city, street-hawkers were everywhere, selling traditional Sahmbal Uhlek's Day fayre: cubes of unidentifi-able meat on skewers covered in chilli sauce, wafer-thin barbecued cuttlefish and bowls of noodle-like eels swimming in jalapeno purée, watery soups seeming to consist entirely of sulphuric acid with a hint of lemon . . . The list was endless –countless ways for devotees to purify their blasphemous mouths in the caustic flames of Sahmbal Uhlek, myriad methods to purge their perjuries and thus achieve true enlightenment. Either that, or they could just stuff them-selves silly with gallons of beer and spicy food.

Mancini mingled warily through the heaving streets, carefully avoiding the plumes of super-heated chillied steam billowing from roadside stalls. Knapp stared about in utter bafflement, amazed by the noise and the smells. People pressed in on all sides, jostling as they scurried from stall to stall, yelling and overdosing on spiced pods, but always heading in the same direction. A torrent of bodies surged from all points of the compass towards a single vast focus, the centre of the Sahmbal Uhlek's Day celebrations. The public choosing of the sacrifice.

Suddenly the air exploded with a hail of shrieks, fire-crackers and whirling katanas. The crowd surged back as eight sword-swirling Imperial Court Bruisers, clad in green and red bamboo armour, made their way past at the head of the Imperial Sacrificial Entourage, goosestepping towards the centre of the Square of the Hundred-Year-Old Eggs. Columns of Palace staff surged into the square, yelling catechisms of holy denial. A vast phalanx of decorated white rhinos lumbered behind, their horns gleaming with ceremonial murderousness. And finally, carried atop the shoulders of a platoon of Palace Berserkers, came the Empress herself in a glistening gold sedan chair. As she rounded a corner into full view a tumultuous cheer went up, followed almost immediately by a wave of terror and a sudden frantic widening of the impromptu passageway as the scuffling crowd pressed back as far as they could.

Mancini strained to see what was happening, craning over the sea of heads, adrenaline rising. Suddenly there was a scream and a figure was pulled out of the throng in a rainbow spray of tom-yum soup and noodles, disappearing instantly beneath a wave of piebald horror. The Imperial Sacrificial Party swept on past as if this was a common occurrence, ignoring the screams from the latest snack in the damnations' seemingly endless buffet.

The advanced guard of the Imperial Court Bruisers halted before a raised dais in the centre of the square, split sideways, formed a corridor and led a single solitary figure up to the bamboo scaffolding at the top, where it joined two other quivering figures.

The crowd exploded into a hail of chanting and screaming, yelling names. Empress Tau leapt from her sedan chair, sprinting up the dais towards the sacrificial pot, her legs buried in a seething mass of red-eyed damnations. Reaching the top she snatched the katana from her shoulder scabbard and demanded silence. She got it.

'Minions of Eternal Vassalage!' she screamed across the ocean of faces. 'The time has come to choose the one!' She waved her gleaming blade at the three terrified figures. 'Who shall it be?'

The crowd yelled back two names at equal ear-splitting volume, each voice eager to sentence their most hated liar of the year. Would it be Mhellah, the ex-Minister for Judicious Accounting, who had not only tried to screw the Empire of Murrha but also the entire women's under-sixteen katana club? Or would it be Makswell, the newsparchment baron whose rag had published a series of defamatory articles proclaiming Empress Tau to be a man? The people would decide, as they always did. Chants for Mhellah clashed against counter-chants for Makswell in swirling bubbles of rising hubbub; curling torrents of contradiction blasted surging neap tides of denial . . .

'Wrong!' yelled the Empress, thigh-deep in growling damnations. 'If anyone in the entirety of the Murrhovian Empire needs to bathe in the cleansing fires of Sahmbal Uhlek and rid himself of the stains of perjurous fabrication then it is *this* worthless creature!' She grabbed Dewlap by the neck and held his struggling body at arm's length over the seething crowd. 'What say you, good minions?' she cried.

'Guilty! Guilty! Guilty!' they shrieked. They had all heard of his wild, lying claims that he owned the infamous Gu-Chi beret. How could any convicted criminal own something so tasteful? It had to be a lie. 'Guilty, Guilty!' Mhellah, overcome with relief, collapsed. Dewlap attempted to scream but Tau's iron grip tightened further around his throat, cutting off his oxygen supply. In a flash she dashed up the scaffolding, dragging the limp figure of Dewlap with her. The crowd erupted with excitement as she balanced atop the structure and held the sacrificial man over the pot.

'My only regret at this time,' she yelled, her biceps bulging beneath her bamboo armour, 'is that I shall have to find a replacement . . . tedious interviews! Goodbye, Dewlap!'

She loosened her grip and the five-hundred-and-thirty-third Court Livestock Image Consultant thrashed momentarily, then plummeted into the cleansing lotion of Sahmbal Uhlek. There was a shriek, a gurgle and after three bubbles Dewlap sank below the red surface of the holy chilli sauce, never to be seen again.

'Hopeful applicants to the Palace at nine tomorrow,' yelled the Empress, wiping her hands and heading back to the sedan chair, surrounded by the seething piebald carpet of damnations.

And as the crowd surged back to the street-hawkers' stalls and the Imperial Sacrificial Entourage left the Square of Hundred-Year-Old Eggs, an idea began to hatch in Mancini's head.

'. . . and this?' asked Empress Tau the next day at just after nine in the morning, hauling a suit of pink raffia body armour out of her wardrobe.

'Certainly, my lady,' fawned Mancini. 'And perhaps for more informal occasions, may I suggest a herd of a coordinated buffalo . . . or perhaps a flock of purple formation humming birds to encircle the Imperial brow.' He clicked his fingers and Knapp produced the latest edition of Annz Hashe's PET catalogue. Mancini waved it under her Imperial nose.

'What would you suggest for this?' she said, raising an inquisitorial starched eyebrow as she withdrew a full-length camouflage exposure suit accessorised with bronze arrow-tip earrings, spearhead lapel brooch and a necklace alternating pure river pearls with miniature jade katanas.

'Oh, Your Supreme Highness, an outfit of such deliciously decorative functionality requires careful selection of matching livestock . . .' oozed Mancini, sensing the interview was going well.

'Can you do it?'

'Certainly. In fact there are two ways one can go. For outdoor, overtly tyrannical functions a rare variegated Ammorettan Death Lizard with gold spines and jade collar would enhance the feel of understated belligerence perfectly . . .'

'The other . . . ?' growled Tau, holding the exposure suit up before her and swaying her hips.

'A string of black Talpine Rock-mice . . .'

'Mice!' shrieked Tau, horrified. 'Mice are for wimps!'

'Generally, that is correct,' answered Mancini, apparently calm, although his stomach seethed. 'However,' he continued, 'beneath the Talpine Rock-mouse's sweet rodent exterior lurks a feral temper with teeth and claws to match.'

Empress Tau's eyes lit up.

'I suggest a string of murine companions when a targeted seduction is called for. By juxtaposing the rodent's vulnerable, pettable exterior and attendant hidden dangers against your harshly aggressive exterior, attention can be drawn to your own Imperial interiors. With a subtle flash of one's regal eyelids even the least hot-blooded of males will simply swoon, gibbering at your feet.'

Tau shrieked with delight.

'Bring the Ammorettan Death Lizard for a trial this afternoon . . . and the job's yours!'

'Your generosity is overwhelming, my lady,' grovelled Mancini. This afternoon! he panicked inside. Why couldn't she just give him the job? He was the only candidate, after all. Surprisingly, nobody else in the entire Empire had turned up. It could be that no-one was insane enough to risk inflaming the Empress' hair-trigger temper. They all knew how picky she could be about her appearance. Or perhaps it had something to do with the fact that Mancini had paid them all off.

The Empress swished and grinned behind the camouflage suit, imagining herself with a fully accessorised death lizard on her arm.

'Until this afternoon, then,' whispered Mancini, bowing low and kicking Knapp to exit in the traditional Murrhovian reverse crawl, their noses a fraction of an inch above the marble floor. Mancini's mind whirred apprehension as he thought of the work he'd need to do. A variegated

Ammorettan Death Lizard . . . in four hours! From memory!

Was it gold spines or gold claws? he squealed to himself as they stood, dashed out of the palace, fled the city and sprinted back to the copse of spiky trees hiding his getaway cart.

Deep in the dark recesses of Losa Llamas, the Technical Wizard, Phlim brushed a stray strand of hair out of his eyes, leaned back from the spherical sneeke monitor and massaged his neck. Bright images of tundra flashed and rocketed by as the tiny insect-like creature buzzed in ever-widening circles.

Phlim yawned expansively and rubbed his red-rimmed eyes. Staring at the monitor all day always made him tired. Right now he was close to comatose. One and a half weeks he'd been down here on Practz's orders, searching, scouring, combing for any sign of Mancini. It looked hopeless.

Countless miles away the sneeke swooped across a track. Phlim stared half-heartedly at the monitor, daydreaming absently of a scantily clad maiden lying upon a sunbleached beach wearing nothing but a becoming smile and a tastefully arranged pattern of cart tracks – just like the one on the glossy parchment of the Peerhelly calendar over there on the cavern wall. Phlim hadn't a clue which whizz-kid of an advertising executive had hit upon the idea of graphically illustrating the road-holding ability of ultra-low profile steel cart tyres by rolling them across the bodies of naked virgins, but he was so glad they had. It didn't half brighten up the cavern. Especially February. The sight of those tanned thighs gleaming with the tracks of Soopah-Slyxx Profile Radials . . . once seen never forgotten.

With a sudden shock he leapt out of his chair and began waving his arms frantically over the control pentagram. Instantly the image angled round as the sneeke wing-overed a full three-sixty and dashed back to the track.

Then he saw it. Stretching away as far as the sneeke's eye could see – the parallel lines of a pair of Peerhelly low-profile racing cart tracks. Exactly the same as those decorating the maiden on February's Soopah-Slyxx Profile Radial beach; precisely the same as those he had found ten days ago leading away from the northern edge of Losa Llamas Forest.

Commanding the sneeke to follow them, he dashed out of the room to inform Practz of his discovery, secretly praising the amazing power of advertising.

'Hold them steady!' snapped Mancini, as Knapp jiggled a pair of psychoterrin crystals boredly. 'And stop sighing. Anyone would think you were bored.'

'I am,' muttered Knapp. 'You've been at this for hours. "Hold this!" "Don't move that!" "Fetch me a psychic screwdriver!" How much longer are you going to be?'

'As long as it takes,' growled Mancini, scowling at the untidy mass of wires, crystals and PCB's*. 'It's got to be perfect. One slip and you'll be wearing your head in your sack!'

Knapp gulped. 'Does that include being late?' he asked.

Mancini squinted at the sun and squealed. It was far too close to the horizon. A mental image of Empress Tau sharpening her katana and glaring irritatedly at her sundial welled up in his mind.

Hurriedly, Mancini jammed a few wires into the tangled mess, detuned one of the hypertaurus generators by one quarter turn and connected half a pound of potatoes in parallel. With a reassuring splutter a chrominence valve glow-wormed into life. Urgently scowling at the racing sun and cursing volubly, he shut his eyes, launched into a low mantra and conjured an image of an Ammorettan Death Lizard into his head, projecting it at the empathy amplifier.

Knapp squealed and leapt behind the Fraree as six foot of spitting saurian exploded from the empathy generator and stood growling angrily, glaring around malevolently. All trace of the empathy generator had vanished – it now hovered inside the lizard, somewhere near where its spleen should be.

* A Pentagram Chalk Board.

141

'Near enough,' grumbled Mancini as he scowled at the creation.

'What happened to perfection?' whimpered Knapp, relishing the idea of strolling into slicing range of Tau's katana with a second-rate pseudo-lizard not a jot.

'Ran out of time,' growled Mancini. 'Let's go.' In a flash the death lizard bounded off across the desert towards the capitol, slavering hungrily.

It was only by mentally shortening its legs enough to slow it down that Mancini eventually caught up with it. Half an hour later, having made a harness, increased the lizard's length to ten feet, added hundreds of spikes, several dozen assorted talons and blood-stained saliva between its teeth, Mancini could see why Ammorettan Death Lizards were so popular with maniacal tyrants. Never in his life had he received so many looks of terrified respect or walked so freely within an eighteen-foot area of free space. Quite remarkable the effect which a pet reptile capable of removing major limbs and spitting acid over fifty ells had on the way people approached one. Very satisfying.

Cheiro Mancini grinned to himself as fourteen Imperial Court Bruisers leapt over fences and hid behind hastily upturned carts. He and Knapp strolled unchallenged through the gate and on towards the Palace. And to think that two short hours ago he wasn't entirely sure if he could remember all the repellent reptilian details. Okay, so maybe he'd overdone the black teeth a bit, and the eighteen inch keratin lances on its tail were his own invention, but that was just VET's licence. So was the reverse polarised empathy field which gave the death lizard such a strongly exuded air of barely contained splenetic fury, wound and ready to explode with the least provocation. The Empress would surely love it.

She did. Her eyes fizzed with childish glee as she shrieked delight when Mancini burst into her quarters scarcely controlling the straining creature on the shoulder harness. It bounded eagerly over the chaise longue, cleared a banqueting table and flattened the Empress beneath a thousand pounds of enthusiastic reptilian affection*. She screamed joyously as the three-foot-long tongue lapped wildly at her face, whilst the death lizard's front claws pinned her shoulders to the floor. Anyone else would have died there and then, but Tau grabbed the creature's horns and shook its scaly head, wrestling it into willing submission, scratching and tickling its hard yellow belly with a quiverful of arrows. Mancini wasn't sure which of the terrifying twosome screamed louder in the playful rough and tumble.

Suddenly a door at the rear of the Empress' quarters burst open and a yapping sea of black and white creatures swarmed in, salivating as they surged forward to save Tau, their goat's milk-supplying mistress, from the grip of the death lizard. Mancini followed Knapp as he dived reflexively under the chaise longue at the sight of one hundred and one pairs of wild red eyes and countless flashing blurs of teeth and claws. The Ammorettan Death Lizard squirmed and roared cheerfully as Tau scratched at its belly, only opening its eyes and staring around as the Empress was snatched away to safety by three hulking damnations.

In a second there was a crash as another door was bowled open by the rushing creatures, a shriek and a series of splashes. The lizard arched its armoured back, rolled itself over and scuttled into the Imperial Bath Room. Wth a surge of alarm Mancini dashed out from beneath the chaise longue and snatched at the shoulder harness of the virtual reptile, grabbing at the hand grips and hanging on. One thing he hadn't sorted yet was the business of making PETs water-tight, let alone milktight. There was no telling what would happen if the ten-foot projected death lizard's power pack was to be suddenly plunged into countless gallons of tepid goat's milk. He was certain it wouldn't do the wallowing Empress much good, though.

The lizard surged on towards the damnation-filled pool, claws skittering on marble as it sprinted eagerly forward.

---

* It was amazing the mass that could be simulated using two giant psychoterrin crystals half-inched from Losa Llamas, detuned and cross-phased against a pulsed hypertaurus accelerator.

143

Mancini cursed himself – why had he not built in a pathological terror of all things liquid? He clawed wildly at the floor, attempting to grab something, anything . . . anything nailed down, counting his last seconds in the frantic scrabbling of fingernails on marble . . .

Abruptly, with a single yell, it was all over.

Mancini stared in disbelief at the Empress, standing dripping in the pool, her arm outstretched, pointing commandingly at the lizard.

'Sit!' she demanded, the emphasised final consonant resonating around the room. Mancini rolled out of the way in the nick of time, avoiding the reptile's backside by scant inches.

In the pool the damnations lapped noisily at the milk, purring contentedly, ignoring the scowling lizard on the side.

Mancini was stunned. In a matter of seconds the hundred and one damnations – the frenzied creatures he had witnessed devour a member of the public at yesterday's event; the wild monsters that had jealously torn Tau from the grips of the death lizard – these same creatures were contentedly gurgling and splashing in the pool. Mancini felt certain that if he threw a ball of wool into the melee it would be as cheerfully chased and playfully swatted at as if they were week-old kittens.

He edged forward for a closer look. A wave of heads snapped around, glaring red eyes and curling black lips to reveal masses of lethal dentition.

Maybe not, he thought, trembling. He would have to work something out if he was to carry out his act of damnation-napping.

Watch and learn, he told himself, edging away from the pool. Watch and learn.

Phlim waved his hands nonchalantly over the sneeke control pentagram and muttered complex catechisms with the consummate ease of an expert. Idly, he sipped at a beaker of ale as he chased the low-profile Peerhelly cart tracks across miles of deserted mountains and tundra.

Then, abruptly, they weren't there. Phlim choked, shook his head and squinted at the sphere again. No doubt about it, the tracks were gone. Stifling a string of expletives, he flashed the sneeke around, panic rising above the questions and sudden doubts. The image dropped lower over the rough road, zooming in over the irregular terrain, flashing past a copse of spiky bushes.

Suddenly, the tracks were back. Phlim expertly spun the sneeke around, homing in as they veered sharply off the main drag. In a second the image stopped at a pile of twigs and branches barely concealing the red getaway cart and a pair of extremely irritated-looking horses-in-harness.

The trail stopped. Lost him.

Unless he could remember what sort of shoes Mancini had been wearing.

'What are you playing at?' growled the sea-scrole in Mancini's head as the VET fiddled with an empathy projector in his new Court Livestock Image Consultant's quarters. 'You're wasting time! You've been at that for hours.'

'Oh, not you as well. Give me some peace. I'm concentrating!' It was four in the morning and the lack of sleep was really beginning to show. On the far side of the quarters, Knapp snored.

'All you've got to do is steal one! In, snatch, out. Easy!' telepathed the sea-scrole.

'Yeah? And then what?' growled Mancini, his teeth clenched around a psychic screwdriver, both hands clutching a pair of psychoterrin crystals.

'Release of Untold Power . . .'

'Wrong. Release of Untold Bouncers . . . after me with a million swords, with my name on!'

'Don't exaggerate! They won't miss one damnation. There's so many of them,' chivvied the scrole, flopping about in its bath.

'I'm not exaggerating! Have you seen the way Tau dotes on those things? She'd miss one in a second!'

'You're scared,' challenged the sea-scrole, pointing an accusing corner at the weary VET.

'How many claws have they got?'

'Er, eight on each paw, I think, but what's that got to do with it? Don't change the subject. If you're not scared why haven't you grabbed it yet, eh?' prattled the scrole.

'You can't just stroll in and walk out with one under your arm.'

'Course you can. That's why you got the job as Livestock Image Consultant, isn't it? So you could have easy access?'

'Yes, but I'm not ready!'

'Scared!'

'I'm not scared,' Mancini growled, concentrating hard on the cross-head screw of the pulsing chrominence filter pre-amplifier, squinting as he adjusted for eight claws. 'I'm terrified. Look!' He hoicked up his cloak to reveal a pair of rapidly trembling osseous kneecaps. 'Have you seen the teeth on those things? Have you?'

'Haven't you got a pair of gauntlets?'

'Is that supposed to be even remotely helpful? They'd be through chainmail in . . . ah!' There was a spark of cerulean flux, a crackle of high potential enchantment and a creature flashed into existence on the table before him, masking the empathy projector. The scrole shrieked mental distress. The creature stood stockily on all fours, glaring around the room through piercing crimson eyes, snarling and oozing piebald menace from every paw. Mancini's knees rang military tattoos beneath his cloak.

'Wow!' thought the terrified scrole. 'Good likeness. What's it for?'

'You'll see,' grunted Mancini, rubbing his hands together warily as he surveyed his latest creation from all sides, sensing victory lurch an unsteady step closer. With a virtual damnation on his side, how could he fail?

Suddenly there was a squeal from behind him followed by a frantic scuffling as Knapp awoke, saw the damnation and attempted, unsuccessfully, to excavate a hiding-hole in the mattress.

Mancini clicked his fingers with a swift flourish of practised prestidigitation, collapsed the empathic field, shoved the projector into his pack and unearthed his assistant from beneath a quaking pile of pillows.

'C'mon,' he snapped, sounding almost infinitely more confident than he felt.

Knapp rubbed his eyes and stared at where the damnation had been as Mancini snatched a bottle of green liquid from his tool kit and hurled it across the room. Reflexively Knapp plucked it out of the air and jammed it into his sack.

Thrusting the protesting sea-scrole into his brine-filled hip flask and grabbing Knapp by the collar, Mancini dashed out of his palace quarters, pausing only long enough to grab a large portable show-case in the other hand and check the darkened corridor for night-guards.

'What are you playing at?' squealed Knapp, and was promptly ignored by the VET.

Sprinting as fast and silently as he could and dragging Knapp when he needed to, Mancini sped through the heart of the Palace, peering cautiously around corners before he moved on, listening at doors and floors to check for approaching security.

Within minutes he screeched to a halt outside a pair of large bamboo doors.

'About time too! What the flip . . . ?' began Knapp indignantly.

Mancini whirled around and slammed Knapp's mouth shut with the palm of his hand, pointing urgently with his other at the sign over the door. Knapp squinted at the string of incomprehensible characters and shrugged his shoulders. Briefly Mancini considered attempting to mime the words 'Imperial Bath Room. Enter on pain of disembowellment' but thought against it. Instead he pressed his hand harder against Knapp's mouth and squirmed quietly through the door, every muscle straining, striving for stealthy silence. Desperately he tried not to choke in the thick, humid atmosphere of souring goat's milk as he grabbed the small green bottle out of Knapp's sack. Knapp took a sharp breath, gagged and turned a pale shade of cream cheese. Mancini edged up to the deserted pool, his breath echoing far too loud for comfort, his heart racing as he upended the bottle of green liquid in the shallow end. Then he cracked open the far door, wafted it three times, crept behind the curtains and waited.

'Tell me what you're up to!' whispered Knapp desperately.

'Wait and see!' whispered Mancini, his voice muffled behind the drapes.

They didn't have to wait long. The warm musty smell of goat's milk floated through the door, round several corners and drifted into the gently twitching nostrils of one hundred and one sleeping damnations. In a flash a host of olfactory systems kicked into action, smacked their associated motor systems into life and leapt out for breakfast. Fortunately for Mancini, none of the damnation's timing centres was disturbed, otherwise they might have noticed that it was still before five in the morning – far too early for brekkies.

They scurried and surged through the corridors, skittering around polished corners, up the aromatic gradient, scampering faster as they approached the bathroom. Mancini held his breath as they exploded through the door and leapt eagerly into the pool. In a matter of moments he would find out if he had guessed right about damnation metabolism, dosage and dilution factors.

An army of tongues lapped at the drugged goat's milk, devouring, relishing the taste, oblivious of the artificial additives. In a few greedy seconds each of the damnations had gulped at least twice the critical dose needed and in the following minutes they would regret it.

Up to its belly in the shallow end, one of the smaller piebald creatures snarled and shook its head in confusion, baffled by the sudden doubling in number of its major limbs. Bewildered, it raised its left front paw and stared at them both. A matching pair; eight razor-sharp retractable claws, four non-stick high-impact resistant hard pads, all-temperature monochrome body fur, perfect. It flexed a single slashing index claw and blinked as two gleaming blades wiggled before its eyes . . . There was something wrong here, something that desperately needed investigating . . . A wave of weariness washed over the damnation's consciousness, sending crashing exhaustion in ripples up its sentient sands. . . . Something that needed investig . . . investig . . . ah, later. Right now it was time for . . . zzzzzzzz.

Mancini thrilled as all over the pool razor-clawed damnations curled up and went to sleep, doped to the back teeth with the sleep-inducing drug, dozamine. He dashed out from behind the curtain, prodded a damnation carefully with his toe, then snatched the snoring creature into the show-cage and locked the door. Swiftly he grabbed his latest tuned empathy projector out of his sack, lay it on the side of the pool and performed a couple of quick hand movements over it. As if by magic a damnation appeared, perfect in every detail, undetectable from the real thing.

Grinning smugly to himself, Mancini dashed stealthily out of the Imperial Bath Room, away down the corridor and out of the Palace, clutching a sleeping damnation.

He was followed by a bewildered, and not entirely relaxed, Knapp.

'You're not bringing that through here!' bellowed the head cement mixer, pointing at Magnus the Carter's laden wagon train.

'Says who?' came the growled reply, rumbling menacingly through the Foh Pass.

'Me and that signpost over there. See? Carriageway closed.'

Magnus scowled at the army of red and white cones protecting the sea of glisteningly delicate virginal roadway. 'And what am I supposed to tell my customers when they've got nothing to sell, eh?'

There was a weary hail of agreement from the other dozen or so hauliers enmeshed in the contraflow system. Arguments had been raging all night, wearing tempers thinner than the meanest after-dinner mints.

Rosch Mh'tonnay squinted out of the window of his porta-hovel and cursed. Grike, the site foreman, was running his way, gesturing frantically. Mh'tonnay shoved desperately at the desk, jamming it against the door and stacking a couple of chairs on top. He had far more important things to deal with than another dispute. In a flash he had snatched the planks from behind the stove, moved the burner and was hammering on the trap door. There was a grunt from below, a struggling, squirming sound and a bearded face appeared just as the porta-hovel door was hit by a whirlwinding Grike. The handle waggled in frantic impotence, accompanied by a tirade of muffled pleadings.

'How long?' demanded Mh'tonnay, his face pressed close to the panting dwarf.

'Ain't you goin' t' answer that?' asked Proph as the door rattled wildly against the desk.

'How long till you reach it?'

'Really should answer . . .' began the dwarf, stopping as he caught Mh'tonnay's wild expression. 'Thaumometer's off th' scale. Couple 'hours an' I'll be right on the thaumafer. If that's what it is.'

The door rattled again.

'What do you mean?' snapped Mh'tonnay.

'Feels weird. Too isolated . . .'

'But it is geomantic, isn't it?'

'Sure as hell . . .'

'Then get it. This job's getting out of hand. I need it!' He shoved the dwarf back down the hole, cursed and sat with his head in his hands. Why couldn't people be more like rocks? he screamed silently – solid, dependable, silent . . . He understood rocks. And with enough explosives they'd do exactly what he wanted them to. An idea sprang into his head. In a flash he stood and sprinted into the back of the porta-hovel, snatching open a locked cupboard and dragging a large case out. Grike pounded harder on the door, panic rising as six dwarf drainage engineers snatched clubs from a pile and surged down to reinforce the angry mob of thirty cement mixers. It was only a matter of time before there were tears. And it was still a long way before bedtime.

A deliberately provocative cone setter, armed with a handful of red and white markers, marched towards the fuming bulk of Magnus the Carter. It was then, with a fanfare of scathing vitriol and cracking whips, that the final strands of Magnus' temper snapped. His lungs fired on all cylinders, freely screaming as three cones were placed before him – a red and white rag to a bullish haulier. Cracking his whip theatrically above the six harnessed animals of his forty-ton wagon train, he advanced. The row of angry-looking cement mixers closed ranks, brandishing shovels. Behind them the sea of freshly laid roadway glistened.

'I don't care if it takes a day to set! You shouldn't have resurfaced both carriageways!' shrieked Magnus. 'I've got deliveries to make.' He cracked his whip again. 'Ho, Donner! Ho, Blitzen!' The wagon train shuddered further forwards.

'Like I said before, you're not bringing that through here!' yelled the chief cement mixer, slapping his shovel threateningly against his open palm. Fifteen mini clubmen stepped forward.

'Says who?' shouted Magnus, advancing his six rhinoceroses steadily. 'Try to stop me!'

Blitzen snorted pachyderm irritation as she crushed three cones underfoot and stepped onto the new roadway. Her vast foot sank several inches into the glistening surface, to the accompaniment of a shriek of wild anger from cement mixers and a roar of encouragement from the massed hauliers.

In a few minutes seven carts began to move and several dozen brawls erupted in what was in danger of turning out to be the largest mud wrestling bout in the history of the Trans-Talpino Trade Route Widening Scheme.

'Okay. That's enough of that!' yelled a man standing on a reinforced trunk, waving a box of matches and a handful of long grey cylinders, each with a bit of string at one end. Stillness fell in seconds, all eyes turning to the madman on the explosives chest.

151

'That's better,' said Mh'tonnay smugly, gathering the hauliers and foremen together and launching into the first ever example of arbitration under threat of explosion.

'But why me?' Thurgia had pleaded.

Practz had turned and stared at the Head of Demonic Possession over his glasses. 'Because you were wearing the backpack thaumatron the first time. You were there. Right now that makes you the nearest we've got to an expert, okay?'

Half an hour later, standing in the middle of the shielded test cavern with the thaumic wave guides glowing aquamarine behind his ears and a cloud of fizzing sapphire motes above him, Thurgia didn't feel any more of an expert.

'Nine kilothaums and steady,' shouted Wat, reading the thaumometer from behind the partial safety of the upturned table. 'You need fifteen!'

A steady high-pitched whine issued from a complex array of traces and readouts by Wat's side, each connected to a different part of the bath-mat shaped creature strapped to the hex-ray table.

Nervously Thurgia reached down and turned the knob. Immediately the fizzing increased in intensity, crackling menacingly.

'Are you *sure* this is a good idea?' he whimpered, knees feeling like jelly.

'No,' answered Wat reassuringly. 'But what Practz says goes. Besides, how else are we going to find out for sure what's on those scrolls?'

'Does it matter?'

'Coo, I should say so! Who knows what information the missing one contained? Could be dangerous in the wrong hands . . . and right now it's definitely in the wrong hands! So come on, zap that one and let's see if it gives us a clue.'

Thurgia squinted apprehensively at the small rectangular object sprouting innumerable monitor wires, positioned his dark glasses firmly on his nose and held his breath. Above him a million cerulean hornets hummed and buzzed, fifteen kilothaums of high energy magic ready for use. He raised his hands, focused on the dead sea-scrole, aimed and let rip. Wat vanished behind the table. Silver-blue lightning crackled from Thurgia's fingertips, leaping across the gap, earthing through the ancient creature's heart, surging through its neural network and firing aged axons. It jolted reflexively, lifting off the hex-ray table. The readouts on Wat's monitors twitched violently, crackled white noise, then settled down again to perfect straight lines and a single high-pitched whine.

'It won't work,' protested Thurgia. 'We cannot bring back to life what is long dead.'

'You did it a few days ago.'

'Are you sure? Did you see it?'

'Go again!' shouted Wat. 'Five-second bursts.'

Thurgia flexed his fingers reluctantly and loosed his captive lightning bolts once more, swaying backwards as the energy powered into the scrole. The cavern interior was flooded with crackling blue, fizzing and lancing off myriad surfaces, powering into the creature strapped to the hex-ray table.

As the scrole bucked and squirmed, needles twitched, traces shuddered and returned to the monotone whine of flat lines as Thurgia broke off.

'See. Won't work! That was full whack,' he declared, powering down and turning towards Wat. 'The other one was vapourised. Fooof!' he added, unbuckling the thaumatron with a wave of relief, shrugging it off his shoulders before Wat decided it would be a good idea to have another go.

The technician leapt over the upturned table and approached the lifeless creature. Miserably he prodded a stick into its middle. 'Move. C'mon. Wakey, wakey!' The drone of flat line traces rang stubbornly around the cavern.

'It's won't work. I think you'd better go and tell Practz,' said Thurgia.

'What? Me? Tell Practz his idea's rubbish? Oh no,' whimpered Wat.

'Well, it's not my department,' argued Thurgia, heading for the door.

'But I'm only a tech . . .'

Suddenly the whine vanished, stuttered and reappeared. Wat stared at Thurgia for a second, wheeled around and stared at the prone bath mat on the hex-ray table.

Was it just his over-eager imagination or did the creature's parchment-like skin look a little less moribund? Nervously he prodded it.

The flat lines jerked as the scrole spasmed, crackled as it twitched and settled back into a weak, but regular pulsing.

'We've got psi emissions!' squealed Wat. 'It's alive!'

A couple of hours later, high above the Foh Pass a small red sports cart screeched to a halt outside a crumbling mountain hideout, two figures leapt out, grabbed a fuming and spitting show-cage and vanished inside, leaving the horses steaming in the chilly talpine air.

'Well done, old chap,' telepathed the sea-scrole rolled in his hip flask. 'Totally undetected.'

Cheiro Mancini landed the show-cage on the rickety table and stared at it from the far side of the hut. Knapp scuttled into the other room and slammed the door. Three days on the road with that thing snarling under the tarpaulin behind him was far too long. A pair of malevolent crimson eyes glared back at Mancini from above a viciously curling lip, framing a terrifying array of gleamingly lethal ten-inch fangs.

'Well, now what?' snapped Mancini, shaking as the damnation howled and thrashed helplessly within its cage.

'Oooh, nice bath, I reckon,' thought the scrole cheerfully. 'This water's getting a bit cold now.'

Mancini snatched the hip flask off his belt and splashed the ancient creature angrily onto the dusty floor. In a flash he grabbed it predator-like, staring wildly into what he hoped were its eyes. 'I've had your wild rantings rattling round my head, taken your jibes about turning lead into gold, risked my life invading the Murrhovian Imperial Palace, kidnapped one of the Empress' pets, and all for what? What the hell am I supposed to do with that rabid thing now? Where's all this untold power, huh?'

Mancini glared at the bath mat-shaped creature, barely managing to contain his frustrated anger as it mutely shrugged its top corners.

'You don't know?' he squealed incredulously. 'You *don't know*? I've got a stolen cageful of livid wildlife capable of stripping a cow in three seconds flat. I am not top of its popularity list, the cage is already creaking more than it should and you say you don't know what to do with it!'

'Sort of . . .' thought the scrole defensively.

'What's *that* supposed to mean? You either do or you don't!'

'You've got to focus some sort of power onto it. It's in the rhyme,' whined the scrole telepathically.

'What? Power? Up here? Don't be ridiculous! Where the hell am I supposed to find power on the top of the Talpa Mountains?'

Half a mile away, fifty feet below the bottom of a certain Chief Engineer's porta-hovel a dwarf swung his pick-axe just a little too enthusiastically. In the darkness of the vertical shaft there was a spark of metal on flint, a seismic cracking and a burst of purple geothaumal energy roared out of the axe hole, slamming the dwarf in the chest and blasting him skyward. Clouds of violet swirled angrily as they accelerated, erupting under the hut, hurling it three hundred feet into the air. Hard-helmeted workers scattered in myriad directions, diving under stationary contraflowed carts.

Mancini scrambled out of his hut, jaw dropping as he watched the spinning hovel arc gracefully over the peak of Tor Teehya.

'You were saying. . . ?' telepathed the sea-scrole smugly.

'What d'you mean, you've lost him?' pressed Practz, glaring at a nervously quivering Phlim.

'Er, Mancini's location is unknown, vanished, information as to his current whereabouts is severely compromised . . . need I go on?' answered the Technical Wizard, brushing a strand of hair out of his eyes.

'I don't believe it!' shrieked Practz, slapping his forehead, his voice hollow in the tiny observation room. 'You've got the best tracking and covert surveillance bug that Losa Llaman technology can supply at your disposal. And you lose him? How?'

'I'm certain he knew I was trailing him,' excused Phlim. 'Why else would he abandon his getaway cart, change mode of transport and double back?'

'Nonsense! He popped into town on foot!'

'Ah. Yes. But he *deliberately* headed straight for the densest crowds to shake off the sneeke.' A wheedling note had crept into Phlim's voice.

'Don't make excuses. There's nowhere in the Murrhovian Empire that isn't seething with millions of people.'

'See?' insisted Phlim, pulling another tissue of lies out from his sleeve. 'You and I know that. Stands to reason that's why he went there. The anonymity of a crowded room.'

'Oh, cut the clichés!' growled Practz. 'Admit it! You've lost him. You mucked up! Blew it! Right now the whole surveillance is in tatters! A disaster!'

Phlim nodded miserably and fiddled with the bottom hem of his lab-cloak.

'Zoom the sneeke into Mancini's getaway cart and we'll pick him up when he moves off.'

Phlim swallowed nervously. 'When he moves off,' he echoed.

'That's right. The sneeke doesn't mind waiting.'

'When he moves off,' whimpered Phlim.

'Yes. Is that a problem?'

The Technical Wizard twitched and turned pale. 'Er . . . you know what you were saying about disasters and things in tatters?'

'Mmmmm?' Practz looked over the top of his glasses. Phlim felt as if he was back at school, hiding his blue hands and flatly denying pouring ink down the boy in front's neck. 'Well . . .' He pointed to the spherical crystal sneeke monitor and cringed.

Practz stared at the tiny monochrome image of a small, empty clump of spiky trees, glanced at the inward and outgoing cart tracks, blinked twice, rubbed his eyes and cursed through tightly clenched teeth. 'Find him!' he snarled, 'or I'll . . .'

Phlim never did find out quite what Practz would have done. The door was kicked open and Wat and Thurgia burst in like stretcher bearers, brimming with excitement. 'It's alive!' they cried in unison and held out the ancient sea-scrole still strapped to the glowing hex-ray table.

Practz peered eagerly at the creature; hoping to have some burning questions extinguished, desperate to know what information the other scrole, the missing scrole, held. His brow, lit by the pale bluish light shining below the creature, knitted into knots of confusion. Instead of the expected, tightly packed scripture of primordial characters super-imposed across the ghostly internal skeleton of the scrole, he stared incoherently at an almost geometric pattern of intersecting lines, criss-crossing a spectral image of a ribcage, flattened skull and proto-spine.

'Is it tuned right?' he snapped, indicating the table. Losa Llaman studies had developed hex-ray technology way beyond the simple unveiling of hidden bone structures or unseen soft tissues. Tuned to the correct micro-wavelengths of acetylcholine molecules and other neurotransmitters, hex-rays could pick up the harmonic fluctuations of the cerebellum, revealing the very thought processes in action and graphically charting the fixed neural networks of memory on a head-up display.

'Sure,' answered Wat, 'three-point-five angstroms. What d'you make of it?'

Phlim, relieved at his temporary reprieve from Practz's temper, edged forward and began to wave his hands across the control pentagram. The image fizzed, dissolved, then reappeared four times larger, revealing the lines in sharper detail.

Practz stroked his beard and sucked his teeth in deep thought. Bisecting lines, intersecting networks . . . in the memory of an ancient sea-scrole. It just didn't make sense.

'What's that?' asked Phlim suddenly, his finger flicking

out, highlighting a tiny mark on the image, just above the scrole's coccyx. Four faces bent over, peered hard, then four sets of shoulders shrugged.

Phlim increased the magnification, revealing microscopic spidery letters.

Dissolve. Zoom. Times fifty.

Barely legible words. Concentric brown lines broken by tiny numbers.

Dissolve. Zoom. Times one hundred.

A gasp rippled around the room as the Thaumaturgical Physicists recognised the perfectly annotated contour map of the Talpa Mountains.

After being blown over the snow-covered peak of Tor Teehya, crashing onto a scree-slope and starting a minor avalanche only to end face down, teetering precariously over a precipice, the last thing Rosch Mh'tonnay needed was an over-enthusiastic dwarf bouncing at him.

'Stand still!' screamed the Chief Engineer as the porta-hovel collapsed around his ears and tumbled over the edge, leaving him clinging white-knuckled to what was left of the back wall, balanced across a ridge of rock in perfect equilibrium with the dwarf.

'Shoot! Look at that readin'!' shouted Proph, eagerly holding out the thaumometer which was still miraculously in his hand. 'Ten an' half kilothaums. Hee hee. I'll be . . . !' He took a step forward and spat a gob of brown saliva over the edge.

'Gobackgobackgoback!' shrieked Mh'tonnay, toes dangling above three hundred feet of bracing mountain air.

'Huh! Thought you was interested?' grumbled the dwarf, his beard, eyebrows and hair charred beyond even expert salvation. 'Wouldn't ha' dug that goddamn hole 'f you ain't said so! Thought you wanted to know 'bout geothaumal energy!' He turned and stomped away down the hovel wall, striding over what was left of a set of shelves.

'IdoIdoIdo!' lied Mh'tonnay. The only energy he was interested in at this instant was biochemical. Several hundred kilocalories of it, straight to the biceps to pull him through the remains of the window frame.

The wall seesawed sickeningly down on the dwarf's side, stopped then swayed back level as Proph stepped back over the shelves, hitching up his trousers, eyes brightening as he had his audience back.

'Tellmefromthere!' blurted Mh'tonnay, panic sparking off every consonant and echoing against the rocks below. 'What happened?'

Keep the dwarf still, he thought, give me a chance to pull. Chin-ups! I hate chin-ups!

'I can hear voices,' telepathed the sea-scrole from Mancini's hip flask as the VET sprinted over the mountain to investigate the projectile porta-hovel.

'I can hear voices,' declared Knapp, still blissfully unaware of the sea-scrole's telepathic abilities.

The threesome crested a rise and screeched to a sudden halt, back-pedalling furiously as the edge of a vast ravine loomed at their feet. A dislodged stone rolled over the edge and tumbled into silence. Directly across the three-hundred-foot drop Mh'tonnay and the dwarf swayed precariously, the former sweating profusely as he practised his chin-ups.

'Thought 'twas too pointy f'ra thaumafer, couldn't trace it,' said Proph, seemingly oblivious of the fact that but for the principle of moments they both would be small, wet, sticky patches on several rocks three hundred feet below. ''Twas a thaumolith-magic nodule, see?' Mancini's ears quivered as the dwarf held out a barely visible chunk of rock shaped like a fragment of an eggshell, smooth on the outside, but the inside crusted with sharp purple crystals, glistening in the thin air.

'Yssssss. Vrry gud!' grunted Mh'tonnay through gnashing teeth as his red face appeared through the window.

'I *can* hear voices!' thought the scrole again.

''Course you can! They're over there!' snapped Mancini. 'Shut up!'

'Just trying to be helpful,' grumbled Knapp, sulkily

turning his attention to the state of his maggots. He was sure that nearly a week in the desert hadn't done them any good at all.

'Shoot! I'd lay a newt to a croc there's a thaumafer 'round 'ere,' rabbited the dwarf. 'Don't get thaumoliths lyin' 'round on their lonesome, no sirree!' He spat another percussive volley over the edge, grinning cheerfully as it tumbled into the distance.

'Gnnnnnnnh!' answered Mh'tonnay, edging an elbow through the hole, threading himself one limb closer to the relative safety of the top of the rocking wall.

'Hear that?' telepathed the sea-scrole. 'Anybody out where?' it thought, appearing to answer an unheard question.

'Look, shut up! We need to know where it is!' snarled Mancini urgently, straining to catch the words whipped on the wind.

'I didn't say a word,' grumbled Knapp as several large bluebottles swarmed around his head.

'That's what I'm trying to work out!' telepathed the scrole. 'Where did the voice come from?'

'No!' growled Mancini. 'I want the thaumafer! Be quiet!'

'Oh. Don't worry about that! I can hear . . .' began the scrole.

'Shut up and listen!' snapped Mancini.

'I'm all ears,' muttered Knapp, scowling at Mancini and wondering if the strain of the last few days hadn't been just a little too much.

'Could do without this darned granite lyin' 'bout,' grumbled the dwarf matter-of-factly across the ravine, rocking up and down as Mh'tonnay cursed, panted and arm-wrestled gravity. One thing that dwarves were really good at was completely ignoring the outside world – centuries of working in the black confines of mines seemed to have bred out the concept of physical discomfort. 'Really mucks divinin' up shockin', does granite.'

Mancini's hopes fell as he heard this.

A squeal of relief echoed through the ravine as Mh'tonnay

pushed and launched himself through the window, landing like a walrus on an ice flow. The seesaw wall lurched sickeningly.

'Can't be *too* far 'way, though,' continued Proph. 'Almost feel it in my bones!'

Gasping in vast lungfuls of air, Mh'tonnay hauled himself along the wall, clawing hand over hand at the wood.

'Yes. I'm here!' telepathed the scrole comfortingly in Mancini's head, answering some distant plea for companionship.

'What?' snapped Mancini. 'Shut up, will you! I'm trying to eavesdrop, in case you hadn't noticed.'

'I didn't say a w . . .' began Knapp.

'Wasn't thinking at you!' grumbled the scrole petulantly. 'I was answering the voice.'

'What voice?'

'The one in my head. My long-lost pool mate, Mytchlin! It's funny, he's in Losa Lla . . .'

'Oh, great! I'm trying to find out where all this geothaumal energy is and you're gossiping with another bath mat! snapped Mancini. Just shut up, will you!' Knapp looked up and scratched his ear worriedly.

'I wouldn't worry about finding . . .' began the scrole.

'Shhh!'

Across the ravine Mh'tonnay got to his feet shakily, hands clenching and unclenching, face an angry red.

'Best bet's under Tor Tellini. Fifteen thousand feet 'f 'stinct volcano, perfec' place t' find thaumafughhh . . . !' Proph's words stopped abruptly as Rosch Mh'tonnay's huge hands clamped around his throat, squeezing and shaking angrily.

'I *don't* want to know!' he growled, lifting the dwarf off the wall. 'I'm *not* interested, okay? You can go right ahead and roast yourself but not me! Oh, no! Give me a pickaxe and a sledgehammer any time of day. You know where you are with a pickaxe and a sledgehammer. *They* don't blow you halfway to Cranachan at the drop of a hat. *Nobody* mentions geothaumal energy within a mile of me, understood? Nobody!'

As the dwarf nodded, Mh'tonnay loosed his grip and stamped off over Tor Teehya.

Mancini cursed and spat. 'Where is it?' he whimpered rhetorically. 'Where the hell is it?'

'What?' chorused Knapp and the sea-scrole.

'The thaumafer!' snapped Mancini, visions of infinite power controlling gleaming kingdoms slipping through his fingers.

'Hold on, I'll ask my mate, Mytchlin,' chirped the scrole. 'He always was good at geography.'

Knapp shrugged and flicked a bluebottle off his leg.

As the pale light of another day struggled to illuminate the vastness of the Murrhovian Empire, a terrified shadow dashed across the swirling gravel expanse of the Xhen Rockery, ducked around the Palace Pagoda, hurled a padded grappling hook up towards the balcony and checked the rope was secure. He knew he was on the right track. The hastily patched repairs everywhere bore testament to that. Aging bones creaked with effort as he hauled himself hand over hand twenty feet straight up.

Itto's grandfather grinned smugly to himself as he leapt over the stone balcony. One hundred and six and still going strong! It must be the early morning regime of ritualistic energy enhancing exercises. He was never the same if he hadn't had his morning Tai Fou.

He stood and listened carefully. Breaking and entering, especially into the Imperial Palace, wasn't a common habit of his. But, after three days of filling out acres of parchmentwork to file for an audience; hours of positive vetting; hours more of negative vetting in triplicate; and then to receive a categorical statement that the Empress would never be even remotely interested in talking to an aging fossil whose pets had been stolen . . . Well, alternatives had to be sought. He wasn't the Guardian of the damnations for nothing.

With swift, stealthy movements he edged along an inch-wide parapet and peered through a small window. Milky condensation covered the inside, obscuring the view of the Imperial Bath room. There was something in there. Or more precisely, a lot of somethings, one hundred and one black and white somethings. His ancient heart leapt.

Balancing precariously on the parapet, he rummaged in his kimono and withdrew a long thin jemmy. A quiet grunt, a small creak and the window was open. Feeling like a lecherous voyeur, he peered down at the woman in the bath.

'Oh, come on, Timmy! The milk's lovely,' urged Empress Tau, wallowing in her regular morning dip. One hundred pairs of malevolent red eyes glared at the single damnation quivering on the side. 'I'll let you lick my elbow pads. You love that.'

The face at the window creased in wonder. Timmy?

A solitary damnation shook its head and backed warily away from the edge of the pool. It almost seemed as if Timmy had developed a phobia. Ever since that night when all the damnations had broken in and spent the night in the bath, he'd been acting *very* strangely, leaping out of the way if any stray droplet of goat's milk came anywhere near him.

Empress Tau erupted from the bath, rivulets of white cascading down her body armour as she stood pointing at the errant creature. 'Come here!' she shrieked. Timmy shook his head and backed away another pace.

Commanding damnations? thought the watcher at the skylight. Nobody has *ever* managed that for very long.

Tau snarled. She was not used to being disobeyed. That damnation was going to have a bath whether it liked it or not. Three days without a dip is *far* too long. Its fur was already beginning to look pale . . . almost transparent in some lights.

'One last chance. Timmy!' growled the Empress, thigh-deep in the seething damnation-filled bath. Four virtual paws remained resolutely dry.

Tau scowled at the two largest damnations and clicked her fingers. 'Pongo. Perdita. Fetch!' she snarled gutturally. The pair of milk-soaked monsters surged from the pool in opposite directions, fountains of white liquid exploding with them as they executed a flurried pincer movement.

The face at the window twitched in disbelief. They obeyed!

163

Damp paws slapped on the marble floor as Pongo and Perdita bounded towards the whimpering Timmy. A change of direction, a skittering of claws on stone and he was surrounded.

'Bath time, Timmy!' snarled the Empress and the two dripping damnations moved forward threateningly, herding the whimpering wayward one towards the milkily lapping deep end. Timmy backed away, playing for time, an inexplicable fear of liquid flooding its programmed thoughts. Suddenly its rear paw touched something cold and hard, rising out of the marble. Up. Away from the pool. The dripping damnations advanced, muscles rippling under milk-plastered fur. Timmy climbed the four steps and reversed down the springboard, terror surging hot through its virtual neurons as it saw the pool below.

Timmy's rear paw struck nothing – the end of the board. Pongo and Perdita glanced at each other, grinned and sprang forward. Eight paws hit hard, the board arched, whiplashed, and three damnations were hurled into thin air, tumbling in helpless somersaulting arcs.

Approximately five milliseconds after the milky surface closed over the body of Timmy, Empress Tau discovered the inherent difficulty in using virtual ecology technology in an aquatic dairy environment. Milk and hypertaurus accelerators do not mix.

Gallons of curdled cheese erupted from the pool, blue veins of thaumic lightning pulsing within. One hundred damnations howled in alarm, springing automatically onto the sides, fur crackling. Empress Tau roared with anger, and her helmet flew off as her hair writhed like that of an epileptic hydra. Whipping her katana from her shoulder holster, she stabbed down through the translucent whey, striking metal and hoicking the fizzing remains of Timmy onto the side.

'Guards! Guards!' she screamed, thigh-deep in rapidly congealing goat's cheese.

The jaw of the face at the window dropped, a terrifying chill of dread growing within its owner. Something was horribly wrong. He couldn't wait around to find out what. In a second he had leapt backwards, abseiled down to ground level and started sprinting across the courtyard.

The doors burst open and eight Imperial Court Bouncers screeched to a halt by the spitting array of crystals, wires, potatoes and PCBs. Questions wriggled for attention and died as they saw the splattered visage of a very angry Empress.

'Bring me the Court Livestock Image Advisor. I want some explanations,' she choked in a voice that defied disobedience, her Imperial torso heaving angrily in the off-white morass. The eight bouncers fled for the door.

'. . . And fetch me a shovel!' she yelled, struggling ineffectually against the cheese clotting around her legs.

'Please look after these jars, thank you.'

Congratulations!
You have won the prize of a lifetime!
Your name has been chosen from millions of hopeful dwarves entered in our prize draw. *Choose* from any of the options
  listed.

  1) Three weeks all-expenses paid holiday in the Eastern Tepid Seas with the woman of *your* choice.
  2) Two weeks erotic massage at the health spa of *your* choice.
  3) More money than you can shake a stick at in untraceable used notes of the currency of *your* choice . . .

Proph blinked as he stared unbelievingly at the glossy parchment in his hands. He was stunned. Nobody had ever sent him his very own letter before. His first letter and it was *giving* him things. He leant against the door of the porta-hovel reserved for the Small Bore Drainage Company and beamed, deciding that he liked letters. One in millions, he was. The winner. And all he had to do was turn up at the address shown, with this introductory letter, listen to a short talk and the prize was his.

Well, what was he waiting for? Come on down!

He dashed through the contraflow system on the Foh Pass, ignoring completely the regular melted lumps of red and white that had once been conical, missing totally the scorch marks caused by the erupting thaumafer on all of the temporary buildings, blinkered by 'the Prize' awaiting him, seduced by its tempting, lip-licking promises.

Puffs of dust flew from his heels as he sprinted down the Trans-Talpino Trade Route, looking for a turning on the left. He rounded a corner and grinned. A small pole was jammed between two rocks, decorated with yellow balloons and a sign which read:

Your prize this way!
Hurry, hurry!

Proph skidded onto the narrow gravel track and sprinted up the steep incline, panting eagerly, every step taking him nearer to his prize. His very own, one in a million prize.

Unseen behind him a brown-gloved hand tugged the pole out of the ground, flung it onto the back of a familiar red getaway cart and screeched away down the shorter, faster, lower track. If the horses held out, there would just be enough time to reach the hideout first. Practice had told Mancini this.

The dwarf ran on, stocky legs eating up the distance, gleefully calculating how much money he was capable of shaking a stick at, oblivious of the circuitous path he was taking.

Mancini cracked his whip across the backs of his horses, powering wildly forward. He hauled on the reins and tugged hard on the handbrake, slewing the cart sideways around a sharp bend, scattering stones and dust – low profile Peerhelly Soopah-Slyxx just didn't give the grip off-road. Shouting eagerly he urged his horses up the last short, sharp incline, skittering to a halt outside his hideaway, leaping down and heading for the door.

'Oi!' yelled a gruffly irritated voice. 'Not so fast there, varmint!'

Mancini gasped.

'I's 'ere first!' insisted the voice. 'My prize! *I* done won it!'

The VET turned around. 'You most *certainly* did, sir!' he oozed, holding out his open hand. 'If I could have the covering letter. We can't be too careful now, can we? Don't want just *anyone* walking away with *your* prize, now do we?'

'*My* prize, dammit. Gimme option . . .'

'Please, please!' interrupted Mancini. 'We can discuss all that inside in a moment.' He coughed loudly, pretending to clear his throat after the dusty dash. Inside the hut a wiry youth snatched at a piece of wire.

167

'After you!' insisted Mancini. He swept his arm out, indicating his hideout, bowing slightly and pushing the dwarf through the the door.

In a second there was a scream, a dull crash and Mancini cannoned in. He skipped over the trip-wire, landing flat on the dwarf's back, wrenching his arms up between his shoulder blades and tying them swiftly. Knapp chuckled and hurled him a length of rope. Mancini coiled it expertly around his victim's ankles and hoisted him, yelling, into the rafters. A row of six other grim-faced dwarves peered at him, shaking their heads miserably, like a wake of bearded bats.

'Welcome!' announced Mancini gleefully, shouting down the latest recruit. 'So glad you could make it!'

Seven different ancient dwarvish curses blasted out between a host of angrily gnashing teeth in various states of stained decay.

'Gratitude is not necessary until after I have explained a few matters of immediate interest. Are you dangling comfortably? Then I'll begin.'

Proph stared in bewildered disbelief as the letter, his letter, slirmed across the care wooden floor, flopped into a bath and began furiously scrubbing at the inscriptions on its back.

'I must apologise for the somewhat underhand nature of the techniques involved in bringing you here,' began Mancini to his captive audience of dangling dwarves, 'but when you hear what I have to say you *will* understand. That's an order, by the way!' He flashed a grin at the captives.

'What 'bout my prize, you varmint?' growled Proph, swinging gently as he struggled with his bonds. 'My prize!'

'Tut, tut! *So* impatient. That's what I like about you dwarves, direct and to the point!'

'Well?' growled Proph, chewing angrily on something. Two others snarled their support.

'We'll discuss that later. At the moment all you need to know is that your co-operation will secure one of the prizes.'

'One! 'tween seven 'f us?'

'No, no! One *each*!' shouted Mancini over the disapproving growling.

168

'Which one?' snapped Proph, spitting a lump of saliva out of the corner of his mouth.

'That's not important right now!'

'Which one?' growled three dwarves simultaneously.

'The holiday! But you can't have it until you've listened to my talk! So shut up!'

Mancini took the chorus of irritable grumbling as agreement, thrust his hands into the small of his back and began strutting about the hut. Knapp watched it all spellbound.

Staring out of the window in studied nonchalance Mancini asked, 'Does the phrase "Geothaumal energy" mean anything to you?'

A sudden expectant silence, broken only by the splashing of the sea-scrole and the constantly chewing dwarves, filled the room. Mancini could feel seven pairs of eyes focusing intently on the back of his neck. He turned dramatically on his heels.

'I hear it's *very* dangerous stuff. I hear that tiny bits of it can blow porta-hovels clear over the top of snow-covered mountains. I hear that handled carelessly it can singe beards and remove eyebrows!' He stared pointedly at Proph's crinkled and blackened whiskers, smirking inwardly as the trussed dwarf cringed. 'I also hear that *any* talk or thought of it within one mile of a certain Chief Engineer is banned under threat of a nasty beating with a big stick,' he added with a sinister whisper, 'True or false?'

'What's it t'you, varmint?' snapped Proph cagily.

'Let's just say I have an interest in vast quantities of geothaumal energy,' countered Mancini. 'And I'm looking for a team to extract it for me.'

'What in tarnation y'want that for?' asked Proph above a background of mumbling and spitting.

'That doesn't concern you. Except in that successful location and tapping of a thaumafer – yes, I know *all* about them – ' he bluffed, 'will secure your prizes. Three-week holidays, all travelling expenses covered, anywhere you like, every year for the rest of your natural lives!'

The mumbling grew by several decibels in curious intensity.

169

'Anywhere?' asked Ghed, one of the other six.

'Absolutely. In fact you can change destinations every year. It's *your* choice,' oozed Mancini, sensing the tides of opinion beginning to turn. '*Your* prize!'

'That ain't no prize!' snapped Proph, writhing frantically. 'That's wages!'

'Semantics, my diminutive friend. Call it what you will. You *never* get something for nothing. I'm offering you a lifetime of thaum-share holidays in return for a little digging. Interested?'

'Thaum-share? What th'hell's that?'

'Correctly harnessed, geothaumal energy can be utilised in a variety of translocational manners, transporting matter vast distances in the blink of an eye,' Mancini lied. 'Each of you will receive a share of this. Three weeks each year to travel where you will!'

Knapp's jaw dropped. 'Can I go to . . . ow!' he finished as Mancini's heel found his delicate toe.

There was a ripple of excitement from the dwarves. And a hail of brown saliva. There were *so* many caves to be explored, vast uncharted underground systems of linked potholes in the Meanlayla Mountains. Three weeks in there, every year . . . heaven!

'Hold ye horses there!' shouted Proph over the greedy chirrupings of his colleagues. ''S just one rinky-dinky rootin'-tootin' snag 'ere.'

Mancini stared, shocked, at the sizzled dwarf. What snag?

'I's tried findin' this fabled thaumafer o' yours . . .'

Six gasps of irritation rang out. How dare he mess their holiday prospects up!

'I's spent days divinin' up 'ere 'fore work started . . .'

Six snarls of mistrust curled back bearded lips.

'Worn eight pairs o' rods t'handles scourin' every nook an' cranny an' . . .'

Six growls of anger erupted. 'An' you kept it secret? What 'appened to teamwork?' They shouted accusingly. 'What 'bout our pension scheme? You forget the Gold Rush *so* soon?'

'Can't be found by divination, no siree bob!' shouted

Proph defensively. "'S granite everywhere, shieldin' it, rods can't get through. You ain't never gonna find it!' Swaying gently, he glared at Mancini.

Expectant silence fell once more as all eyes turned on their captor.

'Hah! I know *exactly* where it is!'

'Where?' snapped the six.

'Fifteen thousand feet below the peak of Tor Tellini . . . oops! Oh no! I've told you! How careless of me,' Mancini smiled arctically. 'I *do* apologise. I'm going to have to kill you all now. Can't risk that information leaking into the wrong hands, now can I? Sorry!'

'. . . !' shrieked the dwarves.

'There are some things that are just *too* valuable. Shame, that. I'll have to start searching for another team . . .' Mancini nonchalantly unsheathed an alarmingly large axe, swinging it around his head noisily as he familiarised himself with the balance. He swayed forward, the gleaming blade whooshing through the air with pent up fatality. Knapp scurried into the far corner and drew his toes out of reach.

'Now hold on!' screamed a quivering dwarf as the blade whistled past his toes, glancing perilously off the sole of his boot. 'I's an idea!'

Mancini whirled once more, closing.

'What if . . . what if . . .' came the stuttered suggestion, '. . . if we worked for you, for nothing?'

Momentum powered the axe onward, swinging in a deadly arc, smashing into the wood of the beam, burying itself inches into the timber.

'Now why didn't *I* think of that?' trilled Mancini. That was what he liked about dwarves – they always got the point. Especially if it was extremely sharp and attached to the rest of a very large axe.

'What do you mean "he's not there"?' screamed Empress Tau as three attendants wiped goat's cheese off her armour. Behind her one hundred crimson tongues lapped at acres of gratinéd fur.

The Chief Imperial Court Bouncer winced. He knew this would be a difficult explanation. He swallowed, making use of a throat he was certain he would no longer retain in a few dreadful minutes.

'Cheiro Mancini, the current Court Livestock Image Consultant, is . . .' He swallowed again. '. . . No longer in his quarters, your Imperiousness.'

'Search the Palace! I want him here. *Now*!' Tau trembled, anger at the petnapping seething through her body. 'He has a lot of explaining to do!' She snarled, glaring at the fizzing heap of cheese-coated thaumatronics on the side of the pool. 'You!' she screamed, pointing at a random bouncer, 'check the gardens for signs of escape!' She pointed again, razor-fingernails slicing the air. 'You! Check my pigeon-hole for ransom demands! And you! Inform the kitchens that cream cheese is banned from *any* menu until further notice.'

The three bouncers scattered in all directions, relief surging through them as they escaped the massing black cloud of Tau's volatile wrath.

A fear-laden head appeared around the corner of the doorframe, smiled wanly at the Chief Bouncer, shook a negative and slunk in.

Why me? he squealed in the privacy of his own head. Why do I have to be on duty right now? Why do *I* have to tell her? I'm too young to die!

'Ahem. Your Imperial Dangerousness, ma'am. I have just been informed that Cheiro Mancini is . . . no longer in the Palace.' The last five words came as a whisper.

The reply didn't.

'Fetch me my Generals! Send out trackers! Bloodhounds! Assassins! Muster the Army! Fire the war-machine! Bring me the head of Cheiro Mancini!'

In the observation room of Losa Llamas, Phlim was staring at the monochrome images racing in from the sneeke. The landscape screamed by below as the fish-eyed insect soared in ever widening circles. But whilst Phlim's eyes were occupied with monitoring the incoming data, his mind was far from it.

Inside his head images of the sea-scrole on the hex-ray table tumbled over and over, completely side-stepping any attempts he made at interpretation. He knew it was a contour map of the Talpa Mountains – he had recognised that instantly – but what were the lines criss-crossing it? Regular geometric lines, bisecting, meeting.

With all the swirling miasma of half-remembered memories dredged from the silt of his past and the cloudy algae of ideas frothing obscurely in his head, it was a wonder he noted the temporary glitch in sneeke transmission at all.

The tiny racing picture in the crystal sphere before him distorted, disappeared in a blizzard of static interference, blacked out totally, then flashed back on as if nothing had happened. Blink and you would have missed it. As it was, the fact that the glitch had occurred was routed through an event buss into a memory buffer and held there as an obscure irrelevance to be reminded of on a Sunday afternoon when there was nothing better to do.

Several dozen speculative line theories and three more glitches later, Phlim was jolted into aquiline attention as the image distorted, disappeared in a blizzard of static interference, blacked out totally then flashed back on as if nothing had happened.

'Damned atmospheric interference!' he cursed, casually flicking his hands over the control pentagram, superimposing a weather chart on the speeding image, browsing through interminable barometric readouts. High pressure inversion layers over the mountains sometimes affected signals. It was then he sat up straight. Columns of nothing above a thousand millibars, everything tediously normal, then . . . bang! Twenty-two thousand millibars, immediately followed by near vacuum. There was only one thing Phlim knew of that caused readings like that . . . a massive explosion.

The image corrupted again. Curiosity, intuition and hunch modes flicked on in Phlim's now whirring mind. His hands darted over the pentagram, pulling down magic menus in a flash of prestidigitation, calling up the sneeke's onboard thaumometer. He shrieked with alarm as the screen's needle jammed firmly into the red before him. Missing scroles, massive explosions *and* extreme thaumic fall-out! It didn't bode well.

Expertly, not daring to hope he was right, he zoomed the sneeke to three different locations, measuring recent atmospheric pressures and fall-out over three hundred and sixty degrees, calculating compression-rarefaction ratios, locating the epicentre of the blast.

The Foh Pass.

He leapt out of his chair, sending it crashing behind him, whirled round to the hex-ray table and adjusted focus, magnification and tuning until the ancient contour map of the Foh Pass swam into view. There, in the centre of the screen, was a pale blue spot coinciding *exactly* with the epicentre of a massive thaumic explosion.

Phlim's knees went weak as the meaning of the intersecting network of pale blue lines suddenly leapt out at him. A user's guide to the thaumafer network!

'Stop. Point to the cave entrance just behind that outcrop to the left and say, "There!" ' telepathed the sea-scrole. 'They'll love it! You watch!'

Cheiro Mancini stopped and pointed. 'There!' he said dramatically. Knapp stared at the hole and looked quizzically at Mancini.

Behind him, seven exhausted and extremely irritable dwarves glared at him from under a jungle of scowling eyebrows. Mountains of pickaxes, shovels and explosives shrugged dismissively on their shoulders.

'There! Behold!' repeated Mancini, gesturing with far more enthusiasm than he felt. Nervously he scowled at the sea-scrole in his hip flask. 'If this is them loving it,' he whispered out of the side of his mouth. 'I'd hate to see them unimpressed.'

'Dwarves have problems expressing feelings of love,' explained the sea-scrole, lying profusely. 'Generations of working in dark, cramped spaces smashing large amounts of rocks into rubble does that to a body.'

'Ain't nothin' special-lookin'' growled Proph, glaring at the cave. 'We passed dozens 'f likely lookin' holes further back. What's so special 'bout this one, hmmm?'

'It's the place,' insisted Mancini. 'Eight hundred feet straight down from the end of that cave and you'll hit the biggest thaumafer in the Talpa Mountains.'

'Know that f' certain, do you, hmmm? I ain't seen you usin' no divinin' rods,' growled Proph irritably. 'Damned queer way 'f findin' things!'

The scowling dwarf with the singed expanse of facial hair hadn't studied long and hard to get his Prophecyship for nothing. There were *ways* of finding things. *Proper* ways. You divined for things, you didn't just stroll up to a likely looking cave entrance on a whim, point and declare, 'There!' Not without divining rods, anyway.

'I don't need divining rods,' argued Mancini. 'I've got *this*.' He held up his hip flask. 'I *know* that's the right place!'

There was a ripple of disbelief, then a flurry of tutting and dubious spitting. Rhett and Guthry tapped their temples and shook their heads doubtfully. They'd all had private doubts, having heard him talking and arguing with himself and never going anywhere without the flask . . .

Knapp was beginning to worry again.

''F it's alright by you, I'll jus' have a quick div . . .' began Proph.

'That won't be necessary!' insisted Mancini.

'Procedure. The way *we* professionals do things.' Proph reached for his holstered rods, drawing them in a second, spinning them around his stubby index fingers and holding them unwavering before him.

He didn't get a chance to use them. Purple sparks erupted from the cave entrance, crackled at the pair of tips, blasting them out of the dwarf's hand with a yelp and the faint smell of burning whiskers. All eyes turned to the blackened pair of fused wires lying uselessly scorched one hundred yards away.

Reluctantly, Proph pointed a gently smouldering finger towards the cave. 'There!' he said.

Mancini grinned.

Knapp scratched his head.

Heavy leather-slippered hoofsteps rang muffled echoes against ancient dressed stone as the laden beast struggled up the final few flights of steps. Wheezing desperately and coughing as the knight spurred it on, the horse approached the vast door to the Palace Fortress of Cranachan. The knight's matt black armour melted into the shadows. In his line of work the watch-words were discretion and professionalism. In, do the job, then out. No fuss, no mess.

Sir Taindeth had all the equipment essential for a swift and ruthless massacre. He bristled with an intense mortality potential, a dealer in death: axes and swords gleaming; myriad devices of entrapment oiled and ready; eighteen types of powdered poison prepared; fifty-three vials of toxins primed; crates of mouth-watering bait diced, marinated and ripe, each in its own essential noxious blend of pernicious venom. Chemical and mechanical murder was his trade, ridding the world of all types of vermin.* Countless thousands of lives had been undone by his very own hands. And today, here in Cranachan, deep in the very heart of the Palace itself an uprising would be eradicated, a nest of vipers destroyed, cut down before it became too big to control. He halted before the vast door, withdrew his sword and struck with his pommel. The wood quivered resonantly, a small panel, four feet up, flew back and a tiny face appeared.

'Go away! We don't want any!' It slammed shut again.

---

* Some of the smaller ones could easily be eradicated using the Little Squisher Patent Rodent Remover. This consisted of two blocks of quarried rock, labelled 'A' and 'B'. The instructions for use were as follows:–

　　1) Placeth ye yon block enscribed 'A' upon a surface of firm integrity and density,

　　2) Graspeth ye yon block enscribed 'B' with a goodly firm grip in ye right hand,

　　3) Placeth ye yon offending rodent in a centralwise position upon ye block enscribed 'A',

　　4) Bringeth ye yon block enscribed 'B' smartleyeth down upon yon block enscribed 'A' for swift and sure despatch of yon rodent.

Sir Taindeth struck again. The panel flicked back, and instantly the knight's armoured foot jammed into the space created. No mean feat for one so encased in armour.

'Is the Master of the Palace Kitchens at home?' asked the knight, black visor glowering at the doorkeeper.

'Yeah. Who wants him?'

A raven dark gauntlet leapt out of the air and handed over a small parchment card. The doorkeeper's face turned pale as he read the name. 'Ohhhh . . .'

'He *is* expecting me . . . which is far more than can be said for the unfortunate creatures I have come here to deal with.'

The doorkeeper could hear the smile of job satisfaction from behind the impenetrable visor. 'Back in a mo!' he squeaked and was gone.

Sir Taindeth sat almost motionless, contemplating strategies and methods of attack. Should it be the short, sharp shock of steel or the dark punishment of deadly poison? Either way it would be the same result – nobody stared Sir Taindeth in the eye and survived.

There was a heavy click and the door eased open on creaking hinges, revealing a cowering doorkeeper and a desperately uneasy Royal Fish-Cook waving his hands for the knight to follow. The cook handed the doorkeeper a small bag of coins, put his finger to his lips and led the horseman away.

At every corner and intersection, the Fish-Cook dashed ahead, nervously ensuring that no-one would see the ruthless dealer in death he was leading in. Surfeit was terrified. In Cranachan, reputation was everything – a man should be able to handle his own problems. Bringing someone else in to do your dirty work – especially a stranger reputed to consume the bodies of his victims grilled with a light garlic sauce – well, it just wasn't done. The small, prematurely grey man raised his hand for Sir Taindeth to halt, dashed ahead into the sweltering clouds of the kitchens and returned a minute later with a white coat and hat. Twitching and glancing over his shoulders every three seconds, he indicated that the knight should put on the cook's uniform and follow him.

A disguise! observed Sir Taindeth with a chuckle; they always gave him a disguise. A wry smile slunk unseen across the knight's face as he considered the lengths to which people went to hide his presence; sneaking him in through back doors, conveniently leaving windows open, attracting everyone's attention to a fictitious happening out there on the lawn. Look! It's amazing! Look, everybody! Funny, though, without fail they *always* forgot about his horse. Although, curiously enough, nobody ever made a fuss about finding a jet black percheron leaning nonchalantly against a wall in a corridor.

Surfeit stopped before a particularly undistinguished door and pointed with grossly overemphasised secrecy, winking and twitching his head melodramatically.

They were in there! Right now, just beyond that door. *That* was their hideout, their den, the retreat of the nest of vipers.

Idly he flicked through the options once more. Careful baited stealth or hack, maim, slash? His black hand quivered expectantly at his sword . . . Then rose to a small pocket in a belt around his waist and pulled out a small, wet and very dead mouse. Expertly he tied a length of twine around its neck, eased open the door and hurled it across the length of the storeroom. Slowly he drew in the line, winding it around his left hand, feeling the tension. There was a hiss, a snatch, a pull. He was on his feet, through the door, sword slashing down, catching the back of his victim's neck, slicing clean through. Hah! Worked every time!

Sir Taindeth, Vermin Eradicator and Infestation Controller, grinned at the viper's severed head. There were times when Pest Control was fun, when it felt like a fight. Outsmarting wily reptiles, second-guessing cunning rodents, rounding them up and blitzing them, that was what it was all about! None of this sprinkling white powder everywhere and watching ants croak. With a wrench he thought back to the good old days, the glorious days when he'd get calls for dragon-slaying or demon-baiting; those were the days when you *knew* you had an infestation. Just look at the holes in the skirting board.

But, unfortunately, there were no dragons any more. The St George Slay-U-Like franchise was too successful by far . . .

Behind the black visor, Sir Taindeth's eyes misted over wistfully. He'd heard rumours that a ninety-foot gold dragon had recently torched the nearby Castell Rhyngill. But nobody had seen it since. He had the horrible feeling that the whole thing was a lie to get the fire insurance claim through.

He sighed. If only there was a dragon to dispose of . . . just one . . . just for him . . . please!

Wistfully he kicked the storeroom door down and cheer-fully began skinning vipers.

Itto's grandfather's aging sandals hardly touched any of the countless steps as he plunged wildly into the depths of his storeroom, hidden in the backstreets of Murrha. His mind fizzed with the desperate panic of the utterly terrified. Discovering the theft of his deadly damnations had been bad enough – but to discover that one had left the city . . . His heart shuddered like a nervous iceberg in the path of an ice-breaker. Such a surgical stealing, cold, calculated, under-hand. Dangerous. Questions, like hungry starlings, squawked for answers. How long had the PET damnation been there? Who could have stolen the real damnation? Where was it? He had to know. The future hung in the balance until he found it again!

The thought of curling up in a dark corner and making blubbering noises was immensely tempting. He had blown it.

Throughout the entirety of eighty-five thousand centuries the damnations had been safely shielded from unscrupulous eyes, hidden and protected by an unbroken succession of Guardians, the responsibility handed down from father to son countless times . . . until him! An evil mockery of a twenty-year-old memory battered at the shutters of his mind, pounding fists of shame smashing painfully. He should have prepared his son better, should have broken it to him gently . . .

But his son *had* been thirty, he had reached the age, he

179

should have been able to take it like a man. It was only the weight of the destiny of the entire future pressing down on his shoulders. That was all.

There was one glimmer of hope. Empress Tau knew nothing of the damnations' potential; she was blissfully, thankfully ignorant of such black arts. He had to take a chance. Leave the hundred with her and find one. Did he have a choice? If someone wanted a damnation badly enough to risk the fury of Empress Tau then that someone *must* have a reason. And it could only be a bad one.

Nervously, the old man removed a key from a pocket in his kimono, moved aside a bamboo fan on the wall and unlocked the tiny reinforced door behind. With trembling hands he withdrew a triangular decorated wooden box, laid it on the table, flipped open the lid and felt his heart shudder as he stared at the contents.

Before him lay a small, translucent orb, held between two closed lash-edged flaps. It was as if he was looking down on a minute head, bald except for the double row of an erect black mohican haircut. He breathed deeply, lit several dozen herb burners, took a sip of bamboo spirit for luck and began to whisper low incantations, the sound ululating edgily around the room. His heart surged with terror as the lids twitched in response, the bald surface of skin moving as the orb roamed within. Then the stripe of mohican lashes parted along its length, unzipping silently. He almost screamed as the fount of knowledge and belief opened and blinked.

The Eye-Ching looked around the room, its dark, seemingly bottomless pupil sucking in light.

The old man took another deep swig and whispered the ancient Focusing Mantra; the words that would home the Eye-Ching's lens onto the object he sought; the timeless Hypermetropic Chant.

'I spy with my little eye something beginning with "D"!' he began, his voice thick with emotions of terror. 'Next letter "A". Then "M" . . .' he continued.

The Eye-Ching rolled epileptically as he continued, its focus seeming to turn from the immediate vicinity to a multitude of distant places. Searching. As the old man added the final 'N' the lids closed with a wet slap and the eyeball thrashed about rapidly, peering around half-seen distant corners, squinting over far, translucent horizons, leaving no stone unturned, no depth unprobed.

Suddenly it stopped, pulling itself out of rem, and opened. The search was over. Now the questioning could begin. This was the bit he hated, the Eye-Ching was *so* pedantic!

'O all-seeing eye, O sentinel,' whispered the old man, gathering his thoughts for the Holy Twenty Questions, 'Hast thou found what I seek?'

The Eye-Ching blinked once for 'yes'.

'Can you tell me where it is?'

Blink.

Eighteen more 'yes/ no' questions to find the lost damnation, thought the Guardian. No problem. At times of acute stress Itto's grandfather could lie through his back teeth to himself.

'Is the damnation safe?' he asked around another swig of bamboo spirit.

Blink.

It's safe! he thought, relief flooding in. Then he stopped. Of course it's safe. With teeth and claws like that it's *perfectly* safe! A question wasted. Try again.

'Did one of the Palace Staff steal it?'

Blink.

'For their own benefit?'

Blink.

The old man's shoulders relaxed a little. Could it be that a downtrodden maid stole it to sell to a jealous head of state for use at official functions?

Blink. Blink.

The old man stared angrily at the Eye-Ching. 'What do you mean, "No"? I didn't ask a question!' Panic and shock edged his voice.

Blink. Blink.

'But you answered me?' he bleated in confusion.

Blink.

181

Can you hear this? he thought, his mouth firmly shut.

Blink.

'You can read my thoughts?' he squeaked, suddenly feeling mentally naked.

Blink.

'That's incredible!'

Blink, answered the Eye-Ching almost smugly.

Then, with a jolt he realised . . . 'Hey! You've just made me waste a load of questions!'

Blink. Blink.

'That was rhetorical! You *do* know what rhetorical means?'

Blink.

'So was that!'

Blink.

'Stop answering me!' he commanded, glaring at the Eye-Ching defiantly, scowling as its lids flickered. 'I only want answers to proper questions. I don't want responses to rhetorical questions. And thoughts don't count as questions. Okay?'

Blink.

'Aahhhgh! I've only got five left now!'

Blink.

The old man panted hard, trying to focus his mind before he did something to the Eye-Ching that he would deeply regret in the future.

'Is the stolen damnation still in the Palace?'

Blink.

'Is the thief still in the Palace?'

Blink. Blink.

The old man jumped. *That* didn't make sense. Then it hit him. They're *all* stolen damnations! Sloppy questions!

'Is the damnation I seek within the Murrhovian Empire?'

Blink. Blink. Then the Eye-Ching closed.

'No!' shouted the old man, panicking again. 'That isn't twenty! You still there?'

Blink. Blink. Then it remained motionless. Twenty questions used up.

'You can't leave me like that! Give me a clue! It's vital. Come on, just a little hint!' he wheedled. 'Please!'

The eyelid opened reluctantly, looked around to make sure no-one was watching, then stared hard at the wall, pointing due west.

'West? Should I go west? Is that where the damnation is?'

The Eye-Ching slammed shut quickly with a wet slap.

The old man leapt up, snatched the carved wooden box and hurled it into a small sack along with a few essential items for long journeys on foot: a sturdy set of boots, a box of corn-plasters, three changes of woolly socks and a bar of white sugary stuff laced with painkillers and mint.*

'Go west, old man!' he growled. Snatching his staff from the wall, he set off, praying he wasn't too late.

'What in tarnation's that stuff an' nonsense?' squealed Proph derisively as Mancini fiddled with a collection of pentagrams, pink psychoterrin crystals and a small hypertaurus generator in the cave entrance. A bunch of yellow flowers turned and looked at the dwarf.

'Security!' snapped the VET irritably, snatching a psychic screwdriver from a heap of tools and adjusting a chrominence filter to achieve the correct yellow.

'Sure looks like a daffodil t' me!'

'Good. It's meant to,' grumbled Mancini. 'Nobody will suspect they're being watched by a daffodil. We plant these in an arc around the cave and when they spot intruders we set the dragon on them. Clever, eh?'

Proph's face fell. Dragon? Sentient daffodils? What kind of a madman had he teamed up with?

'Yup!' he whimpered insincerely.

'Can't possibly fail!' gloated Mancini.

'Nope! Well, not unless yer intruder's a botanist . . .'

'What? These daffodils are perfect!'

---

* Ever since the dawn of time, it seemed, every expedition or invasion force leaving the Murrhovian Empire had carried pocketfuls of the sugary white tablets jammed full of painkilling narcotics. It was said that an entire platoon could march for a week on a single bar of Kendoh's Mint Cake.

'Sure. But it's th'wrong time 'f year fo' daffs,' grunted Proph, stifling a grin as he saw Mancini's face turn crimson. Barely controlling his quivering shoulders, the dwarf scuttled into the darkness of the cave, ready for something he understood. Mining.

At the bottom of a vast cave network a young boy struggles hard against the ropes tying his hands behind his back. Just around the corner a hunched figure chuckles and greedily runs his hands through the once-hidden treasure, the chinking of coins and jewels echoing like some million-groat waterfall. The boy bites his lip and strains once more against the bonds. If only he could escape and return the treasure to its rightful owner . . .

In the third row of curved carpeted seats a small figure chews nervously at a bag of popcorn, totally engrossed in the unfolding drama.

Suddenly a shiny black nose appears around a rock and, with a fanfare blast of triumphant soundtrack, Flossie the Wonder Hound leaps a tall stalagmite with a single bound. Panting with exertion she springs to the aid of the bound boy.

The figure in the carpeted seat lets out a scream of joy, spraying semi-chewed confectionary into the rows in front.

Pausing only to smother the boy's face with a dribbling tongue, Flossie the Wonder Hound chews through the rope in a flash of 80mm Superthaumination trickery, helps him to his feet and edges away wagging her tail and whining. Her expectant eyes glisten in the gloom as she wills him to follow.

'Go on!' yells Rutger, a handful of popcorn poised twixt pot and mouth. 'It's Flossie!'

The boy smiles, takes a step forwards, there is a click and . . .

The magic lantern cavern was flooded with a corona of blinding white light, banishing the eight-foot-high projections from the screen in seconds, shattering the atmosphere.

'Oi!' screamed Rutger, 'I was watching that!'

'Not any more,' growled Practz, stomping to the front of the cavern. 'This is important. Phlim,' he commanded, 'put that over there and everyone sit down. Come on, we haven't got all day!'

Phlim and Wat struggled with the hex-ray table and hooked it onto the wall as the entire staff of Losa Llamas filed into their carpeted seats.

'I don't like it,' complained Thurgia as he entered the cavern, a backpack thaumatron fizzing and spitting as the power levels rose. 'We should let sleeping scroles lie!'

A rumble of opposing views rose in the cavern as they stared apprehensively, or enthusiastically, at the hex-ray table hanging on the wall.

'Shut up! All of you!' snapped Practz, barking at the assembly, tension showing in the hunch of his shoulders. 'I don't like it either, but it's got to be done. We need to know what information the other scrole contained. If it's as valuable as the map of the Thaumafers, then . . .' His voice faded away as his shoulders shrugged higher towards his ears. 'Thurgia, if you would be so kind . . .' Practz pointed to the third sea scrole taped onto the screen.

The enthaumatroned wizard tutted. This was happening far too often for his liking. Why did it have to be him again?

The mass of technical wizardry charged quickly, casting the sorcerous clouds into the air above him, turning darker blue as the power increased.

'Wat, the lights,' shouted Practz.

In a second semi-darkness reigned and eight-foot images of a fleeing boy led by a dog flashed across the wall. Rutger cheered.

'And turn that off!' bellowed Practz. Wat vanished into the magic lantern booth and blew out the candle. Rutger booed, very quietly.

'Now, everybody pay attention!' snapped Practz. 'Thurgia, let the scrole have it.'

In a crackling sapphire flash Thurgia discharged the full seventeen-and-a-half gigathaums into the scrole and hastily shut the thaumatron down with a whimper.

Phlim brushed his hair out of his eyes and turned his attention to the hex-ray table, gesturing frantically and

185

moaning under his breath. It flashed once, shut off, flashed again, then lit with a steady bluish-white light.

Phlim grinned sheepishly. 'Starter's on the blink,' he offered.

All eyes were fixed on the now glistening scrole. Its cartilaginous skeleton showed as ghostly shadows. A shocked hush ran around the cavern as, instead of ancient scripts or age-old cartography glowing against the anatomical backdrop, a badly battle-scarred face appeared. It stared frozen out of the screen in an eighty-five-thousand-century-old expression of utter stage fright.

Suddenly the face twitched, its eyes opened a fraction, its mouth twisted, the billowing orange cloud of fire behind its left shoulder expanded. The whole image moved a jerky frame forward. A subterranean sound growled out, rumbling and roaring as the image began to wind forward. 'I . . . f . . . s . . . some . . . body is watching this,' began the mud-spattered face, creakily accelerating to normal speed, 'then these scroles have been found!' The orange ball of flame raced skywards, curling over itself as it erupted. 'I haven't got long. Can't explain. Show you what's happened. Before it's too late . . .'

The face leant closer, vanished around the edge of the picture and began whispering. Sapphire thaumic lances thudded out of the sky, igniting in vast, destructive plumes of fire. Suddenly the hex-ray screen exploded into a blizzard of static as the scrole indexed back through its memory, beginning a whistle-stop sub-routine of . . . of what? No-one in the whole of Losa Llamas had any clue as to what they were watching. It was something momentous, something ancient, and something very, very important.

The static blizzard ceased abruptly, to be instantly replaced by a jolting, hand-held image of a dark mountain standing before a wan primeval dawn. Strange fern-like trees sprouted in the foreground, rooted in bubbling, steaming swamps. The image bounced and rattled along hard on the trail of two pairs of darting, covert cloaked shoulders.

With a gasp from the assembled audience there was a jolt,

186

a sapphire spark and the image wheeled sickeningly, zooming in on the surface of a fetid pool, closer, the surface reared up, was broken and several thousand startled amoebae and a tentacle scattered.

More antarctic static.

'. . . at was close!' snapped a voice from the hex-ray screen as the running image reappeared. 'Nearly had us! Heads down, keep to the swamps! We can't fail now!' Vast emerald dragonflies fled wildly through the mists between horsetail trees as the sprinting began again.

A wild snowstorm edit forward.

The trees were behind now. A bare, blackened war-zone stretched away to the foot of the now almost horizon-filling mountain, the swamp boiled dry with the intense energy of the fighting, scars drilling through the black primordial mud. And there, atop the mountain, a horned black figure stood – huge, apocalyptic arms crossed arrogantly before its chest, nightmare black cloak of misery swaying heavily down to its ankles – The Prime Evil. It was visible almost by optical vacuum, sucking light into itself. The image shook as the black figure swept vast arms out, cloak eclipsing the young sun struggling skyward, tapping and drawing on immense thaumic forces. It shaped intangible power into three billowing orange fireballs and casually began to juggle them, nonchalantly watching the terrified approach of the last primordial mages.

'That's far enough!' boomed the juggling figure, hurling a fireball. The incendiary orange sphere raced towards the viewpoint, expanding, swelling. On target. The image on the screen wheeled suddenly, lurching to the right, dodging the searing projectile.

'You'll never succeed!' roared the shadow on the mountainside. 'Face it, I have won! *I* am the victor!' The two fireballs hovered for a moment against a black expanse of cloud, a dazzling pair of flaming eyes staring wildly at the mages, and vanished in a magnesium flare of raw power. The battle-scarred landscape heaved.

Throwing back its black head and roaring evil laughter,

the shadow reached into a pocket and withdrew two vast handfuls of smouldering crimson anger. The primordial world reverberated to the cackling death bell of warped amusement, quivering like a scalded rhinoceros as the vast hands hurled the hundred seeds of damnation before him in huge arcs. Where each crimson bullet hit, sheets of flame seared skyward and died, belching scorched earth in all directions. The mages, at both ends of history, screamed.

How long the Prime Evil's cackling resonated through the air was impossible to tell, but suddenly a new sound joined it. The scratching of stiletto claws on rock, the squealing of razor teeth on bones, the screaming cacophany of apocalypse. Midnight black claws scrabbled through the battle-torn landscape, erupting from beneath. One hundred inchoate forearms burst forth, hauling crimson-eyed skulls of black into the chaos of the closing moments of the pre-Cambrian War. Obsidian teeth glinted beneath a defensive hail of thaumic lances centred on each of the emerging creations.

'Fall back and regroup!' cried a terror-edged voice.

Another swirling whirlwind of surging static snowflakes.

Thirteen hastily erected towers of stone stood in a circle at the end of an avenue of cairns lined up on the narrow gap between two hills. Only twelve of the remaining primordial mages could be seen; the thirteenth, the scrole perched on his shoulder, struggled to record everything for a future audience. Unusually for a home recordist he prayed they would never have to see it.

'They're coming!' screamed a disembodied voice, striking adrenalised alarm into every heart, pointing at the hundred crimson-eyed creatures from below. The mages sprinted into place, each in a gap between two stones, each between two mages, a complete, coherent magic circle. They knew what they had to do.

The mage at the entrance to the cairn avenue, the conductor, struck at the block of stone to his left, pummelling at the rock with his bare hands, forcing harmonics from it, his heart surging as an F rang out. Barely waiting to get his breath back he pointed to his right, terror speeding his movements, urging the adjacent mage to match the pitch exactly, willing the geomancer to begin.

A croaked note squeaked into earshot, causing a ripple of cringing around the circle. The mage coughed and tried again, listening to the pitch, absorbing the tone and wailing. The conductor snatched a quick squint over his shoulder at the army advancing between the hills, then pointed to the next mage, his eyes beseeching an F sharp from him. The air filled with beats as the semitones clashed. The third mage cleared his throat, closed his terrified eyes and launched a G into the circle.

A distant roar broke their concentration for a moment. The Prime Evil held its ebony sides and screamed wild derision, laughing at their pathetic attempts at victory, knowing there was no way that thirteen battle-weary geomancers could possibly have enough power to cheat defeat.

An A flat, A and B flat seethed clangorously into earshot, each semitone interval amplified by the stone circle, beating and fighting against the growing wall of discrete frequencies. The activated harmonic rocks started to glow, heat being generated by the raised level of molecular movements. B, C and C sharp sang out, making the air shimmer. And steam, like an army of ghostly wraiths, began to rise from the grass outside the circle. Four converging swathes began to iridesce. D and E flat. The circle was almost complete. Eleven semitones throbbed and fought for attention within the wailing wall of sound. Cracks appeared in the four swathes of glowing ground. And still the Prime Evil's army strode forward, destroying and spoiling, yards away from the mouth of the cairn avenue. The twelfth mage added the final semitone, completing the octave, setting the last of the tonal monoliths vibrating, forming a total impenetrable wall of rock music.

But it wasn't over. Puffs of smoke issued from fissures above the converging swathes. Then the conductor took a deep, terrified breath, opened his mouth, and added the microtonal E sharp. A flare of superharmonics blasted and beat wildly off the sound wall, setting it ringing, driving home the final nail in the cacophony.

The four swathes of power erupted; surging terrathaums powering into the ring. The primordial images had tapped into a throbbing quartet of thaumafers. The conductor screamed as the energy sought its release down the cairn avenue wave-guide. The image on the screen began to scramble in the thaumic fall-out.

Suddenly there was an almighty scream as the Prime Evil realised it was staring down the barrel of the largest thaumic assault rifle ever. The conductor hurled himself to the ground, hugging the grass as countless terrathaums blasted over his body, thudding into the hundred and one demonic creatures at point blank, blasting them into unrecognisable shapes, four limbs, black and white fur. Only the teeth and claws remained. Not a perfect success; someone must have been just off pitch. Inhuman screams and infernal yelled curses assaulted the ears as the hundred and one damnations were rounded up by the victorious primordial mages. Then the screen erupted into a hailstorm of dandruff.

The original mud-splattered face was back, this time on a beach, looking weaker. Behind him, fires raged, horsetail trees and ferns ignited by the thaumic fall-out. Four dead sea-scroles lay at his feet in terracotta pots. One was still empty, a small label tied around its handle with the carefully scribbled request. 'Please look after these jars. Thank you.'

'The battle was too too much. Damnations safe. For now. Hope I've not forgotten anything,' he croaked, wincing as he cut deep into his thumb. Then he tossed the last scrole onto the barbecue, sealing in the memories.

The hex-ray table went blank.

Tryst and Shout

Mhar-Rheanna Pahcheeno had lied.

She lied every afternoon at twelve-thirty, trotting out yet another fictitious reason to be out of the house for several snatched hours of bliss with her sweetheart, Rhomyoh. It was a different lie every day, of course – popping out to the market, or a fitting for a dress to wear at the forthcoming ball – endless excuses dreamt up by a scheming, lovelorn maiden, designed to hide a glorious afternoon's innocent trysting.

She sat on 'their' little outcrop at the foot of Tor Tellini, in a tiny clearing just out of direct sight of the lumbering mass of Cranachan, and pulled leaves off an innocent daisy. Gasping in superstitious alarm as she reached 'He loves me' with three petals left, she peered over her shoulder for anyone watching, tugged off two in one go and ended with a cheerfully wistful sigh. Funny the way daisies always confirmed what she knew.

She loved this place, seething as it was with myths and tales from centuries past, trolls and dragons and dwarves inhabiting the caves behind her, subterranean sounds rumbling mysteriously. Her imagination tripped gaily through the meadows of fantasy, failing totally to see the heads of eight red roses turn and peer at her.

She heard a rustling in the ivy at the base of the outcrop, wary footsteps approaching, checking behind secretively for any signs of pursuit. Mhar-Rheanna, the daughter of the head of the Cranachan 'Family', stifled a coquettish giggle as Rhomyoh neared, her imagination dressing him in gleaming armour, her eyelids fluttering in a rush of anticipation. On a whim she plucked a handful of daisies and arranged them in her jet black hair.

'Oh, Rhomyoh, Rhomyoh!' she bleated. Three more roses stared at her.

'Mhar-Rheanna!' he called, scrambling up the rock with a single bound.

'Oh, Rhomyoh!' she pouted, eyes closed, heart fluttering, waiting . . . yearning in a state of fevered, unrequited trysting. She could sense his heart pounding inches away from hers, feel his tense breaths brush her cheeks, his lips nearing . . . She pouted a little more, leaning forward to expose her neck, then he screamed and ran.

Through the crashing of undergrowth a single word was heard repeated over and over, 'Dragon!'

Mhar-Rheanna spat. 'Come back here and say that! You're not such an angel yourself! You'd better have a good place to hide, 'cause when I find you . . .'

The tiniest of branches cracked behind her, cutting off the fury of the woman scorned. She wheeled round and found herself face to kneecap with the towering expanse of an iguana-green dragon.

A menacing wisp of smoke slunk out of its left nostril as it smiled down at her.

In an instant she was gaining rapidly on Rhomyoh's fleeing heels.

A thick silence hung over the entire cavern. Not a stunned word had been uttered in Losa Llamas since the final image of the pre-Cambrian mage had flashed into final blizzards of whirlwind static.

'Any comments?' asked Practz.

'Never set the box-office alight with editing like that,' grumbled Rutger. 'Besides nobody wants tragedies nowadays!'

'I think I want to go to the toilet,' whimpered the technician Wat, and scuttled out of the cavern.

'Suggestions?' pressed Practz.

There was a grumble of unhelpful murmurings in the dark.

'What did it mean?' he shouted. 'What's the end of a prehistoric war got to do with anything? Especially us?'

'Thaumafers,' said Phlim almost to himself.

'What was that?' shouted Practz, pouncing on the first real answer, however shaky it might be.

Phlim looked up from the scribbles on the parchment pad

before him and into the desperate eyes of Practz. 'Thaumafers,' he repeated, surprised that he had actually made any noise. 'One scrole contained an incredibly detailed map of them, and that one,' he pointed to the bath mat shape still taped to the hex-ray screen, 'that one showed what they could do. If you reckon that they're connected . . .'

'Are you saying that all that business with chanting and rings of stones and swathes of exploding grass was thaumafers?' whimpered a bewildered Thurgia edging nervously away from the still fizzing Thaumatron.

'Accessing a thaumafer . . . yes,' said Phlim, suddenly feeling more confident as inklings of a disturbing sense filtered into his mind. 'Look, here.' He held up the map of the thaumafers, extended a small pointer and indicated a crossing of two lines intersected with a dotted circle. 'That's what we just saw!'

'But what was it all about?' pleaded a voice from the back. It was a question nobody wanted to ask . . . and worse, nobody really wanted answering. 'I mean, it all looks pretty handy to me,' continued the voice of the technician, blissfully unaware of the gravity of the issue. 'Unlimited power at your feet ready to be used, bit like a massive thaumatron. They wiped out a whole army!'

'An army of what?' asked Rutger.

'Nasties!' answered the technician enthusiastically. 'Zzzzzzzzappppp! Gone!'

'Not gone,' shouted Practz with a worried mixture of revelation and utter horror. 'Remember the end!' he cried, slapping his brow with an open palm. 'The "nasties" were only captured, only trapped. The final blast of magic didn't destroy them, only held them somewhere.'

'Uh-oh. After eighty-five thousand centuries I don't think they'll be very happy about it,' whimpered Thurgia. 'I've had dealings with spirits trapped for a week and *they* were really miffed.'

'Why should they be a danger now?' asked Wat re-entering the cavern, an expression of relief plastered across his face. 'They've been there all that time. We only know about them because Phlim brought back . . .'

Phlim and Practz came to exactly the same terrible conclusion at precisely the same time.

'The scroles!' they shouted in unified angst as information, supposition and logic leapt on the accelerator and raced them towards a dizzying conclusion.

'That one told us when!' cried Practz, pointing at the bath mat on the screen.

'This says where!' Phlim stared at the map scrole.

'All things that don't matter . . .'

'. . . if you already know about them!' finished Phlim.

Practz's face went ashen as he struggled out the words, 'The missing scrole contains all the information necessary to . . . to . . . resurrect them. Why else would it alone be stolen?'

The cavern erupted in a deafening plethora of screaming panic.

If we don't find that scrole soon, then maybe not today or tomorrow, but soon, something horrible is going to find those things! yelped Practz inside the privacy of his terrified mind.

Eighteen teams of haulage rhinos tossed their horns and bellowed blasts of pachyderm irritation. The drivers trapped in the contraflow system hurled abuse and any other more solid items they could lay their hands on. Packs of itinerant cone-setters jeered from behind hastily erected piles of red and white striped traffic guides, popping up from the trenches to lob lumps of concrete at the stationary trucks. And that was just the Rhyngillian side of the Trans-Talpino Improvement Scheme. Nothing had moved all day, apart from the lines of cones being rearranged into rudely provocative signs and phrases, and the constant aerial bombardment from both sides.

It was a disaster. And it was all Rosch Mh'Tonnay's fault.

'Come out!' he screamed as he pounded still harder on the door of the porta-hovel occupied by the Small Bore Drainage Company. 'Please!' he cried for the hundred and twelfth time, staring at the large transverse groove in the track surface and the string of red terracotta pipes next to it waiting to be dropped in. 'We can talk money! Nice wage rises, lovely, lovely groats. Three percent? Five?'

A cone with the words 'Sit on thyss' scrawled across it whistled through the air and collided with the back of Mh'tonnay's head, smashing his heavy brow against the weakened door. There was a splitting sound and the Chief Engineer tumbled inside accompanied by a hail of cheering from the Cranachanian side.

Rosch Mh'tonnay's mood took a serious down-turn. He snatched the catalytic cone from the splinters of the door, hefted it angrily and launched himself into the hovel, shrieking as he delivered torrents of abuse and avalanches of scathing blows to the bunks.

Had there actually been anyone in there it was almost certain that Mh'tonnay would have been charged and convicted of seven counts of dwarficide.

As it was it finally took four crates of beer, twelve bulky hauliers and half a dozen mattresses to bring him under some sort of fuming feral control.

And nobody under foor foot six could ever go near him again.

It was little over an hour since Sir Taindeth had polished off a hastily prepared snake kidney pie, three flagons of ale, two large custards and half a dozen fairy cakes, all courtesy of an immensely relieved Surfeit, and right now he felt dreadful.

His head throbbed violently, spasms of skull-wrenching agony exploded as he attempted to move, and cold sweat erupted across his brow. He whimpered feebly.

'Aha! You are awake!' growled Fhet Ucheeni, a vast eclipse of a figure in a pinstripe tunic and slicked back hair, currently staring at the prone knight.

'My head . . .' groaned the captive vermin eradicator.

'Many apologies,' growled Ucheeni, failing totally to inject even the merest hint of sincerity. 'An over-active trainee hit-man. He won't do it again.'

The last phrase gave the distinct impression that he wouldn't be doing *anything* again. Ever.

Dimly, through a fogged windscreen of memory, the knight recalled the rafters outside the Palace Kitchens exploding with horribly enweaponed bodies as he had carefully mounted his trusty horse, his chain-mail trousers groaning. There had been a glint of lethal weapons, one, two, three, they seemed endless, a barked order, the whistle of a vast club through air. Then everything had gone black.

Resignedly he vowed to himself to camouflage his steed next time. Or park it in the kingdom next door.

That was, if there *was* a next time. Fhet Ucheeni clicked a pair of vast fingers and two pinstriped thugs leapt forward, manhandled the knight into a sitting position and whirled the chaise longue around a full mind-numbing hundred and eighty degrees.

Sir Taindeth opened his spinning eyes and stared at the squatting figure before him, glistening across a gleaming walnut table with flaccid wealth, a lifetime of overindulging expensive tastes apparent in the number of chins. The knight was convinced that he was staring at the bastard son of a young maid's illicit trysting with a congenitally obese bull-frog. The bullfrog's ringed fingers stroked at the large white-haired rat in his lap as he stared unblinking at the knight. His left hand reached out, opened a drawer, removed a week-old talpine rock mouse and dropped it casually into the large glass bowl at his side. The rodent blinked and struggled for a moment in the water before there was a rush of bubbles, an aquatic squeak and the faintest trail of red in the suddenly turbulent water.

'Tepeed Sea Snapper!' grinned the oozing figure in his immaculate midnight black suit and matching nihilon shirt.* 'Beautiful creature, you theenk. Streep a rhino clean to da bones een three meenutes! You like?'

---

* nihilon. A finely woven material spun from the fibres derived from the copolymeris-ation of two organic compounds extracted from the decayed bodies of extinct worms, aphids and a comprehensive catalogue of long-dead sea slugs. It was introduced to Cranachan shortly after the end of the now legendary Two-and-a-half-minute War and was an instant hit with the ladies, who promptly leapt into nihilon stockings in a big way, instantly discarding their older outmoded silk. Afterall, who really wants to wear something secreted from a caterpillar's bottom?

'Only grilled with chilli sauce,' answered the knight with forced nonchalance, furiously attempting to ignore his throbbing head and get around the accent. Had he not failed totally to recognise the bullfrog as Khar Pahcheeno, the head of the most powerful of the 'Families' of Cranachan, he might not have been quite so flippant. Over the years the number of enemies buried by Khar Pahcheeno had earned him the title of 'The Undertaker'. Numerous sharp intakes of breath resonated around the room in the suddenly thick silence after the knight's reply.

A flurry of crimson rage flashed across Pahcheeno's face, turning his greying temples momentarily red and raising a squeak of alarm from the rat as he clenched a furious fist around its neck.

'Ha! A sense of humour? We can soon change a dat . . . eef we *have* to!'

Fifteen heads nodded too eagerly. 'Why am I here?' asked the knight.

Pahcheeno stood and dismissed all but Fhet Ucheeni with a casual flick of his wrist.

'Eenformation!' oozed the Undertaker, his blubberous jowls flapping.

'You won't get it! No amount of pain you can inflict can make me crack. I spend five hours a day sitting on hot coals to make me strong! And once a week I thrash myself with burning bushels of nettles whether I need it or not. I am the hard man of vermin eradication! Nothing, absolutely nothing at all can make me talk . . .'

Pahcheeno's right hand appeared from behind the walnut desk clutching a small suede bag which chinked in a very expensively seductive fashion.

'However . . .' began Sir Taindeth, licking his lips. 'As I am always saying to myself "A rule is only as strong as the boots of those who smash it!" What d'you want to know? The best places to find cockroaches? Mating habits of the dung beetle? Three easy steps to eradicate lounge lizardsssssghhh?'

Pahcheeno coughed and instantly Fhet Ucheeni's hand

clamped around the knight's neck and began to tighten. 'Boss wants you to leesten, okay!' growled the owner of the hand, adding a few more pounds per square inch for effect.

Pahcheeno stroked his rat thoughtfully. 'What's a da beeggest crowd ever gathered for a recent extermeenation?'

Ucheeni loosened his grip.

'Last year!' coughed the knight, amazed that anyone could exert such pressure through his armour. 'Huge crowd. For a hornet's nest gassing.'

Pahcheeno's look of pent worry seemed to grow deeper. Something was on his mind. 'How beeg a huge crowd?' he pressed, sweat oozing onto his brow.

'Massive, massive . . .'

Ucheeni squeezed.

'Twelve!' screamed the knight as his collar creaked with metal fatigue.

'Hundred?' snapped Pahcheeno.

'Th . . .' croaked the writhing figure.

'Thousand?!' shrieked the Undertaker, in danger of suffocating his rat. 'Let heem answer!' he yelled at Ucheeni.

'Th . . . thirteen at most!' gasped Taindeth.

'Theerteen thousand for da hornet's nest. Thees ees worse than I thought!'

'Er . . . no,' offered Taindeth. 'Thirteen. Just thirteen. All members of the anti-hornet gassing brigade. There would have been fourteen only one of them got stung the day before and . . .'

Pahcheeno looked up, scowling. 'Gah! I'm not eenterested een da treevia. What about a da theengs you knights are supposed to be famous for? Driveeng ogres out of caves? Riddeeng keengdoms of wild dragons, saveeng damsels and returneeng the stolen treasure? Ever have trouble weeth da press?'

The knight's face fell. 'Don't get jobs like that any more. There's nothing left.'

Pahcheeno and Ucheeni looked at each other in confusion. Could his daughter, Mhar-Rheanna, have lied? Just for the hell of it? After everything he'd taught her about dishonesty?

'Take dragons, for instance,' continued the knight. 'All gone. Apart from that rumour over Rhyngill way, there's been nothing. It's all that Saint George's fault. Too handy with a lance by half, he is . . .'

'Mhar-Rheanna!' bellowed Pahcheeno. 'Get een here!'

The knight was jolted out of his reverie as the doors were hurled open and a young girl burst in, white with shock.

'Deescribe what you say you saw!' snapped Pahcheeno, barely disguising the scepticism in his voice. 'Every detail!'

She looked around and fidgeted under the spotlight of her father's angry inquisition. 'Well . . . I was up on Tor T . . .'

'Not *where*! What!' he bellowed. 'What deed you see?'

'Dragon,' she said to her feet, suddenly feeling ten years younger than she should.

Sir Taindeth's ears leapt upright at the word. It was an Ammorettan Death Lizard . . . *had* to be, dragons were extinct. Still, even disposing of a Death Lizard would be a step up.

'It was huge and green and scaly and smoke came out of its mouth and it was in a cave and it scared me witless!' answered Mhar-Rheanna. 'Dragon!'

Taindeth's mind whirred at the mention of smoke.

'Well?' growled Pahcheeno, scowling firily at the knight. 'Ees eet or eesn't eet?'

'It *sounds* like it could be. A *draco imperialis* by the sound. Mean beggars, they are!' His eyes lit up. 'Thirty-foot torch radius, nineteen-foot tail-whipping arc, stone-hurling . . .'

'Yes or no!' demanded Pahcheeno, his face reddening with desperation, whilst the rat turned crushed-blue.

'I'd have to take a look to confirm . . .' began the knight. 'Er . . . but it does sound promising!' he added sheepishly as he saw the fires of fury receive a few extra buckets of coal.

'And eef anyone heard of thees? Crowds?'

'Heaving!' thrilled Sir Taindeth, his thoughts racing ahead to the multitude gathered expectantly on the hillside, him baiting the beast in his finest gleaming armour, the honour, the glory! 'Everyone must know about it! Let me despatch a messenger to *The Saurian Gazette*, anon. There's a

199

thousand-groat prize for discovery. Oh, the publicity!'

'No!' screamed Khar Pahcheeno, accompanied by a strangled croaking of a rat. 'No publeecity!'

'But this'll do my career wonders!'

'You won't have a career eef anyone finds out. You won't have a life!' Pahcheeno rounded on his daughter. 'And *nobody* else knows about thees . . . thees dragon of yours?'

'N . . . no,' she answered, her fingers crossed behind her back. If her father found out *why* she was up near the cave entrance on Tor Tellini . . . She shuddered. Rhomyoh would be singing falsetto!

Pahcheeno grabbed Fhet Ucheeni's tunic, tugged him down and whispered in his ear. 'Take heem up there, blindfold. Make heem do the dragon. Then do heem! Da next sheepment's almost ready. We lose thees, we lose meellions!'

As Ucheeni dragged Sir Taindeth out of the room, Pahcheeno's thoughts jaunted out to the waving acres of almost ripe poppy heads on the side of Tor Tellini.

Throughout the entirety of the Murrhovian Empire crack troops were bursting through bamboo doors, crashing down decorated paper screens, tearing open sacks of rice, tipping squealing babies out of rickety cots . . . in short, strip-searching the place. All of it. If someone had poked a very big stick into an enormous ants' nest on a hot afternoon there couldn't have been much more seething activity.

When Empress Tau had screamed for the head of Cheiro Mancini she had meant it and if it incensed the Murrhovian people then . . . tough! That was the best thing about being the absolute boss of an absolute dictatorship – public opinion didn't matter. Absolutely.

Tau stamped up and down inside the Palace, gnashing her teeth and muttering angrily as she honed her favourite katana to screaming sharpness. Every hourly report, delivered by increasingly terrified messengers, served to heighten her levels of seething frustration further. The only thing stopping her beheading everyone in sight immediately was the fact that there wouldn't be an audience for Mancini's punishment.

Away across the capitol, a platoon of heavily slippered feet crashed through a locked door and stormed down the flight of stairs revealed behind it. The red beams from the Imperial high-intensity lanterns blasted through the musty darkness, searching, obliterating shadows with each searing sweep. Boxes and crates were smashed apart with flurries of open-handed chops and paradiddles of crushing kicks. In seconds the subterranean storeroom was incapable of hiding anything.

For a moment, blissful silence fell, broken only by the metallic tinkling of the lantern's decorations. Then a shriek erupted from an eager throat, a finger pointing into mid-air. The whole platoon's lantern beams arced round in rapid response, converging on the spot, blasting untold lumens at the thin strand of black and white fur fluttering gently floorward, settling onto a pair of crossed brooms and a pile of hastily abandoned fluff.

General Lehrt's heart leapt. Evidence! Damnation fur. Someone had been trying to cover up the fact that the Empress' stolen pet had been here. Then his heart sank. Been here and gone.

What news was that? Empress Tau's beloved creature was just as horribly missing as before. All he had to show for his troubles was a pile of rustled damnation's whiskers.

That and the alarming feeling that what he sought was no longer within the encircling walls of the Murrhovian Empire.

Squatting like some vast altar in a subterranean cathedral, buried deep in the secretive forests of Losa Llamas, lurked the perfect embodiment of a scrap-metal dealer's heaven. It reared up in dense toroidal elegance – an enormous metal doughnut sprinkled with hundreds and thousands of inorganic treats. Silvery vacuum tubes snaked and writhed across complex jumbles of coils; conduits connected banks of smouldering valves with the giant fingers of cooling fins; and miles of rainbow-hued wires knitted bright nets across the whole surface.

This was the recently refitted thaumatron. Bigger

magnikinetic fields; massively improved thaumic particle acceleration rates and hugely beefier field-flux potentials than the mark one could ever have dreamt of. *This* beastie could belt out thirty-five gigathaums of pure coherent thaumic energy, polarised, purified and ready for anything. The world of thaumatronics had seen nothing to match it. Well, not in eighty-five thousand centuries, anyway.

Phlim grinned to himself as he stood before the runic dials and pentagraphs of the complex control array. He cracked his knuckles noisily, wriggled his fingers experimentally and began to murmur procedural incantations with expert ease. His eager eyes darted across the control array, checking hyperensorcelled steam pressure levels and monitoring thaumic damping requirements as he released the wand-brake slowly and raised the output potential. All across the thaumatron smouldering valves burst into fiery sparks and black steam pipes began to exude a ruddy glow. Power production rose.

Behind him Practz was complaining yet again, this time about backache as he laboriously chalked a series of three almost identical pentagrams on the stone floor. Each chalk figure was aligned very slightly differently to magnetic north, and each one varied infinitesimally in diameter. He stood and thoughtfully rubbed his lower lumbar vertebrae, squinting at the marks on the floor critically and comparing them to that in the vast tome held out by Rutger's aching arms. Translocational pentagrams were so easy to get wrong. One wriggle of a line or slight drift of compass bearing and you could end up appearing at the bottom of a well, or worse.

'You sure there's no other way?' pressed Thurgia, glaring at Practz, expressing his doubts for another countless time. 'I mean, can't we just ride there, or get a cart or something?'

'There's no time!' snapped Practz. 'We may already be too late! If Mancini's found the power source he needs then . . .'

'I would have detected it!' shouted Phlim, working at the control array. 'I've had hypersensitive thaumometers pointed his way since we found the map.'

'But what about the fall-out that interfered with the sneeke?' asked Practz.

'Fall-out? Nobody said anything about fall-out?' squeaked Thurgia, wishing he could just have a quiet possession to sort out. Give me a demon, please! You knew where you were with demons!

'Not powerful enough,' answered the Technical Wizard, ignoring Thurgia's mewling.

'You certain?' growled Practz.

Phlim bit his lip and crossed his fingers surreptitiously, cringing as he attempted to muster some sort of illusion of confidence. 'Oh, yes. It was a thaumolith and no mistake. Short sharp explosion . . .'

'Explosion!' shrieked Thurgia, leaping off the translocational pentagram.

'Mancini would have to tap a thaumafer to free the whole army . . .' continued Phlim, nervously crossing another set of fingers.

'Army!' shouted the Head of Demonic Studies. 'Now hold on. I'm not being thrown about the place with some newfangled machine, to fight an army . . .'

'You won't have to!' snapped Practz. 'Information is what we need right now! All I want you to do is find out where Mancini and the stolen scrole are so we can get it back before it is too late!'

'No fighting?' scrowled Thurgia doubtfully.

'Surveillance. Ears to the ground. Quiet questioning!' assured Practz. 'No fighting, okay? Now please, onto the pentagrams!'

Rutger, Thurgia and Wat stepped reluctantly into the chalk circles and Practz signalled to Phlim.

'Definitely no fighting?' grumbled Thurgia, eyeing Practz with mounting scepticism.

Phlim brushed a strand of hair out of his eyes, swallowed and chanted a sharp, guttural command, thrilling as the power rating surged up to twenty gigathaums and a small hatch opened. With a crackle of raw energy a captive lightning bolt of sapphire energy lashed out, struck Practz in the small of the back and stayed there, flashing and writhing as it poured pure thaums into him. Cerulean sparks crackled

203

and fizzed off his hair and spluttering eyebrows as he flexed his hands and began to chant translocational spell subroutines. The thaumatron throbbed, the sound of high-energy magic bouncing off the rock walls and echoing throughout the cavern.

Suddenly, Practz's hands lanced out, and blue fire sprang from them, pointing at two of the pentagrams, striking the chalk, igniting the shaky lines. In a flash, a third lance of power blasted from somewhere on Practz's anatomy, connecting with Thurgia's pentagram with a loud crack and a shriek of delight from Practz. Phlim released the wandbrake totally, twenty-two gigs surged into Practz and with a triplet of sizzling pops, the three figures vanished.

Phlim never did find out how Practz had controlled all three arcs of power but he felt certain his boss walked differently from then on.

Fhet Ucheeni tugged hard on the reins of his own horse and yanked desperately at those of Sir Taindeth's as he veered round one of the countless dark corners of Cranachan and plunged down a narrow alley. Already the knight was beginning to feel distinctly travel-sick; he wasn't used to riding blindfold. Especially at this breakneck pace.

They wheeled round another right angle, swerved left, careered right and in a flurry of whinnying screeched to a sudden emergency stop. A portion of semi-digested snake kidney pie made an untimely bid for freedom from the knight's churning stomach.

The tiny alley was almost entirely blocked by a single enormous figure. It was clad in a baggy green cardigan seemingly held together with patches of coloured material and ribbons. A vast marquee of what could have passed as a battle kilt swam groundwards, jingling menacingly as metal brooches of leaping whales clashed with enamel rainbows. There was something unnervingly menacing about the way the kilt's swirling canopy somehow just failed to cover the pair of huge knees and boots which stomped unstoppably forward. Behind this green giant surged a forest of screaming, placard-waving peasants in similar attire – a platoon of en-rainbowed warriors swarming towards the Imperial Palace Fortress.

Ucheeni did a double-take as he stared at the legendary Mrs Olivia Beece's ample chest bedecked with the ribbons and patches of a lifetime's campaigns.

'SAVE THE DRAGON!' demanded a placard thrust in Ucheeni's face. 'SAY NO TO SAURIAN SLAUGHTER!' screamed another. 'LIZARDS LOVE LIFE!'

Sir Taindeth tore his blindfold off and stared about, blinking, trying to focus on the barrage of banners. His mind gagged in confusion as he read . . . Save the dragon? Save it? Did they know what havoc an angry full-grown male firedrake could wreak?

'Sign this petition!' screamed a vehemently dreadlocked woman in a green overcloak and matching boots sporting a Campaign for Real Whales tunic. 'Halt dragon-hunting now!'

'Er . . . why?' spluttered the knight.

The petition-wielding woman's eyebrows arched in a terrible V. 'It's barbaric! The slaughter of innocent monsters!' squealed the frantic fanatic.

'Innocent? Have you ever seen a dragon in a tantrum? Have you? Village plus dragon . . . woooof! Dragon plus pile of cinders! They're lethal!' shouted Taindeth.

'They're too rare to see!' shouted Mrs Beece striding forward, her olive green knitted cap tugged ferociously down over her eyebrows in full battle frenzy. 'They've been hunted to the brink of extinction by parades of the rich! Knights and Saints getting dressed up in all their silly costumes, a few quick sherries and off through the woods!'

'Monsters have rights, too!' yelled a voice from the crowd.

'So do I. I've got to make a living somehow!' shouted Taindeth defensively. 'Stabling and armour isn't cheap these days. I'll get a few thousand groats for killing a dr . . .'

His voice trailed away as he suddenly realised the crowd had noticed his armour and weapons, and spotted his proudly displayed crest proclaiming him to be a fully paid up member of 'Ye Aynshent and Nobyle Gyld of Peste Controllers'.

'Dragon-slayer! Murderer!' screamed the crowd, boiling wildly. Ucheeni snatched at Taindeth's reins and spurred his horse into retreat. The knight's steed lurched backwards, almost unseating him into the wild rainbowed throng. He clung on desperately as hands ripped at his cloak; one slip and he'd be stripped in seconds.

A hail of insults exploded from the furious mob, drowning the clatter of skidding hooves as the two horsemen leapt away, swerved madly around a corner and were gone.

'Phew! Bit touchy, weren't they!' shouted Sir Taindeth above the rush of pounding hooves. 'All that fuss about a dra . . .'

'Don't say it! Just don't!' yelled Ucheeni. 'Too many people know about the damn thing already! You could have been killed then!' And I would have had to do the dragon, his thoughts added.

'Nah! They wouldn't. They're totally against killing and slaughter and . . .'

'Only defenceless animals.'

'Defenceless?' squealed the knight. 'There's nothing defenceless about dr . . .'

'That's beside the point. You would've been mincemeat. I know!' shouted Ucheeni, recalling the previous week's riots against indiscriminate burning of phoenixes. Fifteen dead and twelve still suffering.

Ucheeni glared at Sir Taindeth as a flash of blue-white light ignited in front of them, crackled and collapsed.

'Look out . . . !' screamed the knight, clinging desperately to his trusty steed as they flashed out of Cranachan and pounded towards Tor Tellini, only narrowly avoiding a four-foot thrashing body as it dashed from beneath the horses' hooves.

Thaumic lances flashed out of the sky, thudding into the primordial mud, hurling hissing black globs high into the air. Flames lashed out from the vast black figure's fingertips,

206

strafing the horsetail trees, flushing out the mages for the hundredstrong army from below . . .

Then the sea-scrole screamed, thrashed helplessly in its bath and woke up.

Cheiro Mancini leapt off a rock, sprinted urgently across the cave and kicked the bathtub hard. 'Shut up!' he shouted. 'Stop interrupting!'

The scrole whimpered mentally as it sloshed in the settling water.

'What's up now?'

'Nightmares,' sulked the ancient bath mat, unsure where the images had really come from. 'That eel you fed me last night, ugh! This modern food just doesn't agree with me at all.' It shrugged its corners sheepishly.

'Just shut up! I've got my work cut out with these dwarves. They're too slow,' growled Mancini, striding over to the parchment diagram spread over a rock flattened for the purpose.

Three dwarves pored over the sketch-map tutting and grumbling restively, wondering what he had against the bathtub, shielded as they were to any external telepathy by an inch and a half of skull. Generations of inbreeding against unexpected rockfalls. Survival of the thickest.

'You sure this map's right, boy?' queried Guthry, squinting accusingly at Knapp. The wiry youth's head jolted upright, snatched away from his examination of his sack by the direct question. He looked around in shock, feeling dreadfully vulnerable before the intense dwarvish eyes. He squeaked and sprinted away. Ghedd tutted, rolled his tongue and spat across the cave, grinning smugly as the bath rang out a direct hit.

'Of course I'm sure!' snapped the VET, striding back angrily and scowling at the expectorant dwarf. 'Like I said to you before, it's an old map that I've redrawn. It's right, okay?'

'Din't say nothin' like that t' me, boy,' squinted Guthry, his hat brim flopping over his eyes.

'I did! A minute ago.'

'Nope! Mighta said summat similar, but not t'me!'

'I spelt it out clear as anything . . .'

'T'me!' finished Ghedd, squinting out from under a floppy hat brim and a mass of red eyebrows.

'You damn diggers! All look the same to me,' cursed Mancini. Proph coughed and scowled at him from behind a blackened fuzz.

'Give you three days and you'll have a beard down to your ankles again!' ranted the VET. 'It's no wonder you're all so small, putting all that effort into growing hair and beards and eyebrows. Bound to stunt you!'

'You finished there?' snarled Proph.

'For the moment. Now, as I asked before, why the delay? Why aren't you setting explosives or chiselling or whatever else it is you diggers get up to?'

'You ain't ne'er been down a mine 'fore, 'ave you?' tutted Proph. 'Ain't no idea 'bout minin' procedure?'

Reluctantly, Mancini shook his head.

'Whee! A virgin!' shouted Guthry.

'Ahem,' coughed Proph. 'Three Rules 'f Minin' Etiquette. First, ground needs divinin'. We ain't goin' down 'til we know what's down there. Second, we ain't ne'er usin' explosives down here. Look at my face and tell me if I want that again?'

Mancini cringed at the rodenty face peering out from behind a torched bog brush.

'So, we's goin' t' set up f' divinin'. An' if you's got a problem wi' that, well, hell's teeth on a jack-rabbit, we's outta here!'

Mancini nodded begrudgingly. 'And the third rule?' he asked, dreading the answer.

Guthry and Ghedd exchanged furtive glances. This was new to them.

'Third Rule 'f Minin' Etiquette!' Proph drew himself up to his full three-foot-two-inch stature and scowled. 'Down here we's Minin' and Excavation Consultants, y'hear? We ain't no damn diggers!' He whirled on his heel and strode off towards a pile of divining rods. Ghedd and Guthry barely contained

208

their applause as they snatched the map and fell in behind.

Mancini cursed through clenched teeth. The sooner this was over the better. When the power was released he wouldn't have to bother with any more vertically challenged individuals with ideas way above their thick heads.

Growling almost as angrily as the crimson-eyed black and white creature jammed in the cage in the corner of the cave, he spat and went to check on the security roses.

The trail of ripples from the paddles of a solo coracle spread across the still surface of Lake Hellarwyl, and cross-faded into the perfect reflection of the Talpa Mountains. Spam Smith, expert (although strictly amateur) weekend fisherman, gathered in his oars, rummaged in his bait box and cheerfully rammed a juicy maggot on the end of his hook with his smithy-stained fingers. With a thin plop he tossed the length of string into the cold water of the mountain lake and, his part of the fishing done, opened the second of six large pitchers of ale. He was so happy he'd discovered fishing; what better excuse was there to lounge about in the open air guzzling oneself cheerfully senseless? It wouldn't be his fault if he didn't catch anything; it was a big lake, after all, and such a tiny little hook. A fish could *so* easily miss it, especially underwater. It was so very hard to see underwater. He took a long, languid draught of ale. Ah, bliss! Nothing to disturb him, no nagging wife, no shrieking children, no roaring fires of the smithy . . . Peace, perfect peace.

Six feet above the shimmering silver surface of the lake a concentrated bolt of blinding blue-white light arced into view with a crackling shock of echoing discharge, a body appeared, flapped briefly and plummeted squealing and thrashing into the coracle captain's lap.

For several seconds there was only the sound of subsiding waves. That, and the sibilant smashing of shattering placidity ringing inside Spam Smith's seething mind. He snarled as he glared as he rolled up his sleeves.

Wat smiled his most disarming smile. With arms that size threatening his personal integrity, he needed to.

209

'Hello,' he said, grinning a grade five gorgonzola grin, 'I wonder, could you . . .'

It was as far as he got before the coracle sank.

It would be difficult to say which of the rowdy crowd of placard-waving protestors was the most startled by the sudden appearance. A clear favourite, though, had to be Mrs Olivia Beece, the petition-wielding woman with the matching green overcloak and boots. She had heard all about the dark and dingy backstreets of Cranachan through which she had, up until a moment before, been sprinting. She'd been warned of the men that leapt suddenly out of unseen corners, tugging wide their cloaks and exposing their naked bodies before shrieking and dashing wildly away, cackling insanely. But she never quite expected to meet one.

Let alone have one drop out of the sky on her.

Thoroughly incensed by the fact that she had let the first real-live dragon-slayer she had ever met get away without her giving him a large, and very angry, piece of her fuming mind, she was outscreaming the most irate of banshees as she rounded a corner at full tilt, milliseconds ahead of the pursuing crowd. In that instant, there was a blinding bolt of blue-white light, a crack of ionising thaumic discharge, a scream of vertiginous shock, and a body flashed into view six feet above the street. To its immense relief, severe impact damage with the very solid cobbles below was avoided by the cushioning effect offered by a large woman in a matching green overcloak and boots.

Thurgia never had the chance to offer his thanks for such a generous act of altruism. Before he could even open his mouth to speak, a knot of writhing hands snatched him in a straight-jacket of ecologically friendly double-nelsons and frogmarched him to the nearest officer of the law. To Mrs Beece's seething mind and gnashing molars there was only one thing worse than fully armoured dragon murderers. Fully unarmoured flashers.

Into the smoke-filled, alcohol-sodden atmosphere of The

Gutter surged a desperately quivering stranger-in-town. His nerves firing on every terrified cylinder, having recently been milliseconds away from becoming a four-foot sticky patch on just another backstreet of Cranachan, Rutger's adrenaline-drenched system was screaming for a drink. He rattled frantically across the sawdust-strewn floor, ducking expertly between heaving bodies, scaled a stool and leaned across the bar, tongue lolling, begging for a flagon. In a dark corner a group of haulage contractors were yelling raucously bawdy songs and swilling far more ale than was healthy for continued liver function.

Rutger held out a desperate hand as a leather mug hurtled towards him along the bar. He snatched and downed the quart in seconds, drooling his tongue once more in the traditional Cranachanian request for beer.

The haulage contractors launched into a particularly toneless rendition of 'Four and twenty maidens' as Magnus the Carter swayed to near vertical and headed off to get them another round.

'You're in fine voice tonight!' shouted the barmaid, filling a flagon from one of the many stacked barrels.

'Slebratin'' slurred Magnus, playing idly with the coil of his rhino whip in what he hoped was a seductive manner.

'Anythin' nice?' she asked cheerfully.

'Freedom!' he expounded joyously. 'Freedom'n'beer.'

'Been "inside" then, lovey?' cackled a shrill voice from a woman wearing more than a little too much make-up. 'What was it? Brawlin'?' she shrieked, leaning a few degrees further forward and professionally displaying far too much cleavage. 'I like a nice brawny brawler now an' then!'

'Shut up, Maisy!' shouted the barmaid. 'He's my customer. Let 'im 'ave 'is ale first. He can 'ave you anytime! Same again?' she asked Magnus.

The carter nodded, eyeing Maisy's cleavage appreciatively. His eyes misted over as he found himself thinking of the depths of the Foh Pass.

'So what did you do, then?' she asked.

'Eh?'

'How long since you were last free?' Maisy's ankle stroked at his thigh. 'I bet you're yearnin', eh?' she cooed, adjusting a necklace of delicately sculptured crimson and pearl triangles.

'Three days!' shouted Magnus as the necklace faded into a string of red and white cones spreading out for seeming miles before him. 'Three days stuck out on the side of the track! Bleedin' Improvement Scheme! Three days goin' nowhere, an' all 'cause o' those bleedin' dwarves. Gone on strike or summat! Vanished with the track in a right state . . .'

'Still, you're 'ere now, eh?' soothed Maisy, shaking her head as she wondered if, in fact, he was all there.

'And no thanks to those bleedin' dwarv . . .' Suddenly he stopped. Somehow, through the milling crowds around the bar, Magnus' eyes managed to clamp onto the diminutive body of Rutger swigging greedily at his third flagon.

A subterranean growl issued through the clenched teeth of the haulage contractor as his alcohol-sodden mind filled in the details of the last three days. The dwarves, all of them, had *deliberately* left the track in that state and spent all the time here, drinking and laughing in The Gutter – well, where else for supposed Small Bore Drainage Engineers? And they'd done it to spite him, personally. Suddenly, oddly irrelevant connections were made in his mind, turning the last three days spent shivering and brawling in the Foh Pass into something far worse . . . something far more personal.

Rutger sprayed an arcing mouthful of aerosol ale over the vast hand which shot out of the gloom and clamped around his throat, choking as the glistening arm hauled him off his stool and into the air.

'You'll pay for it!' roared Magnus. 'You'll pay!' he screamed, biceps bulging angrily.

Rutger snatched at his money pouch in desperate terror as his face turned red. 'Take it!' he croaked inaudibly, waving the jingling pouch frantically. 'Please, take it all!' he cried, spinning from Magnus' fist in a sweeping over-arm bowl. Fountains of ale exploded sequentially from the bar as he hit, bounced and skidded along the runway of stained wood. In a moment chaos erupted from every quarter. Screams of outrage and cries of protest drowned the tuneless haulage contractors. Stools were hurled backwards as drinkers leapt to their feet brushing off ale, rolling up sodden sleeves in classic brawl-mode.

'Get the dwarf!' screamed Magnus, out for revenge, wading hand over fist into the melee of bodies and stools. A bottle hurled by an unknown hand looped over the throng and smashed against a wall. Rutger shot off the end of the bar, plunging into a terrifying stygian abyss of pounding legs and ale-stained sawdust. For a brief moment he wondered if being crushed to death by the two wildly galloping horses wouldn't have been preferable to having the same operation performed by a riot of drunks. A grim halo of gloom opened above him, framed by a grinning ring of hauliers' faces.

He screamed, darted reflexively through a gap in the legs, and scuttled frantically behind the bar, catching at a ring in the floor and pulling. He lifted a trap door and fell down the ladder into the cellar, hotly pursued by a cascading tsunami of revenge-ridden hauliers.

Magnus, despite his bulk, hit the floor running, scanning for movement, eyes peeled in a rage of dwarficide. He was followed seconds later by a rumble of footfalls as the other haulage contractors crashed in. Rutger trembled behind a stack of barrels, trapped, no way out. 'Here he is!' shrieked Magnus, spotting the trail of wet footprints vanishing behind the barrels. 'Got 'im!' Empty casks were flung across the cellar as he tore at the stack, ripping wildly, exposing Rutger, arms hugging knees, trembling . . .

Then, with a short sizzling pop, he vanished.

In the cellar, there was a very brief period of stunned silence, followed by a raging cacophony of frustrated cask-smashing as the hauliers vented their murderous anger on a heap of innocent barrels.

'Your Imperial Highness,' began General Lehrt as he crawled towards Empress Tau in a perfect display of personal debasement (2nd position), 'O Light of the East, O

Worshipful Illuminator of all that Surrounds Us, O Supplier of . . .'

'You found nothing!' snarled Tau. 'You strip-searched the whole of my kingdom and you found nothing!'

Lehrt swallowed hard, whimpered inside and began, 'With all the respect that wings from on high, erm, on the contrary, I found this.' He bowed still further, expecting to hear the deadly susurration of an unsheathing katana as he held out the small quantity of black and white fur.

'You count *that* a success? I sent you out to find the thief and bring him back to face my katana! And you bring back some tail clippings!'

'There is no other sign in the entirety of your tyranny. He has fled the Empire, but the search will not stop. I have made arrangements for platoons to leave at all points of the compass along the borders. We shall find him!'

'Finished?' snarled Tau. Lehrt nodded nervously.

'Go west.'

'M'lady?'

Tau grinned imperiously and threw a parchment catalogue at the General. 'In his eagerness to convince me of his honest intentions he made a mistake. Such arrogant foolishness.'

Lehrt stared incomprehensibly.

'Annz Hashe's Fur and Feather Fayre, Taxidermy Row, Fort Knumm,' she sneered, quoting mockingly from the back page. 'My cartographers advise me that Fort Knumm lies just beyond the Talpa Mountains. West. Now go!' She hurled a stack of maps at the General. 'And Lehrt?' she added menacingly as he leapt a little too quickly to his sandalled feet and started towards the door. 'Get it right!'

In the Culmen Mountains, far to the north-west of the Murrhovian Empire, straddling the borders of the damp jungle kingdoms of Mynymymm and the temple-strewn provinces of Khambode, lay the cartographically indistinct region known as the Auric Triangle. Despite the fact that no map had ever defined its position with anything remotely resembling accuracy and no signpost or major highway headed towards it, anyone in need of illegal chemical additives could find it.

The dense cloud of lazy blue-brown hallucinogenic smoke that hung above it and the occasional awe-filled cries of sudden mind expansion probably had something to do with it.

Here Ellis Dee, alias 'Hiyzah Kite', alias 'Ohpyum Pappy', alias almost as many other aliases as the kingdoms in which he was wanted, was the King. He'd been here for years, harvesting, distilling, extracting and processing as many different botanical specimens as he could lay his alchemical hands on, and trying the resultant powders, tinctures and balms out on a plethora of willing volunteers. Today was no exception.

Hugh, the Nugh-Age Traveller (modelling the full 'Back to Nature Collection' of open-toed sandals and banana leaf loin-cloth) swayed into the hut and sat down heavily.

'Brought the things you wanted, man, er, King,' he slurred over the constant sound of bubbling and refluxing vessels. 'Havin' a shave?'

Ellis Dee looked up from a strange-smelling pot issuing pinkish blue smoke and squinted at the arrival through the steam. 'Shave? Whatever gave you that impression?'

'Mirror and a razor blade?'

'Ah, yes!' He snatched a small packet of powder from a shelf and sprinkled some onto the smooth surface of the mirror, dividing it into thin lines with the razor. Then he dashed outside, grabbed the long hollow shoot of a tall grass and ran back in, jamming it up Hugh's left nostril, commanding him to 'sniff'.

In a second the two white lines had vanished into the traveller's olfactory system. 'Now what?' asked Hugh.

'Feel anything?'

'Itchy nose.'

'Anything else?' pressed Dee, sounding a little disappointed as he stared at Hugh's shrugging shoulders.

There was a single knock at the door and a small black-haired Khambodian swaggered in, wearing a camouflage

215

green tunic and a pair of crossed webbing knife belts. 'You want me?' he said in heavily accented query.

Ellis Dee tutted at the pot of powder in front of Hugh and turned to Praquat. 'Those vastly overpriced deliveries from that Cranachanian dog, Pahcheeno, still haven't arrived. Check on the progress and report back to me. Supplies are getting far too low.'

Praquat saluted and turned to leave.

'And quick!' added Dee. 'I *don't* want to have to start smuggling again!' The Khambodian grinned and vanished.

Suddenly Hugh shot upright wearing the expression of one who has just witnessed a herd of Ammorettan Death Lizards exploding from his fingertips. His eyes rolled madly as he lucidly declared, 'They're all purple!' and collapsed.

Ellis Dee stepped over him, frowned, added a little more green powder and red chopped root to a beaker, turned up the heat and began to reflux it to dryness.

In the instant that three figures flashed back into existence inside the chalk pentagrams of the thaumatron bay, Practz realised that all had not gone as it should. Whether it was the rapidly growing puddle issuing from a dripping, shivering Wat; the prison uniform being modelled by a dejected Thurgia; or the spreading aroma of stale beer, fear and the corona of a smouldering black eye sported by a fuming Rutger that first tipped him off, he wasn't sure. But in that instant he somehow knew that he was not going to be very popular.

He wasn't wrong.

Three irate voices yelled and screamed a tirade of angry protestations in a densely echoing wall of sound. Phlim edged out of sight behind the thaumatron and winced.

'. . . what information am I supposed to find in the middle of a lake! . . .' shouted Wat.

'. . . accused me of being a dwarf! I ask you . . .' shrieked Rutger.

'. . . mad protestors accusing me of flashing! . . .' squealed Thurgia.

216

'. . . weren't even any decent fish . . .' moaned Wat.

'. . . convinced it was all my fault the dwarves were on strike . . .' complained Rutger.

'. . . "Save the Dragon?" Total fruit-loops! . . .' wailed Thurgia.

Suddenly Practz fixed a feral stare on Thurgia, an eager praying mantis in sight of its prey. 'What did you say?' he asked, eyebrows leaping up his forehead, doubting he had heard correctly. Phlim reappeared around the thaumatron.

'Er . . . total fruit-loops . . .' floundered Thurgia self-consciously.

'Before that. *Before* that!' croaked Practz, homing in on the glinting pearl of wisdom dropped from Thurgia's mouth. 'Something about a . . .' he urged, flapping his hands as if teasing something out.

'Oh! You mean the protestors? Mad! Waving placards and petitions and . . .'

'What about? What were they protesting about?' squealed Practz, bursting with a spasm of explosive hope.

'Saving dragons,' answered Thurgia tutting. 'How stupid! Everyone knows that they can look after themselves.'

Practz wheeled around to Phlim, flares of excitement igniting in his eyes, Catherine wheels of relief surging through his body. 'Dragon!' he mouthed, hoarse with tension. Phlim nodded wildly, his mind flashing to the same spot as Practz's. Level twenty-eight, just round the corner from the library, a vast, shimmering PET dragon.

'Mancini!' shrieked Practz. 'It has to be him. Nobody else can just rustle up dragons. Find the thing and we've got him!'

'Any sightings of it?' queried Phlim, staring at Thurgia predatorially.

'Er, er . . . only one, I think. It's difficult to hear when you're being frogmarched towards . . .'

'Later, later!' snapped Practz. 'Where was it?'

'Some boy came screaming through Cranachan as if his girlfriend had been torched by it and . . .'

'*Where?*' growled Practz.

'A cave on Tor Tellini, I think . . . He was very upset!'

217

Tor Tellini! Phlim clicked his fingers joyously and grinned wildly as connections fizzed in his mind. He wheeled around and dived for a file of parchments, flinging sheets in all directions as he searched. Wat and Rutger scratched their heads in total confusion.

With a squeal of delight and a small impromptu display of celebratory air-punching, Phlim handed over the eighty-five-thousand-century-old *User's Guide to Thaumafers*, rolled up his sleeve and with a showy flourish pointed to a tiny intersection of four lines.

'Tor Tellini!' he said smugly. 'Sited conveniently close to the bustling centre of Cranachan, this disused volcano offers ideal scope for conversion to a hideout for criminals or others seeking solitude away from prying eyes. Other major features include unrivalled access to wild sheep and positioning over four major thaumafers. Yes! All the geothaumal energy you'll ever want right under your very own doorstep. Perfect for resurrecting, let's say, an ancient primeval army.'

'If that *is* what he's trying to do,' growled Practz, tapping his teeth absently.

'Of course it is!' shouted Phlim.

'Not necessarily. What if he doesn't know about them?' growled Practz, chewing his fingernails agitatedly, spitting shards across the cavern. 'Why would he steal that tome about transmogrification? There's nothing in there to help him with this!'

Phlim looked deflated as he brushed nail clippings off his lab-cloak.

'We can't surge in, tempers blazing, until we know what he's really up to,' continued Practz.

'So what do you suggest?' snarled Phlim. 'Sit around and wait for him to dig up the thaumafers? It wouldn't be long before we found out then.'

'How long?' snapped Practz suddenly.

'Eh?' grunted Phlim.

'How long before he tapped into the thaumafers?'

'Well, they're buried under an extinct volcano. Take him

years on his own. He'd need a whole team of dwarves to get anywhere . . .'

Practz and Phlim turned and stared at Rutger.

'Say like a whole missing drainage team, perhaps?' asked Practz, squinting at the battered four-footer, sizing him up, imagining.

'Wat, how long would it take you to rustle up a three-foot-two beard, moustache and matching red eyebrows, complete mining uniform and a pickaxe?'

'Er, about ten minutes if the thaumatron's free.'

'It's free,' grinned Practz. 'You have eight minutes! Now, Rutger, my dear chap. I've got a job for you . . .'

'Walkies'

'I feel ridiculous!' snarled Rutger clad in baggy blue dungarees, rolled-sleeve shirt and floppy black hat. Daggers of extreme irritation lanced out from beneath a pair of heavily forested red eyebrows.

'You look it!' agreed Wat helpfully, cheerfully pasting handfuls of facial hair in place on Rutger and fastening a scarlet ponytail at his collar.

'Are you *sure* this is what dwarves look like?'

'Oh yes. You're just about perfect!'

'Gods! And they walk around like this? In public? No wonder they get beaten up,' grumbled Rutger, pulling grotesque faces – his whiskers tickled incessantly.

'Ready yet?' asked Practz, standing up and rubbing his neck, aching from laboriously redrawing some of the pentagram to change the co-ordinates of the drop.

'Almost,' answered Wat. 'Er, Phlim, the finishing touch, if you please!'

'Finishing touch?' wondered Rutger worriedly. What else could they do to him? Wasn't glueing a herdful of bison hair to his face enough?

It seemed not. Phlim squinted a brief smirk, turned to the thaumatron control array and focused a small glowing ball of iridescent magic five feet above the floor.

'What finishing touch?'

In a moment, Rutger found out. Twelve pounds of gravel, granite dust and building rubble flashed into existence above his head, quivered and plummeted earthwards in a vast billowing cloud. It was followed seconds later by an almighty irritated scream of coughing rage which rattled round the thaumatron bay like a dispossessed banshee on acid.

'It is safe to give him this?' asked Wat, nervously holding out a large pickaxe.

'Er, fire up the thaumatron, Phlim,' said Practz warily. 'I think the sooner our dwarvish friend has a brief mountain holiday the better.'

Rutger glared at them, clenched fist circling in a, literally, filthy mood. 'First one to smirk gets a mouthful!' he snarled from under an architrave of plaster-dust eyebrows.

Phlim gestured before the thaumatron, swiftly coaxing it up to twenty gigathaums as Practz gestured at the altered pentagram. 'That'll put you right outside the cave entrance.'

'Sure?' gnarled Rutger, bristling. 'Absolutely certain?'

'Trust me, I'm a sorcerer!' replied Practz as the tiny hatch opened and the sapphire snake of power flashed and fizzed into action.

Rutger leapt forward, fuming. Wat thrust a pickaxe at him. 'Don't forget this, you'll need it,' he shouted.

'That'll do nicely!' yelled Rutger, snatching the handle, menacingly spilling clouds of dust everywhere. Phlim winced as the bolts of energy arced from Practz's hands, shoving the dwarf back onto the flashing pentagram.

Then, with a final shriek of irritation, he vanished.

'Remind me not to be anywhere near him when he comes back,' said Wat. 'He'll probably never forgive us.'

Murrhovian classical cartography was, it had to be said, far less than entirely accurate. As artistic exercises in fish-eye perspectives the Imperial maps were unbeatable; as detailed and meticulous representations of anything beyond the Murrhovian Borders, readily available in handy waterproof fold-away format, they were worse than utterly useless. Had the map-makers paid the same degree of attention to detailed distance measurements as they had to, say, artistic integrity or colour co-ordination then the entire Imperial Army would not have been huddled around six colourful, but widely differing, views of the Talpa Mountains failing to work out where they were, where they wanted to be and how to get there.

'We are here!' declared General Lehrt, pointing at a wriggly line on the map nearest to him. 'The Trans-Talpino Trade Route.'

'That's a river,' snapped Admiral Ti, his bamboo armour rustling petulantly. 'These three say it is.'

'These three say it's not!' shouted Lehrt, scowling.

'That one says it's a proposed sight for development. As a canal. So it doesn't count,' growled Ti. 'Three against two. This is a river.'

'Are your feet wet?'

'Well, it's a river bed, then,' protested Admiral Ti. 'There's probably a dam upstream, see?' He pointed to two of the maps.

'And you call yourself an Admiral*,' tutted General Lehrt. 'We are lost! I am not going to be the one to tell *that* to the Empress. Therefore, I suggest we find out where we are as soon as possible.'

'How?'

'You could always ask someone,' piped up a voice from the ranks.

'What? There's no-one within miles of here,' shouted Lehrt.

A finger pointed to a lone figure in camouflage green on a horse, sliding slowly down a small track.

General Lehrt clicked his fingers and made a series of wild gestures. In a second two platoons had vanished into the undergrowth, three more had begun to circle around to the left and eight divisions of horse guards were galloping full tilt

* Sadly, being in charge of the Navy in the entirely landlocked desert of the Murrhovian Empire didn't really help much with the understanding of basic hydrodynamics.

The Murrhovian Navy had only existed for three years, having been founded in a fit of pique by Empress Tau after listening to the Chief of the Raft People of the Eastern Tepid Seas bragging about the size of their fleet at a recent Tyrants' Ball. At the drop of a hat she had gone ahead and bought thirty-three battle coracles, sixteen boarding punts and a dozen assault dinghies with optional waterline ramming spikes. Only after they had been delivered did she realise that the largest natural expanse of water was a camel-filled oasis twelve hundred ells away to the south-east.

It was only with a flash of inspiration, under threat of being used as katana practice, that Admiral Ti hit upon the idea of mounting them on wheels, thus saving his neck and Tau's face.

Now the Murrhovian Empire owns the largest land-based Navy anywhere and is utterly impenetrable to attack.

Unless the wind is in the wrong direction.

222

at the rider. Not to be left out, Admiral Ti commanded a flotilla of sand yachts to follow.

Five seconds later a muffled struggle signified the horseman's disappearance under an eager platoon disguised as a small shrubbery and in less than a minute the General was staring at a small figure, and his horse, mummified in a tangle of ropes.

'Afternoon!' greeted Lehrt cheerfully. 'Nice day for a bit of a hack?'

'Mmmf mmmfmmmf!' answered the horseman in choicest Khambodian, the meaning fortunately obscured behind several hundred feet of bamboo rope.

Ti scowled irritably, cursing the fact that the wind had been in the wrong direction to give chase. Five sand yacht crews miserably tacked back to the gathered army under a hail of rude gestures from the lowest ranking privates.

Lehrt barked a few commands and some of the ropes were removed from their captive to reveal the swarthy mustachioed face of an extremely irritated Praquat, mumbling and spitting incomprehensibly. 'Out for a bit of a ride, eh?' asked Lehrt, attempting to appear casual. 'Going anywhere nice?'

Praquat stared around him, baffled by the unusual uniforms of what he had initially taken to be the Cranachanian Vice Squad. 'Could be,' he answered noncomittally, bursting to know why several hundred curiously armoured troopers were milling about in the middle of the Talpa Mountains.

'Travelled far today?' asked Lehrt, trying desperately to sound as if he was having a casual chat in some bar somewhere.

'Maybe,' answered Praquat, glancing over at the group staring at the six maps, scratching their heads.

'Come from anywhere nice . . . anywhere with a name?' questioned Lehrt, a note of pleading entering his voice.

'Mynymymm,' murmured the Khambodian, grinning as six fingers stabbed at six different parts of half a dozen conflicting maps, realigning them to point in an array of different directions.

'Heading anywhere special . . . ?'

'You lost? Need guide?' asked Praquat, suddenly thickening his accent and grinning hungrily. Over the years he had spent in the Auric Triangle offering guided tours around some of the less secret narcotic fields, Praquat had learnt that tourists had a better time if they could understand only about half of what he said. Eight years or so ago he had unceremoniously dumped his native Khambodian accent in favour of a subtle blend of Mynymymmian, D'vanouin and choicest gobbledegook. He was now the most popular guide in the whole of the Auric Triangle. 'Need guide?' he repeated, laying it on thick.

Lehrt shrugged and began investigating a chip in his fingernail.

'Thought so,' grunted the Khambodian. 'Good job you bump into me. I perfect guide. Untie me! Take you where you want to be, good price! Untie me!'

Within seconds Praquat was arranging an hourly rate for Imperial Army Guidance and within minutes he was heading off away from Fort Knumm on a several-hour detour around the local sights of interest, taking in fascinating rock formations and a stack of money.

Carefully steering Sir Taindeth away from Khar Pahcheeno's crop of poppies, Fhet Ucheeni led the vermin eradicator up the foot of Tor Tellini. Cranachan vanished from view as they rounded a small outcrop and stared at the cave entrance before them. It was exactly as Mhar-Rheanna had described it. A single-storey starter-cave with fresh-air frontage, offering commanding views south-easterly across an unspoilt valley. Large expansion potential. Perfect for those with a more reclusive streak or those willing to found a religious community.

The knight stared at the cave with a flurry of competing emotions. Excitement: the last dragon in the world and I'm going to kill it! Mine, mine, mine! Fear: what if it gets me first? Regret: why isn't anyone selling tickets? There should be crowds of thronging people here to witness his finest

224

moment of glory. Minstrels to sing his praises and write him into sonnets and lute songs; poets to capture the moment. Reporters to slam his face across the front page of the *Triumphant Herald* holding aloft the head of the beast before a cheering crowd. And printed tunic sellers . . . oh, the lost merchandising potential. Instead, it was just him and this bouncer. And the promise of rain.

His horse idly chewed at a clump of daisies, snorting with equine confusion as a small rosebud swivelled on its stem, turning slowly and staring up at him unblinkingly. One by one, other roses turned unnoticed and focused on the two mounted riders, transmitting muted thaumic signals into the cave, activating the recently installed saurian security system.

Sir Taindeth squinted at the cave entrance, assessing the size of dragon that would fit inside, contemplating which sword to use to deal the deadly blow – a number five iron, perhaps? Functional, a good chipper. Or should it be the number eight? Better balance, more powerful swing, perfect for hacking. A number two wood was right out. Not least because he'd left his lance at home. Well, he'd never had any cause to lance snakes. And he had never expected to have to deal with a dragon.

A rumble of thunder echoed up the valley, a meteorological knuckle-cracking as the weather readied itself for a damn good precipitation. As he rummaged in his caddy, there was rustle of undergrowth and a sudden shriek of alarm from Fhet Ucheeni to his left. Sir Taindeth looked up, right into the malevolently grinning jaws of the most enormous green dragon he had ever seen in his life. It was the only enormous green dragon he had seen in his life. His mind whirred in the nearest thing to professionalism it could muster. A number eight. Definitely a number eight. Possibly.

'Kill it! Kill it!' croaked Ucheeni through clenched teeth, not daring to move, quaking terror rooting him and his horse to the spot.

The dragon took a step forward and widened his grin,

casually allowing a waft of smoke to curl out of its nostril with lazy malevolence.

The weather could contain its excitement no longer. With a flare of shuddering lightning the heavens opened, spilling sheeting rain into the valley. Sir Taindeth cursed volubly above the roar of the downpour. *How* was he supposed to find his way into the stuff of legends if it was lashing down? It wasn't fair. Heroes were supposed to despatch dragons on beautiful sunny afternoons before adoring crowds of yearning maidens. It wasn't supposed to be like this.

Still, he thought, bring back the head and no-one could argue if he doubled his usual hire fee. He stared at the vast creature, translating it from ninety-odd foot of horribly beweaponed, fire-hurling lizard into a passport to the future, groat signs beginning to sparkle where scales should be. And through this greed-tinted haze he failed to notice anything unusual about the way each individual raindrop stopped an inch short of the dragon's scales and exploded in a tiny puff of steam.

Trying to look as if he knew precisely what he was doing – a feeble attempt to impress Fhet Ucheeni since every fraction of his attention was fixed firmly on the vast green foe – he began to whirl his number eight dragon-cleaver around his head, winding up the momentum necessary to hack clean through the monster's neck. It wouldn't do to get your sword stuck halfway (it was so undignified to have to put your foot on its thrashing neck and yank your sword out) – real heroes did it in one slice. Sir Taindeth gulped and ran forward, spinning and shouting, dodging a plume of spitting flame, blade glinting as it whirled towards the vast expanse of deadly serpentine neck.

And in the instant that Sir Taindeth's sword flashed through the projected empathic dragon with the barest of resistance, and total absence of blood, there were two mysterious sizzling pops. A jolt of tingling sapphire surged down the knight's sword as he unwittingly smashed the creature's aquaflector shield. Rain plummeted straight through the dragon, splashing heavily on the foliage beneath.

The second sizzling pop was followed by the appearance of what looked like a screaming dwarf falling fifteen feet out of thin air. Heavy boots smashed Fhet Ucheeni across the temple, removing him from his horse, and their owner landed tumbling and spitting in the undergrowth. The knight opened his eyes and looked around, terrified of the mess of chopped dragon he was sure he would see. He was startled to discern that his erstwhile employer had vanished from his horse, and turned into a spitting mud-clad dwarf, and worse still, the dragon was still there. After his sword had sliced clean through its neck? Could dragons regrow heads that quickly? If so, where did they keep their brains?

Several thousand feet above the baffled knight a single spot of rain squeezed itself out of a rain cloud and leapt into the freedom of the air, thrilling with the joys of free-fall, accelerating.

Sir Taindeth screamed, realising the truth in a flash. This creature standing before him was no ordinary dragon. Not a straightforward run-of-the-mill fire-breathing beastie with its feet firmly planted in the mortal plane. Oh no. This was different. *This* was a magical ghost-beast, capable of turning grown men into dwarves at the drop of a hat, able to sneak up behind him, possessed of the power to wink out of reality for the merest millisecond to dodge sword strikes . . .

The raindrop spun and cavorted mudwards, savouring the moment before it would hit the sodden soil in a gut-wrenching *splat*. In a flash it hit the smooth silvery surface of . . . metal? Things had changed since last time, it thought curiously, where had all the mud gone? And what about the proto-stream formed by its colleagues? . . . It knew it had been out at sea for a long time before evaporation had pulled it back into the water cycle, but this was ridiculous. The drop squirmed forward, edged along the slippery shimmerings of a wire and . . .

The dragon exploded.

Fragments of hypertaurus accelerator shattered, the power-amplifier shorted in a percussive blinding flash, its energy feeding back into the paired psychoterrin crystals.

There was a brief mauve detonation and the knight turned and fled in a hail of suddenly purple rain. Snatching his horse he stampeded away, far, far away.

Suddenly, there was a chain of rapid fire explosions throughout the valley as the rest of the security system ignited, scattering red petals and thorny stems in every direction, ricocheting noisily off any local boulders.

'Right outside the door!' grumbled Rutger, scowling at the rain and ducking a barrage of high-velocity stamens. ' "Trust me, I'm a sorcerer!" Bah! It's a bleedin' war zone!'

Grinning widely with the exquisitely earthy pleasure of boring holes through mile upon mile of solid granite, seven red-haired dwarves pushed onwards and downwards towards the surging power throbbing and pulsing through the thaumafer. It wouldn't have mattered what they were digging for. All that mattered was the digging. Well, that and the money they'd get for it. It was always the same with dwarves – give them a pickaxe, a picture of a fifteen-pound lump-hammer or even a sketch of a cold-chisel and they'd start dribbling with anticipation. In minutes their genes would be thrilling with countless generations of mining practice; their DNA wriggling and coiling in paroxysms of earth-moving delight. This was pathological job satisfaction with a total hold.

Mancini would never have noticed the series of explosions above the constant frantic hammering, the ringing of pick-axes and the incessant cheery 'hi-ho-ing' of the dwarves had it not been for the sea-scrole bawling telepathically at him from fifty feet above. Waves of alarm flashed through his brain as the scrole flopped in its bath, unable to see what was going on, incapable of interpreting the report of blasts.

The VET screamed at the dwarves to keep digging, which might be considered a mite unnecessary, turned on his heel and scrambled up the ladder out of the mine-shaft, into the back of the cave, questions in his head crowding and yelling for answers all the while.

'What's going on?' he shouted at a trembling Knapp, who

clutched at his sack as if it were a security blanket.

Mancini snarled and repeated the question into the bath, brow beetling.

'Doesn't sound pleasant!' answered the scrole, shrugging and waving a vaguely pointed corner indicating that the trouble was outside.

An incredibly wet, red-haired figure crawled unseen towards the cave entrance through sheeting rain and purple splattered foliage, muttering and complaining to itself about rain, war-zones, weather, fighting and the stupidity of trusting sorcerers.

Mancini sprinted to the cave entrance, dashed into the open and froze. Rain battered down on him as he blinked for a moment in the, comparatively, bright light, convinced that his dark-adjusted eyes were playing tricks. Purple? Everything can't be purple? He scurried back inside to fetch a raincloak.

Rutger broke cover, seizing his chance, and sprinted for the cave entrance. With a yelping curse he tripped on his beard and rolled behind a large mossy rock, nursing his cheeks.

Mancini reappeared, rubbed his eyes, blinked and shook his head to clear it of mind-numbing confusion. Purple rain and rose petals! It was like the debris of a weekend's psychedelic love-in festival. He trudged through the acres of mauve foliage, trying to make some sense . . . Suddenly his toe found the razor edge of a fragment of silver-grey metal. Wincing painfully and snarling a hail of choice Venashtian oaths, he bent to pick up the object.

In that instant Rutger was up and running, beard flung safely over his shoulder, vanishing deep into the shadow of the cave mouth, diving recklessly down the shaft.

An avalanche of terror ran tumbling cold through Mancini's heart as he recognised the metal shard for what it was. With disbelief he stared at the still warm base-plate capacitor of a hypertaurus accelerator. Series five. Exactly the same as the one he had used only yesterday. And unless he was entirely mistaken, over there, just behind that purple-dripping rhododendron lay a charged section of casing from the emp-power driver. All that remained of his PET dragon.

A rose petal fluttered before him. Oh! His best laid plants lay in tatters.

Suddenly he felt the utter agoraphobia of exposure grab at his throat. Bushes which milliseconds before were placid botanical specimens now sprouted malevolent eyes; boulders and rocks harboured spies with hex-ray spectacles, peering at him, examining his underwear. Paranoia seethed close to boiling as he whirled around and fled into the safety of his cave.

His cave. With his thaumafer. And his scrole and his power.

And his time running out . . .

Screaming into the back of the cave, his wet footprints perfectly masking Rutger's, Mancini skidded to a halt at the mouth of the mine-shaft and barked madly at the dwarves.

'Faster, you damn diggers! Faster!'

His words were answered by a roll of eight pick strikes.

Phlim drummed his fingers on the sneeke control pentagram, utterly sick to death of staring at the sphere and the tiny black and white image racing by within it. He'd only been at it half an hour, but after the excitement of the thaumatron and all the hours he'd put in over the last few days, well . . . when you've seen one sneeke's eye view of the Talpa Mountains, you've seen them all. Why Practz couldn't be happy with Rutger's reports over the crystal wristband he hadn't a clue.

'Back-up,' Practz had answered, dripping diplomacy. 'The sneeke will offer communications support in case of difficulty . . . and besides, with the temper Rutger left here in I'm certain he'll do something stupid.'

So Phlim was back driving the sneeke, staring dull-wittedly at whirring tundra, rocks and the odd startled lemming. Dull, dull, dull. Now if it was in colour it would be a bit better, or what about . . . His mind, as it wont to do, spun off at a hundred tangents, mentally attempting feats of fairly low-level technical wizardry, connecting this, rewiring that . . . Suddenly he had it! Leaping up from his stool he snatched a second image globe from a shelf, grabbed a loom of coloured cables and wired them into the back of the pentagram. With an expert flurry of wrist movements and only one singed finger he connected it into the thaumatron supply. There was a crack of static and the second globe lit. Two parallel images . . . much better. Much more enjoyable. Hmmmm . . . now what if . . . His hands whirred again, incanting a series of control programs into the vision processor, altering the left-hand sphere just a little. The image veered round nauseatingly, giving him a bout of vertiginous stomach churning. He edged the image back, tweaking, then suddenly it changed, swinging into view with incredible clarity, almost as if he was there. With one eye on each sphere he could see depth, distance . . . three dimensions. His hands whirred over the pentagram as he played with the sneeke, swooping in wild stall-turns, arcing wing-overs . . . and all in brand-new, bilious clarity.

He dived at the ground, thrilling perversely at the rushing focus-pulling upsurge of muddy roadway, shrieking wildly as he flipped out at the last moment and skimmed inches above the army-pounded surface, marvelling at the pin-sharp clarity of each of the hundreds of footprints whizzing by. A discarded newsparchment shot into view, rearing huge before his eyes, crumpled and . . .

What was he doing? What was he looking at? He'd become so totally engrossed in trivia and detail that he'd lost the overview – couldn't see the mud for the feet. He pulled the sneek up to ten feet and hovered, calming down. Ironically, the increased height allowed him to come back to earth.

With a shock he realised he had almost missed it. Hundreds of military footprints and the newsparchment. It was totally unreadable. Not because it had been trodden on in several places but because of the fact that it was written in utterly alien Murrhovian characters. It was the picture that caught Phlim's attention the most. An artist's impression of an Empress with a pack of piebald animals, holding a collection of wires, pentagrams and crystals. This was next to a reasonable portrait of Cheiro Mancini with the unmistakable sign of money on his head. Phlim put the information together. Tried it a different way round, rejected this and came up with a third conclusion. Disturbingly they all had the same macabre ring to them. The Murrhovian Imperial Army was running about in the Talpa Mountains with the express purpose of doing Mancini in.

Phlim squealed hoarsely and sprinted out of the room.

Practz, he had to tell Practz!

Several decades previously, when the threat of the Linguistics War had loomed omnipresent and thousands of peasants were in danger of being put to death for misuse of vowels and malicious subversion of the imperfect third person, Grand Wizard Prof. Phiynmn had been hard at work perfecting the most subtle of questioning techniques ever devised.

At times of acute crisis he could be heard stalking the corridors of Losa Llamas juggling sentence construction, reinventing adverb co-ordination and concocting heady cocktails of interrogatory euphemisms capable of sucking confessions out of the most reserved of reticent mouths. At the height of his verbal inquisitorial prowess, fellow Losa Llamans would blurt gabbled life stories in response to simple requests for, say, a cup of tea, or break down in floods of tears if asked the time. So honed were his catechismic skills that it was even rumoured Prof. Phiynmn could open the most densely padlocked, barred and bolted of safes armed with just his tongue.

It was an immense shame that Rutger had never met him.

'Er . . . d'you come here often?' he asked a dwarf as it hacked cheerfully away at solid granite with gleeful determination and a very large pickaxe. Plumes of red beard and crimson hair arced and thrashed in all directions.

'What's your favourite colour?' he whispered conspiratorially, barely audible over a cacophany of axe strikes and happy 'Hi-ho's'. 'What size shoes d'you take?' Still no answer.

Rutger growled. 'Find out everything you can about the mining operation.' he mimicked Practz. 'Ask questions. Get right to the very heart of it.'

It was hopeless. He'd been here the best part of half an hour and not one of them had so much as grunted a reply to his barrage of queries.

'Don't you ever stop digging?' he snarled in almost pleading frustration.

'Nope!' grunted Guthry, demonstrating the point with a flurry of ringing strikes.

The voice came as a shock, a brief, shimmering oasis of response in a dusty desert of clanging axes . . . or had it been a mirage? A desperate, eagerly sought answer supplied by his own pitiful mind? The dwarf hadn't stopped to answer, never flinched in its furious pounding, not a hiccup in its driving rhythm.

'Did you just say "Nope"?' asked Rutger. No answer. 'Why won't you answer? Please stop digging for a second!'

'Can't do that, boy!' said Guthry, between strikes. 'Gotta finish!'

'Finish what?'

'Diggin'!'

'For what?' pressed Rutger, suddenly amazed that he was getting some progress.

'Shoot! You ain't no dwarf! Could tell soon as I laid eyes on you! "That ain't no *real* dwarf," I said. Not with those fancy clothes an' them dainty hands!'

The mining ceased abruptly and seven sweating dwarves rounded on Rutger. Proph glared accusingly. 'You from th' Underground Revenue, eh boy? Well, you gotta mighty nerve showin' up round 'ere, stickin' yer nose where it don't belong. We's legit! Pays our taxes . . .'

'No, no!' protested Rutger. 'I'm not! I'm from . . . er . . .' Dare he risk attempting the truth? Would they believe him?

Rutger swallowed hard and began to explain, his mind spinning back across the miles to Losa Llamas, searching for help. Unaccountably, it dashed into the magic lantern cavern, hurling the doors open and tripping over a carpeted chair table, landing in front of the screen as a fountain of credits rolled upwards. Suddenly a plan hatched. 'Look, I really shouldn't tell you this,' he began, looking around as if shaft walls had ears. 'It could ruin the whole thing.' He pointed upwards. 'You've got to give me your word that you won't tell him anything that I'm about to reveal. It's so delicate, one word and . . . If my director finds out . . .'

'What you on about, boy? Where you from?'

'Ever heard of *Your Mortal Coil!*?' he asked nervously. Seven heads shook, dubious but interested.

Rutger rolled his eyes, feigning amazed shock. 'Where've you been all your lives? Down a hole . . . ? Oh. *Your Mortal Coil!* is watched by millions in Magic Lantern Palaces all over the civilised world. They, er, we catch famous people at grossly inconvenient times and bore them witless with elderly aunties recounting their lives and give them a red book at the end. All in 80mm Superthaumination.'

'What in tarnation d'you do that for?' snapped Proph, bewildered.

'Entertainment. People like to watch! I'm a researcher . . .' he lied wildly, pointing up again. '. . . And he's next!'

'Will we be on them newfangled Magic Lanterns, boy?' asked Guthry with a twitch of whiskery excitement.

'Steal yer souls, them things!' snarled Ghedd, spitting across the shaft in disgust.

'I'll have to ask the directo . . .' began Rutger.

'Why you down here talkin' t' us?' asked Proph, scowling suspiciously. 'You ain't from the Underground Revenue, y'say?'

'No, I told you! I need all the information you can give me on what he's like as a boss,' said Rutger.

Proph backed away, shaking his head. 'No questions 'bout money, or bonuses, or . . .'

'Of course not,' oozed Rutger. 'It's him I . . . er, the viewers want to know about. Little tiny trivial bits and bobs.

234

You know, things like what he's doing here in the middle of the Talpa Mountains getting you to dig holes through solid granite. Petty details and trifling minutiae such as how much longer you'll be digging here. Nonsense like what exactly it is that you're digging for and why . . .'

Questions tumbled out of Rutger's mouth as he fulfilled his dream, and miraculously the dwarves were willing to answer.

With only the minutest flash of regret he wished he'd told them he presented the show. But maybe he would get the chance to say it, just once . . . 'This is me shuffling off tilllll next week's mortal coil!'

He could almost hear the more or less trumpet-like theme tune blaring its discordant fanfare over a wall of applause. Oooooh, joy!

Suddenly there was the blood-curdling sound of a scream of frustration exploding from frenzied lungs. This was followed far too swiftly with a rabid sequence of livid, inhuman vociferation and the unmistakable shattering racket of a mainly metallic device colliding with the cave wall at a high rate of knots. Mancini had just discovered the fact that he was completely out of twenty-five microthaum divinators.

He had searched through every box of bits in sight, scoured the minutest corners of each tiny drawer, flinging contents over his shoulders in arcing component fountains, hunted feverishly through unfinished circuits and penta-grams in his chests and found . . . nothing. In a fit of madness he had even upended Knapp's sack, scrabbling desperately through the maggots, mouldy bread and a million other globs of unrecognisable bait in his desperate search. Without twenty-five microthaum divinators it would be impossible to achieve the necessary potential to fire the hypertaurus accelerator, and no amount of twisted bits of silver foil, sticky tape and string could ever hope to solve it. His PET dragon was dead. Totally, irrevocably non-functional. And it was impossible for him to build another.

Mancini was security-less, utterly without protection.

Anyone could just come stomping into the cave, snatch the sea-scrole, steal the damnation, kill him where he cowered. And all before he had a chance to sacrifice the damnation on a crystal altar and release the power trapped inside . . . His absolute power.

He felt naked, vulnerable, completely insecure . . . but there was a way to make him feel better – shout a lot.

After yelling at Knapp for making *such* a mess with the contents of his sack and stamping furiously on the heap, he screamed wildly as he sprinted over to the mine-shaft, snatched a rock from the ground and hurled it into the gloom, grinning as a muffled thud filtered into earshot.

'I can't hear enough hard work from you damn diggers!' he screeched. 'Dig faster! Faster!'

Granite splinters flew as the dwarves snatched their tools and bit once more into the rock.

Unseen, behind Mancini, in the far corner of the cave, the damnation's crimson eyes glared in arrogant malevolence from within the cage as its stygian upper lip curled back, exposing gleaming teeth in a sneer of victory. Its front paw lifted slowly, unsheathing an octet of razor death with the susurration of assassin's blades. Casually, almost pretentiously, it blew cold breath across the savage extensions and polished its gleaming claws on its chest fur, purring in short, contemptuous growls.

High in the Talpa Mountains, standing up to his thighs in thick, clawing heather, an old man was also snarling with fear-laden frustration. He glared at the contents of a carved triangular wooden box, cursing the Eye-Ching's mind-numbing pedantry for the hundredth time.

'Must you be so difficult!' he screamed after sixteen questions had slipped by uselessly.

The all-seeing eyeball blinked twice for 'No'.

'Yeah, yeah, I've got to ask the right questions. I know!' Miserably he stared across the bleak mountain landscape, shuddering as a cold front of rain slunk out of a valley ahead.

'Am I close to the stolen damnation?' he asked.

Blink.

Suddenly he thought of a different line of interrogation.

'As you are the *all*-seeing eye, can you answer questions concerning destiny? The future?'

The eyelid fluttered immodestly and blinked once.

Itto's grandfather's heart surged with acute coronary excitement.

'Will I find the damnation?' he asked desperately, feeling the weight of the future settle heavily on his shoulders.

Blink, answered the Eye-Ching ominously and began to close.

'Soon?' pleaded the old man. 'Will I find it soon?'

There was no reply. His twenty questions were up.

There was a brief, very brief, moment when Sir Taindeth considered the possibility of passing off an Ammorettan Death Lizard's head as that of the recently slain dragon, accepting the congratulatory pats on the back, wolfing down a hearty meal for the returning hero and vanishing with the dosh before anyone suspected a thing. And for a very fleeting period it *had* seemed like a very good idea. Then the problems began wheeling in to land, hopping and kicking up the whirling, nagging duststorms of doubt, shrieking mockery like vultures at a week-dead wildebeest.

First there was the small, but inescapable truth that no matter how many parchment-mache horns you stuck on; irrespective of the level of soot you jammed up each nostril and certainly discounting the numerous layers of green paint that would be required – even *with* all that, an Ammorettan Death Lizard's head looked nothing like a dragon's.

Secondly, there was the difficulty with a certain, undoubtedly furious Fhet Ucheeni who was bound to turn up at the most inappropriate of times.

And thirdly, there was the rabidly angry, rapidly growing throng of placard-waving fanatics surging up the valley hell-bent on destroying anything or anyone who looked even remotely dracicidal.

It was probably this last factor which had most bearing on

Sir Taindeth's executive, and timely, decision to chalk it down to experience and high-tail it out of the Talpa Mountains quick-sharp.

And he was not a moment too soon, for just as he vanished over the horizon heading for pests anew, the entire might of the Murrhovian Imperial Army determinedly entered stage left, their collective mind numbed after listening to a constantly babbled diatribe of falsified histories and snippets of dubious local interest.

'This way! Down here! Follow me, people!' shouted Praquat, beckoning encouragingly to the stomping troops and furiously tacking sand yachts. 'On your left you can see the Three Sacred Green Goats of Goohn!' He pointed at a triplet of insignificant, and far from sacred, mossy rocks, half submerged in ferns. 'Legend has it that if you can touch all three simultaneously without moving, then you will instantly inherit the gift of cheesemaking. Many have tried but without success. You, sir, you're a strapping lad. Would you like to see if there's any truth in the old myth? No? Well, over to your right . . .'

As Praquat's incessant rabbiting continued unchecked, spilling torrents of fatuous fabrications into any ear that would listen, General Lehrt's expression changed from one of extreme boredom, via flickering curiosity, to fully erect, bristling military attention. He wheeled his horse around and galloped frantically towards the flagyacht of Admiral Ti's landlocked fleet. In a flash he leapt off the horse, plunged through a tangle of unnecessarily complex rigging and grabbed the Admiral, pointing eagerly at a spot exactly ninety degrees to the historic site about which Praquat was expounding.

Far down a valley a crowd of placard-wavers surged over a small hillock and scrambled onwards.

'Well, gentlemen and . . . er, gentlemen,' twittered Praquat, 'that brings me to the end of your Talpa Mountain Tour. On behalf of your guide, me, I'd like to say what a pleasure it has been and I sincerely hope to see you in the future. Gratuities *will* be accepted gratefully, thank you.'

238

And with that, positioning himself to one side of the advancing army he stood hand outstretched, palm pointing expectantly skywards.

Far down the valley there was a distance-muffled cry of angst-filled alarm, a flurry of pointing fingers and the crowd hastened their pace, obliviously trampling rare crocuses and wild orchids which a week before they had been trying to save.

Praquat grumbled miserably to himself as the wished-for gleaming pile of monetary token gestures tossed cheerfully by the passing army failed to materialise. He spat at the receding back of the last yacht and dashed off to check on the state of Khar Pahcheeno's poppies.

Within the space of a few minutes, the valley was at an impasse, the air seething with irate chanting and vehemently yelled slogans ping-ponging from the righteously riotous Friends of the Worm to the head-scratching Murrhovian Imperial Army.

General Lehrt was utterly confused. It was ever so nice to be met by a welcoming committee bearing placards displaying their national serpentine emblem and declaring themselves to be friends . . . but why did they look so miffed?

Practz's face was highlighted blue as he leaned over and stared into the image on the hex-ray machine.

'But, what *is* it?' he asked. Thurgia and Wat shrugged. They'd been staring at the latest sea-scrole's secrets for nearly ten minutes and apart from the fact that it was a picture of a powerful-looking shaggy animal with far too many teeth and claws for its own good, they hadn't a clue.

'It could be the legendary katana-clawed wolverine from Upper Thhk,' suggested Wat. 'Amazing creature, lived in cracks in glaciers . . .'

'Yes, *very* interesting!'

'. . . and used its claws as ice-picks . . .'

'Quiet, Wat!' snarled Practz, struggling to access the bit of information chewing at the back of his mind, the feeling that he had seen this thing before.

'. . . diet of yetis and snow geese . . .'

'Shut up!'

'Only trying to help . . .' grumbled Wat miserably.

Where had he seen it? It was a glimpse of more than one of them . . .

Practz's wrist beeped urgently.

There was a frantic dashing of feet outside, a screech of deceleration, and then the door burst open under the momentum of a panting Phlim.

'Army! . . .' he croaked. 'Mancini . . . price on his head . . .' His lungs gulped in air desperately, then he stopped, coughed, blinked and stared disbelievingly at the hex-ray screen. '. . . and one of *them*!'

'What's Mancini doing with a legendary katana-clawed wolver . . .'

'Shut up, Wat!' snarled Practz, his wrist beeping again as he whirled on Phlim, strafing him with questions. 'What army? Who? Why?'

'Stolen from under the nose of Empress Tau,' spluttered Phlim, pointed fixedly at the screen, his eyes peeling with alarm bells. 'Mancini did it!'

Practz's wrist warbled a discordant bleep of irritation. The wizard tugged back his sleeve past his wrist abacus and stared at a tiny crystal on a band. 'What d'you want?' he bellowed at an image of a fuzzy red beard with eyes, clinging to one of the ladders halfway down the mine-shaft.

'Well, thank you *very* much! If that's your attitude I'm not sure I want to . . .'

'Rutger, *please* tell us!'

'Well,' said the face on Practz's wrist, creasing into a juvenile grin of pride, speaking in a thin imitation of Rutger's voice, 'I told them I was a reporter for, you'll never guess! For *Your Mortal Coil!* and guess what? Go on! Guess! Well, they believed me! Isn't that great! Hee hee! Fell for it! So *I* said "Tell me everyth . . ."'

'Get to the point, Rutger,' growled Practz, his thoughts whirling in a hurricane of confused fear. 'Or I might just leave you there.'

240

'Keep your cloak on,' squeaked Rutger thinly. 'There's seven dwarves here digging for one of those thaumy thingies . . .'

'We *know* that, dammit! Why?'

'Mancini wants the power . . .'

'Give me strength!' snarled Practz, his eyes rolling frustratedly heavenwards. 'What for?' he yelled at his wrist.

'Something to do with a sick dog,' answered Rutger.

'What?' shrieked everyone at Losa Llamas.

Three hundred feet below Rutger's toes a monitoring thaumometer needle twitched sharply and bent itself against the stops at maximum deflection.

'Yeah!' continued Rutger in cheerful unawareness. 'He's got this dog thing in a cage and the dwarves reckon he keeps pacing up and down, staring at it muttering things about it all being so much better soon.'

Suddenly Phlim grabbed hold of Practz's wrist and dragged him round to the hex-ray screen.

'Is *that* it?' yelled the Technical Wizard, facing the crystal wristband to the image.

'Now look here!' came the tetchy thin reply. 'What you doing sending me miles across the Talpa Mountains, risking my life, sticking itchy fluff all over my face if you had a picture of it all the time? I'm not happy . . .'

'I take it that's a yes.'

In the bottom of the mine-shaft there was a growing whining sound and with a plaff of wooden casing and shattering mechanics the thaumometer exploded. Over the sound of seven pounding axes it didn't stand a chance of being heard.

'Too right it's a "yes"!' ranted Rutger. 'How dare you . . .' Practz clapped his free hand over the ranting Rutger and stared white-faced at Phlim.

'I can't believe it!' he croaked as his mind hit recall, spinning back through trivia, retrieving the scrole in the lantern cavern. Rewind. Stop. Play. A hundred screaming creatures surged demonically towards the chanting octave of primordial wizards. Four thaumafers erupted in a quartet of blinding light and a hundred throats used to issuing countless decibels of blood-curdling banshee shrieks yelped in protest.

'He is going to resurrect them,' whimpered Practz, his knees suddenly having the urge to quiver uncontrollably.

'What's that?' shouted Thurgia, suddenly interested in the mention of a 'resurrection'.

One of the septet of picks swung through the splinter-filled air, swooping through one hundred and fifty degrees of arc, striking the tiniest split end of a hair-line fracture. The axe's beaten metal tip sent focused shock waves rattling percussively through the last ten feet of granite, weakening the countless-century-old geothaumal containment field.

'Rutger,' shouted Practz at his wrist. 'Rutger! You've got to stop the dwarves!'

'Oh, back, are you?' snapped the thin reply. 'Not good manners to slam your hand over my face when I'm talk . . .'

'Listen to me!' yelled Practz. 'If that thaumafer's breached . . .'

There was a flurry of static on Rutger's wrist crystal, wiping the screen and distorting the audio signal momentarily. The message came across as, 'Listen to me!. . . fat . . . on of a bitch . . .'

Rutger didn't have a chance to reply. Below him the ladder shook as seven pairs of tiny booted feet began to pound their way up and out screaming 'Abandon pit!'. The bottom of the mine-shaft twitched and shuddered like a stone troll wracked by nightmares, bulging uncontrollably as immense geothaumal forces fought for supremacy. In a second eight pairs of boots were scrambling upwards, the eighth pointedly ignoring a battery of thin, panicky requests to tell him 'What the hell's going on!'

A single tongue of crimson flame lashed through a breach in the containment field, spitting and fizzing erratically, then vanished, leaving a dark subterranean rumble echoing below.

Mancini shrieked, dropped the half-completed iguana circuit he'd been stripping of six microthaum divinators and hurtled wildly towards the mine-shaft.

'What have you done?' he screamed as a series of eight dwarves launched themselves out of the hole.

At the bottom of the pit the tongue lashed out again, this time seeming to know where it had to strike, thrashing at tiny flaws, striking a million minuscule weaknesses, flailing at microscopic fissures in a wild crimson frenzy. The rumble increased; an immense flexing of immeasurable effort in a vast power struggle. And with a seismic scream of releasing energy the granite geothaumal containment field lost.

Rutger pummelled at his crystal wristband, cursing as it squeaked irritably at him, swearing at the crackling red static. With a flash and a tirade of Practz's favourite oaths it flashed on.

'. . . appened? What's going on?'

Rutger stared at Practz's tiny image and fought to keep his voice steady above the roar of terrathaums. 'Ha! Practz, sir, er. What would happen if, say, er, perhaps I didn't manage to stop the dwarves? What would happen? And would it affect my chances of ever getting a promotion?'

'What's that noise?' asked Practz.

'Ooooh, static, I should think. Nothing to worry about. Well, what would happen if the thaumafer *was* just broken into just a teeny weeny bit, sort of, hmmm?' wheedled Rutger, cringing.

'Usual sort of thing that happens when countless terrathaums of absolutely corrupting power are loosed on an unsuspecting world . . . Why?'

'Ahem. Would it, perhaps, look a little like that? Maybe?' He held his wrist up. There was a thin scream of terror, then silence.

'Practz? . . . Practz? Cooee? You still there?' whimpered Rutger in the cave.

'Practz? . . . Practz?' shouted Wat, rattling the shoulder of the Thaumaturgical Physicist's unconscious body. Nervously he tapped his cheeks in an attempt to rouse him.

'Stand back,' commanded Phlim, conjuring several gallons of iced water out of his sleeves. 'There have been times when I've wanted to do this *so* much.' He grinned and disassembled the anti-gravity spell with a wrist flick.

Practz shrieked a host of obscenities, leaping up from the growing puddle and staring at his wrist in disbelief.

Phlim grabbed Wat's shoulder, spinning him round. 'C'mon!' he barked, all trace of frivolity gone. 'We've got some work to do.' And in a flash they were gone, a trail of wet footprints fading towards the door.

'Thurgia! Fetch me that Map of the Thaumafers,' croaked Practz, dripping. 'Fast. Now! Yesterday!' he demanded, his voice rising shaky octaves with each snapped command. 'Oh. And bring me some willow bark. I'm getting a migraine.'

'Greetings. O welcoming committee of Cranachan,' began General Lehrt, spurring his horse a few steps towards the seething throng of anti-dragon-slayers. Placards waved wildly, bristling like some angry giant spiny porcupine. A hail of abuse and a few rocks were spat back.

Lehrt squinted over his shoulder. He knew the Cranachanians had some peculiar customs but was *this* how they welcomed strangers? Should he hurl back a stone in acknowledgement? Would it be deemed impolite not to?

He stared at the most vocal member of the throng, correctly judged her expression to be one of extreme displeasure and began to dismount. With a grin of acute diplomacy he grabbed a large stone, flinging it at the woman in the ferocious woollen cap and matching green cardigan. The diplomatic projectile arced through the thin mountain air with a slight whistle and struck her with a resounding crack on the forehead.

At that precise instant the ground seemed to shudder. The mob of protestors stared wildly around, suddenly quivering, unsure of what to do. Seething with indignation, Mrs Beece leapt up off the ground, rubbing her forehead, waving her 'Save the Dragon' placard and yelling. 'It awakes! It witnessed the act of violence and stirs! It wants us to fight!'

'Er, excuse me?' said a man waving a 'Stop the Saurian Slaughter!' banner. 'Have you perchance noticed that we are facing an army?'

'The slogan is mightier than the sword! Right will conquer all!' shrieked Mrs Beece, surging with high-octane righteousness.

'Are you sure they've come here to kill the dragon?' asked the man trembling as he looked at the massed army. 'I mean, really certain?'

'Of course! They're Murrhovian!' she shouted, as if it were a crime in itself, spitting the word with acute distaste.

'So what?'

'Have you never heard of the things they do with dragon's teeth?' she shrieked, rounding on the man, her fiery eyes blazing. 'Aphrodisiacs, erotic balms and potions that give the word "sex" an entirely new dimension! It's disgusting!'

'What sort of new dimension?' he asked, raising his eyebrows with mounting interest.

He never found out. At the instant that he was about to be torn off a strip 'for even thinking about sex at a time like this!' the side of Tor Tellini shuddered as a series of crimson cracks appeared, spreading and widening like an enormous blood-shot eye first thing in the morning.

Terrathaums erupted skyward, gushing eddying swirls of power, blasting a ten-foot hole through the side of the mountain and witnessing sunlight for the first time in eighty-five thousand centuries. A crimson fountain spewed thousands of feet into the air.

The vast majority of the placard-wavers screamed and ran.

'The dragon has been disturbed! A cry for help!' shrieked Mrs Beece joyously.

'Cry for help? . . . I hate to sound like I'm wimping out of anything, or making excuses or the like, but . . .' began the man, trembling. 'Do you *really* think that something capable of breathing *that* much fire is actually in need of *our* help?'

The woman turned on him, screaming. 'The most powerful of beasts has its weak spot! We must protect it!' And with that she wrestled herself from his grip and sprinted towards the cave mouth, placing herself between the 'dragon' and the entire Murrhovian Imperial Army.

Inside the cave the damnation could barely control its

excitement. It leapt and cavorted in the confines of its cage, thrilling as the power surged around it, crackling off its fur, warming its very bones.

Watched by a terrified clump of quivering dwarves hiding behind a large pile of granite chippings and an equally petrified Knapp attempting to climb inside his sack, Mancini tugged a large cloth off a device squatting in the corner. Its four legs were attached to flat skis of wood with short lengths of string and rose up to what looked like a barbecue grill. Suspended from this swung two large pink crystals in an adjustable harness.

Feverishly, the thought of unrivalled power surging through his brain faster than the worst bout of acute gold fever, Mancini grabbed the damnation's cage and hurled it onto the device, wincing only slightly as it trembled precariously. Then he began to shove the whole thing towards the throbbing eruptions of energy surging from the mine-shaft. Whether it was simply reflected light or something far, far more deeply fundamental Mancini didn't care, but the pink psychoterrin crystals began to glow, their intensity pulsing stronger as they neared the shaft mouth.

Knapp peered out of his sack and wished he had a very large sofa to hide behind.

Mancini's face arched into a greedy grin as the damnation whined and shrieked. 'Ha! You've guessed, have you!' shouted the VET. 'You're my passport to power!'

His thoughts scrolled backwards as he chanted evilly,

> 'Powyr from ye rocks and,
> Fohcuss threw ye stone,
> Onto ye boddey of ye damned-nation.'

'Don't worry, you snivelling creature!' he yelped as he showed the platform forward. 'This won't hurt a bit!'

Despite the fact that the Eye-Ching had prophesied that he was close to the damnation and that he would find it, Itto's grandfather hadn't expected such a clue as to its location. Balls of piebald fluff hidden under masses of vegetation –

perhaps; eight-clawed footprints glistening in tiny areas of soft ground – maybe; but continent-shaking blasts of crimson geothaumal energy erupting skywards in such an illuminating manner, pinpointing the spot like some Neon from the Gods – well, no.

Recalling an ancient Murrhovian proverb about never peering into the buccal cavities of horses bearing presents, he yanked his robe up around his waist and with a surge of adrenaline hurtled off towards a previously insignificant cave entrance in the side of Tor Tellini.

One stubby forefinger followed the faint tracks of the maze of thaumafers on the *User's Guide* whilst the other had its fingernail chewed off in a flurry of nervousness. The finger pored over the scrole desperately, tracing the eastern network around Tor Tellini with the avidity of an expert forger.

Suddenly it stopped. A single thaumafer snaked underground and passed directly beneath the Tor.

Holding this finger where it was, Practz wrenched the second out of his mouth and began to trace thaumafers from the west, spitting fragments of nail across the cavern.

In seconds his fingertips met across the Tor. With a squeal he leapt upright, snatched the scrole up and dashed out in search of Phlim, a glimmer of hope spluttering in his kidneys.

In a cave a few minutes' mad dash from where Practz was now sprinting, the bees of industry were swarming. Psychic screwdrivers whirred eagerly; large metallic rods arced huge plumes of silver sparks; chants and incantations fused alloy to component and strap to chassis. Phlim directed three technicians, yelling impatiently if the wrong value divinator was delivered or if a hypertaurus accelerator was dropped. Sweat seeped from his brow with the strain of concentration. Nobody had ever attempted to manufacture two backpack thaumatrons at the same time. And right now, Wat was wishing that was still the case.

'No! Blue to green, *yellow* to mauve!' shrieked Phlim, brushing at his hair with fraught desperation. 'Have you forgotten everything I told you about Quantum Thaumics? Polarity is vital! One twist in the destiny loom netting and you'll unstick all your gluons,' he snapped, snatching three screws from an emotion-proof box and forcing himself to feel calm.

Wat swore, held the dark visor before his eyes, raised a thaumic lance and reattached the wires in a flurry of sparks.

Suddenly the door to the workshop burst open and Practz lurched in panting and waving the scrole. 'I've got it, I've got it!' he shrieked breathlessly, screeching to a halt before Phlim. 'One thaumafer . . . just one, that's all. Mancini's placed all his eggs on one conduit. Are you listening? I've worked it all out. Me! Put that . . . that thing down and pay attention. Phlim. Phlim? Hello, you listening?'

The Technical Wizard took three cross-headed screws out of his mouth and looked at the red-faced head of Losa Llamas. 'Yes, heard every word crystal clear,' he said calmly, put two of the screws back in his mouth and returned to the mass of untidy high-energy thaumodynamics on the table. With a flurry of efficiency and a whirring psychic screwdriver the screw was tightened down.

'Well?' squeaked Practz, hopping up and down impatiently. 'What about it?'

Phlim shrugged with highly concentrated nonchalance as he wound another screw in.

'We can stop him!' ranted Practz, tugging on Phlim's sleeve as he tightened the last screw.

'Yes, I know we can stop him. Given a following wind, a stack of luck and a total lack of interruptions we can,' snapped the Technical Wizard suddenly, his aura of calm shattered. The screw picked up on the change in mood, turned crimson and hurled itself out of the hole, catapulting madly across the cavern.

'Duck!' yelled Phlim as it ricocheted off the far wall, bounced off the doorframe and vanished under a table in a clatter of sparks.

'What the . . . ?' whimpered Practz with his hands clutched firmly around his head.

'Psychic screws,' snarled Phlim. 'This batch are so sensitive. It'll take that one weeks to calm down. I hate cross-head screws. Just hope there's enough left to finish off.'

'Finish off what?' blustered Practz.

'Backpack thaumatrons. We'll need them for the mining.'

'Mining?' shrieked Practz, unable to believe his ears. None of them knew how much time they had before the nastiest army in eighty-five thousand centuries was loosed on them and here was Phlim proposing a couple of mining expeditions as if it was a sunny afternoon.

'Have you taken leave of what little sense you have ever had?' squealed Practz, turning red. 'This is no time to be dabbling with your own pet projects. While you have been in here wasting time *I* have been working out a way of trying to stop that madman!'

A boxful of screws started to vibrate on the table.

'I have worked out a plan,' declared Practz. 'All we have to do is . . .'

'Pull the plug out,' interrupted Phlim.

'Ahhh, you know,' spluttered Practz, deflating rapidly.

'Yes,' spat Phlim, barely disguising his irritation as he turned back to the thaumatron.

There was a short pause filled with the sounds of industry and the whirring of Practz's brain.

'So why are you messing about with these things instead of saddling the horses and shoe-ing the carts, or whatever it is you're supposed to do?' he asked.

Phlim turned around and stared at Practz. 'How do you pull the plug on a thaumafer?'

'I . . . er . . .'

'Where do you find thaumafers?'

'Well . . .'

'How much magic is there in one?'

'I don't know!' growled Practz. 'You're the Technical Wizard, you're supposed to know these things.'

'I do. Wandbrake. Buried in several hundred feet of granite. And haven't a clue,' scorned Phlim. 'In that order.'

'I think this is ready to try,' said Wat, screwing the back

249

cover onto a thaumatron with a whirring psychic screw-driver.

'Yeah, sure,' grunted Phlim absently, his mind fogged by Practz's ridiculous naivety. There were times when he wondered about the old goat's mental prowess . . .

Wat shrugged the thaumatron onto his back, fired up the magi-kinetic field and increased the flux potential, thrilling as it began to glow pale aquamarine.

'But what's that got to do with thaumatrons?' stuttered Practz.

The tone of Wat's thaumatron changed from a hum to a deep throb, aquamarine glow turning to blue then purple, like spring daylight dissolving into a discontented winter night.

Gradually Phlim became alarmingly aware of the noise, the terrifying pulsing throb of contained magic building up inside an enclosed space.

'What are you doing?' he screamed, 'It's going into overload!'

Wat cast a hail of sub-commands and cascades of wrist-flicking prestidigitations, panic rising with the decibels. Phlim stared horrified above Wat's head. By now there should have been swarms of agitated purple hornets hovering in a cloud of magic ready to be controlled and channelled for a multitude of thaumic purposes. But there was nothing, simply clear air almost totally unensorcelled.

Fifteen kilothaums surged about inside the thaumatron, whirring and fighting for escape, seconds away from critical . . .

Desperate beads of sweat cascaded down Wat's forehead, terror rising, a faint hint of burning rubber and singed ozone filling the air. Wildly he mentally leapt through all the prespell checks, his arms flailing. Phlim wheeled around gesturing frantically for everyone to take cover. They already had.

Wat's left hand dropped almost to his waist, mentally gripping a bar, his thumb arched over the psychic button on the end. Purple fire was turning to a blazing midnight . . . He

250

depressed his thumb and in his psyche released the lever. Eighteen kilothaums of ensorcelled purple fury blasted out of the thaumatron looping over his head, exploding from his extended right finger with a splitting crack. And a swirling cloud of dust filled the room.

Even before the snowstorm of dandruff-fine granite settled over the room Phlim was tearing Wat off a strip.

'You should have checked it . . .' screamed Phlim.

'I . . .'

'. . . should've run a diagnostic nano-sprite test . . .'

'It . . .'

'. . . could've at least made certain of . . .'

'It was user error!' shouted Wat. 'My fault, okay! I'm sorry!'

'Sorry! *Sorry!* You've almost destroyed the place!' Phlim cried, pointing at the ten-foot-deep hole in the floor. 'What the hell did you do?'

At this point Wat looked extremely embarrassed and crossed his toes, pretending he hadn't heard Phlim's question.

'What the hell did you do?' yelled the Technical Wizard once more.

'Forgot . . .' whimpered Wat.

'Forgot what?'

'I forgot to let off the wandbrake, okay? Happy?' Wat yelled, angry at his own stupidity being so publicly and dramatically demonstrated, especially in front of the Head of Losa Llamas. 'It's easy to do . . .'

Practz's face executed a change that Wat had never expected to see. It was crimson with rage, seething with wild vexation, steam almost exploding from ears and nostrils, but then he glanced at the hole, stared at Wat and grinned, all traces of irritation vanishing in a flutter.

'Oh, I see,' he said to Phlim looking up from the steaming hole.

'Mining. Yes. er, do carry on,' he added and ran out of the door.

251

'No! No! You've got it all wrong!' shouted General Lehrt to the small clump of murderously fanatical protestors sitting in front of the cave, waving placards furiously. 'Tell them we don't do *anything* with dragon's teeth any more!' he snapped at a hastily selected trooper, the nearest thing they had to a translator. He shouted a series of shaky conversational Cranachanian phrases, supplementing them with a string of over-exaggerated semaphoric gestures and, for the sake of his neck, hoped for the best.

A shrieked reply soared defiantly across the valley from the large woman in green. To the interpreter it could have meant anything from, 'We are prepared to discuss terms and conditions relating to your withdrawal from Cranachanian territory in return for the safety of the dragon,' to 'Up yours, dogbreath!' via 'Your mother was rabbit pâté!' It was only the accompanying flurry of obscene hand gestures that allowed the quaking trooper to conclude it was option two.

Lehrt turned an angry red as one last strand of diplomacy strained desperately to prevent the eruption of an inter-kingdomnal incident. 'We only want Mancini and the damnation!' he yelled.

It was the height of misfortune really. The interpreter tried his best, but armed with a series of fluent questions, such as 'How do I get to the swimming baths?' or 'How much is that doggy in the window?', Lehrt's last statement ended up as, 'I'll personally spread your livers on the barbecues of Hell, just see if I don't!'

There was a blood-curdling scream of inarticulate fury and the en-rainbowed warriors rushed the army, sharpened placard poles shouldered and fixed.

'Rutger! Rutger, come in!' shouted Practz, glaring at the stubbornly static-ridden crystal strapped to his wrist. It was becoming more and more apparent by the minute that contact with the undercover dwarf had been totally severed. According to Phlim it was 'a series of powerful, random fluctuations in the geothaumal fall-out giving rise to excess presto particle production affecting reception'. Practz preferred using the shorter, but less accurate word 'interference'.

'Rutger!' shrieked Practz, banging the wristband on the table. What was going on? He needed to know. If only he could see what was happening.

Suddenly he clicked his fingers and sprinted off down the corridors of Losa Llamas, twisting and turning expertly, screeching to a halt outside the sneeke control room. Now *this* was thaumatronics he understood.

In a matter of seconds he had fired up the receivers and was thrilling at the added joy of binocular vision, swooping the sneeke through the Talpa Mountains, powering on towards Tor Tellini. Unfamiliar territory surged by, feeling as if it was comfortable inches beneath his feet, changing from harsh heather to gentler lower altitude flora, talpine crocuses and idlewhites. Then, in a flash of geography he was in the valley, his heart surging as he saw the powering plume of crimson erupting skywards and spotted the cave entrance. For a second the shock of the view beat his vertigo to the tape.

But only a second.

Heaving suddenly he dropped altitude and, with only the fewest of static snowstorm flashes, swooped over what looked like a vast army being set upon by a gang of frantic placard-waving protestors and plunged into the snug darkness of the cave.

Rutger squatted behind the pile of granite chippings alternatively cursing the wristband for not working and calling blasphemies down on Practz for not answering. All around him geothaumal fall-out was sprinkling stalagmite seedlings on the cave floor. Tiny etiolated rock columns pushed their way upwards, swirling with unsteadily circling tips. He swore unashamedly as he bashed the wristband, blaming it for the sudden breakdown. Absently he brushed an insect from his face.

Cheiro Mancini stood in the middle of the cave, the end of his makeshift sacrificial platform inches away from the seething torrent of energy blasting from the ground. The air was saturated with magic, every movement releasing coruscating flares of static sparks. All he had to do was push the damnation into the uproar, focus the power onto its body and . . . victory! From a safe distance the sea-scrole telepathed encouragement, flopping and squirming in its bath. Knapp had, somehow, finally managed to fasten the catch on his sack. He peered out in whimpering terror.

Rutger swept the insect away again and irritably prised the back off the wristband. There was a thin squeak of alarm, a buzz and the insect was back, staring up at Rutger with its head on one side, whining for attention. A tangle of unidentifiable components bulged disturbingly out of the back of the wrist crystal set, smugly defying interpretation and, worryingly for Rutger, repair. He could see nothing wrong with it, all looked fine. It was. Rutger, it has to be said, was not at all aware of the effect which high-velocity presto particles had on the reception of tight-beam signalling devices. The insect buzzed in front of his face again, seeming to frown at him from a pair of bulbous eyes. 'Go away. Shoo!' he grunted.

Dozens of miles away Practz moved his hands swiftly over the sneeke control pentagram. The insect shook its head. A stereo image of Rutgerian puzzlement appeared in Losa Llamas. How could he get through to that magic-lantern obsessed idiot?

In a flash Practz clicked his fingers, prestidigitated furiously and somehow managed to make the sneeke stare imploringly at Rutger. It edged backwards away from him wagging its antennae and whining pitifully.

Suddenly the insect changed in Rutger's mind, growing ears, a black shining nose and oh! those expectant eyes . . . In an instant the sneeke had become Flossie the Wonder Hound. It was that imploring look.

The diminutive Losa Llaman began to follow, eagerly crawling forward a few feet. Then he frowned and stopped, scowling suddenly at the sentient insect, recalling a terrifying episode when Flossie had been kidnapped by the evil Count Blackfinger and had been hypnotised and commanded to betray her owner . . .

'Hold on. Friend or foe?' snarled Rutger suspiciously. It could be an evil scheme to trap him!

Practz slapped his forehead in despair, vowing to severely restrict Rutger's time in front of the magic lantern. Nervously he peered over his shoulder, afraid to admit that he had actually seen the kidnapping episode. He chanted a series of guttural commands, making the sneeke flip over onto its back and wave its legs endearingly. Rutger's eyes lit up moistly. 'Had to make sure, Flossie. Nothing personal.' He whispered to himself, following the sneeke once more, although where it would lead him he hadn't a clue. Would somebody need rescuing from a rock fall or an avalanche . . .

A shriek of pent-up excitement erupted from Mancini's lips as he edged the damnation nearer to the mine-shaft.

Away behind another pile of granite chips a septet of dwarves quivered in uncertain terror. 'Go on!' snapped Guthry anxiously.

'Why me?' shouted Proph over the roar of energy.

'Shoot! You struck this deal! Go on! 'Fore it's t' late!'

With a scathing tirade of dwarvish, Proph headed miserably over towards the crimson silhouetted figure of Mancini and the howling damnation. Quivering in a way totally unsuitable for a dwarf of Proph's experience, he coughed twice for Mancini's attention, swore and reached out to tug on his cloak.

The VET's eyes burned and smouldered with the fires of the greed within. He was so close to having it all! Without a trace of anything remotely resembling regret he looked back scornfully on his feeble past, scraping a living from the scrapings off the Trans-Talpino Trade Route, living from hand to mouth . . . Well, no more animals after this one. A final despatching and the future would be as rosy as he ordered it to be.

He gripped the frame and sneered at the damnation.

Suddenly, sparks of red ochre shorted between a dwarvish hand and his cloak, stabbing Mancini in the thigh. He wheeled around wincing, towering over the red-haired midget.

'You damn digger! Get out of my sight!' screamed Mancini, power crazing his mind.

Proph stared up at him, holding out his palm. 'Wages!'

Mancini, framed by a corona of crimson, hurled back his head and laughed the shrieking hyenic laugh of a power-corrupted madman. 'Do not concern me with such trifles! You have been useful, get out before you bore me!' Mancini slapped Proph across the face, sending him spinning over the pile of granite chips to land with a grunt on top of Rutger.

The sneeke whirled and buzzed excitedly, flashing its attention from Rutger to the dwarves, and pointing outside with its antennae. Amazingly, Rutger understood almost immediately, grinning happily as the sneeke mugged furiously. Well, he *always* knew what Flossie was trying to say.

'Double your wages if you come with me now!' shouted Rutger to Proph, straining to be heard above the rushing din of the geothaumal release. Seven heads nodded and dashed out of the cave behind Rutger, hot on the wings of the sneeke.

Mancini pushed the table forward. The front edge of the frame touched the tower of power, disappearing for a second into the crimson oblivion before flaring violently, igniting in a flash of barbecueing wood. In a second the whole frame was ablaze.

'Save it!' yelled the sea-scrole inside Mancini's head. He screamed and panicked, snatching the damnation off the table of cinders and making a wild grab at the pair of scorching psychoterrin crystals. With a yelp he hurled the burning rocks to the ground, sprinted across the cave and plunged his hands into the bath. Wisps of steam rose from the water.

'What did you make me do that for?' he shouted at the sea-scrole.

'Fohcuss threw ye stone!' came the reply in the front of his mind. '*Focus*! Remember? Not hurl the thing into the flames and hope!'

Mancini smashed his fists against the bottom of the bath and released a hail of curses.

It was agony. Such a painfully trivial frustration. Ultimate power out of reach for lack of a non-inflammable hostess trolley.

A mountainous slag heap of unidentifiable valve fragments, chanting boards, coils and high-velocity presto particle accelerometers had been tossed over Phlim's shoulders in his desperate search through the Losa Llamas Projects cupboard – the thaumic equivalent of that cardboard box stuffed full of old switches and broken electric motors that lurks long-forgotten in the shed. One and a half semi-completed devices sprouted gay fronds of curling cable and lay miserably discarded on the bench. Next to them, in an equal state of dejection, strings of calculations lurked – scribbled on parchment, crossed out, smudged, reworked and eventually abandoned.

'It's no good!' sulked Phlim beneath a single swaying tallow candle as Wat entered and blinked at the chaos. 'No good at all!'

'Eh? No, it's fine! Filled the hole in easy!' replied Wat.

Phlim wheeled round on his stool and stared at the technician. 'Seven and a half dozen terrathaums! Can you believe that!' he wailed.

Wat furrowed his brow and counted on his fingers, mouthing as he did so. 'No. Six and a bit (remainder one) gigathaums and three buckets of concrete. It wasn't as deep as it looked. Of course it's not set properly, yet.'

'It's too big. Eight orders of magnitude bigger than anything I can make out of that junk!' wailed Phlim, wallowing in defeat.

It dawned on Wat that perhaps he wasn't talking about floor repairs after all.

' "You're the Technical Wizard! Think of something!" ' said Phlim in a passable mockery of Practz. 'I told him we shouldn't have gone for miniaturisation. Look at where we've ended up! I can't even shut off seven and a half dozen terrathaums of raging energy. Not with a backpack wand-brake!'

'Oh!'

'Need at least the pair out of the main thaumatron coil to have a hope, and even then, if my guesstimates are wrong . . . !'

'Er!' grunted Wat helpfully.

'What if there's an emergency diverter on the thaumafer trunking?' whined Phlim, locked in a deep internal argument. 'It would be madness to shut down . . . !'

'Why?' asked Wat.

Phlim fixed Wat with a wild glare, waving with ripening fields of scorn. 'The shut-off sites are miles away! Are you going to lug hundreds of pounds of thaumatronics across the Talpa Mountains without dropping it, eh? I couldn't even lift the damned thing, remember!'

'We could use a cart,' whimpered Wat defensively. 'Load them with pulleys . . .'

Phlim's eyes glazed over and his voice faded away. '. . . Couldn't even lift the damn . . .'

'If we wrap them up carefully they should be alright . . . are you feeling okay?'

Phlim stared at Wat, sizing him up, estimating as his mind whirred back to before his holiday, the work, the effort of lifting tons of thaumatronics into pinpoint positions and shutting down the thaumatron. . . Suddenly with a flash of gleaming eye, he snatched a sheet of parchment, grabbed a quill, stabbed it into the ink pot with deadly accuracy and began scribbling manically. Figures surged from the scratching tip . . . laden mass . . . acceleration due to gravity . . . thaumic output coefficient . . . power conversion . . . wind chill factor . . . plimsoll line. He paused only once to snatch two tomes from a shelf and feverishly cross-reference the peak height of the Foh Pass with a table of oxygen depletion related to altitude. In a flash he totalled up the columns, added ten percent and stared at the conclusion. 'Yes!' he cried, whirled on his stool and dashed off.

'Tell Practz to meet me in the thaumatron bay!' he shrieked over his shoulder and the pounding of his desperate feet.

Tell Practz, thought Wat. Nobody tells Practz what to do! They ask. I'll ask!

The sneeke hurtled out of the cave entrance milliseconds ahead of the sprinting figure of Rutger, his beard flung over his shoulder and his ponytail streaming behind him like a tangled windsock in a hurricane. A second later, rattling mountains of clattering hand-held mining equipment, seven dwarves erupted into daylight, blinked and almost smashed into the middle of what looked like an extremely ugly war of attrition.

A vast army still fought hard against a tiny band of green-clad defenders wielding strange weapons. Sharpened planks of wood with boards attached, each emblazoned with an oath, thrust bravely against an onslaught of whirling katanas. It was a war of petititions. Rutger didn't remember seeing *that* when he came in.

Suddenly there was a yell. A finger pointed, the fighting stopped and countless eyes stared in disbelief at the eight figures.

General Lehrt spurred his horse into action, raising his hand in greeting, unsure whether to hurl a rock of diplomacy. He reined in, dismounted in a fluid movement and began to speak. 'Greeting, O diminutive ones . . .' was as far as he got before the green overcloak-clad figure of Mrs Olivia Beece thundered up behind him, panting.

'This is a protected area!' she shouted indignantly. 'You shouldn't be here!'

'Have you seen this man?' yelled Lehrt, unfurling a parchment illustration.

'Have you seen a dragon?' bustled Mrs Beece, scowling from beneath her woollen cap.

'Yes,' croaked Rutger under the twin spotlights of indignant inquisition. The sneeke buzzed in tiny circles whining impatiently. 'Nice of you to take an interest but we really must fly!' And with that he was off, hotly pursued by the rattling septet of the Small Bore Drainage Company.

'Still in the cave?' chorused Lehrt and Mrs Beece.

'Yes and no!' yelled Rutger over his bearded shoulder, keeping the sneeke firmly in his sights as he vanished over the top of the outcrop.

'Well, there you are!' snapped Lehrt, scowling with military smugness at Mrs Beece. 'No dragon! Go home!'

'Ha!' came the indignant reply. 'He was a gentleman! Answered me first!'

'I am a *General*! He answered me!'

'There *is* a dragon . . . !'

'Isn't!'

'And while there's a dragon in the cave you are not allowed in!'

'Even if it's dead!' shouted Lehrt, drawing his katana menacingly.

Mrs Beece squealed several unprintable somethings and launched herself at the bamboo-armoured general, her fury stripping him of rank and protection in her eyes.

Within seconds the ceaseflail was over and weapons clashed again, percussion echoing through the valley.

The sneeke, controlled by Practz, dipped and weaved through underbrush, hovering impatiently on occasion as the dwarves caught up. Short legs, steep terrain and mountains of earth-moving equipment don't make for fast travelling.

And as Rutger dashed on and on, the panted grumbles growing restive behind him, he did begin to wonder where the sneeke might be leading them.

He was about to find out.

Suddenly it stopped. In the middle of nowhere in particular it flittered above the rocky ground and made strange swooping motions.

Proph stared at the panting figure of Rutger with growing scepticism.

'Now what?' he asked, hands leaning on his knees, gasping for breath. Guthry dropped his shovels, roof joists and half dozen ladders, chewed noisily and spat a derisive glob at a rock.

Rutger shrugged, trying to fathom what the sneeke was attempting to tell, scatching his beard irritably as a dribble of sweat made a bid for freedom. In countless episodes he had never seen Flossie the Wonder Hound do anything like that. And unfortunately he had never been any good at charades.

In Losa Llamas Practz sobbed and cradled his head in his hands. So close! Such an idiot!

Before Rutger's eyes the sneeke dropped out of the air, landing in the rocky dust. And, accompanied by a crescendo of whines, with spindly insect legs it began to scratch desperately at the ground.

Rutger stared. This was more like it. This looked familiar . . .

'Come on!' squealed Practz at the double witless image in the spherical monitors. With a flurry of fingers he made the sneeke scratch harder.

Rutger's nose bulged out of the fish-eye monitors as he knelt down and stared intently at the sneeke's antics.

'Come on! You *can* do it!' Practz flourished another few whimpers.

And then, through moist eyes, Rutger saw before him not the inch-long sneeke, but the shaggy, delightful Flossie the Wonder Hound in an episode called 'The Stolen Gold of Goblin Bay'. In an instant he understood. His journey was over, *this* was the spot – the treasure was there below his feet.

'Dig!' he cried, scrambling upright. 'Dig! There! Now!'

Several dozen miles away Practz leapt to his feet and punched the air in victory as he watched the dwarves heave their shovels off their shoulders and begin attacking the ground.

All he had to do now was watch them burrow down through the ground straight for the thaumaf . . .

Suddenly the monitors buzzed and went totally blank.

'Phlim! It's a disaster!' shrieked Practz, bursting into the thaumatron bay and stomping across to address a pair of feet sticking out of a small hatch in the side of the vast mountain of cold thaumatronics. 'Disaster,' he repeated, hopping up and down for effect. 'We've lost contact with Rutger. The screens have gone blank.' In his state of agitation he failed to

261

notice the complete lack of anything even remotely resembling a charged thaumic particle emanating from the thaumatron.

'Just went blank,' he ranted. 'As if something had pulled the plug out.'

'Yes. It was me,' answered the voice of Phlim from deep within the body of the thaumatron.

'It was on, then it wasn't . . . You what?' shrieked Practz, suddenly registering what Phlim had said. 'Have you taken complete leave of your senses?'

'No, I . . .'

'You're mad! Mad! An eighty-five-thousand-century-old army is about to be resurrected at any moment and now, not only will we not have a clue when they have been, but we won't be able to do anything about it. Brilliant! Absolutely brilliant!'

The feet twitched and an impatient sound of banging metal rattled out of the hatch.

'If you think I'm just going to let you pull the plug . . .' ranted Practz.

'Look, if you *want* to put this wandbrake back, then go ahead!' came Phlim's voice. 'Do it, and we really will be powerless!'

'Come out of there!' shouted Practz, snatching at the feet and tugging.

A sooty-faced technician appeared in a stained lab-cloak, jerked a thumb over the horizon of pipes and hyperensor-celled steam tubes and tugged himself back inside, grunting. 'He's over there!'

'You said it yourself!' came Phlim's voice from within the thaumatron casing, grimacing with the effort of using a psychic spanner. 'Shut off the thaumafers and Mancini's powerless!'

'So are we, without the thaumatron!' shrieked Practz, scraping soot off his hands. 'You should know that!' quivering with a mixture of extreme anger and terror.

'Oh yeah?' answered Phlim cockily. There was a whooshing crackling noise and a sapphire glow shone from behind the thaumatron casing. In a flash, Phlim appeared ten feet above the casing, hovering on two jets of spitting aquamarine blasting out of his tightly clenched fists. A pair of enormous ropes hung straight down from a belt around his waist, quivering as if under extreme tension. His mouth worked rapidly, re-engineering the incantation control parameters and increasing thrust. Then, like a bulky, pale-blue coronaded sun of interlaced wiring, a twenty-foot wandbrake rose over the horizon, hovered for a moment and began to move out into the middle of the cavern. A widely grinning Phlim, backpack thaumatron spitting gigs of power into the air below his feet, hovered almost casually into view.

'What the . . . ?' began Practz.

'The Daedelian Lift Harness!' shouted Phlim above the whooshing of the thrust, carefully balancing upward power vectors with small rotating wrist motions. 'I've tweaked it a bit since the thaumatron refit.'

'Yes, yes, *very* good, I'm sure,' answered Practz, seething as he edged nervously away from beneath the massive doughnut of floating thaumatronics. 'Now put it back and get the thaumatron back on line!'

'Hush, a minute! It's a bit fiddly landing this. Not quite used to . . . ooooh.' Phlim and the wandbrake slipped sideways violently as he closed his left-hand beam down a little too fast. In an instant he had regained control. 'Close! . . . Wooops, nearly lost it . . . ahem . . .' confessed Phlim as he lowered power, placed the wandbrake carefully onto the ground and landed in front of it.

'Well that's just great!' yelled Practz, fuming as he glowered at the ring of the wandbrake towering behind Phlim's grin. 'I hope you're having fun!' ranted Practz. 'Some of us are concerned about what Mancini's up to. Some of us are actually doing something about it! Unlike certain Technical Wizards I am currently staring at who seem content to dally with gadget-magic, I have been attempting to stop Mancini in his tracks! Even as we speak Rutger is digging towards a thaumafer! At least he was until I lost contact.' He glared once again at Phlim in case the message hadn't sunk in.

'How? Surely the crystal wristband would have been useless with all that fall-out . . .' began Phlim.

'I used the sneeke!'

'Oh! It's fine for *you* to use gadget-magic, is it?' snapped the Technical Wizard.

Practz opened his mouth, raised his finger in protest, thought better of it and blustered. 'Yes, yes, yes. I needed to, okay?'

'Tell me,' growled Phlim, knowing that Practz knew that *he* knew the score was now fifteen-love, and also knowing that Practz *didn't* know it would soon be thirty-love. 'What will Rutger do when he reaches the thaumafer?'

'Shut it off, of course! Pull the plug on that madman Mancini!'

'How?' pressed Phlim, the question soaring over the net in a rocketing smash.

'Ahhhhhh.'

Thirty-love. The crowd went wild!

'He doesn't stand a chance without the biggest wand-brakes we can possibly lay our hands on. This and the other one that'll be out in a minute,' said Phlim. 'Ship these over, drop 'em in the hole and we might come out of this ahead! Now, what?'

Practz's face glowed crimson, his mouth working in silent rage as it tried to keep up with his boiling temper. 'You idiot! I can't believe . . . "Ship these over"! Trips off the tongue, doesn't it? What are you thinking? Roll them there? Just trundle the bleedin' things over the Talpa Mountains? It's a nice afternoon! Why not?'

'You've just seen . . .' protested Phlim.

'You just barely cleared fifteen feet of metal with that one. It may have escaped your attention but the Talpa Mountains are a *lot* bigger than that. With two wandbrakes, you'd need at least . . .'

'. . . three more backpacks!' finished Phlim.

'And where, in all the Gods' names, d'you expect to find them? What top hat are those darling little bunnies hiding in, eh?'

264

Barely containing himself, Phlim pointed casually at the cart which Thurgia was shoving through the door. Practz wheeled around and stared unbelievingly at the triplet of gleaming, glowing thaumatrons whirring gently at tick-over. His jaw opened and closed feebly as the Head of Demonic Possession slipped on a backpack, fastened the waist strap and increased power.

'One each,' said Phlim. 'For Wat, Thurgia and, er, you.'

'Now wait a minute. Hold on here!' declared Practz, throwing up his hands in horror. 'If you think I'm going to strap one of them on and go hiking across the mountains . . .'

'Who said anything about hiking?' asked Phlim as he and Thurgia ramped up the power output, clenched their fists, directed the thrust at the floor and launched themselves into the air.

'Of course,' said Phlim, looking down and grinning as Practz forgot once again to close his mouth, 'you *can* hike if you insist!'

It hadn't taken long for the dwarves to drop their mining equipment off their shoulders and begin attacking the ground with frantic geocidal tendencies. To Rutger's amazement the lack of pickaxes didn't seem to be hindering their rapid downward progress. In fact within minutes of the first foot-propelled shovel blade slicing into the terrified topsoil all he could see was a constant shower of erupting dirt, pebbles and the occasional startled mole. Now, after an hour's work, even that had vanished below the lip of the hole.

Proph struggled into daylight beneath a mountain of leather buckets, emptied them on the pile and scurried over to Rutger.

'Hey boy, what we diggin' fer?'

'Twice what Mancini gave you,' answered Rutger, staring apprehensively at Tor Tellini and the bank of crimson clouds building above the constant gush of geothaumal energy.

'Gee! That's mighty generous. Twice nothin's hardly more

'n a poke in th'eye wi' a stick!' scorned Proph, recalling Mancini's generously non-existent time-share offer.

'Hey, I'll pay. Name your currency! Groats, gold, diamonds?' It didn't matter to Rutger – it all started as just so much scrappy lead piping anyway. It wouldn't be a problem to pay them an enormous bonus, as soon as he got back to Losa Llamas. *If* he got back to Losa Llamas. Nervously he looked at the now inert sneeke on the ground, its eyes strangely lifeless. He shuddered, recalling the shock he'd had when it had fallen out of the sky in front of him, shattering the illusion of Flossie the Wonder Hound and severing contact with Losa Llamas in an instant.

'Gold's fine!' said Proph, 'Know where y' are wi' gold!' He grinned and walked away, turned and came back. 'Hey boy, what we diggin' fer?' he asked.

A shock of *déjà vu* rattled Rutger into full alertness. He knew very well the way magic could be used to warp the folds of time, shattering continuity in a flash, screwing cause and effect up into a ball and tossing it into a small raffia-work basket. If *this* was Mancini's doing . . . ?

'Didn't you just ask me that?' asked Rutger, almost dreading the answer.

'Sure did!' grinned the dwarf. 'Only I git th' wrong answer! What we diggin' *fer*?'

Rutger flushed. 'Oh, I . . . Actually, I don't know. Didn't you do any divining? I thought you always did that.'

It was Proph's turn to flush. 'Din't think there was no need, you pointin' at ground so insistent, like you knew!'

'I was told where to dig.'

'I din't see no-one, boy!'

'It was a sneeke . . .' he began, saw the direction the conversation would go, about saying an insect told him where to dig and that he trusted it because it reminded him of a dog and . . . and finished, '. . . sneeke . . . sneaking suspicion, that's all! Ha! Just looked like the right place. Meant to ask you to have a check around, but in all the excitement . . . you know how it is.' He offered Proph a very weak smile.

'Lookin' fer anythin' in particular?'

'Er, nope. Just tell me what you find, will you,' he hedged, wishing he had even the slightest clue.

As Proph tugged his divining rods out of his belt with a flourish and scampered eagerly away, feelings of doubt began to creep into Rutger's mind. Why had he suddenly lost contact? Had he been right to trust the sneeke? What was going on? And why could he suddenly smell burning?

Rutger looked up as a waft of freshly singed whiskers floated into his nostrils. With an incomprehensible squeal and a cry of, 'Not again!' Proph appeared at the top of the hole, blackened and lacking several inches in the hair department, like a rabbit that had just bored through an underground ring main.

'If I'd wanted to be involved in magic minin' I'd 'ave said so!' he shouted, small puffs of smoke drifting from the brim of his hat. He flung a pair of charred divining rods at Rutger and cursed several of his favourite dwarvish oaths. 'My bes' rods! Ruined, ruined!'

Hurling his hands into the air, he spat and vanished down the hole to take his fury out in some honest toil shifting some honest soil, promising himself three weeks of nice relaxing non-stop potholing when all this was over.

As a discarded pickaxe head smashed Mancini on the toe for the third time the cave was filled with another blaspheming tirade of choice curses, the majority of which were directed at himself for never paying attention at boy scout knot classes.

'Up through the hole, round the tree and back down again,' telepathed the sea-scrole helpfully. 'Now pull and you'll have it!'

Snarling almost as volubly as the frustrated damnation, Mancini tugged and attached a fourth pickaxe head to make a bowed square, just slightly smaller than the base of the cage. Then he turned, raised an intact pick over his head and smashed another handle off the last three in the corner. Half an hour ago it had seemed such a stroke of genius. A hostess trolley made from eight lengths of cast iron would be perfect, totally flame-proof!

A couple of his more perceptive neurones had flashed queries, addressing the house on the topic of why seven dwarves armed each with two upper limbs would be in need of eight picks, requiring a total of sixteen limbs to wield effectively. Was the apparent limb disparity due to the fact that one dwarf had four arms? Or that one dwarf could wield two axes? Or one axe was a spare? Discuss.

Drenched in a deluge of surging ennui, the neurones gave up and, giggling quietly over several very large Dopamine Slings, turned their critical attention on Mancini's feeble attempts to recall the intracacies of the half-hitch.

Mancini snatched the pick-head off the ground and lashed it to the rest of the contraption, cursing as he tied his thumb and left forefinger into a tangle of twine.

His head whirled round, power-hungry eyes glaring at the damnation. Was that thing actually laughing at him? At him!

Well, it'd soon see who was boss, soon be engulfed in the throbbing geothaumal release.

And who'd be laughing then, eh?

From a distance it looked as if a gigantic cheshire cat had just vanished in a shock of sapphire alarm. Two black spots quivered above a startled doughnut, floating fifty feet above the ground.

'I don't want to look!' yelled Practz, his brow writhing in concentration as he struggled to retain his position as the left eye above the twenty-ton wandbrake. He would be the first to admit that balancing thrust vectors against the unpredictably uneven terrain flashing by beneath whilst attempting to prevent the mass of delicate thaumatronics suspended from the thaumatrons swinging uncontrollably about, wasn't the easiest thing he had ever tried to do. Especially after only two wobbly circuits of the thaumatron bay for practice. And especially since even climbing the stairs gave him vertigo.

'But it's fun!' shouted Wat above the combined noise of wo backpack thaumatrons spitting and crackling over the rushing of thin Talpine air. 'I've never looked down on goats before!'

'Shut up! Shut up! Don't say "down". Just tell me when we get there!' snapped Practz, wincing as one fist-thruster beam ducked down a rabbit hole. 'If wizards had been intended to fly we wouldn't suffer vertigo! Couldn't you have found some witches for this?'

Suddenly Wat shouted with glee. 'Over there!' he shouted and only just managed not to unclench his fist and point. 'That's the spot. Ready for touchdown . . . er, landing.'

'What?' shrieked Practz. 'We can't be there already! Can we?'

'Time is of the essence,' grinned Wat, surveying the hollow in the ground carefully for any obstacles.

'How fast have we been . . .'

'You don't really want to know,' advised Wat, painfully aware of the nervousness of the newly aerial wizard.

'Tell me!' commanded Practz, pulling rank and a series of terrified faces in almost equal proportions.

'Er, about nag six.'

'What's that mean?'

'About six times the speed of flight of an unladen horse. It's my idea! Ooooh, up a bit, that hillock's higher than I thought!' Practz increased thrust, his eyes still firmly shut. 'Slow forward motion,' said Wat, 'and ease back to your left! Down . . . er lower, now.'

The spitting magic users dropped slowly into a tiny bowl-shaped valley and vanished out of sight.

Suddenly Practz opened his eyes as the hawser connecting him to the wandbrake slackened. He stared nauseously at the thirty foot of nothingness below him, whimpered and shut his eyes again, concentrating on lowering the vast mass of thaumatronics gently onto a slope of bracken.

'Power down, power down!' shouted Wat off to his left, sounding strangely low.

'Don't say "down"!' screamed Practz, easing off thrust, then letting out a startled cry as a very small section of the Talpa Mountains nuzzled affectionately at his feet. With an even larger scream he shut off the thaumatron and leapt towards a vast expanse of heather, burying his face in its yielding softness, clinging to its solidity. 'Hello, heather!' he whimpered. 'I love you, heather! I'll never leave you again! Oh, soil, oh, rocks, oh muddy bits!'

Wat shook his head, unfastened the hawsers, and consulted the *User's Guide to Thaumafers*.

This was the place. Eighty-five feet six inches below the surface was the other end of the sub-Tellini Thaumafer.

With a grim face he attempted a smile.

They were in the right place, with the right equipment.

All they needed was the right amount of time.

Nervously he shivered as images of rampaging ancient armies surged through his mind, then he turned to his backpack thaumatron and began to whip up an all terrain vertical disruptor set to remove a twenty-foot diameter hole to a depth of eighty-five feet six inches.

'Abandon pit!' came a muffled shriek on the far side of the Talpa Mountains, immediately followed by seven rapidly moving dwarves. Rutger stared in shocked horror as the ground bucked, writhed and vomited half a dozen tons of granite several hundred feet into the mountain air. Moments later a column of crimson geothaumal energy gushed skywards to join the growing cloud spreading from Tor Tellini.

Rutger screamed. This wasn't supposed to happen. This never happened for Flossie the Wonder Hound.

'What've you done?' shouted Rutger above the throbbing gush of energy.

'Dig there, y' said. Can't blame us, boy!' shouted Proph.

Rutger grabbed his head, rubbed his eyes and tried furiously to tell the part of him that thought there was a vast column of escaping energy erupting before him that there wasn't a vast column of escaping energy erupting before him. He failed. Eight times.

'So what's ye gonna do now, hmmmm?' yelled Proph, his arms folded across the handle of his slightly scorched shovel.

Rutger's mind whirled. He was certain that digging there was supposed to help. The sneeke had told him. Hadn't it? It *had* made digging motions above that spot. Hadn't it? He sprinted over to the tiny insect perched on a leaf and stared imploringly into its vast fish-eye lenses. No response.

Behind him seven dwarves looked pityingly at him and shook their heads. Amazing how pressure affects people, talking to insects. Sad. Very sad.

Rutger squatted on the ground and held his head. It was a disaster. He'd come here to gather information on Mancini and report back, not to release countless millions of terrathaums into the air. Losa Llamos suddenly felt as far away as a million ducat-winning lottery ticket or a night out with the magic-lantern goddess. Would he ever see the place again, or hear the familiar throb of the thaumatron? As if to comfort him his ears began to ring tinnitically, conjuring a thin imitation of agitated thaumic particle streams blasting against rock. Miserably he stared at his feet, the sound getting louder in his head . . . the sound of two thaumatrons!

He looked up into the sky and stared in bewilderment. Behind the fidgeting dwarves two dots winged into view, a huge doughnut of thaumatronics slung between them. Veiled by a cloud of sapphire sparks they raced towards the gushing fountain of energy, eating up the distance at over nag eight, suspended on hyperensorcelled thrust. Phlim yelled final approach commands to Thurgia as they swooped in as close to the gusher as possible, dust blasting everywhere in the downdraught.

The dwarves scattered.

Barely audible commands flashed between Phlim and Thurgia as they lined up to touchdown, ten feet of hawser and four columns of magic the only things holding twenty tons of dedicate wandbrake aloft.

Suddenly an aberrant flash of energy snaked sideways out of the surging fountain of the geothaumal gusher, blasting Thurgia's thaumatron in a flash of destruction and sending him into a tailspin. In a millisecond the hypertaurus coils were a mass of molten magic and showers of crimson sparks.

271

With a scream, the Head of Demonic Possession dropped out of the sky. The wandbrake lurched, hawsers screamed in overload. Phlim's brow was a fountain of sweat, furrowing with intense concentration as he fought to control the power thrusting from his fists, struggling to support the wandbrake and the added terrified figure dangling from it. His struggle was accompanied by the sickening whine of a backpack thaumatron attempting to produce far more thrust than it was ever designed to and the yells of a Technical Wizard under far more stress than *he* was designed for, and Losa Llamas' finest swooped out of sight behind the crimson upthrust.

And was never seen flying again.

'Yes, yes, I *know* you're intensely happy to feel the ground beneath your body again,' snapped Wat at Practz, 'but I really need your help here, okay?'

He stared at the prone wizard rubbing his cheek against the heather in the small hollow valley and cursed under his breath. 'We're running out of time!' he screamed. 'Hello? Wat to Practz? Come in!' He tapped the gibbering Thaumaturgical Physicist sharply on the head.

Practz looked up, startled, saw the sky above him, heaved vertiginously and grabbed at the heather once more, burying his head beneath a particularly comforting frond and making a series of gurgling noises.

'I can't risk lowering the wandbrake into place without your help!' screamed Wat. 'One jolt and I could ruin it! I've dug the hole! Come on!' He gritted his teeth, grabbed Practz's cloak firmly in his hand and snatched him to his feet. In times of crisis, decorum could go whistle.

In a matter of seconds Wat had buckled the thaumatron firmly onto Practz's back and was slapping him around the face to make sure he was listening.

'. . . Look, just nod if you can remember how to keep a level three containment field operational,' yelled Wat.

Nod.

'Right, keep it trained on the bottom of that hole. There's

only an inch of granite between us and that thaumafer.' With a flick of his fingers Wat fired up Practz's thaumatron and watched as he cracked a blanket of shimmering green anti-magic into the hole. In a couple of seconds Wat had shrugged on his thaumatron, fired it up and hooked the hawsers onto the wandbrake. With a deep breath he tucked his arms in close to his sides, bent his elbows and appeared to grasp at a pair of invisible handles. Spurred by a barely audible whisper of commands, the cloud of aquamarine motes swarming above his head swam five fathoms deeper, throbbing and spitting louder. With a flick of his thumbs two forks of magical lightning arced over, plunged through his fists and smashed groundwards. In a second he was fifteen feet above the wandbrake and gunning for more thrust, straining against the dead weight below. He gritted his teeth and chanted for more power, thrilling as he felt the wandbrake move, sparks shooting randomly in all directions, earthing off stray insects and small frazzled butterflies. Sweat exploded across his brow as he concentrated his will totally to align himself and the wandbrake above the hole.

Painfully, slowly, the vast doughnut of cutting edge thaumodynamics was manoeuvred into place, settling leadenly down like some gargantuan gravid bluebottle, disappearing out of sight. After what seemed to Wat to be a lifetime of mental strain, he too vanished beneath the lip of the hole.

'Are you ready for this?' he shouted up to Practz. 'You know what to do?'

Practz nodded, fighting attacks of vertigo as he peered down the hole, took a deep breath and released the temporary containment field. Crimson sparks exploded in all directions, swarming and spitting wildly. Wat ramped up the power on his thaumatron with a squeal, blasting a neat twenty-foot slot in the granite. Sweat covered his body now, dripping onto the thrusting magic and exploding into puffs of steam. Then, with a sound like a million fingernails on freshly painted blackboards, the torus wrenched through the surging thaumafer and settled into place with a thump – a

273

ring of technical wizardry encircled the surging terrathaumic finger of energy.

Hardly pausing long enough to breathe, Wat swooped down to land on the wandbrake casing. In an instant he had unhitched the hawsers, his hands trembling as he felt the power torrenting through, inches below him. Flipping open a small pentagrammed panel he prayed he could remember all that Phlim had said. Frantic hand gestures and fraught, panic-ridden, semi-mantraic chants were rewarded a few moments later by the glow of crystals deep within the matrix of the wandbrake. Vibrations throbbed beneath his feet as a permanent, and incredibly powerful, magikinetic field was generated and began to close, fighting against the vast terrathaums of surging resistance.

Rocks quivered, strata struggled and seismic shriekings erupted all around as the magical power struggle raged. And in a matter of moments an impenetrable tourniquet snapped tight, stemming the geothaumal rushing.

The sudden silence was deafening. The only sound Wat could discern was the hum of his backpack thaumatron and the pounding of blood in his temples.

With a squeal of celebration and relief he launched himself into the air, arcing out of the hole and victory-rolling recklessly into a heap of heather. He lay there panting, secure in the unshakable knowledge that just as soon as the other wandbrake was in place, Mancini's plan would be doomed.

'. . . doomed!' wailed Phlim glaring accusingly at Thurgia. 'Doomed!'

'It wasn't my fault!' protested the Head of Demonic Possession, 'It came out of nowhere. I didn't see it!'

'I've heard some excuses!'

'It's true . . .'

Rutger jumped up and down and screamed for attention. 'What's going on? Why are you here? And what *is* that thing?'

'Useless!' snapped Phlim. 'Stuffed up! Worthless! Twenty tons of scrappy thaumatronics!'

274

'But what *was* it? Why was I digging . . . ?'

'Ahem,' coughed a voice at his elbow, reminding him precisely who was digging. Rutger winced.

'Have you never seen a wandbrake?' snarled Phlim derisively. 'I guess not. Well, the plan was to dig a hole, drop it in and stop the thaumafer. Easy peasy! But Thurgia here cocked all that up.'

'It wasn't my fault,' insisted Thurgia resentfully.

'You mean it won't work?' asked Rutger.

'You don't just go dropping delicate bits of thaumatronics twenty feet onto solid rock and expect them to work!' yelled Phlim. 'It won't even fire the primary containment field. I've checked. No purple indicator light. Not even a glow!'

'So . . . ?'

'Aghhh! First basic rule of advanced thaumatronics. No glow, no go!'

'What's this?' asked Thurgia, picking up a small round crystal lying next to him.

'Is that it then?' asked Rutger. 'Mancini's won?'

'Yes! Any more stunning questions before the monsters of hell come storming over the top?' snapped Phlim.

'Er, yes. Why does this look familiar?' said Thurgia, turning the crystal around in his hands.

'Because it's a primary containment field indicator light, that's why!' shrieked Phlim, raising his open palms to heaven. 'Gods, give me a break. I'm surrounded by idiots!'

'But, where did it come from?' asked Thurgia. 'I mean, you don't normally find things like this just lying about in the middle of nowhere . . .'

'I don't *believe* this!' bawled Phlim, angrily snatching the crystal, stomping over to the wandbrake and shoving it into a small hole. 'There! That's where it comes from! Happy now?' he shouted, turning away and glaring at Thurgia. Behind him the crystal flashed intermittently, then began to glow with a warm, comforting, all-systems-go sort of purple radiance.

There was something about the way nine pairs of eyes were staring a foot to the right of Phlim's shoulder that gave

275

him a hollow feeling. Something was not as it should be.

Almost reluctantly he turned around. And instantly rewrote the first basic rule of advanced thaumatronics.

No glow, no bulb.

A second later he had a backpack thaumatron throbbing eagerly between his shoulder blades and was yelling a torrent of desperate instruction to anything within a half mile radius.

Two and a half miles away, in the cave at the foot of Tor Tellini, bathed deep in fiery crimson light, Cheiro Mancini squealed with delight as he leapt onto his impromptu pickaxe hostess trolley and discovered that it remained rock solid. The damnation curled back its lips, tiny glows of scarlet fire shooting from its shaggy fur as it scowled arrogantly upwards from the corner at the cavorting VET.

In less time than it takes to skin a lemming Mancini had covered the distance to the cage and was staring sneeringly inside. 'Barbecue time!' he cackled, manhandling the creature onto the trolley.

'In a very few minutes, yes!' gloated the damnation to itself, flicking a deadly drum roll of eight claws on the cage mesh.

Two and a half miles away Phlim was screaming desperately at Thurgia as a vast doughnut of thaumatronics hovered precariously beneath two flashes of sapphire sparks. There was still a chance. Rutger and the dwarves stared open-mouthed as Phlim expertly dropped it into the spitting hole, casting searing pyrotechnics in all directions.

Mancini kept up a constant deluge of wild murmurings, his thoughts whirring with the absolute power he knew he was going to release in a matter of a very, very few seconds. Pulling his tongue into paroxysms of concentration he checked the orientation of the psychoterrin crystal in the harness below the cage and grinned. It was all in place – Powyr from ye rocks and, fohcuss threw ye stone, onto ye boddey of ye damned-naytion.

He was seconds away from everything he had ever dreamed of – total, infinite power!

As the wandbrake settled into the spitting tumult of the

breached thaumafer Phlim leapt in afterwards, praying that it wasn't too late, his mind rehearsing the start-up sequence as he dropped down on two columns of hyperensorcelled steam.

At precisely the same moment Mancini spat across his grubby palms, cracked his fingers noisily and began to push the damnation into the seething, surging torrents of geothaumal energy erupting before him, thrilling as he sensed the dawning of a momentous occasion.

And yet again he failed totally to witness the thrill of glee in the creature's eyes.

Blackboard fingers screeched klaxons of anguish as the metal axe blades passed through the fire, tiny virtual vortices spinning and snapping off into oblivion . . . and still Mancini pushed on.

Phlim leapt across the surface of the wandbrake, incanting, murmuring, praying. A host of tiny purple crystals lit. It was going to work.

Cracks of crimson coruscation writhed and lashed from the damnation's fur, its ancient feral howl adding to the deafening uproar of energy in the cave . . . and still Mancini pushed on, cackling madly.

Phlim felt a vibration beneath his feet: surging magikinetic fields growing, blossoming, fighting the forces of evil erupting from the spawning fey-lines of geothaumal energy. And dying with a spluttering cough.

As the suspended psychoterrin crystal entered the uprush below the damnation, a calm, smooth silence fell across the entire spilling thaumafer. Crushing random wavelengths of surging terrathaums were adjusted, turned coherent. Each compression added to countless others and formed a vast punch of power which cannoned into the caged damnation.

The silence lasted perhaps half a millisecond.

Then the roaring began.

Mancini stared at the creature in his cage, his knees turning to blancmange as he saw red eyes of utter malevolence flash into the ultra-violet of ultimate greed; his horrified jaw hanging loosely as the piebald damnation expanded within the confines of its feeble cage. He screamed uselessly as the skin changed from shaggy dog fur to glistening inchoate leather, gleaming with stygian epaulets . . . and, as the wrenched debris of the cage bounced off his nose, Cheiro Mancini wondered for the first time if he had in fact just made a teensy-weensy mistake.

The cave shook as the Prime Evil chuckled and stretched, revelling in its first moment of freedom for eighty-five thousand centuries.

'I really suppose I ought to thank you,' began the seismic bellowing of the very ex-damnation, 'but greed and stupidity are *so* worthless these days I don't think I shall. Had you been *just* greedy you might have stood a chance, but falling for the old talking bath mat gag. Shocking, some things never change! However, one turn deserves another so I'll count to ten before coming after you, alright? One . . . two . . . I'd like to chat but . . . three . . . there's so *much* to do . . . four . . .'

In the far corner of the cave a small sack suddenly sprouted hands, opened and spilled out a terrified wiry youth. In a split second Knapp snatched his sack and sprinted out of the cave faster than a scalded whippet, ducked sideways and sprinted on towards Cranachan.

It was only as a belch of superheated foetid gases licked affectionately at Mancini's chin that he finally screamed and thrashed his way out of the cave in hot pursuit, full speed into the glaring sunlight and the waiting throng of the Imperial Murrhovian Army.

'You!' screamed General Lehrt, his finger lancing daggers at the wanted criminal. 'Get him!' he yelled and cannoned towards the cave entrance.

'You can't go in there without proper representation from a Dragon's Rights Front Committee Member!' yelled Mrs Beece, bridling furiously as five platoons vanished into the cave hot on Mancini's trail. 'Wait for me!' she screamed, accelerating into the gloom.

Two and a half miles away Phlim hurled psychic screwdrivers at the inert lump of thaumatronics beneath his feet, waggled bits of trunking and screamed as the wandbrake stubbornly refused to even fizz a bit.

It was just as well he wasn't aware of all the goings on in the valley at the foot of Tor Tellini. The sound of adamantine claws stamping gleefully on a host of Murrhovian warriors, and hurling what sounded like wet rags against rock walls in a long overdue frenzy of destruction, was drowned by the cacophony of survivors erupting from the cave mouth and diving for cover. In seconds most of the Imperial Murrhovian Army were not in any fit state to talk straight, let alone fight coherently.

General Lehrt screamed at Mrs Beece as they sprinted into the daylight once more. 'Is that your idea of a poor defenceless creature who needs its rights protecting, eh?'

'I didn't think dragons were so vicious! Claws are for mating rituals, aren't they?'

'That's no dragon!' bawled Lehrt above the screaming of the fleeing army making a bee-line for the horizon. 'Everybody knows that dragons have faces that look like red and white peckingese dogs with long beards and they launch fireworks and wear sandals!'

'So what's that thing . . . ?'

'Your problem. I only want Mancini!'

Abruptly the ground shook. Rocks that had remained perched on ledges on the side of the Tor Tellini since the retreat of the last ice age cascaded down, whirling and bouncing unpredictably as they gained momentum. Something was kicking.

As unchecked terrathaums poured into the Prime Evil, giving it strength, inflating its already arrogant ego, it grew. With a seismic jolt an inchoate fist several hundred feet across burst through the side of the ancient volcano. Followed moments later by a pair of enormous shoulders crowned by a horned mockery of a head.

It was then that Thurgia knew it was too late.

But too late for what?

Instead of following the mountainous crimson pangs of rebirth with a frenzied orgy of senseless destruction, violence and rampaging carnage, the Prime Evil stuck four talons into its vast mouth, took a deep breath and whistled.

'Walkies!' it cried, still up to what passed for its waist in the side of the mountain, and whistled again, a deep, hard, evil sound. 'Come on, boys. Walkies!'

Far away to the East, the rough and tumble splashing of four hundred paws in goat's milk echoed through the Murrhovian Imperial Palace as Empress Tau revelled in her mid-afternoon damnation tickling. Cascades of emulsioned white torrented down her bamboo armour as she wrestled and fought the pool of beasts, ducking one here, drenching another there. Out of the corner of a milk-soaked eye she could sense three of her favourites readying an attack, growling to each other in dark cover. She pretended they weren't in sight, thrilling as their pincer movement homed in on her. The milk frothed about their legs as they dashed through the throng of piebald creatures . . . and at the last minute she ducked, vanishing below the opaque surface, holding her breath, waiting. And waiting.

Was this a new kind of attack? Her lungs began to hurt. Why hadn't they come for her? They always did. Suddenly the aching in her lungs grew too much as her blood screamed for oxygen.

With a gasp of defeat she erupted from the goat's milk, bracing her arms over her head for the inevitable onslaught of a hundred sodden creatures. It didn't come.

With a shock her eyes flashed open, sucking in the unbelievable sight in seconds.

The pool was totally empty.

All that remained to show the damnations had been there were a few bundles of stray piebald fluff, a fast-drying path of milk-soaked paw-prints and the creaking wreckage of a large paper patio door.

Empress Tau whimpered, snarled and finally screamed as she stared at the swathe of destruction visible out of the shattered portal heading due West.

Had she bawled furious fulminations at anything less than

the level of shrieking anger to which she had become accustomed, she might, just possibly, have heard a frail, distance-dulled whistle and a definite 'Come on, boys. Walkies!'

The blackened grimy face of Phlim breasted the horizon of the hole on a column of sapphire, swooped miserably over in front of Thurgia and landed in a heap of dejection, his back to Tor Tellini. 'Damned wandbrake's totally up the creek! Either the secondary thaumostat's fried or the marvinsky drive's shot! I can't fix it out here . . . Hello? Hello?'

Phlim waved his grimy hand into the face of Thurgia, getting no response. Eight small figures were standing in a row staring in the same direction, hirsute jaws dragging awestruck against terrified sternums. With an immense sense of really not wanting to, Phlim turned and looked over his shoulder.

A surging wave of bodies tumbled out of the valley, fleeing the towering form of the Prime Evil. Their arms flailing madly, the ex-placard wavers scrambled towards Cranachan, whilst a cloud of dust was the only reminder of the Imperial Murrhovian Army. And there in the distance, one solitary, bearded figure was sprinting desperately for its life: Cheiro Mancini.

Rage seared through Phlim's mind as he forced the thaumatron into full power and sputtered madly into the stratosphere on a trail of sapphire steam. Crimson clouds flashed by as he leaned into a neat stall turn at thirty thousand feet, blissfully unaware that he should need oxygen, and thrusted head down at the fleeing Virtual Ecology Technician. Clouds. Sparks. Tundra. Target. Scarce feet above the heads of terrified ptarmigans he plummeted into the back of the fleeing figure, wrapping his toes into Mancini's belt, gunning the thaumatron skywards, snatching the VET from the ground, dropping him moments later at Thurgia's feet.

'What are you playing at?' shrieked Phlim, barely missing roasting Mancini in a blast of magic as he rattled his cloak collar.

'Y . . . you?' came the feebly croaked reply.

'Do you know what *that* thing is? Eh!' barraged Phlim, itching for a chance to rip Mancini limb from petty limb . . . and wearing a fully charged thaumatron on his back which could do the job and then some.

'Was a cute little cuddly . . .' whimpered Mancini.

'. . . Bloody Prime Evil!' finished Phlim. 'What are you going to do about it?'

Mancini pulled his arms round his knees and began rocking gently on the ground, whispering, 'Bah, bah blacknyss, haven't any sowel, to Hel, sire, Hel, sire, ye hundryd and one . . .' Too much had happened over the last few minutes – facts sat unabsorbed on top of his mind like the results of a very hard fast flood.

'Oh great! He's gone loopy now,' yelled Phlim, close to panic. 'What are we supposed to do now? Sing campfire songs round that till it's all too late?' He gestured madly at the flaming thaumafer behind him.

'Powyr from ye rocks and . . .' murmured Mancini, staring intently at his toes. Ten pairs of eyes stared expectantly at Phlim.

The Prime Evil's whistling sound echoed harshly across the valley, summoning.

'What are we going to do?' screamed Phlim against a barrage of dull faces.

'Hold on a few minutes,' said a thin papery voice. 'There's no rush yet!'

There was a flurry of activity from the Thaumaturgical Physicists as Thurgia and Rutger wheeled around. 'Who are you? Where d'you come from?' snapped Phlim, rounding on an old man in a kimono, carrying a carved triangular box. 'I suppose you're some sort of expert on eight-hundred-foot-high demons popping out of mountainsides!'

'Questions! It's a little over five hundred feet. And, yes,' answered the man, enigmatically. 'Wait for the others,' he added and squatted on the ground.

'Others? What others?' panicked Rutger, reality starting to look a little bit fuzzy around the edges.

The old man tugged a long, slender ear trumpet out of his pack, touched one tip against the rocks and one against his ear, 'About five minutes.'

'The whole army?' burbled Rutger.

'Be here soon, we'll work out what to do then,' said Itto's grandfather, poking curiously at Thurgia's discarded backpack. 'What's this?'

'Are you just going to sit here and watch that . . . ?' began Phlim at a tone far higher than his voicebox was designed to make.

'Does it look dangerous now? Five minutes, then it'll be dangerous,' said the old man glaring impatiently at Phlim, then he turned to Rutger. 'You. What's this?'

Phlim turned to Thurgia. 'We've seen what that Prime Evil thing can do. The scrole, the ancient message, remember? We've got to stop it!'

There was a tug on his sleeve. He looked down into the singed face of Proph.

''Scuse me buttin' in, but, with all this talk o' armies and stuff, boys'n'me's wonderin' f'you can see yer way free t' payin' us th'wages we's owed?' He grinned.

'Not now!' growled Phlim, turning back to Thurgia.

'That ain't th' right answer,' growled Proph, swinging on Phlim's sleeve. 'Ghedd's gettin' a bit jumpy,' he added significantly. 'An' when Ghedd gets jumpy he might jes' hop on a valyooble piece o' kit, see? An' smash it all up! Nah, I ain't sayin' 'e will but . . .'

'Yes, yes!' growled Phlim. 'Talk to Rutger!'

'What does this switch do?' asked Itto's grandfather, rapidly coming to grips with the intricacies of the backpack thaumatron.

'That's dangerous!' protested Rutger, moving the old man's spidery fingers away from the red knob. 'It's a phase switch. Some spells need a slight inversion vector to produce a stable reality mobius. You don't want to know about that!'

'And this?'

'Gigathaum selector . . .'

'Pay day, boy!' growled Proph, shuffling up to the two

figures poring over the silvery grey fluorescent heap of thaumatronics. 'Our job's done!'

Rutger winced. No lead. He stared at the seething throng of dwarves and cringed. He'd only ever tried lead into gold. With a grimace he fired the thaumatron up to full power, snatched the arcing globe of sapphire bees and, offering a silent prayer, flung them at the heap of rock and soil piled by the mine workings. There was a shriek, and the best part of twenty-five tons of twenty-eight carat gold shimmered into existence. A slow-moving mole winced as its eyes beheld a very snazzy new gold fur coat.

'That fer us?' shrieked Proph.

Rutger opened his eyes. 'Er, ahem, yes. Overtime! Enjoy!'

'Sheeeyoot! You ever need a job an' we'll be round!' Proph flicked Rutger a card and vanished after his six colleagues into the vast glistering pile, dreaming of several months' potholing in very very tight places.

'I think I got that,' mused the old man, stepping out from behind Rutger. 'Very good demonstration.'

'You were watching?'

'Oh course . . . uh-oh. *Now* it's very dangerous. Look.'

Phlim and Thurgia stood, open-mouthed.

Even across the Talpa Mountains, hidden as they were in the bowl-shaped valley, Wat was tugging at Practz's attention, firing up his thaumatron and preparing to steam out of there fast.

Had any of Mrs Beece's hunt saboteurs been unfortunate enough to be near the baying tumult of frenzied piebald madness which catapulted over the horizon and swept madly towards the mouth of the cave, it is immensely doubtful whether they would have had a chance to raise more than a finger in protest. Claws, teeth and a vast array of bounding bodies swarmed over the mountain, hacking and destroying anything even remotely sentient in sight and, like a black tide, vanished into the stygian depths of Tor Tellini, sparks of crimson arcing off their bodies.

Screams of feral pleasure rebounded off the walls of the cave as strings of damnations flung themselves into the unstoppable torrent of energy erupting from the mine. One after another their bodies melted in a flash of devilish red, tearing off their piebald prison uniform with yelps of delight. Yapping jaws entered the force, howling slavering maws emerged; curved gleaming claws slashed at the curtains of power, ten-foot crimson scythes erupted. Throughout the cave the eighty-five-thousand-century-old shackles twisting their bodies into an eternity of suffering were shattered, evil fulminating freedom smashing the restrictive ribcages, freeing the ancient army of the Prime Evil.

'Are you absolutely sure this is such a good idea?' whispered Rutger to anyone who would listen. 'I don't really want to put a damper on the whole plan but . . . well, I'd rather not be here!'

'Shut up,' snarled Wat, his hair a wild mess after another high-speed hop. Practz, not normally famed for his ruddy complexion, looked the colour of month-old milk. He had spent today *far* too far above the ground for his liking even as a blindfolded passenger.

Phlim turned and glared at Rutger, his head silhouetted by cavorting crimson spires of flame, his eyes wild with utter terror and overwhelming excitement. He made a gesture and the three enthaumatronned physicists melted into the shadows – Practz was still too shaken up to be trusted with one.

Itto's grandfather watched carefully, trying to piece together the wreckage of Thurgia's thaumatron as he attempted to recall a tiny strip of race memory wriggling irritatingly at the edge of his consciousness.

Five more damnations leapt through the fountain of geothaumal energy, paw in paw, and emerged moments later with raving eyes, blaring horns, razor-tipped tails and gleefully slashing claws to match.

All around the cave, three thaumatrons could barely be heard powering up, hypertaurus coils glowing in the crimson gloom, thaumometers registering sixteen gigs. A few moments more and the time would be perfect.

A dozen damnations cartwheeled through the column, flashing and sparking into their full, twenty-eight foot six, mean black bulk.

Nineteen-point-five gigs.

The last three flick-flacked in as Empress Tau's pets and erupted in a final cinder-spitting blast of transmutation. Now the entire army was free. No-one and nothing to stand in its way. In hours kingdoms would fall, in days continents would be smashed, wreckage strewn across countless millions of acres of desolation. If there was one thing the Prime Evil really hated, it was order: higher orders of plants and animals, speciation, regimentation. How it longed for a wallow in its favourite ooze. And in a matter of days it would have it again.

Extending its arms theatrically around the gathered swarm of its army, the Prime Evil readied itself for the frenzied orgy of onslaught and took a vast step forward.

'Not so fast,' shouted Phlim, trying to make his voice sound big and grown-up and several thousand years old. He furiously cast a Grade One Gullibility Field in the beast's general direction.

The Prime Evil's face clouded over, peering down at the tiny solitary figure before him. '*Who dares to attempt to hinder the inevitable*?' he bellowed, succeeding far better than Phlim. The twenty-six-foot voicebox probably helped.

'Well I do, of course!' yelled Phlim, trusting all to the Gullibility Field and leaping in with both feet. 'If you think you can just pop up here and start rampaging wherever you want you've got another thing coming!' He fervently wished his voice sounded a little more confident than he felt. 'We've got rules now!'

'*Rules! Pah! Speak not to me of such petty matters. Out of my way!*'

'No!' said Phlim, wishing he hadn't. 'Er . . . make me!' he added, straining to keep his feet from turning and running away very, very fast.

The cave shook as the Prime Evil laughed a nine-point-five on the richter scale. Aftershocks of savage amusement tittered amongst the damnations.

'Can't, can you?' taunted Phlim.

'*I could remove you in a matter of sec . . .*' growled the Prime Evil.

'Can't!' blurted Phlim. 'Well, you think you can but you haven't seen one of these before, have you?' he snarled, sounding incredibly mean-and-not-to-be-messed-with (he hoped) and patting the thaumatron.

Three stifled screams whispered out from behind an array of rocks as Practz, Wat and Rutger mentally wrote Phlim off. The pressure had got to him . . . and after that nice holiday, too.

Phlim was still talking. 'Well, if you won't keep up with current trends what *do* you expect?'

'*What is it*?' snarled a seismic query from overhead.

'Standard issue Mercenary-matic personnel carrier. Five hundred and sixty-three of the meanest, hardest assassins, killers and cutthroats in an easily portable quick-release deployment pouch. They'll do your lot in a couple of minutes!' A pair of fingers on Phlim's hand crossed involuntarily as he lied with utter barefaced gall.

'*All that, in there*?' growled the Prime Evil sceptically.

'Yup! Whole army. Age of miniaturisation, innit? Everything that *really* matters is getting smaller and smaller. Armies, governments, everything,' blustered Phlim. 'If it can't be miniaturised it doesn't count.'

'*Until now! I'm the greatest force of evil ever to have blackened the face of the universe*,' snarled the Prime Evil.

'Pull the other one,' yelled Phlim. 'You can't exactly sneak up on people with feet like that, can you? How can you win without the element of surprise?'

'*Brute force!*' roared the Prime Evil.

'Oh, come on. My army could outmanoeuvre you without even thinking about it. You'd be slinging thunderbolts all over the place, tiring yourself out, and you wouldn't hit any of them. I tell you, if you've got plans for invading anywhere you've got to lose a bit of that bulk.'

'*What? How dare you*?' bellowed the Prime Evil, looking down at itself. '*There's nothing wrong with my size!*'

'Oh no? How many rulers can you name with a hundred-foot waistline, eh?' Three more pairs of fingers crossed behind Phlim's back.

'*I could lose a few feet*,' the monster growled. '*If I wanted to*,' it added doubtfully, comparing the size of its army and itself with the tiny backpack on Phlim's shoulders.

'You're just saying that. Never do it. Face it, you're a dinosaur. Past it!' taunted Phlim.

The cave rumbled as the Prime Evil's temper snarled and spat.

'Never get you and your army to lose that much. Never wrap that belly of yours up in there!' jibed Phlim, staring at the bulging inchoate curve as he unbuckled his thaumatron and laid it provocatively before the demonic manifestation.

The Prime Evil's face turned bottomless-pit black as he grabbed a clump of damnations, snatching them from his side, crushing them mercilessly into a microscopic stain of pure malevolence and thrusting it through a small opening in the thaumatron with a crackle. '*See? Easy!*' it roared with a glimmer of pride.

'Bet you can't get the rest in there.'

An immense roar of frustration exploded from the caverns of the Prime Evil's lungs as it rolled dozens of damnations into greasy stains, forcing them into the thaumatron.

It was only as the forty-eighth damnation was rammed in that the Prime Evil realised what was happening. With a squeal of anger that covered every audio frequency in the spectrum and stunned several fruit bats, it fixed its crimson gaze on Phlim, leapt forward and snatched at the thaumatron. With one talon it tore the guts out of it releasing the captured damnations in a burst of rage.

'*Nice try*,' boomed the Prime Evil, its face creasing into a rictus of a grin. '*Now, prepare to die, insect!*'

'Fire!' screamed Phlim, dropping to the ground. 'Blow all tubes! Zap, maim, fry!'

Rutger and Wat leapt from their cover rolling, then aimed and launched spitting fusillades of cerulean flame, gunning straight for the centre of the malevolent mob. Sapphire ignitions erupted in dense showers of light, driving the raging Prime Evil's army back into the gloom.

Rutger spun the thaumistor on his backpack, sending the power output whirling into the red, his nostrils flaring as he launched close to thirty gigs in a strafing run across the mob, just the way Clint Machismo would. High voltage ricochets flashed in the air, barely missing Phlim as he snatched his thaumatron and fled. Wat screamed at the top of his voice, pinning a dozen damnations into a corner, drilling into them with countless gigs. Million kilowatt pyrotechnic displays crashed and burned across the inside of the cave, burning damnation outlines into the walls, smoke-haloed claws obliterating ancient neanderthal paintings. They had them on the run. Rounding them up. It smelled like a hunt and a barbecue at the same time.

Phlim stared at the wreckage of the thaumatron and whimpered, wishing he could join the fray.

With a shudder he realised that something had gone horribly wrong.

The damnations' retreat had stopped. They huddled together in the cave countering the thaumic onslaught, ricocheting twenty-five gig thaumic lance strikes harmlessly into the walls, sidestepping high-velocity strafing runs . . . and all the time behind them the Prime Evil was feeding off the constant gush of terrathaums erupting from the mine.

Defeat grinned across the cave at the Thaumaturgical Physicists.

At this rate the remaining two thaumatrons would burn out way before any real headway was made. If only they had more firepower.

'Need some help?' whispered a paper-dry voice in Phlim's ear. Phlim wheeled around and stared at the kimonoed man wearing a very battered but apparently functional thaumatron on his back, fired up and ready to go.

'. . . ?' whimpered Phlim.

Itto's grandfather nodded sagely and patted a small triangular box – the Eye-Ching was a very useful diagnostic tool. Then he tucked his hands into his silken sleeves, closed his eyes and shuffled forward mumbling a complex series of heavily accented mantras. At the exact instant he intoned the final consonant, instead of sheets of focused beams searing away from his fingertips to mould or shape or destroy, a stampede of frenzied magics torrented towards him. Vast slabs of earthmagic bouldered madly forward, wraiths screamed from the ground, feral incantations and curses seethed and crawled at him, netted in the beating, sweeping, cleaning action of the rebuilt thaumatron.

And into the whirlwind vortex of vacuumagic were caught the entire army of damnations, their feet kicking, clawing helplessly at the walls, clinging hopelessly in the turbine draft. A hundred damnations flashed past Phlim wailing and flailing into oblivion, tumbling madly towards the balding guardian. Then, gradually, like a vast landslide, the Prime Evil's grip began to fail. Leviathan talons lost their grip on the rocks, sounding like glaciers arguing over who kept the calves after a messy break-up. For a few seconds stygian darkness was all, light a brief memory as the Prime Evil was sucked, kicking, spinning and cursing after its erstwhile army.

Suddenly the crimson fountain of roaring geothaumal energy arched over, curving gracefully up to the vaulted heights of the cavern and plunging towards Itto's grandfather and the rapidly overcrowding thaumatron on his back.

'Stop!' yelled Phlim desperately. 'Enough!'

'C . . . c . . . can't!' screamed the old man, vibrating wildly as the energy torrented through him.

'Two beams into the fountain!' bawled Rutger, aiming at the rim of the mine. Wat nodded, very dubiously.

'Fire!'

A pair of lightning strikes launched hole-wards, blasting into the surging eruption, momentarily holding the fountain in check as Itto's grandfather smashed at the thaumatron quick-release mechanism. A stray spark of energy had fused it, welding the two halves of the buckle together.

'Hurry up!' screamed Rutger, his thaumatron beam vibrating and fizzing wildly with the effort. 'Can't hold this much longer . . .'

Phlim smashed at the old man's clip with a rock, panic lending weight to his actions.

'You done?' yelled Wat, glancing away from his beam. In that instant the snake of sapphire sparks fizzed, arced sideways and shorted across Rutger's beam, flaring into a cerulean corona, blasting all the Thaumaturgical Physicists in totally different directions.

Phlim just managed to unbuckle his quick-release clip and vault for cover before the thaumafer ignited.

How long Phlim remained under the pile of rubble simply thrilling to the lack of thaumic bombardment, he couldn't tell. But it felt wonderful. Total blissful silence in the dark. This was probably the first time he had ever really appreciated the advantages of hibernation. Peace, the glorious, utter lack of cacophony . . . unless of course the blast had done something permanent to his ears.

Suddenly the ground above Phlim bucked, and in perfect silence a slab of stone was wrenched out of the way. Daylight strobed into his eyes as Rutger bounded up and down excitedly after having found him, his mouth firing a silent barrage of questions.

Phlim sat up and looked around, fear rising as he failed to hear anything of what was going on. The blast . . . oh gods! He'd never play the euphonium again.

Rutger leaned over, pulled Phlim's index fingers out of his ears and grinned. 'Can you hear me now?'

Phlim grinned foolishly.

'D'you know where the thaumatron is?' repeated Rutger.

'Oh great! Hello, Phlim. You okay, Phlim?' he growled.

'Hello, Phlim. You okay, Phlim? Where's the thaumatron?'

'Respect! pah!'

'Thaumatron?'

'Up my bottom!' spat Phlim.

'Look, this is important . . .'

'There is something hard and metallic pressing uncomfortably in my nether regions. It is my guess it may well be what you are seeking!' frowned Phlim.

291

'Why didn't you say?' scowled Rutger.

'I did!'

Rutger stood and made a series of gestures to a group of dishevelled-looking Murrhovian Imperial Bouncers. They stood eagerly and dashed forward. 'Mancini? Find Mancini?' they babbled and looked very sad when Phlim returned their smile. In a few moments he was brushing himself cleanish and peering over the ancient shoulder of Itto's grandfather as he squinted suspiciously at the thaumatron.

'They're in there?' asked Rutger, bewildered. 'All one hundred and one?'

'Think so!' grinned the aged figure with not a little relief as he tightened up the straps and made to leave.

'Hold on!' shouted Phlim. 'Where's he going with that? I built that!'

'I did!' objected Wat.

'Yeah, yeah! That's one of our thaumatrons, he can't just walk off with it!'

'Want your damnations back?' asked the old man over his shoulder.

'I . . . er, no, but . . .'

'So!' said Itto's grandfather and strolled away, the thaumatron glowing and peeping softly with its contents of evil.

'But, who is he?' struggled a bewildered Phlim, wondering quite how long he had been under the rubble.

'Great guy!' said Wat, 'taught me how to make this!' He held out a small red piece of paper folded into the shape of a three-dimensional dragon.

'Who is he?'

'One of the Guardians,' said Thurgia. 'Last of a line of genetically unbroken sequence all the way back to the first primordial mages!'

'And you've just given him his very own thaumatron full of nasties? Oh, great!'

Suddenly the group of Murrhovian Imperial Bouncers exploded into a frothing flurry of excitement, leapt off their haunches and sprinted away across the rubble-strewn valley.

A tiny figure near the horizon turned, squealed and ran for his life. Mancini was not likely to escape them, he was their ticket back into the army. Empress Tau would be delighted to see him, whole, and introduce him to a host of very, *very* freshly sharpened katanas.

It was only then that Phlim noticed the full extent of the damage.

Stretching approximately thirty-five miles in a dead straight line from where he stood, between the two wand-brakes, a trench hacked its way through the Talpa Mountains.

'I see you're admiring the new Trans-Talpino Trade Canal,' said Practz, grinning. 'Few months, when it's full of water, it'll be great. Fancy a nice cruise?'

'I could do with a holiday.'

A cloud of dust blew up as Rutger steamed in with a thaumatron, landing gently. 'I'm getting the hang of this now!' he grinned. In an instant Thurgia had donned the other one and was revving up.

'Last one back to Losa Llamas comes back for these two!' shouted Rutger, tightening his grips and arcing skywards.

'Hey! That's not fair,' yelled Thurgia. 'I've got to carry Wat!' And in a moment Rutger was followed by two dots, one dangling on a length of hawser, powering towards the sunset.

Sitting in a small cloud of smoke, in a field of strange-shaped botanicals, a pair of figures watched the three Thauma-turgical physicists vanish into the corona of the sun and didn't really believe their eyes.

'Ees good stuff,' grunted the Khambodian through a bluish haze.

'The best!' drawled Fhet Ucheeni, smiling crookedly.